C000108401

EYES OF A HAWK

EYES OF A HAWK

Yggdrasil's Gaze

A fantasy novel by

SEAN CROWE

Copyright © 2023 Sean Crowe

The moral right of the author has been asserted.

Apart from any fair dealing for the purposes of research or private study,
or criticism or review, as permitted under the Copyright, Designs and Patents
Act 1988, this publication may only be reproduced, stored or transmitted, in
any form or by any means, with the prior permission in writing of the
publishers, or in the case of reprographic reproduction in accordance with
the terms of licences issued by the Copyright Licensing Agency. Enquiries
concerning reproduction outside those terms should be sent to the publishers.

This is a work of fiction. Names, characters, businesses, places, events
and incidents are either the products of the author's imagination
or used in a fictitious manner. Any resemblance to actual persons,
living or dead, or actual events is purely coincidental.

Matador
Unit E2 Airfield Business Park,
Harrison Road, Market Harborough,
Leicestershire LE16 7UL
Tel: 0116 279 2299
Email: books@troubador.co.uk
Web: www.troubador.co.uk/matador
Twitter: @matadorbooks

ISBN 978 1803135 496

British Library Cataloguing in Publication Data.
A catalogue record for this book is available from the British Library.

Printed and bound by CPI Group (UK) Ltd, Croydon, CR0 4YY
Typeset in 11pt Minion by Troubador Publishing Ltd, Leicester, UK

Matador is an imprint of Troubador Publishing Ltd

To my family and friends, who sat through countlessly long conversations, and provided limitless love and support.

To all the stationery fallen along the way.

There are just three words
That drain the darkness from hue.
They are: ....

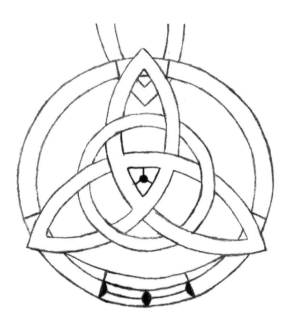

Krylei Amulet of Stewardship, 0 PIA

CONTENTS[1]

(2ᴺᴰ ERA: DATE IN YEARS PIA [POST ICE-AGE])

---

1   To better explain our translation of the Contents page: We
    have scattered the maps and documents originally found in the
    Appendices; we have also added to the documents with resources
    provided by the Yeli Archaeological Society.
    Moreover, the footnotes beyond this front matter are Intrif's own
    original notations.

LIST OF FIGURES

INTRODUCTION FROM THE AUTHOR(S)

*Once, long ago, I stood before the cold vast vacuum of the
unknown. I took the dragon's tail tightly in my hand, and fell
headfirst into the deep, dusky depths that pit us all.*
—Herodbheri, *The First Hedonist Historian* (220 PIA)

It is often said that trying times produce trying texts, and
in the trying tests of Valestia's movement across the sparse
Shorelands, we will sample a multitude of tales and trials to
anchor our souls.

The stories we've collected within this tome weave
the waxing yarn of Hawk, somewhat of a hero; a traveller
of varying fortunes, a foreseer of a few too many vicious,
unfortunate truths. His adventures were fortuitous enough
to undergo custodianship by the noble and esteemed
House of Berihtos, collated from the various documents
scribed during his life in the centuries following his death,
preserved within their copious libraries to last through
the thousands upon thousands of years of the tumultuous,

despotic diminuendo of the Fourth Era. A tattered pamphlet manifesto left long ago in silence; all in fitting tribute to the first hedonist historian, Herodbheri, who, with his work *The Glyphstories* [215 PIA], set the tone and standard used by our later historian Intrif II, a loathed descendant of Berosia's founder, Berihtos, the Glorious First King, to construct an autobiography.

Intrif II [1401–1475 PIA] is commonly described as a fear-dripped malingerer on the outskirts of civilised Berosian conversation. His many contemporaries declared that his calling to the creed of their primordial ancestor was never only to stoke the tide of virtue, but instead an obsessive compulsion of his own sense of grandeur and misguided need for attention. Critics often cited his ancestor's loss of the throne in the period before the First Berosian Civil War [1015–1097 PIA], the formation of the Republic [1127–1152 PIA], and the atrocities committed by Isinof II "The Vicious" during the first decades of the Second Berosian Civil War, while Intrif repeatedly referred to the importance of his grandfather and great-grandfather, Emytos II and Hawlik II, respectively, during the Second Berosian Civil War [1307–1357 PIA], both of whom were significantly less vicious. Many of these critics and contemporaries were removed from power following the Pre-Albensian Crisis [1480 PIA], an exhibition of which is permanently featured in the Royal Casidian Museum.

Intrif II used the vast family-kept compendium of documents regarding these tales as the foundation to his moralistic allegory, representing the stories as a call to arms and justice, a hawk of vigilance before the face of impending dark tumultuousness.

Tumultuousness is still an accurate historical term, even now, with the knowledge of the ever-tempestuous times existing prior to the Fourth Era, or Post Ice Age (PIA). The icy tempests of the "Ice Age" begin our textual chronology. Yet still, reservations must be kept to the truly "riotous" nature often ascribed by Intrif "The Rambler" (Iessios of Casidia, 1432), "Herald of the Dark Loom" (Byoini Stronyar, 1453), "the apolitical parasitic mosquito" (Goyal Buirs, 1467).

Intrif himself was a well-known, and extremely ignored, doomseer of his times; the constant calls for protection against the Albensians that rolled from his lips were never heeded. When the war between Albensia and Ristos began, the Berosian Legions were late to arms, having primarily given up the notion of organised conflict for "sedentary hedonism".[2]

The translation that we've provided hopefully keeps the tempo of the original piece, scribed from an oratory tale in ballad form. The need for detail was abandoned for a belief in necessary moralism in the preserved original manuscript.

We collectively chose to drop the hexameter structure to the verse, mostly due to the fact that the original Casidas script was designed as a response to the notion of a "song language", its strongly created aspects allowing flourishes and witticisms that can never truly be translated as efficiently or as beautifully.

The maps are copies of originals provided by the Preserved Libraries at Dzeriko. However, it is important

---

2 (Eds: Are you sure you want to include this?)

to note that Intrif's accuracy in copying these documents cannot be critically examined, as no originals have been recovered to verify their authenticity.

All other figures have been provided by the Yeli Post-First People's Landscape Initiative.

The premise of the collection appears to be a description of the death of a civilisation. The terms and descriptions given by Intrif describe the encroachment of the Valestian superpower amongst lands peripheral to the cosmopolitan confederacy of Ristos. The text regularly devolves into long strings of commentary and terminology that seems out of place; however, references to cultures long developed past our current level are subtly inferred, having enculturated Hawk's vocabulary. They could also be references to recently developed knowledge from the Berosian Second Golden Era. The inclusion of a series of documents referencing a series of deductions regarding the ecological state of Valestia suggests that the original archivists had some choice and intention in the formalisation of this collection.

The biggest issue in translating the original manuscript was the evasive and shifting sense of narration. Often the fabric of the text bleeds between the personal and the omnipresent, questions and perspective merging and shifting in ways often times confusing. Unfortunately the Casidian cultural progenitors of the Berosian style were amorphous in their delineation of perspective and identity. To them the nature of reality was as much a negotiation between the external drivers, and the internal consciousness, as it was the accumulation of all individual people. Even though the Berosian style developed a more stable sense of self, the original text has maintained its surreal sense of self, preserved by archivists in their copying and translations.

In a similar fashion the metre in which the original script was written often uses disjunctive and dissonant phrasing to split the flows, to mirror the cycle of conflict and harmony. Unsure as to whether it would detract too much from the feel and texture of the writing some parts were kept, and others remoulded to provide an easier read.

Previous works of Intrif mention the semi-mythical city state on an island amidst oceans, referred to simply as the Valestian Primacy, which could be a literary reference to the stories of Aitlati and Albuoisi, both first mentioned in oratory tales from the Ebonheart region. For a long time, the literary reference argument was the predominant understanding of Valestia's nature; however, there have always been scholars, of various disreputability, who have suggested the island was real. To that aim, the volcanic dust-caked island of Tubarik has long been argued to be the ancient and mystical Valestia. Previously there has never been conclusive evidence to substantiate such a claim; however, recent excavations undertaken by the Great Yeli Museum have yielded results with significant substance.

Now that we can be more than certain that the Valestian Primacy existed – not just as an allegorical story to encourage conflict with the First Albensian Imperiality, but as a thing with consequences and a significant importance – the annihilation of the Valestians has become an even more pressing question for archaeological concerns. How and what caused the complete destruction of the civilisation is mentioned within Intrif's collection of stories. As befitting these kinds of new and scientific insights into what was once the realm of historical gospel and oratory retention, perhaps there is greater validity in providing an informed and nuanced translation of one of the earliest historical pamphlets.

It is without a doubt that the tales of Hawk, son of Jiha and Ishni, have inspired countless heroes through the long, blood-soaked history of the Shorelands. Except, as usual, all references to these exploits have been long lost in the deep passage of time; not every hero is fitted with a story that lives on. Neither is every story of a hero fitful for them. What is undeniably clear is that the mythological actions of Hawk and Ilyia, the scribe-wrought claim of a genocidal consequence of their behaviour, and the vivid, complex landscape they fought within, might eventually be seen as more fact than fiction.

We hope you enjoy this particular translation.

ACKNOWLEDGEMENTS

We are forever indebted to the Yeli Archaeological Society (YAS) for their sustained and permanent endeavours in uncovering the sequence of events during the Valestian Conquest Period. As non-historians and translators, we have been greatly aided in our task by their help. With their provision of historically accurate representations, we have some understanding of the places where these events happened. Without them, this book and assemblage of documents' fragments would still be a dream in the pipeworks.

Throughout the text we have been able to include figures and maps detailing the places and artifacts mentioned – and not mentioned – within the stories of Hawk. We are therefore wholeheartedly thankful to the artists and archaeologists who have spent their spare time in the production of the multimedia we have packaged alongside the original narrative.

There has been a continuing discussion within epistemological circles about whether truth needs to be explicit or implicit. My pedagogical companions attest to the use of modal logic in creating a broad understanding of perspective amongst their students. We ourselves are fervent and zealous exponents of the benefits of modal logic and historical eternalism, but that is a conversation for another day.

We are further indebted to the University of Yeli for their archaeological work on the Island of Valestia. Their excavations through what can only be assumed is a thick volcanic layer[3] across the whole of the island has given insights into the final days of the island's inhabitants, and an incredibly precise and clean lens into the everyday mundanity of Valestian society and practice.

They are currently planning several more excavations on the island, as both long-term research projects and field schools, and have been given a grant by the Great Yelite Museum to produce an exhibition of their collective finds in the coming years.

The excavations of Etribuy and the village of Ist'Lindg have given immeasurable insight into the events that happened there. We have attached the produced resources associated, with thanks to the University of Yeli.

The strong relationship between the YAS, the Yeli Museum Service, and the University of Yeli has always enabled the

---

3   Trace residues discovered in the Untya Valley, surprisingly on the clothing and equipment of the deceased, has given an approximate date of 746 PIA, +/− 150 years, as the time that the volcanic activity occurred, which unfortunately doesn't correlate with any known volcano activity in the region. Similar trace residue has been uncovered across the Shorelands. The only corresponding historical data is a record by an Albensian Monk who records a "star implosion".

collection of evidence, and the further articulation of events during the Valestian Period – the research significance of this period being the occurrence of a large atomic explosion,[4] prior to any technology capable of supporting such an occurrence.

As has been apparent with each and every research project, Intrif's representations of the societies in his documents are sufficiently accurate for there to be no disclaimers of further necessary facts, untruths or false representations.

We would therefore like to begin this book at once. We apologise for the vitriolic introduction by Intrif. But doomseers do as doomseers do.

---

4   In particular the University of Yeli's physics department has always found this of serious and (dis)concer(t)ning interest. [Eds: Really…?]

Map of the Shorelands: "The Shorelands As We've Let Them Become", commissioned by Ilyia of Nostos, 624 PIA

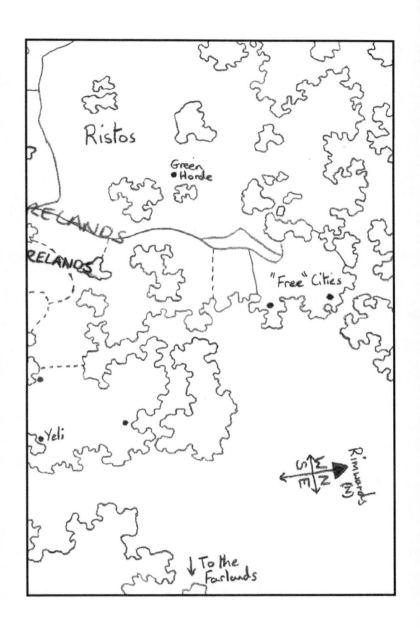

Ristos

Green
Horde

RELANDS

RELANOS

"Free" Cities

Yeli

Rimwards
(N)

N
W   E
S

↓ To the
Farlands

THE VALESTIAN/ RISTOS WARSCAPE (736–737 PIA)

(OR "THE SHORT'ST WAR")

By Intrif II,
Son of Asnof,
Descendant of Berihtos III

Originally published
in the Year 1467 PIA

ON THE ARTFULNESS
OF VIOLENCE

OR THE VALESTIAN
ENCROACHMENT, AND HOW IT
RELATES TO US

Pass power like an ox. Castrate kings with your first kick.
—Berihtos, First King of Berosia (703 PIA)

Once more it is I, Intrif II, the last living descendant of our nation's great and glorious founder Berihtos: Berihtos the Brave; Berihtos the Blue-Blooded; Berihtos the Bountifully Brilliant. The last enamel-forged foghorn before the deep denial-engraved walls of our city Dzeriko, our Illustrious Capital of the Invincible Berihtoni.

It is I, the self who is called Mad Prophet of Venomous Tongue, if you wish to believe the brain-dead propaganda of the despair-soaked windbags pretending to play power. The one and only, casually defenestrating oneself most sincerely in a task beseeched on horror of soul-scorched death. Beseeched by who but the very emerald ethereality we all permeate through?

Yggdrasil, the very same.

I am therefore left committed in true spirit to denounce and verbally defecate on the idiotic idletry ever present in our piss-soaked society. The bottomless, contemptuous foot-shrugging; the repeated enunciations of ever-clotting mounds of bone dust and blood stains. The foul, debilitating, ever-present stench of apathetic, putrescent, malcontent-tempered psychopathy, left to cradle and curdle in our collective mass grave; left to creep and crawl, and insidiously thread its way deep into our political gut, a tapeworm of diabolic endorsement.

As I have numerously endowed the leaves of many pages, once more I call forth to bring a torturous and treacherous tale. A tale drawn from the strands of fateful history to provide a fitting fabric for us to trace our design from. "What tale?" you ask, but alas, as barbarians barrage our walls and gates, no elation permeates from our crestfallen throes. Therefore, this story rings forth woe-smelt and sorrow-seared, a tale tailed by unstomachable fear and despondency.

Some might lament that my metaphors sting truer than their sense of actuality. They bemoan their latent feelings that argue we move to break the back of the seven-headed beast below us, the dark rising shadow of the Albensian Imperiality rearing viciously to engorge itself upon our lame body politic, the beast of fury and destruction that seeks only to renew the slumbering darkness of Azga, all towards a new gruesome dawn of a blood-soaked sun.

I, personally, find the gutless, stomach-split, vilely indecent scum that govern our republic to be the only spineless stains of malformed pustulation that have driven our esteemed paradise to the ground.

We, the noble crowd, are those few burdened to understand that the effect of life is only ever through truly justified cause. As they sit up high and denigrate the fragrant loss of life that shreds, sears, and subsumes the lands beneath us, it is up to us to choose the path of what we have to do.

To make my point, I call upon the last time this tragedy occurred, the time when a civilisation was annihilated in the blink of an eye. A time when every complicit character in the malicious macabre was cindered into absolute dust. The heroes I am to mention saw fit to kill every person in the civilisation of Valestia for their heinous crimes against the manascape. And it will do us well to remember that those same heroes are the ones who fight Albensia now.

The fiend-state in question, Valestia, was an ever-present source of pain and damnation – an inquisitor-collective intent on nothing but void-scarring sorcery. Their foul conflict and mana-genocide raged for far too long, far too furiously. The Shorelands are now a barren steppe, lamenting beneath our verdant and emerald inset heartland. Their zealous idolatry burn the very souls of those afflicted, scorching the once-fertile farmland that sustained sanctity into a desolate, demon-seared oblivion. The very natures of those afflicted and their children, soul-scarred and fate-scorned, are left as reminders to all those who deem the dark macabre an art worth exploring.

The harrowed and decimated states have all taken too long to recover. In some places. they are still recovering. The

Isle itself, now a salt-strewn graveyard, suffers putrescence and insensibility.

Maybe someday it will be inhabitable.

Maybe not.

This meander is not the purpose of my point purely a noted and notable fact of what happens when such a violent power meets such a resolutely destructive stance. For our interest in petty politics, and prosaic preening, the question is why such a resolute decimation occurred. Notably, the opposing answer only emerged four hundred years after the first true stresses of the Valestians. After their incursion into Yeli, their malignant power was left for centuries to move north and gain traction, before unceremoniously having their lives and agency permanently revoked.

Primarily, there were other factors that limited the Valestian advance, keeping a slight form of freedom for the people caught in their grasp. A freedom that, even if caught amidst malfurious intricacies, had the foresight to aid and abet the movements of the Guild, and our point of authorial insight: the hero called Hawk. Where now we see the diatribe-laden blabberings of idiocy in the Valestians and their colonialism, corrupted by ritualistic and militaristic perversions, they saw supremacy and power, selfhood and idolatry.

It is through the actions of the Guild that we were given the historical respite to draw true notions about the Valestians and the nature of their crimes against the manascape. And maybe more. Crimes that, even when readily acknowledged in the past, still seep into the present, and ever more into the future we are befitted to protect.

The current conflicts devastating the Albensian Imperiality also come as a natural consequence of their severance of the manascape from the landscape. The erection of their new gods and the bleeding of the old gods has allowed a self-consuming chaos to breed to the south of us. A chaos we will soon face, or consider facing, throughout the far future.

This is why I have brought this tome before you, to warn you of those times to come through reference to these times past. Therefore we find ourselves on the precipice of our odyssey into the realm of Hawk.

The realm of incidental chaos and dramatic catastrophe. Auspicious omens and fortuitous epiphany.

It is to that end that we allow one final anchor in this liminal pre-becoming. One last reference to the future already written by the breath strokes of those contained within this leafy, origami ensemble. One last image par eternality.

The defining moment of the Valestian/Ristos conflict was its final battle in the Untya Valley, a vicious, sharp, discordant conclusion to tempestuous and tumultuous times. When what can only be described as an atomic[5] incineration was unleashed, and, even then, the understatement of that premise left a gargantuan chasm. It is to this purpose that the following arguments will be drawn; if there is to be conflict in the future against forces of dark macabre, the stories of the Guild are a watermark in our defence.

Or maybe our avoidance of sheer obliteration.

Please enjoy,

> Intrif II, son of Asnof II,
> Descendant of Asnof,
> Son of Berihtos III,

---

5   *Atomic* definition: as in pertaining to the individual particles of the universe.

Son of Hawlik,
Son of Entrif,
Son of Berihtos II, The Grey,
Son of Isili, The Wedded,
Son of Intrif, The Fastidious,
Son of Berihtos I, The First King.

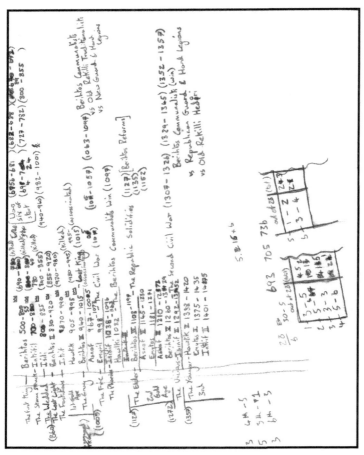

Intrif's Genealogy, "Notes From an Unorganised Archivist" by Unknown, 1557 PIA

XXX

ONE

A twinkling emerald, sat at the centre of the universe, blinked a couple of times more, trying to strain the dirt from its eye. Finally, the dust scattered into the untidy and roaring cosmos – food for fishes swimming throughout eternity. The dust was consumed by the effervescent shrapnel of a billion incandescent explosions rippling across the twilight night sky, their licking flames coddling the swallowing darkness cast between them.

Shining high above the Shorelands, the constellated star forges flexed their being and bearings, speaking through the infinitude of time and space, each shred of sizzling primordial ecstasy breaking the boundaries of cold vacuum, bringing flittering descendants in particularly bright waves of extension, their illumination of existence burning out into an interweaving incendiary blossoming.

The not-so-ends-of-themselves, dissipated by the light's touch, refracted and radiated onwards and upwards through into the dusk grey pre-rain clouds, where they gathered and mulched in precipitous, atmospheric bulks. Half-wanted cues and semi-destructive cures littered the space between damp, cloying molecules, their hermetic perspiratory isolation soon to come to an end. The masses unleashed, the tidal waves of zealots expelled, each and all fervent missionaries for the primordial Cloud Dwellers.

The newly anointed and expelled were to leave their soft pink sheens and descend towards the godless ground, moisturising zealots with chemical contributions, their repetitive, ricocheting cycle to continue evermore again. All before the eyes looking upwards, gathering in vast quantities beneath the cosmological ballet; the sun descending, the moon in stoic vigilance, sitting and settling, ever so slightly, above the line of mountains marking the world's endridge.

The Shoreland's dark serene tranquillity was sporadically broken by protrusions of flickering orange-red firelight. Campsites and shadowed selves moved softly between settlements, cities, markets and fortresses; hunters, raiders, pirates, seers and perseverers, all trekking their odysseys, and journeys, through the maddened decline of their once-civilised society. Deep in the green forest shelf, along the cresting grey mountains, before the sheer drop into rich, verdant farmland, lay the campsites of the Krylei, their fluctuating illumination bringing out the flights and soars of birds and bats, brightening red, purple and green expressions.

Soft-feathered owls graced overhead as the teeming forest life quickly shifted into a thick, linen-clad tent village, the wooden stakes-as-barriers quickly giving way into rows of blue-, red-, yellow- and green-painted cloth. The colours were a sparkling patchwork of blossoming life, the dyes chosen and daubed without care, rank, honours, or dare, speaking of an intricate collation of will and sense.

The only tent that would catch naïve attention was the largest, placed securely in the camp's centre. Its walls were consumed with flickering shadow plays, rapturous orange and red rising in tense rumination. Rippling candlelight flowed throughout the tent's interior, illuminating the voluminous scatterings of rich, thick furs; brown, white, pink, green and black, soft, silky and mesmerising. Like their tittering lovers cloaked inside, they were hung heavily and lazily amidst a tranquilising heat.

A warm movement was ebbing across the giggling walls of the tent; there, entwined in the centre, lay two forms, both beneath a deep, tender, all-enveloping bed-dressing mountain. A serene sea softly lit, seamed and unseaming, covering domesticated and deep breathing, encompassing all thoughts of action. Deep laziness settled in glazed and fired contentment.

Flower petals in wooden bowls curled out tender streams of soft, sweet fragrances, their auras collecting together into compounded sublime. Their hues flickered, and the radiant glisten of light wove a slow wave over them.

Her breath steadied, her head lilted. Her lips moved, slowly producing, "*Soooo.*" Her hand emphasised her stresses with long strokes across her companion's skin. "You've not told me one of your '*epics*' in a long time." She scoffed.

The tension resonated across her companion's chest, his hairs gently prickling.

"It's getting *awfully* long since you *really* entertained me. I could start to grow *bored…*"

She yawned, inhaling and rolling her body away from her exacerbated partner, his eyes too rolling in protest. She contested with a sea of limiting softness. "You mock, *but* I can feel it happening, the waxing tides of *your* ocean falling short of *my* shell-studded beach. *Your* lapping a vast shadow in the recesses of *my* Divined memory... *Perhaps* I don't even know you anymore?"

The wind outside grew in terrifying tenor, the skirts of the tent grasped, accosted, jostled. Threads were beckoned by air to unravel. A shrill birdsong dominating the background grew with a flurry of furious, shrieked objections.

"Perhaps you've become a figment of my imagination, a *rolling* crescendo that, with *each... single... flourish*, passes into insignificance." Her hand slowly followed the harmony of her tone. "*Never* to be heard again. *Perhaps* I imagine these encounters as a way to pass the time in this *incessant pit* of a world."

The silhouetted backdrop gasped in thoughtful refraction.

The wind chilled, its tone falling to a mournful silence. The shadowed hands reached to hide their coming folly. The birds fell silent too, awaiting the harrowed call soon to follow.

"Perhaps I've ceased to exist materially; *you* having escaped me long ago, *me* an ethereal immortal, crestfallen by the darkness of the Sun. *A cosmic interlude of silent retrospection.* The *lives I never was* flashing before... The *lives I never had* the preoccupation of shadowed boredom..."

She paused for breath, the intensity of her soliloquy both spiritually and physically demanding. The room breathed deeply with her, the shadows falling closer and closer, the gathering dusk oscillating and flickering gently in rhythm. Her chewed lips drew the words out gently, and quietly, from her magmatic viscosity.

4

"*Perhaps...* I don't even exist in reference to myself. My whole life a lie, all constructed to deceive myself from a truer truth. The acknowledgement that *I'm* truly alone out here, or *there*, or wherever I was needed to be... or not."

Magnets shivered as his hand gently palmed her back.

The tension eased in gentle communion with the flickering candlelight. A slow motion brought the wolf-skin blanket higher, the tension creeping from shoulder to den.

"*Maybe*, if you tell me one of your *stories*, it will preoccupy the desolation flowing freely through my being."

She paused, her fingers running in idle estimation, abstract equations and existential geometry to be resolved and chartered between the ridges of her lover's stomach. Cryptic commonality crept out in hushed tones.

"I'm not sure what I want, though." Ambiguity trailing absolution.

The radiating warmth of the tent returned to her skin and touch, the skirts assured, swept threads relaxed. The tension of the wind dissipating into tranquil harmony as soft birdsong slowly rejoiced into the soundscape, trailing choruses interjecting after harsh call and response verse.

She rolled back into conversation.

The blankets and sheets were luxuriously gentle. The oceans of bed space receded as the two bodies came close.

"Why don't you tell me about *that* scar?" A soft direction outlined a ragged slice moving across Hawk's right ribs.

He shrugged, entering dubiously into the dialogue. "I *highly* doubt it's appropriate."

Her laugh was facetious. Her nails skirted his flesh.

His hand was running concentric circuits.

With hushed voice, words were formed. "I'd been paid

Map of Askilt: "The Western Twinned City" by Scout Captain Kleos, Valestian Scout Order, 453 PIA

to rescue the daughter of Askilt's rector from a group of gnashing and gnawing Hill Giants, and as you can imagine, it went, well… well and truly, *titillatingly*, up."

THE RECTOR

SHORELY KNOT
(715 PIA)

Red sky at night, shepherd's delight.
Black-stained morning, Azga's dawning.
—*The Shepherd's Call to Rise,* an Entoilee folk song

A deep, vivid, waxing rainbow etched lilac dreams across the sky. Shimmers of thin, violet cloud trails threaded and scored behind the luminescent arch, shafts and columns of sublime light drawing radiant marches down through the atmosphere, speckled empyreality washing out into crystallised Divine.

The floating aromas of finely dusted flower fragrances shifted waves and streams of sweet and lush, mellow and vibrant wafts and gushes moved past the picnicking couple. Sunned and scorched, they lay there, her head gently, gracefully and warmly abutting his stomach, her hair rippling softly across his torso, both adrift in cloud-etched contortion, her mouth pursed in perpetual rolls. With effortless energy, her tongue lolled out syllable after soliloquy, all into the gentle oblivion of the roasted afternoon epitome.

The shimmering green glade they rested within had begun its ascent into verdant sublime. A sublimating choral chimed in with upcasts of cricket calls and whisperings of bird songs, chirrups of voles and shrews and field mice, the footfall and echoed stamps of passing herds, dragonflies and butterfly flutters, all rebounding and sounding around the couple, an enchanting and enthralling throng in encapsulating choral rise.

Flocks of feathered flights dipped and wove around them, permeating the ethereal, emerald essence they were enshrined within. Shades of twinkling orange crept into vision as a few of the scattered trees cast off their summer skin, their dry and rigid fur dropping gracefully to the ground.

A scuttle of grey-white fur purred into perception. Chasing tails before the nightly curfew, the scurry of furred forest critters erupted as a blossoming dust-scuffle. The chaos flummoxed its way across the foliaged coliseum, set to Ilyia's gentle ringing laughter. Her melody settled with an intonated twinkle, gem-set flecks of radiance washing through in prickling, satisfying waves.

The rolling bass and baritone of the wind slid across their exposed arms, warm enough to provoke a gentle shiver, cold enough to heighten their sensation.

Their bodies inched ever inwards.

A deep-lavender crested deer followed the meandering conflict with besotted awe and glee, the symbolic warden of the encroaching despair, warding warily away from the loving couple.

The red-emanating sun was sitting half-lazily in the sky, burgundy drunk from the rude wine of their picnic; it settled, feet unshrugged, and feats finally resting, the tips of the mountain range below waiting to finally provide its privacy.

Likewise, the heroic, loving couple were attempting some form of intimacy.

Hawk's arms and body were resting gently; Ilyia was supposedly comfortable sheathed within his "godly" form. Her voice chattered away, the inflection of her tongue stressing the odd word or sound. The trace of each syllable etched a silver-strung web through the quietly bustling serenity, Ilyia at the centre, half-woven, half-weaver, mostly fidgeting and gurning through the sentences she felt caged within.

The wine was from Berihtos – an anniversary present. He had laughed his deep laugh when he handed it across to Ilyia at the last Winter Unfurling, the laugh that ran like a warm stream over geyser cobbles. He said it had a certain stimulating effect – the intoxicating effect of the Ko'ko leaf.

Hawk felt the blackness starting to ebb and flow, his eyes drifting steadily upwards towards the shadowed sky. He felt the flickering twitches at the backs of his retinas. A retinue of iridescent stars crept through the red-stained sunset, the vast balled sheets of atmosphere ruptured by pulsating purple glimmers. Constellation lines emerged to create fractured patterns and form shifting shapes, traces of entoptic pixelation searing across his vision, inciting tides of visual snow.

They wove themselves intricately into a vivid and garish summer circus, circles and pendulum swings of vibrant red, burgundy and orange, shifting and simmering into an entangling kaleidoscopic carousel; hands and feet clashing and calling, murmurs, shouts and uproars abounding, all cascading round the growing festivities and forthcoming noises. Inebriated sensations trickled around and above the growing extravaganza before they ran down the colourful and bunted dancers, spritely bashing feet and hands with glee.

The periphery of the fairground fiasco became bolder and sturdier; deep-brown wood and shreds of torn beige linen span out from mechanistic chains. The bazaar constrained the bizarre, a flurry of constructed cell walls splitting the footfalls and flailings of fun, a meld of mystical mitosis bludgeoning out into the free-flowing being. The wooden frames, emboldened, split inwards, dividing the cyclical mirage of complex and colourful dancing.

Marketeers, merchants and militants fostered and shuffled their way through into the concentricity of dancers. With sharp tempo snaps, they began berating and battering the twirling motions away from their unconscious symphony. The shop stands continued to extend, clutters of baskets and furniture shrapnelling upwards and outwards, tools and trinkets scattering and slicing at the kettled protestations.

Howls of anguish pierced Hawk's ears, sharp nails shredding his head. The mass of harmonious artistry was haemorrhaged and beaten before him, Hawk left horrified by the sharp deterioration of his blossoming hallucination. Blackened blood accumulated in deep pools of dark black-red coagulation, the sordid mess and mass of flesh and death embellished a grim image of awesome pretence. His head cracked with stress, his cranium splitting as the force and pressure fragmented and split; uninvited abyssal blackness ebbed and flowed once more through his tepid stream of consciousness.

The word "Funny" was seared across his darkened sight.

Consciousness rejoined him, late as usual, five pints deep. Hawk spluttered, drenching the interior of the rag binding around his face. The adjunct around his head was suffocating, the restraints around his arms annoying. The strain and pain of their tightness was a testament to their poor persuasion.

He was starting to lose his temper. His chest tingled, rippled, burn. There was an internal crescendo; his heart pain started again. Oh fuck, he couldn't deal with an aneurism. Not at this time.

Breathing became slow and steady.

In, out. Repetitive cycles.

Consciousness settling at a pleasantly inebriated rhythm, his heart rate dipped. The sharp, stabbing, shooting pains ceased. Well, ceased for this moment. He felt the bubbling chest sensation subside. Psychosis was not his strong suit. Perhaps a strong suit wasn't right? He tasted salt on his lips. They were out to sea; a strong suit would drown him.

Trills of birdsong emerged to guide him home.

It was garbage. Absolute trite. Territorial shite. Sea-bird nonsense of foolishness and gnashing, glaring guilt. Lost shit and abandoned whims. Sins aplenty.

Fuck.

Why were they trying to kill him? What had he done... this time? Yeah, definitely this time, no one else knew of his whereabouts. He was tucked away safely from the others who wanted him, "The Felonious Monks". But if not them, the Siblings of the Scourged Sigil, then whom? Or, to rephrase the question, how? How could he find out?

He strained his chained hands and the soft grey manacles shattered with ease; the shrapnel ricocheted off the backs of the two armed guards. They had been left to oversee the entrance to the brig, lest someone get behind the guards at the door, their burgundy-and-red tunics dyed to hide any lapdog's blood.

They quickly turned to meet an awaiting rock-hard fist. One for each. Compassionate care; community orientated. They fell too quickly to speak, and were subsequently trodden over as the escapee née detainee rushed for the poop deck. But not for that reason, mind you. There was a different kind of shit he had to take care of.

He passed a weapons rack and stopped momentarily. The axe, sword and small blades he needed being present at first glance. Moments, though, are a reflexive thing. The weapons rack would remember the ransacking for the rest of its days. Bereft of the easily susceptible weapons it had sought fit to shelter and protect from the warring and worrisome world outside, it whimpered for their safety as it felt its bundled wards snatched up.

A dark and vicious malcontent of a storm was bracing to rage above the ship so avidly sliding across sea waves. Dark, sombre strokes of black and grey washed through cloudscape, rinsing the gentle whites of fortuitous sailing, stoking an agonising gale and kleptomaniac winds. Instead of soft and slender communication, the apocryphalic etchings of lightning and flame maliciously spat static intent at one another, their bustle and battery smashing high above the sauntering and meandering missteps of the sailing vessel.

The sails were a sharp blur of crimson and burgundy, the ship adorned in black waterproof pitch, decorated with gold and silver, blood-red gemstones dazzling from the aft and bow – the hull a fortress of destiny-destroying intent.

Enios'Kul, the red-and-brown leather-clad commander-in-chief, was ardently striding the upper deck barking orders in a slicing and sharp staccato, a totalitarian den mother snapping at her bundle of pawing, yelping mutts, viciously demarcated syllables cutting through the cacophony of the sea's energy.

The mutts cowered and crawled and crept quickly and quiveringly over to their posts and positions. The sails were unfurled by the crew mightily, but the storm was mightier; the pitch-black clouds, lightning-veined, imposed an aura of all-hell-breaking-loose upon the seas.

Seamen speak of the monster deathly deep below, in the suffocating depths of an eternal slumbering creep, ready and waiting to rise. To rise and consume from its sodden, crushing tomb, to shake the golden sands of the Shorelands with dark, suffocating obscenity; a smothering tentacled predator of pelagic misfortune.

The oali-hewn doors to the deck of the black and foreboding imperial ship splintered under the weight of the ominous preposition. The proposition, undaunted and unbridled by the snowballing storm, continued in his path towards destruction and escape. The shimmer of a silver blade flew cleanly through the atmosphere, splitting the air of majesty projected by Admiral Kul, swiftly and solemnly bequeathed. The blood splurt usurped the chain of command over to his lieutenant, Dio'Tor. He was bequeathed by another severing blade, dropped like the maggot-bearing fly-on-the-wall he pretended to be. Gias'Drul, the third in command, shat himself, an unleashed sail frame bluntly colliding with his lungs, his ribs splitting and tearing within him.

Impacted, Gias wheezed and whooshed a stream of blood as he was sent straight over the deck and down into the drenching, tumultuous waves. Some of the crew quickly waved goodbye and joined him, jumping into the lapping and sloshing sea. The others drew their short, stunted, sterile weapons, attempting to take up a projected pretence. The proposition was still one-ended about the whole scenario; having silently leapt to a rowboat, he sliced the ropes, gently splooshing to the surface of the black shuddering sea. The paddling began, with no Valestian asses presented.

Unsure of what to do next, the crew, vexed, rushed to the rescue of the bewildered, newly, and nearly anointed commander-in-chief of the Valestian Grand Armada: the severely wet and washed-out, two-named Inquisitor Admiral Gias'Drul.

Hawk eventually made it to the glistening tan shore. He saw the promise of rest under soft trees lined abreast tender grass. Pulling the rowboat ashore, he started his journey into the Sleeping God's realm, softly abutting a tree.

The pursuers didn't even notice the purple, slimy, reaching tentacles, the protruding prongs of Poseidic, deadly intent.

They were just gone.

Hawk awoke severely sweaty and cantankerous. It was to be expected. It was always expected when undertaking the vast, starless odyssey. He reached for his water. Fuck. He cursed his lack of foresight and made swift sight for campfire wood. He took out the hand axe he'd stowed in his caged rebuke and sought out a fresh-feeling wood. He found it quickly enough, hefting his axe and splitting the tree. He shifted the wood over to his hastily made beach-stone fire pit, eventually forming a small blaze to purify some saltwater. The blaze comforting, Hawk's thoughts drifted to the task at hand. He was obviously knackered, trying to investigate the murder of Rector Arnest's daughter, the beloved and pious Ariel, the queen of charity who was soon approaching her thirty-first year. Getting mugged by thugs and press-ganged aboard a Valestian ship wasn't his idea of smoothly investigating the death of a prominent city dweller. However, it had narrowed his list of suspects down to a solitary and unsubtle one.

He guessed it was Rector Arnest himself who had sold him out to the Valestians. Those sanctimonious wretches would pay. Perhaps that was next? He could kill Rector Arnest, find the daughter's body in the basement – the one the Rector was so adamant led to nowhere – and then saunter slowly back off to Ristos. Ristos was serenely beautiful this time of year.

Well, Ristos was always serenely beautiful. Figuratively enchanting. A sublime expression of the idyllic to the extreme, untouched by the violent warfare that proliferated below it. Compared to the sparsely vibrant buzz of the Shorelands' southern steppe coast, Ristos was a patchwork of forests, lakes, rivers, glades, groves, snow-dipped mountains and receding glacial valleys. Occasionally ice would melt and the valleys flooded, beautiful fenlands and marsh isles emerging from previously canopied and bush-strewn valley floors.

Askilt, in comparison, was sparse of life; there was very little that edged itself out, and what did was hidden from the predators that soared high above and burrowed far below. Although there were some who said that was just the curse of the Urm'gil, the tread marks of a time long gone, still staining the landscape, from now until forever.

The campsite didn't take long to pack up, which tended to be the case when you didn't have a tent.

He could join in with some of the tournaments, earn some barterables and livestock, then go back home for the Winter Unfurling.

They had stolen his sword, though.

He pushed the stolen boat onto the coastline, the low tide shifting like the trace lines of snails. The slow and steady bob brought him out into focus.

Hawk corrected himself. Not HIS sword. She was safe with Tiani. The *substitute* sword. The one that could get lost when investigating self-absorbed assholes who never held respect for the Warrior Right.

He would definitely make that last journey back to Askilt. Samrost would still have a blade for him; he could pick up supplies for the hit he'd already been paid to make. He would finish the job. He had the seal of the guild if caught beside the Rector's body; Samrost's seal would keep them off his back. One job, then finally freedom from this pimper's paradise. He was getting sick of prostituting himself like this. It made him the money. It kept Ilyia happy and well-fed, his tribe in good stock. But it was a trying time. His sword arm was particularly tried.

Was this his one hundredth consecutive year making the journey around this part of the continent?

That was much too long, and definitely a form of hermetic enclosure. The Farlands sat in the back of his mind. Always. When was the last time he had seen the Dragon's Throat? Lain beneath the Blood Star? Far too long ago. Maybe the last time had been his and Ilyia's honeymoon.

There was never really a need to come here. His treatment was petty, unfittingly dire. His ribs stressed this fact exasperatedly, painful in their exposition, savage in their residual tear and begrudging nudge.

He had a loving family, a happy home, a plentiful future. This was just leftover political manipulation he adored engaging in. Absentee gerrymandering from beyond the grave.

He winced in paranoia. Caught himself. Took stock.

He might be back before nightfall. The soft waves welcomed the life raft onwards. Oh well.

The sound of the oars was a zen-like serene.

The coastline he was following to Askilt was gentle; seabirds flew overhead, muttering in garbled dialects and accents. With a mocking tone they spat at intruders from foreign shores, cursing denigrates who left to venture further inland, far away from the righteous and holy flock.

The soft gentle undulation that lifted the beach coast up from the soft shore waters sat in communion with the clans of skittering crabs; a few steppe otters were sat star-watching atop the estuary's tan skin. The red shells of the crabs were a second tide over the sand shores, the islands of otters brief patches of brown imbued with white.

*

The stench still clung to his nostrils, an asphyxiating aroma of hysterically stressful despair. Samrost had been well and truly stressed out, agitated and flea-bitten; twitching and traumatised. It was a shame to see him in such a state, woe-bidden, crestfallen, ajar. A jar ajar, smashed to bits on the star-studded floors adorning his fortress's interior. Samrost the impeccably impenetrable. *Well*, laughed Hawk, *not for much longer*.

Not many would have known how to spot Samrost's emotions. Samrost could be expressive enough if you knew where to look – or, more accurately, how. He pretended not to. He pretended to keep an eyesight, or perhaps he pretended to pretend not to. Perhaps everyone knew of Samrost's flagrantly expressive fragrances.

He cackled. Perhaps not.

The street signs swung around him as he wandered through the cramped settlement, the revelry of tavern time boiling out into the city atmosphere. The trails and tentacles of song and dance, conversation and chatter, spread discussion and consequence out through the settled expanse. In frigid comparison, the sparse steppe landscape didn't encourage much.

Swathes of thick rivers cut the Shorelands, like transcendental children's traces across scrunched-up paper: rich, eclectic carvings of pearlescent blue caught between oceans of green, brown and dark purple. He thought of his children's traces back home, wonderous etchings adorning the stout walls of the stronghold, of seeing their incantations of colour, vegetation, people and animals all again soon enough. It had been too long since their inscriptions had dazzled his eyes. Too long in a land marked by chaos and crisis. Too long looking over the skimming lines of axeheads, far from the warmth of their art and laughter.

Too long readjourning indolence and idiotry. The Shorelands had never been butchered by the rivers. Life had been brought here far before the interloping Askian and Denbois families and their colonial creeds of despotic industry. Life had skirted the Shorelands' sparse flora long before Askilt and Denilt's Twin City Schism.

Their families cared little for life, valuing gold and prestige instead.

Their patrician palaces stood aloof, facing each other viciously, dog-eared from decades of dedicated generational conflict. This was all committed above the looming Treborz Strait, a narrow path of a waterway that separated the Islekind from the Shores. The Islekind were too fastidious and vengeful for the Valestian Primacy to annoy, even though they had tried, failing dismally. The Valestian Primacy was too weak, pathetic and dreary for the Islekind to enjoy.

If politics had ever been of any value, the Valestians would hold an immensely greater sway; hence they had established the Twin Cities, bringing about the war between them, all in a catastrophic and devastating interplay. Now the once-peaceful Shorelands encroached on Ristos; Ristos, being too grand and mighty, let the waves lap and diminish. The only ones who suffered were the previously Free Cities. They had clung to their idolatry for fear of sharing power.

Now they sat the lice-ridden lapdogs of lepers... though at least it made for a quick buck. A quick buck to make the least.

A quick buck bounding through a dense forest of chaos and mischief, refreshing grove brimming eternally on the horizon. Scores of feathered fiends and horned atrocities waiting hungrily by either flank. The mobs of deer-kin had been funnelled quickly into their city, and now, surrounded by Valestian poachers, they held their hide and hooves with dread-induced worry. Their footsteps could always be accompanied by a welcoming ricochet of arrow paths, their sides the ever-glistening marked trophy of aristocratic dreams. Bloodlust-bearing brethren bore down on them at sundown, hunters in devout addiction to their monstrosity.

His footsteps had reached the epitome of their ascension. He now stood at the top of the ridge that overlooked the "Lesser Quarters", so named because it was at the base of the hill, not because it housed those the family sought to exploit. He could see the difference; it was still considerably better than the Krylei Ghetto tucked away by the gatehouse. The tides of slate roof tiles clustered in small communities, clutches of cityscape diversified into economic and social allegiance. The main streets extended out as two market squares dealt with internal and external markets. The ethnic hostility was palpable, as it always is in cities like Askilt.

The Primacy said they had put a lot of effort into rebuilding the settlements they had stolen. Well, "at least they did this close to Askilt", which talking about the Twinned Lands wasn't saying much. Did it really help? Previously the structures had been wooden and stone, thatched and insulated, warm and cosy. Now they were barren, bleak, stoic structures of frozen solitude. Cold-capped hospices exposed to the crucifying steppe wind.

As someone who normally lived amidst snow-capped peaks, this seemed an insanity. There was, of course, violence when they announced their plans, rioting and looting amongst the more formal settlements along the south coast. The erection of the Twin Cities came about because the original settlement, Akil-Kemyi (or Lake-Dawn-Place), was ravaged in the "attempt" to retake it from its original occupants. A blessing for the rebuilding Valestians, who had let all the traditional places of worship and authority go up in flames.

The few-and-far-between farms, hamlets and estates had been encroached upon as the Valestians moved out to provide "peace", pantries raided and left destitute, families assaulted and indentured, their livestock and stockpiles stolen to feed the murderous intent of the invaders.

The Borsi rebels amongst the So'Ultai (the sons of Ultai) were put to a viciously stunted flight; many guild historians claimed that the small skirmishes were purposeful traps, the Valestians choosing to murder rather than capture, deciding to provoke partisan resistance for the pleasure of perpetuated torture and battle.

For a peninsula where conflict lasting more than a month was long, this was a titanic gutting. Lives were lost, though not as many on both sides. The Valestians' banning of mention did not allow precise insights, but for an island people it wasn't a particularly healthy course of action for them to have undertaken.

Samrost was perhaps the smartest Valestian he knew, and even he was adamant that this so-called "Primacy" was absolute batshit crazy.

A sign of the times.

It might have been why he was emitting such strong pheromones.

But what did it truly tell him, though?

Hmmmm. He pondered, perplexed, pausing in thought. His feet caught up with him, to carry him onwards. Onwards into the Rector's abode, to put this abysmal affair all to boot. The cobblestone steps steeping the steppe stronghold made for ill-footing. His feet were sick of it. They slugged and slogged heroically up past the benches and perches he could have easily stopped upon. The bastard above wanted to continue, so forced they were. Finally they caught rest underneath that fatefully out-fitting symbol of respite, the Rector's Retreat.

Branding a bishopric puts emphasis on the latter.

He checked his holster. Yep. Perfect.

She whispered in excitement.

He kicked in the door.

The splinters caught everyone else off guard... Well, because there was no everyone else. The entrance hallway was unfitted with guards. He let out a chuckle, swiftly taking a defensive posture. Here came some footfalls. Two sets of ricochet footfalls gave promise of an open affair.

Thereafter, a squad of infantrymen met a squadron of infantrymen. Both heralding differences quite liveryly, they met each other, accusing the other in the ruins of their defendee's exhibitionist opening.

"We received word of a fugitive being held in sanctuary here."

"Under the authority of the Rector, town guards are strictly forbidden from entering these premises."

A gateway to paradise... in many a sense.

All it took was the heat of the moment. The lock would melt away, and the warmth would test everybody's patience. Sharp slides of steel from scabbards rang in beckoning testimony. They fell upon each other like armoured porcupines, spearing and piercing with premeditated wit.

His defensive position was discreet enough for him to avoid the ribaldry of rough and tumble. Jawbones, knee bones, head bones, hipbones, all swaying and flaying in sanctimonious synchronicity. He left the way the house guards came, making a quick step up through the defensive stone maze separating entrance and chapel house from Rector's "heavenly abode".

The steps were cold and hard. Silent, thus deadly.

He heard the chink of metal, the clunk of heavy armour. He readied his serrated axe and handheld billhook.

The first guard came down the stairs with sword and shield. The symbol of the Rector's house was emblazoned on the shield's shining face, a deep-brown eagle daubed with red on its feet and wingtips, a heart caught between the eagle's beak. Hawk flashed the billhook left, tearing the shield away towards the external bend of the staircase; he jabbed with the serrated axe, pushing it through a gap in the armadillo.

With a violent tear, the armoured hero was pulled down past him to clatter and bounce. Stood behind was a knight with a spear.

Perfect.

He lanced before the knight could strike, aiming for the jugular. His billhook struck and severed. The spear clattered down as hands flew to close the gushing tear. The knight glided down the stairway as well, deflating as he passed.

Perfect.

This was not the time for theatrics.

After violently hacking and slashing several more of his fellow pedestrians through pain; after leaving a wake to wake the vagrants that might come to loot and despoil next – the vagrants who might next try to set up shop in exploitation and denigration, vagrants with no sense of vagrancy, the indecent ones. The ones with too—

His unspoken monologue interrupted the raw, violent hedonism of the room, his interruption a breath of respite, an air of civility, a quick breeze of, "Get the fuck out of here before heads start to roll."

The orgy's fight-or-flight response was to go catatonic. It's a good thing an orgy is made of a good many people. Not all were quite so sticky and dense. They flew and scattered, coup spooked; no pleasant "thank you" slipped from the lips of the previously entertaining occupiers; indeed, they sought unoccupation several times over before finally they were free, free from the rampage they probably should have guessed was coming when all those guards were posted. "I mean, they were pretty heavily armoured and scarred." / "I mean, one of them was the winner of the local tournament the other year."

I would say hindsight is a daeva. Maybe foresight is a djinn. But stupidity is a serendipitously sardonic siren.

Where was the Rector, one may ask oneself, at such a tense and turmoil-torn time?

An astute question to ask, an askew person to answer.

The blood gurgled from his lips with pox-shaped pulsations.

His guilt dripped over the blade perched between ribs, severing just enough of the lungs to cause pain and slow suffocation.

The sword slipped out. As the Rector paused with his last moments, he thought he saw a light.

Hawk was only a few steps out from Samrost's lair when the guards grabbed him. The roaring flames consuming the "Pastor's" palace provided a shining beacon, asking for rapid guard intervention.

They would have to grab him. Several of them, if they wished an arrest or wanted to enshrine him within a steel cage. Maybe an adamantium web. Something physically strong enough to cease whatever rampant rampage of destruction he might have been unleashing if he was getting to the point of needing to get grabbed.

This was a polite formality. A kind "I know you can't really do this, but if I go along with you, remember I'll tear your legs off at the first sign of you being an ass."

That kind of polite gesture. Knowing but firm. He didn't like to reiterate after the initial over-step, lose-a-leg statement.

They took him straight to the keep.

They sat him straight down in the basement.

They Gordianed him, I shit you not.

*

"So, where are you going today, my friend?"

"East, across the so-called 'Border'. I need to make a quick journey to Ustgart."

"I can do that for you, my friend. I can do that. Take a seat; we'll set off shortly."

*

They found Ariel's body.

She was in the basement of the Chapel house. They were not looking forward to the apologetic conversation with Hawk. It wasn't a conversation to cherish. They were sure he would understand, but still, locking somebody up is a deep sign of disrespect.

It was Cleo, "Head of King Hedorah's Guard, Cleo", who was sent down to talk to him.

Well, to try to talk to him. Normally, holding a conversation with Hawk was hard. He's never really all that there at the best of times. And in the worst, he's just never really there. Never there.

"Oh, for fuck's sake."

Echoed across the empty series of cells that where now empty of any occupants.

*

The girl across from him was crying, her parents busy discussing their market plans. He gave her a padded plaything from his travelling pack – a small woollen brown bear he had bought for Elipse. She quietened down, fascinated with the fabric form.

The gentle cantor of the cart beckoned the long journey.

'Twas a night they might all come to fondly remember as that good old, finely fashioned, bonfire of the vanities.

(But that might take some time).

*

Samrost was accosting a guard, one of the ones who had managed to coerce Hawk to go to the City Prison, which was crammed beneath the military fort on Askilt's middle tier. Apparently, Hawk had vanished into plain sight, something signified by the previous rush of feet past his guild house.

When he left later that evening, there was the guard in the red-and-yellow heraldry of Askilt's patrician.

"I'm sorry, you won't find that sore thumb here."

The guard sighed deeply, unsure as to whether to muster up the effort for all the unanswerable questions that could be thrown Samrost's way.

"Have you got any idea of where he '*supposedly*' could be?"

It was a simple question; the guard hoped there would be a simple answer in response for her.

"I imagine he's as far away from your missteps as possible by this point. He's got quite a good two-step, you know." Samrost mimicked the quick footsteps that accompany jabs and lunges, his hands unconsciously riffing on an imaginary blade pointed out into the open in pure rebellion. "When I began working for the guild, Hawk was a living legend; that must have been about..." Samrost stopped for brevity and feigned calculation. "Oh, about thirty years ago. I remember I was assigned to his tutelage for my ascension to rank. I wasn't looking forward to working with him; he has a reputation for being casually obtuse."

The guard was not taken with Samrost's harassment; her patrol required her to be by the east gate guardhouse in the next twenty minutes, and she still had to do a closing of the pub just south of Samrost's shop.

"He has a tendency to cause trouble wherever he can."

In continuing with his speech, Samrost, however, had taken no notice of her fidgeting. "We killed a sand wyvern together, you know. We executed it viciously as our last breaths were nearly carved into fate. Hawk had clambered on its back, and I was left to harass and coax it through a labyrinth gorge near the Dragon's Throat."

Samrost paused as the memory deepened, consuming his senses, the lashing of the tail chasing behind him, the colossal teeth gnashing and gnawing as the golden-yellow-scaled behemoth chased him through the ancient trackway of the Uiss. "Eventually, Hawk made his climb onto its head, and then, after managing to lever away a few scales…" Samrost split his hand with his fist, a brief thunderclap dissolving into delicate silence. "And then he slit its nervous system."

The guard was shocked, fear and awe dredged across her face. The legends of the sand wyverns from the Shuush Desert had reached the Shorelands, though like whisper ripples, their forms and momentums grew and reshaped, re-fused into spectral abominations miles high and decades long.

"Killed it with one thrust of his blade."

Samrost lowered his emotional tension. He could remember the glint of the sun off the sharpened tusk extending like a horn beneath the wyvern's jaw. The teeth the size of arms, reaching out to hold him in a tenderising hug. His heart battering against his chest, a maddened, chained beast, raging as his veins sought to split his skin, the earth-splitting wake caused as the obscenity's body seized and locked, appendages freezing into an impacting point.

A long chain of sweat dripped down the left side of Samrost's face. "Nearly killed me as it fell through itself with the charge's momentum."

He took a long drag of his pipe, acrid smoke flushing from his face, his hand having found it for comfort. "Funny thing is, that wasn't the only time Hawk's tried to kill me with a dead monstrosity's corpse."

A dereliction of duty composed the guard's face. Disrespect for a worker's life. "They should give you worker protection; do you not get given any rights as an apprentice?"

"None." Samrost took another deep drag, his death wish in nostalgic assession. "They factor in that your belief in the job's satisfaction of your existence will be enough to pay you for any traumatic atrocities that get dished your way."

They kicked up a scatter of dirt, the clump dissipating into the many small bodies that composed it, the guard resuming her journey through the city's night, Samrost in tow.

Samrost continued, "They reimburse you for anything you've not been willingly a part of yourself. And how would anybody claim against them?"

"Ridiculous. We get fully insured with the guard's union."

The guard kicked at a drunk who had passed out oblivious in the street. The beer-soaked breath that escaped him told the two of them he was going to be there until morning. It was a standard procedure for many of the city's drunks and loiterers: double-padding their trousers and shirts, and finding the cheapest, closest building porch they could cuddle themselves under.

"And all our training is subsidised."

Samrost was gobsmacked. "Wow."

She continued, "You know that we're not even regarded as a specialisation? You guild members are seen as some kind of Divine extension of the laws of history, and yet you tell me you're all left out to dry. That's truly absurd."

Samrost began his last tangent.

"There was once a strike by the Denilt City Guard, who demanded that they be given better working conditions and better pay."

The guard wasn't surprised; their Denilt equivalents were notoriously underpaid, underserviced and overworked, mostly because Denilt was the richer of the Twinned Lands of the Valestian Colonial Protectorate scheme.

"They sent in a guild member to do the negotiating." Samrost took a last, long smoke to take the memory's taste out of his mouth. "They went back to work straightaway."

Some idle pebbles followed the meandering direction of Samrost's commentary. "Apparently, all he'd done was show them his list of non-negotiables."

TWO

Her laughter dripped across the room. Intoxicatingly rich, voluptuous and warm, it merged with the candlelit sheen in unrivalled beauty. Her face was forcefully contorted into a shape of disaffirmation, her skin taut and prickled, the soft hairs across her skin standing aggressively. Her eyes broke the façade: swollen blackness orbited by submerging blue. Deep and sublimely enchanting. A gentle pink settling across her cheeks, slowly cooling.

"That was *so incredibly inappropriate...* I *cannot* believe *you* would *think* to tell a lady such an *incredulous* tale. *I am well and truly disgusted.*"

The shadows elicited a large gasp behind her, noiseless and strained, their arms exclaiming in serious adjudication.

Her posture became cold and disjunct. Her cheeks, however, were still awaiting their message. "I'm *wont* to call this *whole* charade off by this point. *Where* is the rescuer of beasts and nature *who* brought me flowers this morning?"

Her gestures articulated her intense displeasure. Her

head turned, right hand covering her mouth, left hand pushing against him, the shy wrinkles of a grimace or smile showing. The flowers had been set in water; she could see them out of the corner of her eye. Thick swathes of purple and red, embellished by traces of yellow and white.

"Woe befall me to let *such* a brute into *my* bedchamber. The spirits of my ancestors *must* look down on me in *shame*."

The tent walls shook in shocked insight.

Hawk stifled his growing laughter, his words jauntily stepped. "*Perhaps* if this *lady* would prefer a *different* tale, she might be wont to provide some *direction*."

His breath was a warm hearth; the furred blankets were pulled over them both. She felt the heaviness become all-encompassing. The web of sensation sent soft shivers up her spine, the tingling collecting in her shoulders. She half-nuzzled Hawk and stretched her back and legs through the bed. The feelings followed her example and extended through her body towards her ends. She felt the ache and itch knotted deep in the pit of her stomach.

They wrapped themselves around each other with feigned disinterest.

"How about that time when I helped Lirizia?"

She laughed. The tent laughed too, unsure as to whether the mounting tension would fracture and split, whether it was innately faulted or secure.

The fleshy fault line between ridged tectonic plates sparked with epochal momentum, the trails of forestry and bare stone abutting under a glaring, bright vigil of existential catastrophe. "You'd tell *me* the tale of *your illicit adventures* with another *woman*? *You really are a cur*."

Sharp flickerings of candlelight began as the wicks

33

discussed in soft significance the coming storm. Would they truly be safe? Especially in the epicentre?

Her hand pulled away and mock-motioned a sword thrust through his abdomen. "If I ran a blade through you no one would care; *I doubt anyone* would even *attend* your funeral." Her balled fist separated; she sketched her finger's sharpness around his belly. "*All alone you would die.*" Her fingertips felt the goosebumps prickle along the pattern of her path. She weighted tension, her tongue straining the roof of her mouth. "*All alone* to pass into the eternal night, *without* a single follower or sign of affection."

The tent hung low, the atmosphere shattered by lightning and thunderous atrophy. The conversation scuttled and speared.

Hawk laughed, his tongue tracing his teeth. Puppy-dog eyes sat above a drawn grin, his lips speaking loving energy. "You would *curse* me so? You'd leave me a *soulless shade* with *nowhere* to rest but the twilight of existence?" The shadow of a forlorn afterlife hung over the couple, a spectral, shorn soul, waiting to enmesh itself with its cursed victim. "Better a *landless vagabond*, and a *braindead cur*, than an eater of souls… *Better to lose one than to sell one.*"

Silence. The type of dark, void-encrusted silence that always befores befalls.

She stabbed hard through his abdomen with vicious intent, her rough fingers swiftly shanking his stomach, jabbing and assaulting, repetitively extending and surfacing pain. "Perhaps I should just cut out your tongue, to remind myself of what happens to those without the foresight to shut up?"

His laughter was soft and sweet, enchanted by her emphatic disposition, her flurry of blows a symbolic savagery.

He began to speak. The tent skirts held themselves, anxiously awaiting the words that would thread another inappropriate tale.

"Despite your vitriolic intent, you know full well my tale with Lirizia is little more than the heroic vanquishing of a sultry demonic atoll."

They casually conjoined, their heat and tension resonating and welcoming ecstatic resolution.

"Although it does start with us in bed."

A dark exhalation mixed with prophetic resolution, meandering to a dusky simmer in the atmosphere.

The words began to creep from his mouth but were interrupted by her grasp –

"Fuck!" –

placed firmly in his gut.

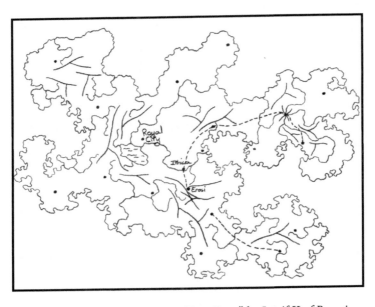

*Map of Kyia: "Where Footsteps Have Been" by Intrif II of Berosia,
1453 PIA*

THE APPRENTICE
KYIA ME A RIVER (727 PIA)

I once saw the blackness spread out across rocks,
Its guts are the tents of the darkness that rots.
It could be much more, but it's never the same,
The darkness that haunts us: a Mineral Vain.
—*The Ballad of Azga*, a Krylei voyage song

He awoke next to her...

What? Lirizia?... *Both of them* safely tucked into bed? Looking just a bit too comfy for things to sit right with him, her hair matted, his body feeling slightly strained.

His thoughtful musings were interrupted by the pronounced shattering of the wooden door.

That explains it.

Lirizia bolted upright, pulling the crossbow out from

underneath the covers, which explained the arm. And the bulge. And maybe the uncomfortable feeling near his ass.

Ahhh, well.

The bolt flew cleanly through the air, piercing the first entrant. A crimson shower of blood spread across the room's atmosphere. A second erupted through the throat of another cutthroat, quick to follow, the body crumpling to the floor with a soft thud, a blood rainbow signalling their demise. Hawk rolled out from the covers, grabbing his sword and shield from their sheaths of mattress and bed. A flourish bloomed two more bolts. Flying from the crossbow, they slew two cronies climbing in through the window.

Hawk's head was fazed; he felt the suffocating fog of heat and humidity sapping his effort and sense. If only he'd drunk more water last night, instead of the leftover wine and spirits who had flowed in fitting revelry. Regardless, he charged head-first into the fray. The blood-thirsty intruders quickly stumbled backwards in response to the bold, scuffling spearhead, causing a shimmering cascade. Hawk continued, stumbling forwards more so, shield drawn, flowing towards the door, his blade nicking the legs of a leather-armoured soldier, blood streaking in crimson arc. His shield battered the body aside and she, the blade, lunged for the chest of the next.

Lirizia, discarding her crossbow, drew her long sword, a dark sheen of primordial metal hilted with glistening rubies. The handle long and stocky, the blade reached, requiring two hands. She swiftly eviscerated several soldiers who had established themselves by the bedroom's window.

She had paid good money for this place. It was a rare treat to work a job with Hawk. And fortunately, this was the perfect battleground.

Well, it was essentially still a small- to medium-sized bedroom. Or, more accurately, with spite the room's conditions were severely hampering the efficiency of the Shadow Knights. Their long blades and serrated shields were too large and ungainly to be truly effective inside the tight space, and they only wore light bronze breastplates, instead of the formidable attire they were fitted with on the battlefield. Therefore, their bodies were quickly accruing on the floor. Mounds of butchered and beaten assailants piled with maleficent essence, their whisps of tarnished life force slowly leaking from themselves, their demonic substance severed by the encroached-upon heroes.

This particular order of Shadow Knights that they were intent on taking down was the Forbidden Order of Unbridled Extent, a shadowy and secretive pact dedicated to the dark god Azga, and the many melds and forms Azga's prejudice took. The Forbidden Order were wont to assassinate interlopers into their estate, and thus Lirizia's plan had been formed.

Having "accidentally" let slip that he was staying in this room, she booked it for Hawk. Hers was next door; she'd snuck in late last night to set the perfect trap to catch some devious and devilish Shadow Knights. She was getting experience hunting the aforementioned band, which was sworn to slay the heir to the Kyian throne. Well, she *was* still technically hunting them.

She called this the "watering hole" strategy. It seemed to be working.

Lirizia dispatched her pair of Shadow Knights with three sharp slashes of her blade. The thick heft of its edge cleanly ruptured the neck of the first intruder. Her second and third slices broke the battered breastplate, with a red sash produced across the chest of her other attacker.

They both fell to the floor with a single *thump*, a brief staccato signal to the end of her trial by combat. She exhaled and felt her pulse start to slow. She felt sweat across her brow, wiping it and looking to see how Hawk was faring.

Hawk was bludgeoning the last Shadow Knight lackey to death by the doorway to the room. He looked confused. These souls were too easy for him, even with the element of surprise. He looked more intruded-upon than anything, etched into a situation he didn't feel comfortable ethically resolving, like an elephant trampling cutthroat shrews.

Or maybe he was just constipated.

He walked over. There was no word, just an inaudible muttering resembling, "Breakfast?"

After name-tagging each of the bodies, she saw to it that the guards were notified. She repeatedly apologised for the fact that their reputation must have gotten out, leading to this fantastical fiasco.

The mighty Hawk drew a crowd, and who was she to know what that could have entailed? She was still naive and needed to learn. They listened and sighed and pitied. She tried to offer them restitutions, but they said they couldn't inflict such a thing on her. "Such a shame. Such a brave woman, doing a man's job."

Lirizia secretly laughed. She looked and saw that Hawk was standing towards the end of the estate spa, a luxurious reminder of what the Valestian Primacy does for its ruling elite, having bought the land and built the retreat as part of a friendship contract with Kyia. Kyianese peasant children were gathered around him as he attempted to lean against an apple-bearing gastoir tree.

Eventually coerced into tricks, he began throwing his sword slowly between his hands, bringing it into gentle arcing spins and whirls. He slipped, the sword ascended, the children gasped as it looked like his fall might slay him. By the time they'd finished gasping he'd rolled, caught the sword, and proceeded to bite the apple half-caught along the sharp blade's edge.

The children guffawed. They rolled around on the floor in a tulip-head scatter, all in slow rotation through time. The waves of laughter that echoed out from their tumbling bodies hung around the warm atmosphere. Hawk carefully stepped over the children to begin the journey away from the buildings and workers, their families, and patrons of the establishment. He then stood, foot-tapping in idle syncopation with the flurry of activity that gathered behind him, as the estate's daily business began.

She caught up with him a few moments later. He'd stepped off as she was tending to her mighty and heroic steed Esseni in the stables, harnessing her and laying her bag and gear across the horse's broad back. At a leisurely pace, it hadn't taken her long to reach him, Esseni in tow. Hawk turned, apple in hand. Esseni took a bite. Hawk discarded the core.

They set out for Kyia.

Hawk had wanted to stop for a detour. Lirizia's protests hadn't helped. Her voice wasn't heard. She had tried to sway with her sounds but they fell upon deaf ears, and dead intent to act against deterring her from her noble quest.

The temple that would break their trek was only a half-hour walk off their road. They took a turn north-west, then north, then west through an everglade forest. The shimmering green foliage retreated into sparkling teal and cyan. The twinkling lights of enchantment clung as a rich luminescent sheen. Verdance in abundance.

They were getting close.

The temple was neither elaborate nor ostentatious. Indeed, it was barely visible. A grove of trees emerged from a well-tended but wild thicket. A spring in the centre bubbled into four drizzling streams that ran a concentric pattern before disappearing. They'd had to ascend the gently rising hillscape of the Gebbis peninsula during this "necessary" distraction. This central plateau that housed the grove was the foundation of the four Emerald Gebbis rivers.

They were widely renowned for their healing properties. Not from the water itself, but the consecrated culmination of the stream's flow. There had been tales told of them since the beginning of the first people's spoken history. The Gebbis peninsula being an old territory of the Urm'gil, these tales were renownedly old, ancient root-swallowed and wizened tree-bearing.

The evergreen barrow was truly sublime. Breathlessly so. The rich green-gold flow of enchanted fey foliage beckoned them forwards, evermore into a fold of dazzling envelopment.

He would be happy to meet Knope. He could hear of his exploits. Learn of his passions. Remember the first time they'd met so many decades ago. Would Knope still remember him? It had been around 130 years since last they'd met. He'd only recently been allowed back into Kyia since that incident.

That incident. Yes, that one. The one he wasn't supposed to talk about.

Knope was deep in a trance when they arrived. He wasn't supposed to be woken; his attendants were adamant about that. Instead they were supposed to wait several hours for him to emerge. After his communion with the barrow-king came theirs, in the name of an enlightened disposition.

Or some other batshit religious mumbo-jumbo resembling that. Knope was deep in a trance, a.k.a. joyfully asleep, under an oali tree. The fruit of the tree perched ever so precariously above him. Hawk kicked out Lirizia's feet as they were both waiting, and she fell, causing the crossbow's mechanism to catch and accidentally expel the bolt.

He uttered some vague apologies to Lirizia as he stretched out his hand; the attendant monk sighed exasperatedly.

There was a thud.

Maybe they wouldn't have to wait so long after all. Knope was clutching his brightly bruised bonce.

"How was the trance?"

The glare of the sun was amplified, the conversation eclipsed.

So apparently, according to Knope, they were "to head west to Ithica". *Apparently*, that was where their rendezvous with the courier would take place. Elaborate names for elaborate games. Bullshit, more like. The journey would be good. Quiet. Mellow. Tranquil. Anything to offshoot the occasional annoying intrusion by the locals.

Lirizia wasn't impressed with any of it.

The Shadow Knights she was hunting had been working through several groups of middle-people in their quest to kill the king, creating a chain of pure confusion, which she believed added an utmost of importance to their task. They were wont for secrecy and disguise, either because they were nobility or because they were just really fucking disfigured. You could never know; that was one of the major draws, the whole hooded cloak and mask. A classic benefit and massive attraction to the people who suffered through the beauty-beguiled society of Kyia.

The landscape around them was euphoric in full bloom. Vivid swathes of flowerheads had burst out from the forest shrubs, a cornucopia of insects and birds gently flowing through the plantscape. The enchanting Gebbis rivers all descended to enrich the peninsula, and from their coursing forms a diverse ecology blissfully grew.

The village they were passing was called Elabora. It was an ancient Krylei (née Urm'gil) settlement. Hawk remembered it fondly from paintings, the gardens dotted with pink and purple perennials, the splashing ripples of light across fairy dust trees, mud-brick buildings and white-stained rooftops. Dusted red chimneys and walls used to sit idly by the river's course. Now it was a trickling stream abutted by a marketplace of stench and decay. The Ultai had moved into the Shorelands. The Krylei Gem had become the Garden Island of Kyia. The times had changed. So had he.

What was Ithica's old name?

He couldn't remember. It was lost to him. It had never been his playground during those times. He'd been born after the time of Azga's fall, after the Ice Age Accord.

Ilyia's great-great-grandfather had written of the ancient times in his recorded histories, having become an adult during the Falling Spires, the time when the enlightened Urm'gil settlements fell to infighting and brutal ideologies, their technological marvels and prowess lost to the treading march of the Ice. To be honest, there were times when it all sounded like garbled nonsense, self-satisfying notions of previous grandiosity; bygone ages of gold, silver, bronze recurring ever onwards into the faint black traces of the past. Even after the fey laced adventures he had cherished with Ilyia, he was still strained by the zeal and fanaticism that belched pain and suffering into the sky of the Shorelands.

It was the remnants of an ancient script of symbols navigating a surreal landscape. Ristos was established when the climates stabilised after the Winter Titans were beaten and finally negotiated into balance – when the Last (Great) Ice Age came and went, and the Accord was struck.

First Ristos, then the Ultai, then the Valestians. The Urm'gil still trod the land when the moon grew full. They still marched across the plains when Yggdrasil's ascendency allowed, when rites of belief allowed manifestation of the Divine source.

Some bullshit like that got chanted by itchy robe-wearing monks hogging good seats, good food, good wine and good times.

Hawk didn't really care for the traditions that allowed such frivolity; he respected them as his place in Krylei society demanded. As his place as council to a warchief commanded. It didn't mean he acknowledged them as the be-all and end-all of truth. Just that he had seen what he had seen, even with Ilyia, reminded him he wasn't hallucinating, and he was loath to surrender the complexity of life to any organised mythology.

Out of all the mythology he'd heard and lived through, his favourite tale must have been the ballad of Istarig. Father used to sing it to him when he helped with chores. He could sometimes still remember the traces of his father's words, how his accent cut the silence of work to begin rolling lush syllables and hair-stoking resonance.

Istarig was his father's favourite figure to tell tales of. Often at night when Hawk had failed to sleep, another fable or anecdote describing a venture of forthcoming would be woven before him.

"Have you heard of Istarig?" The question followed naturally from his trail of thoughts.

Lirizia mulled over the question. She thought she found the answer. "The Monkey King?"

To Lirizia, Istarig was a person told of in children's tales, an old wives' tale passed down through the centuries by Kyianese islanders, describing the acquisition of fire and society by the Ultai before they left the cradle of Ebonheart. Kyianese society had been foundered by Ultai not willing to return to their home continent after the death of Azga. They had chosen to stay amidst their garden island while the frozen wastes expanded across the Shorelands. The Kyianese had been nurtured and nourished by Kyia's blessing, and in return they sent their sons and daughters to die against the Winter Titans. The shrines to their blooded and buried still marked the Shorelands, a hidden network of pox marks and power, long ago left to rest. The Kyianese clans still claimed blood lineage with the warriors who had sold themselves an early death against the ethereal forces far before them.

"Hmmmm." Hawk paused, vexed. "Yeah, maybe. Monkey King seems similar." His pace slowed, and meaningful thoughts expanded out. "He's known as the First Light Bloods amongst the Krylei. The Icitopi call him the Furred Flurry."

Lirizia joined in, emboldened. "When my siblings and I were younger, we would sneak out to the market square at night to catch the Storyteller. I remember the story of the Monkey Prince's ascension." Lirizia paused, straining the memories through her consciousness.

She remembered the bright fires that lit the courtyard, and the rich smell of living that blustered about when that many adults gathered. Her siblings would scatter between the crowd to get a better view; however, Lirizia would always stay behind, anxious over the crowd and mass. She never caught the intricate story woven before the people's eyes; smoke charmers, sat either side of the stage, made anamorphic clouds, vivid rainbow hues billowing from their pipes.

Lirizia would always be fixated on the heroes who gathered outside the tavern. She would watch them with earnest, waiting for the first spilt drink and violent brawl, fixated on the skills and arts of the inebriated and foam-soaked patrons.

"The Monkey Prince story was about his return to Ebonheart. His arrival and conflict with the Vishidyai Kings who had enslaved the Ultai. His capture outside the city of Erruik by Anktoir, and his eventual civilisation into the world."

Lirizia had seen this particular one regularly at the high solstice festival; it heralded the marking of the Ultai as a true people, and their freedom from the valley of the Monkey Kings. It was the penultimate story of the Kyianese Early Mythology. After the Monkey King came the Dying Triology: the Falling Gods; the death of Azga; the Winter Titans.

"He eventually led the army of Anktoir into the Vishidyai Kingdom and slew the Monkey Gods. I remember that bit well. The spray of blood as the Monkey God heads were hewn and split, and then cast asunder." Her smile etched a nostalgic path across her mouth. "I remember that's when I knew I wanted to join the Guild."

Hawk laughed jovially, the light embers of his tone encouraging. He remembered the stories of Anktoir, who went by another name for Hawk, who was a fabled friend of the nobody Odyci.

"I remember that story well. My father used to sing it constantly. However, with significantly less blood. I held to it when I joined the Guild, the idea that heroes were some sort of bulwark against the tides of horrifying evil. Now I'm older, I'm not so sure... perhaps it's the people who are really more important than the heroes?"

Hawk was about to solemnly continue when they crested the hill, and out shouted Ithica: "Welcome, sweet hospitality."

Hawk stood still reminiscing. The Ithica he remembered had never had walls. Had never needed walls. It was still lacking any such demanding quandaries. There wouldn't be any Krylei left here now. Kyia had been bestowed to the Ultai in thanks thousands of years ago, in reward for their help in the wars against the Ehmr'gil, one of the many such places granted to the hordes of fresh-faced newcomers. The many-facing hordes of fresh-faced newcomers. Yet the land was far greater than any, and all, of them. The Ultai footprint was miniscule.

Even after the many centuries since the war with Azga, it was only with the passing of metallurgy and agriculture, pastoralism and healing magic, that the Ultai's successors multiplied so quickly.

Or maybe not.

They bred like rabbits, and were viewed as egocentric barbarians by the Krylei.

That was facetious of Hawk.

There were xenophobic tendencies on both sides. Unfortunately the Ultai's descendants, the So'Ultai, acted more on these tendencies than was particularly healthy.

His dwindling internal monologue was interrupted by the encompassing noise of the tavern.

Lirizia was behind him, tending to Esseni. He walked through the doorway and towards the bar. The crowd were milling around tables – a few were spare – and in one corner sat a crowded dice game. Towards the far end of the bar there was a space. He walked over and motioned to the barkeep. He passed over the glistening shards of metal and waited for the drinks to be poured.

Lirizia joined him.

There was one particular piece of news spreading across the tavern. Valestia had struck and taken Askilt in the past week. They had declared no war, just sailed ships into the harbour and landed. There were no forces to defend the city, no pillaging undertaken. Just a simple march into the Palace of the Patrician King… and his summary execution. Apparently, a sacrosanct bishop of the Silver Order had been placed in charge. He was granted powers empyreality and told to reshape the city into a Northern Paradise. Now refugees flocked across the continent, and mercenaries were drawn to Valestian employment. They looked to advance on Denilt with armies from the Untya Valley.

It explained the foreboding clouds accumulating in the rafters, the resonance of discontent and ill repute. Locally, Kyia was away from Valestia's interests. The alliance with the Islekind would keep them safe.

A surly figure sat down with them by the table. He remembered Hawk. He interrupted the chaos of conversation overhead. "You're the Nifilost slayer, aren't you?" His eyes were jaded.

Hawk's grimace was obvious beyond conceit.

"I remember you. Unfortunately, that wasn't me. I did have to kill the ones that did kill it." He finished his drink with a cough. "Perhaps best we don't talk about that tragedy. What brings you to these parts?"

"I heard you might be entering the mountain?" the man continued, his voice cutting through the silent cacophony. "There was a braggart courier in here earlier; he drank too much, so I took him to bed. He said you were heading to Mount Erosi. That's where the Shadow Knights...?" The man paused quizzically. "That's where they reside. He said it's up to you to kill them and stop them from causing any kind of great catastrophe." He motioned to the barmaid to bring over a fresh round. "So imagine you'll need a healer in case everything goes south?"

Hawk was sceptical, but from the look of the man's frayed robes, he didn't feel he had a choice.

They finished up their drinks and set out. The old man said the journey wouldn't take the night. Apparently. They kept their torches lit as they ascended the road. There was a rustle straight ahead.

An arrow emerged. It split on his blade, but still bit his flesh. Hawk acknowledged the pain, readying his sword and shield. "Awww, fuck... Where did that arrow come from?"

"I think to the left, in the trees and the shrub." Lirizia had drawn her crossbow, taking sight.

The healer began muttering a few words, and a green energy amassed between his hands and dissipated. A swarm of incandescence emerged from the trees. Lirizia shot her bolts towards the shining target.

They both connected, and an effervescent font gushed forth.

Two more patterns of bright energy entered into the healer's enchantment. Lirizia began reloading her crossbow.

Hawk stepped forward, and with a prepared arc caught the interlopers as they protruded from the foliage. They were cleaved with one blow, and crumpled to the floor. "Fuck. That was too painful for something so simple."

The people hadn't unnerved Lirizia; a few interlopers was nothing to give her more than a slight quickness of breath. Her lungs were slowing, and her aim had rung true. "As always," she liked to add.

Hawk stood aggrieved, with two trickles of blood flowing down his leg. "Kind 'Healer', if you would be so kind, please?"

The healer laughed. "See, I'm sure the fates divined our passing. Were it not for me, you would die out here, wounded, pissed and cantankerous." He approached Hawk with open arms.

Hawk had been injured, not mortally wounded... she wished. That would be so much better, and it was obvious that the healer was more than capable. His tourniquet was done unconsciously mid-conversation. Instead of concentrating, the healer rambled sullenly about grotesque attitudes. He was bitter. He was unkempt with contempt.

He laid his hands out suddenly. Closing his eyes, the healer muttered a few inaudible syllables. She thought she saw a shimmer of green resonate from the healer's fingertips. With that, he was done. An expletive described the current King of Kyia. Two more described the king's ancestry.

Hawk couldn't really disagree with him. She couldn't really, either.

They continued the journey towards their goal.

They were close to the mountain now. They would reach it tomorrow. They had been feeling the earth beneath their feet shake momentarily at irregular intervals that had increased in frequency since the start of the day. The healer had rippled with tension as each one hit, stopping briefly to close his eyes and take note.

That concerned Hawk. She noticed it in his quick glances to the sky. Was he looking for animals moving, or shifting trees? She couldn't tell, and he was deep in concentration.

As they'd gotten closer, the intensity of the vibrations passing through their surroundings had increased as well. This especially concerned Hawk. He was thoughtful as to whether the actions of the cultists had caused something to awaken in the mountain. He knew they couldn't have done enough to cause the emergence of some dark chaotic force, but what if their sacrifices had corrupted a Manakind nestled deep within the rocks?

The cultists were sat amidst this pox-marked cave. The entrance was daubed with what she hoped to be ochre, red-stained pictographs of sacrifice and gluttony.

The healer fingered the pictograph closest to him. He licked the substance and grimaced. "That's blood. Fresh blood, and it's human."

Was every healer so comfortable with cannibalism? Lirizia hoped not.

They entered. The crevice that gave passage to the interior was only a couple of metres wide. The passage in was a snaking dark pathway to the underworld. They could hear currents of water passing overhead; the strange echoes of cave life, bats, fish and spiders rustling above and below.

They caught brief glimpses of passageways veering off to the left and right, smaller, less worn paths that didn't whisper to Hawk. The way to the cultists shimmered in his vision, the ethereal wisp-hook that aided his perception pulling him down, deeper into the labyrinth beneath Mount Erosi. If he had been nurtured on Kyianese fantasy, he would know he was reaching the lair of the Ulgash, the dark tormentor and slayer of souls, the eater of essences.

The Kyianese cultural imagination could be a pit of despair at times.

She was extremely anxious about this endeavour now.

Ulgash was a ferocious spirit that would consume those of the night; not the guilty, but the innocent. Ulgash would wait and torment, eliciting fear before consumption, valuing a scared prey beyond all else. Ulgash would lick tainted teeth and spread the curse across his tongue, a lashing of which would sear away skin and burn sorrow deep into the heart of the unlucky, soon to be gone.

As they entered deeper into the mountain's belly, she would come to terms more and more with the consequence of conscious creativity.

They eventually saw a flickering flame's shadow, the fluid movements of darkness projected by light, a backdropped rippling, shimmering against the dripping passage wall. Imprints of silhouetted figures dancing were etched onto the rockface. Hawk made the first steps around the corner; she was perched behind, crossbow readied, the bolt reflecting an amber resonance. The healer had vanished some junction past, sneaking off from the rear-guard to attend to some shifty disposition Hawk had suspected he had intended for some time. That's why he had *been* on the rear guard; better to avoid confrontation and just let the sneaky fuck shift off into the backdrop.

Now he was gone, though, he'd kind of miss him. His sullen attitude. His flimsy attire. His lack of conversation. Even when he'd been tending Hawk's wound, he'd mentioned very little. He'd seen the edge of a tattoo peeking out from under his stuffed collar. It was pitch-blue, a blueness in hue whose intensity increased the longer you focused upon it. Mystifying.

The blade of a cultist nearly caught him off guard. His fist connected with the first of several faces that emerged around the jagged corner of the tunnel. The others scraped to push past the first. Hawk's blade rushed forth, stabbing several times, and then several times more. The florid of blood rushed forth until, eventually, the fresh flesh-based palisade could be trodden over.

Lirizia was gobsmacked, even more so than the first cultist.

They turned the rest of the bend and met what remained of an incantation. They must have heard the racket of the fighting and decided to perform dark macabre arts.

They'd performed the incantation wrong. Oops.

Hawk bent down; his fingers intruded into a chasm of a wound across a cultist's chest. He retrieved his fingertips and licked them. Lirizia nearly barfed.

"They died ever so recently. It's painful; we could have saved them if we hadn't got caught up with those idiots who wouldn't lay down their arms."

He was right, although she failed to understand how they would have stopped them without the edge of a weapon.

"Ah, well. I just hope whatever it is didn't cause any further damage. It doesn't look like the incantation merged a Manakind into some kind of corrupt entity."

"Hawk."

"It looks like they were missing a person, though."

"Hawk… behind you."

He heard the snicker of serrated teeth; he felt the edge of a sharp blade tenderly caress his shoulder. It traced a bead of sweat. His throat tightened. Hawk braced for impact.

He heard the thudding slam of the crossbow mechanism as two bolts flew past, one by each ear. They punctured the manifestation, which let out a chilling howl. He reached for his sword hilt. The blade swung cleanly out of the scabbard as he shifted on his right foot and brought his left leg round; the sword sang as it cleaved into the charred leathery flesh of the beast.

The beast howled again, stabbing its right blade at Hawk's left calf. It nicked his leg, and blood spurted. Hawk swore and rolled to his right. Two more bolts were spat at the beast; they pierced and lodged themselves into its left scapula. Green blood pustulated and pissed from the wound.

The beast was an eruption of bone from what must have been the final member of their abhorrent entourage. Their pink fleshy fingers had melded into white-tan, single-bladed protrusions. Their face had warped; jutting barbs and tusks tore and contorted through the former skin, which had become a deep, tattered, red-brown leather. Horns had perforated said skin everywhere, spearing upwards out from every appendage. The skin, straining to contain them, had split and ripped, becoming weathered and tough. The eyes were pitch-black onyx sockets, nose and teeth forming a gnashing chain of rusty blades.

The blades whirled as it tried to chew at Hawk. He held it at bay with several consecutive blows – *left, right, right, left, up*, the clash of his sword parrying the flayed blades of the monstrosity, his fleeting defences sparking against the abrasive strikes of the horror.

Lirizia was perspiring. She wasn't expecting this kind of horror. She was used to dealing with banditry and brigands, not inept cultists with too much free time and too few language skills to cast a spell properly.

This was a malformed horror from the seventh dimension.

This wasn't Ulgash, the red-black premonition of life's twilight and suffocated dreams. This was a darkness far worse. This was the immediacy of life-threatening danger. Red flares culminated in her vision. Her thoughts had aided in distracting her from fear, and two more bolts were let loose. They lodged themselves into the perches that were once eyes. The beast was unfazed, though, and ravenously hungry.

She moaned. Throwing the crossbow to the floor, she drew her polearm.

Hawk yelled something about magma seams. Something about how dormant mountains often contain pockets of seeping, burning fire and flames. He must have meant the bodies of Ulgash. She remembered the tale. Something about an internal pit from which Ulgash spoke with putrescent black smoke. How would they get the demon there?

They felt the cave begin to vibrate.

With clashes and slashes, the noise of the melee was spread throughout the cave system. There was a close echo that Hawk just about discerned. It was worth it; it might be all they had. He motioned to Lirizia to push the incantation towards a pathway to the left of the forum. He braced himself behind his shield and began pummelling the serrated shape.

It gnashed at his brim; the flicker of blades sliced at his exposed flesh, his face becoming a patchwork quilt of nicks and cuts.

Between the two of them, the maleficence was pushed ever slowly backwards through the tunnel. After a long and tedious slog, they arrived at an opening into Ulgash's lair.

They were on a precipice that overlooked a flaming inferno of a pit. Further below them, on another jutting rock, stood the healer, arm outstretched. Vivid blue words flowed from his mouth. As they pushed the beast into the inferno, he looked up at them, smiling.

A blue simmering blanket lay across the bubbling magma.

The sharp form fell through the layers of sublime silken shadow.

The incandescent ripples of energy fused into the malformation, weaving rich webs of warming motion,

The bones retreated, the fires calmed, the volcano breathed a sigh of relief, let out a gasp of exultation. After drawing deep for breath, they were finally expelled.

*

They landed with a thud.

57

A soft thud.

A thud softer than any thud she could have imagined, but still a thud.

And fuck, do thuds hurt.

She'd had to tell everybody the story.

*

It wasn't just the officiator who suffered her regales. She had triumphed victoriously, and would now be regarded as a fully certified guild member.

She hadn't requested a post. She didn't need to be stationed anywhere. She had decided to follow in the footsteps of the champions who went before her. She would range across the mainlands, maybe travel south-east towards the Ultai homelands of Ebonheart. She had heard the stories of technological marvels and martial prowess. If she studied the arts of war, she could return and ready herself for the time that would come.

The time when Valestia would sail north.

This would be her time to prepare. This would be the start of her arduous journey across the realm of progress.

She had been given her steed Esseni on full terms, which she was glad for. She hadn't wanted a different mount on graduation. She had been given her bursary, a bag of gold, a full set of blue-and-white melding moon-crusted armour, a sharp sword and manasmote shield, vigilant and stoic.

She had been directed towards the keep of Strenis Bargif, a baron suspected of dabbling in demonic sorcery. He wasn't very powerful or intelligent, and therefore this was both of utmost importance and the minutest of duties.

Esseni had set off at a gentle canter. She revelled in the soft breeze rushing past her furred face. Lirizia's legs were tenderly wrapped around her flanks: not too soft to be loose, not too hard to be uncomfortable, the bridle a fluffy weight of sheepskin and hardened cattleskin.

Esseni felt the joy rippling through Lirizia, and therefore highly suspected they were off to have more fun.

THREE

Rows upon rows of fathomless coloured tents marked out the boundaries of Hawk's eyesight. His return from the "urgent" foraging assignment was going well; the soldiers he passed knew better than to waylay him and interrupt their commander's midnight snack.

Their passing parties patrolled for alcohol and meat, the campfires consistently harassed by skulking shadows. Laughter and camaraderie doused any sense of chilling fear, or sinking dread, before the battle tomorrow. There would be anticipation on the lips of the soldiers spread across the campsite, but not a harrowed anticipation. It was the offering of glory and honour, of long overdue rest from the weariness of the world.

The soft linen structures dissolved like flowers in a meadow, his careful footsteps dodging guide ropes and near-invisible tufts and mounds of grass and dirt. Insects and birds chirruped as he passed, the forest soundscape merging with the songs and chatter of the Krylei soldiers.

He strolled past the pitched tents, the nightscape above them twinkling, brilliant lights smitten. He was laden with food and drink: a pack stuffed with meats, crackers, and cheese, and waterskins of Ristosian wine and spirits.

She might be asleep by the time he returned. He half hoped not, but maybe she should be. Tomorrow would be busy, and she'd need her rest. There was no place on the battlefield for a deep tiredness.

He returned to her wakeful gaze. She was standing by the dresser preparing her clothing and armour. The waves of candlelight wove over her body, shadows cresting her shoulders and trickling down her spine. He unpacked the food, watching her serene movements. Her armour was made from an ironesque material that could be re-smelt into itself at whim. Her blade was sharp enough to cut stone and light enough to hew through as many foes as dared stand before her. White inlaid patterns told her clan and lineage, and noted that she was the seventeenth of her line to be their regional warlord.

The soft concentric circuits imprinted into her vestige shone and sparkled in harsh juxtaposition to the fields of battle they were often found in, the beautiful piece of art a testament to the ideals of the Krylei.

Preparing a tower of food, he slowly and carefully returned to the bed. He waited on her return; her arrival stunk of gluttony, and she descended. He watched scatterings of crumbs fall across the bed; reaching for the covers, he pulled it into the debitage zone. Their midden began to mound.

The food was good; he didn't have the stomach for thought. Glancing over to his pile of equipment, he checked that he was ready. The scabbard shined with anticipation. The blade was keen and giggling. She was far too eager for the coming dawn, yet it was good of Tiana to return her for this trial.

He checked; she was finished with the food, spread feline. He took the plate, moving it to the table next to their bed.

"I feel a bit friendlier now. Now that I've had food. I think, though, you'd be rude to forget how crude you were being earlier. Your lewdness is unbecoming in my presence." She sniffed the air and held her head high.

The rising melodies of the night bird's songs crept into the tent.

The glance towards his weapons and armour was quick.

They enmeshed. Her hair cast silkily across him as her head took stock of nourishment and sought to nestle into the deepest of slumbers.

Her eyes were slits of stars, all-encompassing twilight burning bright in cosmic crescendo. Starfire hues dancing before the dawn of oblivion.

"I think I might sleep now. Will you as well?"

"I'm okay. I think I'll think about tomorrow's strategy. It'll be an early start for the troops."

She laughed. "You should get some sleep. Can I have one more for the road?" Her voice was becoming blurry and slurred. Her head nuzzled. "One more that I can pay the Sleeping God with?"

"How about that time I slew the witch Kin'Yif?"

She drifted off to tousled hair.

"That was the time Malicath saved me from death. I remember the murder of crows gathering at my feet like it was any other day of my life. There was a rich black tide that swallowed the sun, casting vigil over my soul before I passed into the pestilent underbelly of Yggdrasil."

He checked to make sure she was comfortable, her expression and breath soft and cosy. Reddy pink hues gathered on her cheeks. He felt the faint trace of her exhalations as she slowly drifted off into the Sleeping God's realm.

"If he hadn't arrived, I would surely have been dead. I would have seen no more sunstrokes across the clouds. I would have entered solemnly into the cursed existence of an afterthought, like so many others before me."

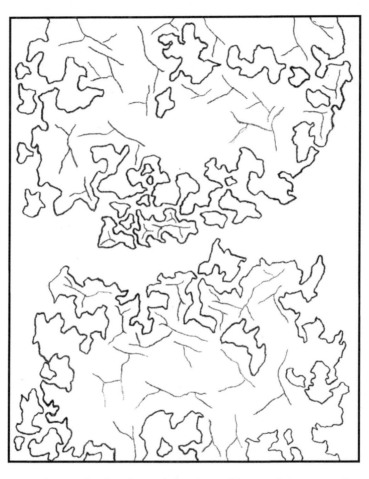

Map of First Isles: "A Charcoaled Calamity" by Nyarl, Dragon Rider,
~236 PIA

THE CYCLE

A PITTED OLIVE
(710 PIA)

At first there was crystal water,
Then in a second, came the torrent,
by the third came all oxygen,
And then finally fourth, a meteoric light.
—Usstrix, *The Dragon Rider Creed of Creation*

The thick, toxic stench clung to him, painfully stinging his eyes. He still hadn't lost it. He'd been stamping through pox pain for days. Weeks since the incident that led to pungosity Divine. Now he was fucked, any bath he took, every lake he passed; pestilence if he dared take a dip. Wholescale contamination would be his wake. A lifetime of decay to trail his momentary slip into demise.

The baths were fine; if he dissipated the bath water, it wouldn't damage the local environment. It wouldn't poison the other livings within a bubonic minute. He couldn't risk touching any of the fresh water he was surrounded by, though.

The druid was ahead. Supposedly ahead. Malicath the Murderous. No pun intended.

He heard a caw, some crowing in front of him. He was overwhelmed by a swallowing tide of black feathers.

He hoped he'd been quick enough. He knew he probably hadn't been. Blurred images started to form in the shadowy recesses of his mind.

Putrefying toxic abbreviations of raw fluctuating chaos submerged him. Rupturous belches of carrion-spreading lamentation that singed the threadbare thoughts swimming, drowning, suffocating, corroding in the depths of his pain.

The swirling shadow mass melded into a plethora of misty, noxious forms, shapes protruding, revolving, rotating inwards into themselves in time-warping dissonance, intensely colliding into particle-imploding revolutions. A geodesic dome of cosmically creative carnage. The synergic mental mass and stimulated reception; tingling effervescence rippling in spasmodic elastications. Creeping tentacles and cloying, suckling attachments masticating like limpets through the electrical shadows of his body's nervous system.

Ilyia emerged, draped in her blood-red cloak. Ruby gemstones inset around the clasp created a kaleidoscopic shine, the refractions and splittings of light enticing Hawk's vision and perception. Beneath the searing red ran a rich turquoise lining, inlaid with concentric sparkling silver mazes.

Her hand outstretched, he reached forwards, tumbling into the wispy mass of tendrils. Her face shifted, tentacles emerging, turquoise-red melding into deep, dark, antagonising green, shifting lines solidifying, rays of light gathering substance and shadow. They began to concrete as cagey brown oali bars, a looming force, a brown snare to entrap a beast, to crush its spirit before its death. Shrinking ever inwards, ever more tight and claustrophobic. Pushing him ever closer into the chaotic storm-cloud epicentre.

Chains of synaptic discord brought memories forward from the eye into his throes. He gleaned the night at the farm. A raging inferno, and him a crestfallen child. Stern resolve – bitter, stern resolve. Decimation, destruction, and pure unbridled hatred.

He felt the choking smog, grasping for his throat. Silent screams to the two fallen by the fire in the doorway, the shedding wood burning and shattering his conscious.

There was a sharp intake of breath as water flooded his lungs. His arms leapt out to drag his body upwards, out from the lake's sodden choking hold.

He was drowning, trying to escape; he was weak and starved. Pushed to the brink and nearly catatonic. Frozen shivers tore at his body. His captors wrapped him in blankets and chains, the cold steel biting his wrists.

There were hands encompassing him, pulling him, tugging him, forcing him out from the hold of the cage as it tightened. Thudding his chest, impacting his lungs. A thick torrent of water burst from his throat…

He awoke, sweaty and cantankerous, to his first death.

The titan Axi;Fli-Yly, the unspeakable; a young buck ready to prove himself.

The weeks spent in preparation. Several moon-scorned

nights of dedicated practice and patience. The Brightscale's endowment to the sword. The blessing to the steed. The last rites. He chanted his lineage, spoke the words of his ancestors.

He recited what needed to be done in the mind and mental foreboding.

"Before the lost times, there was no one to be lost, and thus our task was simple. Now there are many, and without a reaping the crop will strangle us all. As is the way of all things natural. The gardener knows they are just a mobile tree."

His steed, Elstess, wasn't nervous. She cackled malevolently at the hymn, prescience of death satisfying her whims.

Toying with some cattle, she bit a chunk from one, bringing the fresh carcass over to her young. The hatchlings were doing well. Their sharp faces and serrated teeth gnashed the corpse of their mother's final meal.

They would be good for his brood, at least. His broodborne, if more. His broodkind, if most.

They set out at dawn. He would let her have this last moment. After tonight, it would be done.

He readied his weapon. The Brightscale Yiz-Gil had lain the last few enchantments. His blades were sharp. They were sharp last time this happened, too. It nearly hadn't been enough. Nearly. Twenty years hadn't dulled their keenness. The shimmer of the sky-forge was caught by his first blade, a shafted polearm smart enough to sever any foul Manaborn with the first nick.

They could both taste the coming blood.

The sun shed itself; the cattle fell silent. Mournful. He left before they returned home from service. They knew he would. The children shed a tear and held their own.

68

It was just that time.

They weren't the last. They weren't the first. They were the first middle. The first uninspired slump. The first scatter of laziness and hedonism to plague a raw primordial middling. There weren't many of them during this time. There needn't be. Too much of a good thing is a problem. Problems were plenty outside the islands. Problems were plenty *inside* the islands.

They knew there were others of their kind scattered throughout the lands, this strange world of vicious, scaled drackind and malformed titans, energy possession and emerging Divinity. They had lived on the islands long enough for their existence to have affected the network of raw, powerful symbols that clashed around them. They had seen the fluctuations and vortices that swirled around their social minutia. The carrion crows of infinite volume that would appear, transform, then dissipate into the astral ether that sat just above their earthly bearing.

The Manakind, they were called. The ones from time begun, to be feared and respected, and especially avoided. A genetic conditioning so deeply engrained and important to the foundation of the universe that some said that Yggdrasil themself was entwined with the fates of the Manakind, making them the true children of "God".

The first who came to the islands were from the Volcanoes of Klaxc, a raging cataclysmic land of sweltering magma and eruption, its location lost to all but the Priestcadre of the East Isle. These Dragon Riders slept under the mountains' gazes and found refuge. They anointed their blades and slew the first Great Beast to trespass and bring trauma and travesty, sharing in the feast and blessing their homes, erecting the first cairn and the spiritual platform that became the Priestcadre's illustrious halls.

After centuries, there were eventually settlements across both islands. Twelve, to be precise. Others had also arrived from the many nameless places under the sun. In times like these, that was considered significantly good.

Now, further centuries on, there are the twenty-five dragon-rider clans on Wxil-Lix; now there is the Iriyas Priestcadre of Exil-Lix. All before the behemothic intent of Axi;Fli-Yly the unspeakable, a larger titan than any he had previously killed, a Divinity that would need to be recast through sublime rhinestones.

Elstess huffed in warning. Time to clip the wings, so to speak.

They arrived at the lair with ease, under the gentle breeze of the wind, and the soft murmur of fauna scampering the other way. Being new to the manascape, Axi was still shaping with raw will manifest. The threads of Axi's being were still entwining themselves into the spirit-scape. The life-dipped, blooming hills that used to rest here, just last season, were wrought with ironesque foliage. Strewn metallic shimmers streaked the dirt-grass patchwork. The copses of trees bled a viscous, mercury shine.

For a month's work, this was quick intent. It worried him deeply. All the more that Axi needed to be moved away from the islands. It was as much fact as fiction by this point in their destiny.

In death, Axi's energy would rejuvenate, would be reborn in the stories and tales woven in the shade of their death. Axi would continue not as a blight but as a blessing, a cloak of sobriety following intoxicating roots.

That was the way. That was the accord with a;Giz-Kos, the primordial. The order to chaos and approximation. The seal between the steps of Manakind. The chain that bound the Dragon Riders and the Illyuom city Sstates to the islands, to the coursing tide of causality. Axi was the next cog in the wheel. The totem would be crafted on his deathbed, the cairn established, the defence against future encroachment further strengthened and developed.

Axi was the seventh greater titan since the Settling. His fall would chart the dawn of the Seventh Caste of Priesthood, the Children of the Voiceless.

A searing red-orange burst of flame licked past his face as Axi gave chase, joining the ferocious sky-climb. He clung to Elstess's body, Axi's raging voice booming far behind them. He clung for their lives, thinking about his next move. He knew what had to be done. There. The brief stench of flame rushed past them once again. His legs loosened; he fell backwards through the cloud of post-shout smoke. He drew his blade; she giggled hysterically.

They landed in the belly of the beast.

Only temporarily, mind you; you never want to be close to one of those things when they go off.

The light punctured Hawk's daze. He awoke in tremendous pain. Winced. Gasped. Cursed. Strove to lessen the burden and relax his mind. It didn't work. Where was he?

The room was below ground-level. He could smell the atmosphere and pressure change. The scent of cave spiders and troglodytes suggested he was deep underground.

Malicath. He must have found him.

Or worse.

There was a voice amidst the shadows: a wispy, thin, sharp voice. Like the caress of a razor over his ears. He couldn't understand the language. It cut through the pain, and thus came sleepening darkness.

The voice shifted in register. It became the tenor cry of someone specifically calling him. Sheer immediacy. She was in danger. They were all in danger. His brood had helped him lessen it, but still.

This was his second death. He remembered his first so fondly. He had done his brood proud. They had done *their* brood proud. His steed Elstess had been the finest. Her litter had exceeded her, as expected, in only the best ways. Now he rode her grandchild, Elsteir, the silver-tipped. He spoke to her in her kin-tongue. Elsteir was ready for this. She had helped persuade the others that escape was the only option now; the fanatical zealots would be the end of their time here on the islands.

Would be the end of the islands altogether.

He fed the two mice, taken from their carry case, some brown-green tea leaves from their pouch, letting them chew on the prophetic herb, then placed them down on the ring board. They eventually traced their visions across the sand; with rambling gaits they divined. If he was of either island's zealous priest castes, he would have disembowelled them. A disgusting practice. The zealots would remain to wage their war. The refugees of both sides had already been gathered. He was the last.

Well, the last, but not. He would be here to see it happen. To say the rites of passing and face the consequence.

The great consequence of everything they'd done.

Everything the others had done to kill themselves.

Decimate the landscape. Drown the population in a demagogue-drenched deluge. They suffocated, embittered by the two factions. They expressed their flaming rage as a desolating inferno. They ate the earth, vomiting walls and temples, leading the land into pestilence. Corrupted rotting soil turned foul for destitution to populate amidst. The waters ran crimson with the blood of sailors and sea slaughter.

The last of the dragons would leave, the last of the Dragon Riders with them. The ships of Tizki, the one named, would sail north under the dragon shadows. And there would raise the ashes of despair.

The mice traced their vision.

A crumbling shelf. Two movements beneath igniting, buried magma churning. Burning, fiery destruction erupting from air-touched seams, spewing tremendous expenditures of bottled energy, chasmically beneath the depths, inciting violent tides of rising water and large breaths of heat.

The islands slowly sauntering ever inwards. The gentle, protracted crushing of land against land. The deafening death howl of two blood-drenched civilisations. Engulfing screams. Drowning tsunamis. Settlements drenched in volcanic flames. Suffocated by earthquakes.

The ones left would all be dead.

The mice-seers ceased their sand shaping scribblings.

The totality of it didn't astonish him. The islands would collide.

The sun dipped from the sky, down behind its mountain shield, saving its eyes from the sight.

It happened, beginning with one large snap – the shredding of calcified tendons. With an expanding crack, they severed and one dropped, pulled under by an unknown strain, the other curling inwards on itself, snagged by the same elemental hook. The water leapt up, reaching for the sky. It missed, beginning its descent.

Elsteir spoke calming words, sibilating sentences slipping through the signs of coming apocalypse. Eventually, the water collided with the land. Then came the drowning. He could see the islands slowly being ripped into the deep-sea crevice. He saw great wings emerge from the ensuing destruction, quickly cresting the skies and ferrying away.

All the while, the island masses were drawn closer, slowly but surely meeting their certain fate.

Eventually, the crushing carnage ceased.

Then there was quiet. Not the golden silence of joy, serenity, tranquillity... the silence of the apocalypse.

There, shredding through the atmosphere with a jagged crunch, an infuriating crash came. Tentacled appendage after tentacled appendage appeared, barbed, in gigantic fetish, and violent fury, to the armoured inklings of the Isles. In gigantic totemic emblemage came the consequence – the consequence to be faced, lest it decimate. Lest it unbalance the flow of the great cycle. Cataclysmic consequences for cataclysmic choices. Apocalypse for apostatehood. Demons for Dragons.

They both gulped. He grabbed his lance. The world took note.

They began their descent, knowing it would be their last.

Deep silence is the premonition of death;
engulfing winter the prediction of all life.
To drown an island is an immense test of the
universe's patience,

74

But luckily there's always a harpoon on hand.
—*The Dragon Riders' Sermon*

Rows upon rows of serrated black teeth welcomed them both into the void-drenched unknown. It began to fizzle and burn, ignited by their flaming entrance, then eventually it began to implode. With implosions come headaches, and back pains, and dull aching semblances of past trauma.

They ignited Hawk's brain, rapturing him from his medicinalised slumber. He was in a temple. Your average, everyday temple. A temple to whom? Who's to know? Well, obviously Malicath, of course. That was where he was heading. To rid himself of that curse: the permanent, pustulating endowment saucily provided by the she-witch Kin'Yif. He had had to slay her after that. Collect her blood. Collect some aspects of her form and substance. For the antidote. The potion. He'd then walked for how long? A week? Two weeks? Three weeks? His body was used to withstanding this kind of torture and agony. His physiology was stoic to most of the threats this side of Ristos. But this had been a magic curse. It must have been someone providing Kin'Yif with the weapon. She didn't have the power.

He winced in pain as his brain surpassed the painkillers lodged in his synapses.

She didn't have the power for something this insidious. He would need rest. Need to rest. Then he would find the person who did this. Someone with this kind of malicious intent was ill fit to rule, but likely destined to if no one were to stop it.

The hooded figure turned around. He hadn't noticed the shape in front of him. He was food, a mouthful of hot broth. There were vegetables and a taste, but he couldn't… he couldn't quite get his brain to put together what it tasted of, what it contained. He felt a dullness.

He was soon asleep, journeying to Yggdrasil's realm.

He awoke to the sounds of battle, to the sounds of indentured servitude towards death; noble or not, the gruesome reality of an impending knowledge of one's own doom. The intoxicating thread that can so quickly turn to dread-inducing dissonance.

But it wasn't here.

There was a golden chord. A resolution beneath the harrowing harmony overlain. Good.

They hadn't faltered while he was in communion with Tael'gar, the barrow-king. He needed the time away from the discord to ready his breath. Azga'Kilnof, the Demon of the Void, the Stones-So-Sullened, the Usurper, the Mountain before the Abyss, the Rim-Turned-Inwards. His forces had amassed by the edge of the peninsula. They had flocked in multitudes to his banner, those he had corrupted. Those who were darkened.

Azga continued their journey into the depths of their biology. He ruptured the threads that bound them to their personhoods. Reborn, they were sinful souls, sinful souls that sought to slay the light. Usurp the might of Yggdrasil. Plunge the world back into Manakind-led genocide. Tael'gar was the highest order of Divinity he could have contacted. The very soil of the Earth had felt the armies approaching, had wanted to see response, had helped persuade the various Manakind to join in union with the Urm'gil and Ultai. Had helped organise the First Peoples and their cities. Helped them find the First Forged, the Bladed Lance of the Dragon Riders. They planned to hunt the abomination.

Now, he held it.

To kill a mountain range is a terrifying idea, nigh on impossible to imagine. He had thought they would have to descend to the very centre. Plunge the blade into the flaming heart of the North Rim Mountains.

Instead, the mountain range had come to them, embodied and emboldened. Tael'gar had told him the transformation would make Azga vulnerable. Not weak, but vulnerable. It would be up to him to find the body. Slay the beast. Save the day. He didn't like that idea. He knew what would come. Tael'gar told him of the great consequence. That this was both one of theirs to slay, but also to bask in.

Bask was such a strange word for what Tael'gar meant.

Not a soul would survive the inferno.

Was *inferno* the right word? It wouldn't be flames. But it would be cleansing…

Slaying a mountain range expends an enormous amount of energy.

*

He caught sight of the gigantic beast, its horrific scaled belly bulging over a plain of slain challengers, their corpses a valley of dead, putrefying dunes. Blood and flesh dripped from its rows of fangs; a sea of black-purple fur coated its thick, leathery skin. Azga had taken the form of a six-legged rhinoesque monstrosity. A large flat-snouted face protruded; it snarled with fanged teeth and expulsed terrifying roars of deafening blades. The waves that roared outwards from the eldritch monstrosity caused horror and soldier alike to fall. The fields of lustrous grass resting between glistening hills were now drenched with blood, and had washed into several miles of dank, or desiccating, cesspits of despair.

Azga strode through the ranks of soldiers, a behemothic demon hellbent on the mutilation of the manascape; the visceral evisceration and severing of living sentiment, scouring phenomena into pure null abyss.

He swallowed hard and reached for his stirrups to mount Algir. Algir stood firm, and they began their journey down into the fray, loose stitching and stained carcasses leading the way.

He had reached Azga. Sweat dripped, rolling from his brow. He clung to Azga. His hand was strained, pain searing through tendon and muscle alike. He roared in distress. Azga was shivved by him. Precariously perched on the nape of Azga's neck, he readied his long sword.

He plunged it into Azga, simultaneously levering his right blade out of the flesh.

He plunged it back in, securing his footing, using the weapons to holster his body atop the titanic fiend. He anxiously felt for the bladed lance.

He panicked, breath strained and nervous chills resonating throughout his spine. It was still there. Tension rippled. The cacophony of sword clashes and shield blocks overwhelmed his senses. Azga stank to the high heavens of unadulterated foulness. His stomach gurgled with poisoned ripples.

He forced the two swords deeper, wrapping his legs to their hilts. He made the plunge. This was the one shot. If he missed or let go, they would all be fucked. He swallowed hard.

As sweat slowly dripped down his brow, he made his mark. A current of energy shimmered through the lance's shaft into the blade, down into Azga. Forked lightning electrified Azga's interior. The demonic form was illuminated; the ripple of neurons buzzed, then burn. Enflamed, they roared, then engulfed, then soared outwards across the battlefield, like purifying light.

Like...

The searing white energy jolted Hawk awake. There was a figure above him: Malicath, that old bastard. Malicath smiled and laughed. Some sounds emerged, his lips pursing, but the meaning and nature were lost to Hawk. They etched themselves over him, ringing him into a deep sleep, deeper than the ones prior. Deep, and again deep.

He saw shapes form from the eternal darkness.

Wisps transformed into clouds, which melded into substantial patterns: concentricity merging into personhood. The meaning and images were lost to him. Ethereal sentences of transcendental identity. Outstretched arms of blurred purpose. Skewed hands grasping for contact.

But there was none.

The shadows parted, illuminating the vision, the manifestation of rupturing mountains, rolling cloudscapes teeming with fields of water and charges of energy. A bolt shot down to the valley floor, igniting a tree. Another shot out. A third burst, chasing the second. Soon the forest was alight with fire and smoke.

The clouds in pity cried, tears streaming across the scarred forest. They smothered the roaring screams.

Soon came silence.

Then shoots blooming amidst ash-caked silence;

animals returning, life renewing the cycle; culminations of intent and nurtured consequence. The river shifted, sifting the ash-laden silt. The animals began their slow build, managing their portions they fought, and shared, and moved towards.

He saw Malicath, collecting herbs. Befriending a deer; several more emerged from a grove to nuzzle against the druid's robe and posture.

Malicath, with hand lent, stood in appreciation. Eventually, he was coerced into handing out some more of his bounty. Satisfied, the deer thanked him and moved on, chatting with glee for prospective tides.

Hawk awoke for the final time. He felt it in his bones: the buzz of resourced energy, left to stew and culminate, finally emerging from a cocoon of surrealist hallucinations as a vicious, enraged butterfly.

Hmmmm. That was a pretty shit metaphor. He was still dazed. He looked for his sword and pack. If Malicath had done his job properly, which he was eternally thankful for, he could finally have a wash. He couldn't risk a fresh stream, though, not in the slightest.

He looked for a bowl. There was one on the counter opposite his bedframe. A deep, dark red Tyani-wood counter. Hewn from freshly cut wood. The bowl was a piece of coppiced Tyani-wood, hollowed out and coated. It was filled with fresh water.

He dipped his finger. He waited. He moved and some bubbles amassed, rising to the surface, the slow chase of fear following through Hawk's stomach. As the bubble burst, he was greeted with a sigh of relief.

No pungent black skull emerged from the bowl. Nice.

He took a long soak and dwelt upon how much he hated magical curses. And hallucinations. But most definitely magical fucking curses.

(DOES TIME REALLY EXIST WHEN YOU GO THIS FAR BACK?)

Nin awoke to the sounds of roaring winds. The chaos of the storm that surrounded them had crept into the dwelling they had built atop the back of the Drakarch Alexios, the Great, Beautiful, Scaled Sublime.

The others were already up and working, Nin still too young to bear any responsibility. The Dragon Rider creed said work was a luxury for those old enough to not need to learn. Therefore, Nin was still owed many more years of idle joy and serene experiments.

He resolved to draw the birds that often flew alongside them atop their cloud city. Their wings gracefully flickered through shades of the rainbow as they crested the tides of air. Their faces relaxed into the breeze and rested into joy.

That was the life Nin aspired towards.

Breakfast was already set aside for him as he left his small, cloth-walled room division. The main part of the structure housed the family room, and on the table rested his bowl, filled with nuts and salted meat.

His drawing kit had been prepared by his mother before she left for the day's hunt. She would be out all day on her steed Sias; he knew she would enjoy her time trailing skywhales. Nin gathered it up after wolfing down the bowl of food, and set out to Alexios' head ridge to say his morning prayer.

The settlement they had constructed when their voyage began had grown to a fairly large size of forty-six families. They were only one of several, and the other four Drakarchs were currently elsewhere, scattered across the sparkling skyscape of the world. Nin had learned all their names with glee as a young hatchling, starting with Alexios, his favourite. There were:

Alexios, the Great, Beautiful, Scaled Sublime, the oldest of the Drakarchs to heed the Ancients' advice. They were currently flying north towards the edge of the world, under the leadership of Nin's father's blood-bonded kin, Gyian.

Fias, the Wise, Gorgeous, Rippling Wind, the youngest Drakarch at 26,858 years old, and heralded by Gyian's cousin Suh. They were currently involved with the Cloud Dweller Issshi'l, who was helping them find new land to settle.

Samos, the Brave, Illustrious, Tempestuous Tide. A Drakarch renowned for her violence and courage, she was heralded by a community of warriors who still carried on the ancient tradition of the Manahunters. Gyian was never too sure where they were at any particular time, but when they were eventually seen it was always a forewarning of terrible danger.

Ocelotus, the Bold, Enchanting, Cascading Shimmer.

Ocelotus was the smallest of the Drakarchs; her heralds were originally renegade members of the East Island's Priestcadre. They had resolved to build a new temple to the covenant with a;Giz'Kos, and renew their ties of priesthood to the fallen godkind.

Brionis, the Glorious, Exquisite, Unbridled Destruction. The last of the Drakarchs to leave the island. Brionis originally carried no one, having ruptured the ground above her tomb just as the islands were dragged devastatingly inwards. No one knew why Brionis had joined them, but she rescued those who had sought to escape the island apocalypse by boat from the chasing tsunami, and it was fabled that she had been persuaded by the captors of Jysk.

As he reached Alexios's throat, the wind's velocity decreased to a slower speed that would grant Nin the reprieve he needed to observe the birds. Their waves of red, blue, green and yellow feathers twinkled, an eclectic chorus of biomes beautifully balanced atop a tortoise shell.

Their early morning free-forms of song and harmonies were slowly blurring into the tides of work chants and clan tenors, their identities and purposes slipping across the sky to be woven into the communal loom, the sparkling trills and sweet dipped melodies singing of fealty and folly, tasks and tirades. All in soft, adjoining communion with the key notes and gust symphonies serenading and subsuming Alexios the conductor, illuminating their charges.

Nin settled down to the whipping winds and began his traces with charcoal. The birds flittered around Alexios's head; they always gathered in large flocks before perching atop the shimmering Drakarch scales and pecking at the parasites and life that got caught atop the continent with wings.

Nin's day of drawing had been going successfully. He had produced several drawings of birds that had crept closer and closer to him as he spent the early hours of the day nested atop Alexios's scaled and sturdy head.

Mother had returned from her hunt with a treasure trove of fish, which were promptly roasted for lunch, seared over their home's campfire. The bright scales, some rainbow, others deep blue and purple, a few green and red, rippled with the fire tides. Eventually the succulent wafts drifted into Nin's nose, and salivation foretold sustenance.

His drool accumulated, and he helped prepare the table for the arrival of his father, Tyalis, and his brother Ashae.

They would both arrive together, Father having spent the day teaching Ashae how to ride his soon-to-be dragon mount. Yelissi was his name, and together with Ashae they were destined for the clan's standard of powerful and stoic greatness. Nin himself would be off to join the Bright Scales soon, having been chosen two years ago to be sent to the Shimmering Scale Temple atop Brionus, to learn and steep in the ancient arts of universal persuasion. His life would consist of little but study, with the occasional breaks for research. This would continue *ad infinitum* until he would be reborn into whatever tier was deemed worthy of him, to join their mission, a trickle in the grand stream of existential renewal.

His thoughts were broken by the stride of his father.

"Now that the Earth's sundered, we need to know where we go next."

In daily repetition, his father was referring to the Great Cataclysm, the moment the islands the Dragon Riders had lived upon were drawn into each other. It had been accompanied by the meteors, then the smog-apocalypse.

Luckily, now the skies were clear, and soon the Earth would be liveable again. This had nearly not been the case; their life sailing the skies owed to the unfallen hero Jysk, who persuaded the very Earth itself to withhold from its wish to fall back to its old ways as a roaring ocean of lava.

His brother joined the conversation. "If we knew where fertile land was, we could settle again?"

"There might not be fertile land for a long time." His father's response was tinted with sorrow. "Plus, we don't know what'll happen now that the balance with the titans has been overturned."

Since the circumvention of their pact with the primordial one, the titans' sway over the landscape had increased. Volatility broke out at every passage of a moment; infinite streams of conflict subsiding and re-emerging, casting fracturing tides, explosive eruptions, shattering earthquakes.

The memories would be burnt into their existence until the sundering of time. It might be that they would never find a homeland to rest lazily amidst.

These solemn words Nin carried through into his post-lunch malaise.

He returned to awareness by the evening. They were collected within the Great Hall, which was neither Great nor a Hall but just a large, sturdy, linen-and-bone concoction that adorned the centre of Alexios's back.

Ceremonial words slipped from the clan chief's mouth. With them the gathered Dragon Riders bowed their heads and raised their hands forward. "Since time immemorial, blessed are those without the eyes to see, who instead gaze up at the stars." With that, the great feast began.

By the third rainbow of breadcrumbs, the evening meal was heartily underway, scatterings of leftovers and crumbs spewing forth over the deluge of food that had been cooked for the riders of Alexios. They took their evening meals collectively, sifting through the day's earnings and gossip. Every family was normally in attendance, and the large feast was conducted in the large hall central to the Drakarch-hitched settlement. There were only a few people missing from the gathering. Kessip and Nyuil had led a band out to explore for suitable land to dock upon; Byis and Alri had gone looking for signs of Manakind; Iseyio had volunteered for night watch and was absent with the rest of the Drakarch night-watch wardens.

Nin's father, Tyalis, sat with the clan chief, the position a rotating title handed around between comrades-in-arms. Nin's mother, Eris, and brother Ashae sat with him and their extended friends and family. Among those with them were his mother's brother, Vaair, and his partner, Dorss, alongside their children Tyrr, Giour, and Kai. Nin's father was an only child whose parents had been killed during their great migration.

They were all casually sat discussing the woes of life, while Nin and Ashae were discussing potential manaspawn spottings with Giour. They enjoyed Giour's company and were often found exploring the skies with her on their freeday. Her steed was called Pyuis, her scales glistening with rich colours of emerald, amethyst and sapphire.

The adults laughed at one of Eris's jokes; she spoke quickly, with wit, and would often be found when a solution to a problem was needed. The joke was spoken in the adult's tongue, a hunter's dialect they also used to speak beyond the children's knowledge.

Nin had worked out the code, but gladly followed the rules that kept him from sharing the lewd anecdote regarding an iguana attacking Nin's father, biting him deep in the tail joining. Even with Nin's father's status, these jokes were acceptable; the Dragon Riders of Alexios's held to the ancient warrior code, with humility and blasphemy going hand in hand.

The wind chimed through the spacious and capacious hall; it was a mind-bending feat that the hall stood the tests of time.

Scattered across a cornucopia of bowls and plates was their feast-to-be. Various plants and animals had been served in weird and wonderful ways. Crispy redskin birds from the skies adorned with fruits and vegetables; golden flecks of corn from the highlands they had just passed.

As the feast drew on towards the end the conversation eventually turned to Iseyio.

"I hear the best way is to keep yourself busy. Perhaps we should offer him something better to do with his time?"

"He does seem quite lazy; busyness would suit him."

"I do think idleness is his own fault. We offered him partnership on a venture, and he just ignored us."

Many of the clan were wont to pass time causelessly speculating on the dos and don'ts of each other's productive ability.

"His wife did pass last winter. Since then, he's just let himself go adrift."

"He doesn't handle himself properly."

"It's a problem of him keeping his mood permanently low."

"If only he took the time to actually do the work on himself."

The cacophony of voices trailed in meaningless circles around the plethora of pedantic excuses, the comments and criticisms sounding up before unceremoniously falling down, throwaway attitudes towards acceptance and expression rippling around the mess and mash of voiced opinions.

"If only he had more positive energy."

"He hasn't been making any of the ritual prayers."

"His family shrine has been silent for an eternity."

"And all he does is sit and sullenly mull over whatever atrocity he has brought into himself."

"We could give him a chemical medicine to help ease his pain. Mental anguish is a physical sensation."

"True, we could rebalance his sense of being. The chemical nature of his ailment can't be ignored."

Nin was hoping the commentary collection would soon come to an end. The range of potentials was soon falling short, despite the collective testament to truth.

"There is definitely some chemical component to it; if he doesn't feel joy, he'll never want to persist."

"And that'll always undo everything."

"We'll rest on it tonight, and discuss this further tomorrow. Let's enjoy the rest of this feast and leave the work talk for tomorrow's new dawn." That was Gyian, who was speaking with the authority that preserved ties.

"Wouldn't it just be better to show him he is cared for? You know, circumvent the problem by an expression of acceptance?"

This was Gyian's son Uilt, who was clearly destined for greatness.

"You heard your father. Leave this problem for another time." A classic stifling comment.

Ashae broke the silence with a thoughtful divergence.

"Soon I'll be done with chores. Are you ready to play Usk afterwards?"

Usk was a game they played with bone dice. They were stained black and painted with sweet-orange runes. The game's rules were a constant flux of change towards the potential of annoyance. There were no recorded examples to show to new participants. Ashae and Nin played it often enough, enjoying the chance for unbridled chaos.

"Yes, I look forward to it. Definitely to the part where I thrash you."

Ashae laughed and accosted Nin, grabbing his head with the fold of his arm, his free hand agitating Nin's forehead.

"Let's see if you beat me yet; I'm still wiser and quicker than you. And hubris is the mark of the misfortunate."

Ashae let him go free, Nin quickly gulping air into his lungs. His brother stood towering over him, muscles and appendages beaming out intimidatingly.

"With tactics like that you are fit to be beaten."

Nin's leg lashed out and caught Ashae; he fell bluntly and the two quickly fell into a protracted scuffle, hues of chaos and joy blending into the sublime.

Nin decided he would go back to Alexios's head, where he would take some time to draw the varieties of insects that settled as night time slipped over them, the glaring sun retreating behind the mountain wall. The camp was quiet. The silent calls of insects and whispering birds slowly hummed and vibrated. Alexios was flying away from the winds, and it left a serene shimmer to the noise-dampened backdrop.

There were some people about, finishing chores that

kept them from the festivities in the central hall. There were also the night watch attending to their duties around Alexios's gargantuan back. The night watch, with their scales of ancient beaten metal, their bone-hilted weapons the characters of many famous stories and tales; the mythic and fabled naginatas that encased raw moonlight into scale-defying sharpness.

"Have you seen anything today?" Nin asked the closest two night-watch wardens. He couldn't see their faces and bodies behind their deep violet, all-encasing moon-set armour.

"There's been word of an emergent Divinity, a near-titan, born into the world by the Spine Shatter Mountains."

"Wooooow." Nin was enthralled, twinkling radiances beaming out towards the yarn weavers. "What does it look like?"

"A chunk of old meteor merged with a lesser mountain range."

The night watch stopped for thought, their polearms gently tapping out a pondering rhythm. "Apparently, it's become a malformed spider the size of a forest, with black, scaly legs that divert rivers and dredge lakes, his fangs the size of estuaries."

The flickering torchlight illuminated a horrifying image in the recesses of Nin's mind. That sounded truly terrifying.

They all wondered when they would be free to return to the land, and rebuild their settlements, homes and traditions. Many of them were probably never going to see that wonder satisfied.

It had gotten even darker as their piece of existence had been dragged into the deep night of the central mountain shade. The sun rotated through the sky between the mountain ranges that ringed their vision, and its shadow constantly revolved.

The last of the sunlight was creeping over the cold grey crag that signified night's ascent. The silver and tan scales shimmered and glistened as Nin's footsteps trekked out over the greater neck of Alexios. Eventually, after hopping through several games of scale-step, Nin arrived back to rest atop Alexios's neck. The Drakarch was trailing something in full totality. Nin was cautious not to disturb the One Esteemed Enough to Grant Us Reprieve; however, the trail of a voice hissed out of Alexios's gargantuan mouth.

"Have you seen that moody shit Iseyio?"

Nin replied courteously, "No, Esteemed One, he was missing from the gathering this evening. Perhaps he has left on an odyssey?"

Smoke sifted Alexios's thought and words. "The glum one was lurking around here sullenly earlier."

There was a pause as several birds were netted in the Drakarch's giant maw.

"Make sure you check up on him. It's easy enough for depression to sow itself through you all. You might think it's a personal problem to be solved." A feathery smoke ball escaped Alexios's teeth. "It's not; it's strictly communal."

Alexios left the chasm of silence there for pure reiteration.

"Now fuck off, I have to hunt."

Nin scurried away, surprised the Scaled Sublime had chosen *him* to reveal their words of wisdom to.

FOUR

The sound of her snores reverberated around the tent, her face a tranquil sheen in pure reflection of twilight, the rough waves echoing out from her nasal cavity a comforting clash of swords scraping across his ears.

The evening's thought had fallen into a dark-edged sombreness.

He wondered how all this began; how the fraying strands of fate had drawn them both here now. How this would be the final end of it, their last few moments together. Then... maybe nothing, no reconnection, no future conversations beyond their talk tomorrow before the battle, into bleak and absolute nihilistic separation.

He wondered what his wife would think of this. He was sure she would be irritated by the scenario. Ilyia would have harsh words.

He was allowed these moments as befitted a consort of a warchief – an ever-busy, prestigious warchief at that. Ilyia would tell him to stop being maudlin, to focus on the good things the future had to offer. The roots of his planted tree.

The forces would gather in the Untya Valley. They would fight their battle and rage their conflict. Smash whatever unneeded sovereignty they viewed as foiling their freedoms. Stain the grass with the blood of those who probably didn't care beyond personal gain and status. A sad loss of life without purpose or honour, or respect for any shred of life.

He remembered the valley from his early life. It had always been beautiful. From his times as a kid amidst the bustling city of Yeli; from his journeys into the city's hinterlands to meet with the various clans that still roamed and periodically settled in summer and winter towns. They held vivid markets with fascinating rituals. Gaudy linen roofs housed arcane secrets generations old, laced in combining patters of silk and gold. The odd jobs he'd had to do to support his young life; the indentured servitude to the Brightscale Nin'Gyuili. He'd been sworn to secrecy about that. Forced to keep that secret for longer than Nin would have deemed necessary, lest corrupted powers sought access to secrets and knowledge which would only enable their genocidal prophecies.

Only Ilyia knew the full extent of his apprenticeship to Nin, and the ancient compendium of Manakind knowledge that had been passed on from master to student. Diamond-inset esoteric treasures from long before the Ice Ages, from before any of their experience of life's stability. Nin had frequently called Divinities from every part of their spectrum into the sigil- and rune-strewn crux of his tower; Hawk had always watched, awash with glee and awe. He remembered the pink and white wisps of the empyreally gilded Cloud Dwellers, the harsh, crushing darkness of brown, black and grey of the Rock Dwellers, the blue-white frost lightning of the Ice

Crofters, the prodigious and all-consuming immolation of the Fire Lights.

They were all incorporeal, appearing as solidifications of pure premise. Then they spoke with deep vacuums of silence, strings of words and syllables struck and tempered together with intonations non-verbal but heard intensely. They often requested favours from Nin, who was always happy to oblige; Hawk, as always, would tremble in fear of the metaphysical behind his master.

Nin might have been the last of his kind. The final Brightscale of a once-shimmering world armour, now a single incandescent plate. Nin might have even founded the Guild in the years before the ruling houses of Yeli.

Hawk was constantly bewildered and besotted by the comings and goings of Nin's residence.

There would be dwellers tomorrow. They might not see them, but they would be watching. With adamant interest.

He sat with crossed legs, as Nin had taught him, and began the mantra that brought communion with the many-faced fabric of Yggdrasil.

Map of Yeli: "The Crownless Jewel" by Scout Erinoi, Valestian Scout Order, 632 PIA

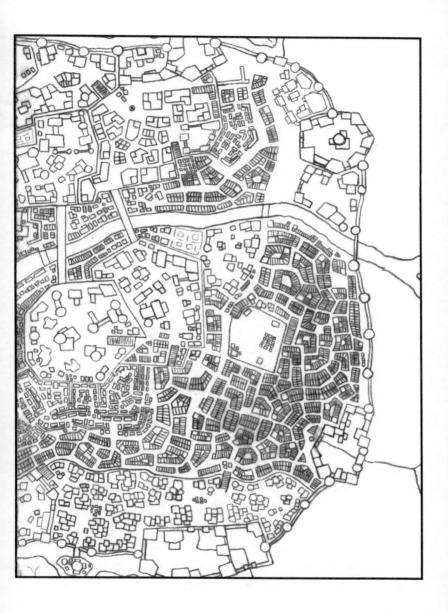

97

THE ENERGY

A TROLLEY PROBLEM (706 PIA)

'Annoyances come in a variety of forms.
From the dark shapeless entity that persists,
exists beyond all aspects of fractured creation;
To deep, sweet serenity that's scorned.'
—Herodbheri, *On the Nature of Ideology* (256 PIA)

Bustling cities reminded Hawk of the incessant need for people to find other people to annoy. The deafening and disconcerting clamour and furore of voices in obnoxious uproar always slid a sharp knife-blade slowly down his back, the trickle of enticed nerves sparking with stress-induced intensity, like coarse-grained sand sitting chummily between machinery.

It was terrifyingly ridiculous seeing the lengths people went to, just to get into one another's way. You wouldn't get these kinds of baseless shenanigans amidst the utopic paradise of Ristos.

In fitting example, two people ahead of him, just further up the street, had broken out into full-frontal physical violence. The crowd around him was unfazed; still they milled and trundled about the growing commotion. Conflict and crisis like this was common amongst the hot-headed Krylei, but the incessant need for it was seen as the self-involved vainglorious act it truly was.

A couple of people looked like they were heading to intervene; they pushed through those agape and mawful. They gently moved the pink-skinned obstacles gawping around the crisis; their gesticulations looked socially responsible and consciously warning. Then they reached the epicentre, and instead they began to beckon to passers-by for bets, yelling out odds and guarantees. A fitting commentary. Hawk remembered then who the contestants were, two ex-members of the private guards who had aided the royal Hhouses in their previous subjugation of the civilian masses.

Hawk had been in Yeli for a few days, waiting to hear from the Guild about something or other. He didn't care that much for specificity, and was supposedly laying low since he'd broken free from Valestian imprisonment last year. Right after Berihtos's wedding, they had bundled him with some form of incantation and incarceration. He had broken free when the "magician" responsible for the spell had gone to sleep. Proceeded to slip out in the call of twilight. He was successful in not killing anyone, which ensured they were still hesitant to publicly lay arms upon him.

Which was why he was now free to laze around the semi-Valestian territory of Yeli.

As the jewelled city central to the Shorelands, perched

along the golden coastline of the Untya Valley, that was a right he adamantly held onto. It was also the place he fondly remembered as his second childhood home.

Yeli was an old So'Ultai city, its original population having risen solely from one of the five roaming clans that took refuge in the region, from whom it inherited its name. The Yelites were noble and prestigious in their ancestry tales, fitting leaders and diplomats given to founding the first sense of neutrality amongst the clans – the first space for them to safely congregate, away from blood feuds.

After the Winter Titan's War, the sons of Ultai (or So'Ultai) were given reprieve to settle the previously icy tundra. Several clans sought out their own spaces to finally grow and prosper amongst the verdant, emerald glistening valleys of the Crossing Peninsula. Others moved north and east, skirting the Krylei Confederacy of Ristos; some were given safe passage through its blooming and effervescent valleys and forests.

Yeli was founded in the midst of the So'Ultai departure, in the first fifty years, in the broken bleakness that followed the Ice Age Accord and the death of the Winter Titan Fyoojrmin. It was, and still is, a pivotal passing point. However, now the deep vivid canopy of lushness that once welcomed the Ultai as they strode into the heroic and mythic lands of the First Peoples has been turned into a life-consuming, bric-a-brac stack of metropolitan sparsity.

Even the following Entoile migration remained at the borders of the city for five years, under the truce of their Yeli kinspeople, before pushing through the other hostile So'Ultai clans that had taken up settlement along the Shorelands. They were hounded because of their Peshya-Ultai ancestry, and the atrocities their clan had committed during the time that the Ultai returned to their desert homeland. These blood feuds were still being continued in the one hundred and sixteenth year after the Ice Age, long before Hawk's time. Although, like all such things before Hawk's time, it had set the pace and tempo of his life. A vivid butterfly wing-flap wrought with sweltering carnage. The final wreckage of the Entoile's nihilistic destruction still bearing bright, cast for all to see.

During the one hundred and thirty-sixth year following the permafrost's retreat, the first of the other cities began to emerge. The Korsif clans had gathered around Yeli; the Abresh and Borsi clans had already taken further routes inland, forcing the Entoile to encroach further and further north. The Yeli were unique in their early settling. Now they were at the cultural head of their world.

Yeli blossomed. By the turn of the second century, it housed a university, a hospital, a monastery with a hermetic order, a lordship, and a council that extended voting rights to the local landed aristocracy.

The Korsif clan subsumed themselves into the stratigraphic society of their urbane mother. They became cleaners, toilers, tinkerers, labourers, artisans of the mechanistic cog that churned out prosperity.

Yeli capped itself with bright red and rich blue roofs. Their conical constructions raised fingers high in cosmological questioning. They spoke in hushed whispers of the clouds of chaos to come; the twinkling horizons of nightscape intruding on the peaceful slumbers deep below. The Magisterial Order of the Dusk-Robed Sorcerers still sits in the tallest of the tantric towers. In the darkest of shadows they still glean the dusky, esoteric truth that skirts the lines of vivid, unfolding plenitude and facetious fluctuation.

They were enshrined into the mechanism of political stability by the two hundred and twelfth year. Eventually the Korsif, who moved like tides around the lighthouse of a city, wrought their own unified truth. They built the other two cities of the Golden Shore. Yeli the magnificent stood first and southmost, Etris the unshaven stood second and westmost, and Tyrni the resolute stood third and eastmost.

They sat in quiet contemplation of dazzling brilliance. They meditated on harmony and effortless action, as all cities do to empower the ones that scurry amidst their in-betweens. They continued this way until the three hundred and twenty-eighth year. The year of the dark dawn.

That was the year the Valestian Navy appeared on the shore. It was approximately twenty years before the rise of the Twin Cities. Around three years after the Entoile-Ristos conflict.

Hawk was eleven and a Yeli slave, having been sold by Entoile raiders to Borsi traders. Borsi traders had sold him east to a Korsif named Erinori. Erinori had brought him to Yeli a year before the first Valestian ships arrived. That was a long, and sharp, journey into adolescence.

The true Valestians were more closely related to the Ultai of legend than the So'Ultai that migrated to Yeli after the Winter Titans were dethroned. They had persisted through the Ice Age, carving their future in the glacial tracks scouring the Shorelands. They had done *something*, though no one outside the Valestian priesthood had access to the historical documents describing exactly what, and they were stored in the High Valestian Cathedral at Ingiria – the battered, ancient tomes that held the collective history of how to survive an ardent frostbite. They lauded it as the miracle of their society, and now touted it on the streets of Yeli.

The first ships brought warriors and trebuchets. The second brought missionaries and knights. Civic virtue and courageous complicity.

It wasn't long before the first signs of monster encroachment brought worry and panic to the Untya peninsula. In response, Erinori had sold him on to the Brightscale Nin. He had watched the unfolding tides of the universe before him, and saw the essence of what was and was still to come. An encapsulating dream.

War broke out at the turn of the fourth century.

Within ten years, the war was finished. The cities of Etris and Tyrni were subjugated. Claims were brought forward that the cities' nobles who declared war were on Valestian pay. The accusations and accusers were silenced brutally and efficaciously.

Erections of symbolic solidarity had been hung from the walls, eyeless and handless. Within Yeli custom, that was one of the worst offences: robbing their means of finding the final starlight; leaving them to wander the eternal night without a final restful berth.

The royal houses had maintained their grasp on Yeli, until they had been purged in the Valestian's faux-liberation in the year following the plague.

Hawk had performed odd jobs for Nin up until his final passing, long after he'd moved on from living in the tower and found his new home wandering far away from Yeli's cream-stone walls.

It was on one of the early days of his apprenticeship that

he ran through the bazaar and saw his first sight of a Guild member.

An armoured shell of a titan stood bartering for alchemy ingredients and potions. Their green-and-black armour was adorned with scrolls, weapons, and a litany of violence. A steel foot tapped slowly in annoyance. Eventually, a coin purse was exchanged; a bundle was passed over to a squire. The squire moved it over to a horse and led the horse firmly away.

Spotting Hawk, the guild member stooped down, passing him a gold and crusted coin. It had a symbolic face displayed, etched into the small, circular piece of metallic significance. "Remember, kid, when you hit the right age, take this to the Guild. We'll definitely have a place for someone like you."

Apart from Nin, who didn't really count, it might have been the kindest gesture a Yelite had ever given him.

The coin was unnecessary, though. The Guild would definitely accept him. Nin had already performed the necessary accommodations, and his parents were legends from the time before.

Yet, still, it made Hawk smile.

He continued with his cart up the street, the alchemist having loaded the appropriate parcels. It was at that moment that another cart collided with Hawk.

He swore profane as the memory trundled away.

He was in the Great Yeli Bazaar. Or just the "bizarre bazaar", as it was known to the locals.

The kid pulling the cart was already off up the streets. It would probably be the apprentice of Nin's apprentice's apprentice. That lineage still stood the test of time, even if Nin had not.

He was distracted from his task, which involved doing nothing; therefore, he decided to relax near the Speakers' corner. There were three brightly dressed peacocks toting their aestheticism, their spiritual salvation fresh from the source.

Hawk hated this kind of fop-headed tomfoolery. Those who speak don't know. Those who don't speak? Fucked if you can draw a conclusion about them.

Well, fucked if you can't. Hawk recognised his own inalienable rights and knowledge. Skills and expertise. Perceptive advantages the sons of Ultai lacked. Having had a Krylei mother and an Ultai father, Hawk was far from the three preachers and their flocks of naïve dialectical accumulation deceivingly drizzled over discourse.

He sought rest from himself, and abutted a wall. It was a sombre and fading red, crumbling dust, flecks and chips parting to make way for him.

There was a hazel-green-cloaked man next to him. Tension carried itself around him in a curious fashion. He seemed truly inert to it. Therefore, Hawk began his auditory fixation on the spoken words of the prophets while his visual fixation followed the swirl of the crowd. Plumes of smoke billowed from consecrated caskets either side of the speaker.

In true Spokrakt tradition, they would undertake their oratory odyssey in three parts. The first speaker was mid-flow. He wore a red cloak, inlaid with gold stitching and hems that ran at geometric angles of precisely forty-five degrees. Isometric diamonds protruded in vibrant esoteric shine. Their ley lines soared throughout the crowd, exciting the vibrating particulars of flesh and blood. All gathered before the yellow chiselled-stone stage.

A hum of vibrating energy resonated out from the podium.

"It is in the equiangular eye of our Divine lord that our will manifests itself."

A good, strong *in medias res*. He must have been referring to Geodis, the single-eyed triangle deity.

"In the speechless spoken of geometric precision, certainty and attained singularity present our universal accord."

The speaker appeared to have a velvet tongue, stroking itself voluptuously.

"Rigid structures of meaning are framed along all our vectors of life. We are all merely trajectories along the plotted transformations we pertain to."

The speakers of Geodissi were renowned for their single-minded obsession with vector matrix transformation.

"They coincide with tantalising truth and bear brilliance to all the cosmological pyramids that enshrine our reality. A rich perpendicularity for us all to bear witness to."

A sort of high-minded mathematically fluffery, wrapping simple broad statements about mechanics with flowers and finery.

"The beams of light, emanating Divine, persist our sublimation cycle."

It always ended with sublimation, an easy word to lose yourself in. There must have been as many endings as there had been beginnings by now, each copied by many masses of musing tongues.

"Golden, red-kissed spheres adjudicate the fates of man and time, the maths of life and existence providing solid, stoic, stable truth, telling the truths of all temporalities. The sand grains that clock each's destiny are but a simple diametric producement of patterned presence. The pronounced abutment of linear being frames our discourse far, far, far beyond people's agency."

The crowds before him stood gossiping and quietly speaking of small matters; not trivial, but things that trivialise grandiose thinking.

"To be is the fallacy of being; we are but the dripping dregs of sand glasses shattered on time's periphery, the immortal undertaking of not being too certain of how we correspond to the immortal abstraction underlining us."

Many of the people in the crowd would have no idea what the ornate speaker was chiming on about. His language was purposefully convoluted, Hawk liked to think, to avoid any criticism. More accurately, it was too wow and showboat, a glazing to entice people into suffering.

"The shining veneer of stability forever out of our reach and touch. Further, a fingertip-trace away from the grasp of knowledge and certitude. We are left the earless recipients of a mouthless speaker, the doomed retainers of that which ekes and permeates way beyond our disposition to know."

There came a point to this kind of speech where the only intent was to cause audiences to despair. Not outwardly, but inside, in their sense of self the seed of doubt would be laid, buried to sprout and consume during chasms of self-doubt.

"There is little for us to find safety and security in this world with, bar the shining solidarity with incomprehensible solidity; to integrate ourselves into the perpetual and singular function holding us from aloft. The cosmological pattern that reifies all geometric truth in self-referential definition. An eternity of prismatic partitions revealing particular propulsion. A purposefully produced perpendicularity. The drawing of resolute pyramidic postulations. Aggrieved and agitated. Antagonised into decimation."

This was the turn of speech that would evoke the most darkened of the crowd to truly turn their ear.

"Agonised into pure decadent decimality. And with each new point of refraction, the light of our Lord can beam, can shed and seem, and anoint with attained accuracy a newer sense of felt reason."

As always, time makes dogma more apparent in its insidiousness. There was a rule of thumb to this kind of thing: the more you tell yourself "you're better than alright at this", the less better than alright you'll be.

Next would come the bait on the hook.

"This is where we emerge and decide to rest. Beneath the eye of our Lord, and in deep commitment to the renewal of oneness.

"We sit with no bonds or brokerings to commit ourselves to. We sit in pure self-fulfilment. Pure contentment and satisfaction.

"Plucking delightful consumption, we taste and sip and proffer our salivation in full delight.

"We find ourselves truly the benevolent benefactors of joy-stained intention, all in the sharp axiomatic doctrine of our Lord."

A shopping list of appeals to offer to those still too destitute to turn away from the free but foul intent.

"In pure eye, our Lord conceives everything; in pure heart, our Lord feels the totality; in pure soul, our Lord delivers wholly."

The crowd murmured and bickered; some seemed to have fallen enthralled or attuned to the testimony of the speaker.

Others were still dawdling through half-conversations at a mull pace. There would come a point to this speech when the hook was returned to its nest.

"It seems a shame that their Lord doesn't have ears. Perhaps he would be able to better train his orator."

The green-cloaked figure had spoken suddenly, without warning of want.

"Perhaps communication with the Lord is so esoteric it garbles his sense? Lunacy and genius are close compatriots," opined Hawk.

"They are indeed. A god that sees everything is wont to go blind, lest they end up like Azga."

An upcast of birds graced overhead, in a rich cacophony of black and blue plumage.

Hawk's mind drifted to slight connotations; the odd black feather sparked through a memory, or reminiscence.

A large murder came to the forefront of his thoughts. He had passed one once on a journey north of Yeli. As he strolled along the road north of the port of Askilt, he had come to an intersection. Travelling to the east would take him into the realms of Denilt; north would take him to Ristos, west to Berosia. As he tried to remember where exactly he was supposed to be heading, a large swarm of crows arrived, discussing a matter of grave importance. He overheard a few of them more clearly then the raucous scrawing of the rest. They in particular seemed to be defending the actions of one of the murder's youngest members.

The crow in question, Kauos, was found guilty of allowing another to die from eating poisoned seeds. Apparently, Kauos had seen the perpetrator of the crime applying the poison, and let his brother suffer. Kauos had tried to get help, but regardless, the victim died; and now they debated the price that Kauos would pay.

"Fool's folly is to repeat the madness of history."

The cloaked man's voice ruptured the memory; he coughed once, then twice more, and then thrice in staccato sign-shaping. He wore a shimmering green cape of flecked brown-threaded leaves.

The roots of universal harmony expanded through him.

The cloak wove a profound wilderness wisdom that rippled against the chaotic backdrop hustle of the city. The leaves glistened with arcane truth.

The fumes from the speaker's opinie caskets had started to take effect.

"So, how do you think the next will fair? I've still got time to kill."

"Perhaps criminal ventures best be left to the shadows? Seems a shame to silence such sibilant charlatanry."

Hawk was certain he didn't want to try to pass more blood through stone.

The crowd buzzed with discussion over the speaker's esoteric musings. Many of them would already been intoxicated by the opinie misting out; many more would be plastered in a few moments.

The second speaker approached the lectern he'd brought with him; it was a pale white-stained synthesis of blind-eyed wormkin, merged together to form a bone-lain pulpit.

The speaker drew a long breath; the words crystallised in his throat.

"The binding roots of time and being flow through the worm-tilled, that which we are from and forever move towards. The very nature of our existence is the underlying harmony with all of nature's aspects that govern before and after. Without uttering in devout dedication, I find myself chosen by Untiyal, the true lord of the land, the Silent God who rests beneath us."

The tendrils of sound merged with the clouds of enticing fragrances. The audience's ruptures of noise were quietly muffled and silenced by the overbearing resonance of mist and soundwaves.

"I have met him. I have travelled to the deepest caves of our kingdom. I have spoken to those that know all, and see all. They have revealed to me the truest incantation of excellence. The harmony that unites us, is that which I have found. And I bring it all to you. You who deserve to hear the tunes that bring good being and prosperity."

Creeping sociality plucked forlorn heartstrings. Dense hands of vapour extended hands of solace to the lonely and vulnerable.

"Who deserve to live their lives sublimely mandated by Untiyal. Untiyal is the God that gives, and has given me indefinitely, and now I bring this to you."

The hands moved comforting, a symbiosis of false fact and enticed sensation. The use of gesture would breach the unconscious of those truly observing, and subtly sway with subliminal messages and imprints, in true inversion to the raw truth of the speaker's glossy, dead eyes.

"Don't listen to my compatriots; they provide false gods with black-laced tongues. They don't provide the eternal light to cleanse the path to fortune. We have a settlement in the north-west, Nestya. Come join me and my comrades in devout dedication. Come join us in eternal servitude to the sublime splendour of Untiyal."

The speaker finished with a final visceral offering.

"The false gods that seek to speak to you through prophets are long dead. Untiyal exists and broaches us his knowledge at our behest. Join him now, or dwell forever in deep regret."

With that final sweeping declaration, he lifted the pulpit and was gone.

Some words casually fell out of the green-cloaked man's mouth. "I feel he missed the mark, like a drunken archer. All this talk of the God of the Land, and yet how is one to know how he feels? Have you ever spoken to him?"

Hawk was equally lamenting. "Even if I'd ever spoken to a god, I'm not sure I could quite easily find one ready enough to call themselves so. Perhaps they were orphaned? No one around to name them, and now this eponymous obsession?"

"I, for one, would rather speak to a god who asks me how I feel than worship one who's still without a voice. Perhaps the scheme will result in a tomb."

"A totemic pyramid scheming grave?"

"Abysmally so."

Hawk remembered the look of dread that had been cast upon Kauos's face when his execution had been agreed upon.

Kauos's friends had clustered in his defence, but unfortunately the Elder Council had decided that Kauos's naïve experiment to see what the poison would do was irresponsible. The knowledge that the poison killed was enough for their group, and Kauos was deemed to have gone too far.

The green-cloaked man jostled him from the waking nightmare vision of the murder.

The final speaker wore a berth of dread and disdain. His form dripped with death and decay; a black trail of decimation clung to his footsteps.

He approached, the tetrarch of fate's unholy trinity: Death, Disease, Desiccation. His master's name lisped from the cavine that came to be where his teeth should have rested.

"Aszialisk is the god of a thousand black nights. They are the one that calls to your mortal flesh at dusk, at dawn, at the eclipse of your soul's departure from this vain affair. If all of you who stand before me kneel before the darkest lord to ever lay the threads of despair before thee, you will be saved the pestilent rancour that will throw this world into haunt."

He inhaled a gale of insidious ruinance.

"Kneel before the violent usurper of the holy bodies of flesh. Yield before the final utterance of death's righteous breath. Steel your soul to face the toll of the silent bell that comes last, rings truest, and condemns your being to an eternal oblivion. All who cast their fates to the forge of dire destitution bear heed to this final warning. Soon the times will come. Soon the lords of darkness will rain fiery hellspawn upon thee. The sins that you cast amongst yourselves will be the utterance of your final hours of damnation."

The deep, dark shadow of a gasp absolved itself through the crowd. The gathered mob struggled for breath in its wake. Shivers began their slow, scraped crawls up the audience's spines, creeping out across exposed skin.

"Praise the one true lord. Praise the bearer of our final judgement. Praise he who will destroy and reunite the final forms of our being in a glorious oneness beneath his ultimate resolution. There may be life after death for the ungainly lot I see before thee: those that choose to live their lives without foresight. But beware, for he will come to claim those who live in foolish idolatry."

The hazel-green-cloaked man next to him turned. Some

words escaped his lips. "I find these jackasses always miss the point by a wide margin."

He took a breath to continue his stifled expression.

"They 'speak' fine words; they forget the soundscape doesn't only include them. Or us. I pity them. Have they ever felt a connection with anything other than themselves? Or do they drift on the ocean of their pedantic *language*?"

The last word spoke more than the others, and not just literally.

Hawk was more careful with his response. "I find the sheep often forget their calls are in equal measure to wolf and sheep alike."

The cloaked man laughed. "Most people forget the calls of nature when they forget to hear others... Perhaps you could get a pulpit?"

Hawk remembered Kauos's execution acutely: death by bludgeoning, to be done by the elders.

The murder of crows gathered in an acidic mourning, and a few large rocks were gathered and carried to the top of a tree. Kauos was asked to sit beneath the drop, and of course he complied.

Hawk remembered the snaps as the rocks fell. They quickly crushed Kauos in awe-strained silence. His head caved in, blood trails detailing his inner conflict, now left to rest in a still silence.

Hawk was stone-faced. "There's only one executioner. I wouldn't want to displace them."

They clasped hands and parted way, the tides of words falling on deaf ears, the low tide calling a few drunkards to listen without hearing, the collected acculturation departing in semiotic drift.

Hawk continued some-way through the Yeli bazaar.

The sound of his name broke out from the crowd, striking his nonchalance. A red-faced man, giddy and winded, stood oppositionally. "I just wanted to say thank you for warning my grandfather's captain about the situation in the city."

Hawk was confused; that could have been anybody.

"My grandfather served during the Plague. He told me you advised his captain to quote, unquote 'stop being an' – excuse me – 'idiot'. And to 'keep his soldiers alive'. They resigned their positions that day before the Great Riot, and then, when the Valestians arrived after the city was clean, they had already escaped. My grandfather found his partner out in the mountains near Ustgart, and they adopted my father and his siblings and well. Well, him and my mother one evening decided that they would…"

Hawk abruptly coughed, his response staccato.

"… procreate to elevate?"

The man was red with nostalgia, lost in memories of decades enchanted.

"Yes, well, I just wanted to say thank you. He used to ramble on about them, and he said he enjoyed his time working as a magain for the villages much more than his time working for the royal houses."

The man paused, his face sharply disjunct.

"And, well, he survived the purges that killed those who hadn't resigned…"

Hawk nodded and shook the man's hand affirmatively, politely thanking him for his acknowledgement before striding quickly off into the dissipating crowd.

He remembered his time with Nin all those years ago fondly; he found his memories had attained a golden resonance, although behind the tranquillity was the cleansing flame of purification, which in of itself was quite sublime.

Well… at least, far more sublime than the bullshit those "sorcerers" were spewing.

And then, as if on cue, bang came the trolley.

*

Untiyal was slipping through the earth one dark evening, sliding through an ancient silted-up cavern system once carved by the ancient Kyushuush Sand Worms. Untiyal enjoyed spreading themself through the earthen accumulation that had settled in the previously hide-hewn igneous rock. The mountain ranges that surrounded the Shuush Desert were filled with these passageways, once filled with water, now solidified into a dirt ocean.

These allowed Untiyal and his fellow Kyushuush-descended brethren free rein to roam between the sand mounds known to the walkers as the Ultai Deserts, and the sheltered valleys that surrounded its ephemerality. They had carved out a veritable underworld paradise beneath the sun-soaked landscape, an otherworldly mineral extravaganza to be feasted upon out through the infinite.

Untiyal had been minding his business when the skinned sorcerers had appeared deep in his cave one day, broaching and passing through the symbolic liminality the other-skinned ones signified and respected.

The sorcerers descended deeper, Untiyal feeling the vibrations and tremors that spoke of a quickening pace and tempo.

Untiyal could sense the heat emanating from the

descenders, could feel their trajectory towards the central cove, the space where the holy people could enter into communion with the Rock Dweller Theil'Be-ois. Untiyal acted as a diligent intermediary between those that came, and them that stood throughout.

However, these weren't here to pay tribute, and Untiyal detected something else. The leader carried a long, hewn staff that resonated with the soul and spirit of Untiyal's smaller brethren. There were also metal knives among the others, some shackled, others moving angrily. Their heat and voice spoke in a swift and vicious pattern, like the footfalls of predators soon to kill their prey. Untiyal could feel the anticipation of a bloodthirst quenched.

The party ceased their movements as they entered the prophetic chamber.

There was a commotion; arms were grabbed, and three of the party seized. They were taken before the carved rock altar that had been used as the Theil'Be-ois shrine, and they were split and haemorrhaged in two.

Untiyal could hear the pitter-patter of blood that trickled out to contaminate the sanctified site. The reverberation of screams whose waves and ripples echoed through the sand, dirt and stone. The blood leached forwards through the earth to gather and pool, an unclean expression of desecrating obscenity.

Loudness grew in the chamber as the survivors voiced a strange opinion. The atmosphere was charged with a dark energy, maleficence rebounding from the dripping, damp, cave walls.

As the party left to ceremonial chants and shouts, Untiyal got to work, leaching the blood out of the silty earth the party of skinned had stood upon. It was sweet and refreshing, and he only imagined the taste of the bloodstained stone formally debilitated.

Untiyal shimmered back through the cavern, listening for Theil'Be-ois.

This would be a fun message to deliver.

The sweetness returned to what we'll refer to as Untiyal's lips.

A very fun message to deliver indeed.

Untiyal's slither spread the dirt with sublime expertise, creating the space for his catechistic epitome.

Theil'Be-ois, however, was definitively aggrieved.

T H E Y - D I D - W H A T?

He asked for the third time, Untiyal once more complying with the request.

Shatters of stalactites fell to floor as the Rock Dweller churned the existential proposition around itself, careful not to free any debitage near Untiyal's shine-covered flesh.

H O W - V E R Y - I N T E R E S T I N G.

Several more fractures of rock split to roll around the thoughtful open chamber, splashes of water matching the synaptic action, ripples syncopating their mind into auditory.

Y O U - M A Y - G O.

Untiyal shivered back into the silt tunnel that led back through the mountain range, back into the warm soil of the under-desert.

T H A N K - Y O U.

Theil'Be-ois receded back into itself. It heard the scatter of soil and the shifting of mounded sediment, pebbles and earth swaying in lively reaction. This was a sign of titillating times; how long ago had it been since the last cluster of catastrophes? Apparently, as always, not long enough.

Theil'Be-ois breathed through itself. Perhaps it would tell Djor-Zis as it passed. The winds across the mountain tip spoke of their coming occurrence.

T I M E – T O – H A V E – S O M E – F U N.

FIVE

A pillow punctured and truncated his meditative trance.

It was a kinetically fluffy awakening from his nostalgic reimmersal; a soft, firm prod back into actuality.

She giggled and leapt from the bed to tackle him. The full force of her weight impacted his chest, balancing the butterflies that held him upright. They fell into a snuggled stance amidst cushions, pillows, bed throws and fabrics, the warmth of her breath forming the atmosphere of their linen worldscape. They embroiled in symbolic symmetry, like the first fuses of primordial essence deep within the eternal ocean. Under intense pressure, diamonds amidst coal.

The coal caught fire, and the flickering flames of the tent's fireplace cast a multitude of shadowy protrusions and obfuscations.

Their cheeks reddened and giggles slipped from their mouths. They wrestled sporadically, catching breath and whispering cutting remarks through each other's faux despair.

Far above the interweaving harmony of chemicals and hormones, twinkling stars spoke out amongst the pitch black.

The softly drawn semblances of cloudscapes nested their radiated wisdom. Vibrations rose and edged, nudged and prodded the collected masses of semi-inert flurries caught amongst them.

The first of the countless many sneezed. The chilled tension looming high above the battlefield, née dandelion-dashed pastures, gasped. The first drops of snow began to fall, to catch the imminent death with a pristine white easel, to chart the coming constellation of chaos with surgical precision. Sterility recoursing into fertility. Recycle and renewal.

The clouds cried, wept, drenched the pastures beneath them. The droplets dove away from their mothers in droves, hordes, cascading crumples and chilled crushes of compaction. The collection of corpses left from the day's ceaseless slog gave thanks and prayers as Tyingr's soft white cloak clothed over them, sublimating them into the eternal cosmos.

The spirits rose to join the Cloud Dwellers: white ethereal spectators, flocking to the bosom of incandescent pink-white wisps of speckled grey intent, reminisces of electrical currents reverberating through rapids and aggregations of subatomic persuasion. Torrents of electrical water fizzling and crackling. Lightning shimmered upwards, leaping between souls of primordial slush.

Catching on the clusters of water, the spirits caught rest. They began their muster upwards into the magnetic field that buzzed over the world. Their resonance dissolved into the ethereal vibration of Yggdrasil's being.

Her breath was heavy and damp. It, too, had caught clusters of soul in its inhalations and exhalations. She too was finally catching rest between swift breaths. She laughed through her words with sparkling essence.

"You're easier than the giants, that I can say for sure."

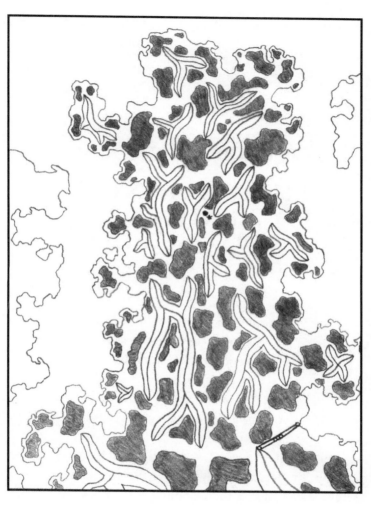

Map of Berosia: "The Forests That Bore Us" by Eioni Byer, Scout Master, of the Berosian Forestry Admission, 721 PIA

THE BRIDEGROOM

THE WEDDING OF BERIHTOS
(705–736 PIA)

They told me to come quickly,
there was nobody there to help.
So of course I came quickly,
and yes,
there was nobody there to help.
—*Brognind's Lament*, a giant's ballad

A gentle rustle of wind whistled through the thick leaf canopy. The forest was always tranquil this time of year, a serene sheen glazing the blooming bioluminescence of life. The buzz of coexistence creeped through the air, lightly gracing the flora and fauna nesting beneath it.

Hawk was walking at a leisurely pace through the forest, quietly meandering through his journey, lost in blissful thought. He strode past den and denizen, settlement and settler, place and person alike. He was evidently in deep communication with himself.

He was preparing himself for the coming trauma, the excruciating event that he had been dreading for days. Weeks. Months in advance. He knew he had to be there in support of Berihtos. He couldn't falter in this line of duty, lest something ill befall them both.

He'd even had to shave.

Berosian culture demanded a clean face at this hour, and now he meandered, half out of spite, half out of anxiety, waiting for that ill time to come when he would arrive and begin the trial and tribulation. Why did he, in particular, have to have a clean-shaven face when Berihtos himself personally designed Berosian culture, based on his own fickle interests and frivolities?

He knew he'd have to make do on his oath. He knew it deep to the core of his self, but that didn't make it any easier.

He trudged on, wishing for death to find him first.

Death tried its hardest to produce, to craft and machinate, and what of its production? A squalid squad of six ne'er-do-wells craftily hidden with care just over by the bushes there. As Hawk's lazy footstep fell into place, the rope tightened. His foot jutted upwards, bringing him full tilt.

He lamented and lurched upwards, trying to seize the rope. By the time the motley crew had accumulated beneath him, he had it in both hands.

They started pelting him with stones. "Oi, stop that!" one called. "It's not like you can break the rope, you half-wit. That's iron-enlaced twine fresh from the mines of Askilt. Hey! I said oi, you better listen to me, or we'll fuck you up!"

The rope snapped. Hawk plummeted, landing on four of the six.

The other two pulled him up. When he regained his footing, he pulled them together. They crumpled in swift imitation of the others.

This shit was always way too easy, Hawk usually lamented when brushing the dirt from his clothes. This happened more often than he, or his assailants, ever liked to admit.

He moved his pack and gear out of the way. Now that they were getting up, he drew his sword. He readied his throat. He had prepared a speech about the due diligence needed to protect yourself from a life of brigandry. Then he noticed their symbols, and decided he might as well just end their lives now.

This wasn't a random waylay by vagabonds. These were assassins. Inept assassins, but assassins still. It was a shame they didn't have more spunk; he could have done with letting out some of his pre-court jitters. It was going to be an ordeal, to say the least.

They got up simultaneously; he'd seen them do their secretive group check. He flexed his blade and let out a laugh. "I know that for me this is a fight to the death, but I don't feel comfortable extending that courtesy to you. If you tell me who hired you, we won't even need to cross blades."

The first two lunged at him. He parried the first's blade and ran it into parry with the second. He kicked the first square in the genitals; that one gasped and fell quickly. His left hand connected with the jaw of the second. The two fell to the ground too quickly for their price.

The next four began their descent. The flicker of light across Hawk's blade met the throat of the fourth, furthest to the right. Hawk continued his momentum as a roll; he threw dirt as he rose into the eyes of the closest would-be assailant. The second closest lunged forwards, darting his blade. Hawk parried, and the third danced inwards, swinging his blade down to connect with Hawk's sword arm. Hawk's left leg leapt out and broke the leg of the third assailant. He dodged left to avoid the altered downward curve of the sword, his right foot stamping on the calf of the second.

His blade pierced the torso of the first. He brought it upwards, severing it free at the neck. The third had taken several steps back. He took several more when the second was beheaded, body collapsing and blood draining.

Hawk spat towards him. He promptly dropped his weapon and fled. It was a sad day for his honour.

It was a sad day for Hawk; this would be his last bit of fun before being cooped up, stuffed beyond despair.

He took a quick breath under the shade of a lambis tree. The blue petal/leaf bush above him rippled with the wind. A gentle breeze rustled the leaves. A fruit fell; the catch was quick, and so was his bite. The fruit was sweet and refreshing.

One of the better things in life.

He had made it to Berihtos's court. He wasn't sure that was a good thing. It stank – stank to the pitch-black beams of sickness unto death, a defecation of personhood in the worst sense. He cursed courtroom proclivities. Berihtos saw him and signalled him over with a smile, raising a hand. His teeth were clean of wine for once. Hawk wondered for how long.

"Hawk, how are you, you hefty swine? Did you have a mighty adventure on the way, waylaid by dragons and demons and such?"

The question was typical of Berihtos's jovial demeanour, the near-perpetual hyperbolic expression in speech. Classical Casidas.

"Just a few assassins, Berihtos, nothing to break a sweat about or astound your guests with."

"Alas, not a cadre of corrupted knights quick to cut you down? Now *that* would make for a story."

A pretty shit story, Hawk thought, wondering how long he could last here.

The courtroom stood stoic and stout around him, shouldering the assemblage of mass and posturing into a carnivalesque cornucopia of clandestine camaraderie.

"I remember such a time that Hawk could dispatch the souls of any destitute ones bold enough to bring woe before any of you, my esteemed company."

The accompanying besotteds laughed.

Thick, rich, cacophonies of colour beamed from the walls, a multitude of lighthouses shining through smoke-furled wallflowers. Crimsons, burgundies, ceruleans, teals, cyans, and golds all burst through alongside emerald greens and amethyst purples.

"I remember the time that Hawk lambasted a beast of no less than forty heads. Maybe forty-five heads, of height, I dare add; there were only two heads proper. One that breathed a fire rich to sting and cut the soul; the other a torturous noise that tormented and tinnitused the ears."

The heraldry spoke of the diversity encased. Every clan in Berosia had gathered here, each bringing the faux-royal images they adorned their castrums with.

"Hawk, no more a master of blade and sword, has slain a beast with little more than the quickness of wit and finger, has slain men with no more than a pained glance of premonition."

Berihtos could continue like this for eternities; it had been a wise move for him to subordinate a kingdom rather than attend to the democracy of his homelands.

"Maybe Hawk is the eternal form that all warriors speak through? Perhaps an avatar of the eternal recurrence that pains our place in time and space?"

Hawk reached for a jug of wine; they were currently abreast the royal table, a table lain with breasts of every type, and tendered to by many more.

Berihtos' wedding was the event of the year. Perhaps the decade, or century.

For a king who had come to claim his lands far from ancestry or right to rule, he and his battalion of mercenaries now lived well and were well-loved. They were previously light specialists in the art of city pacification. They had come to the lands west of Yeli, had settled amongst the Entoile chiefdoms that warred and ravaged each other. It had taken four hundred men only a decade to carve out a real territory. Now Berihtos's legions claimed ownership of the whole kingdom, were the safeguard for thousands, and protected duchies of free citizens, not despotic chiefdoms full to the brim with serfs.

Berihtos used the splendour to turn to Hawk. "Could Ilyia make it with you?"

"Unfortunately, she is at the Jotuncall... well, I say unfortunately, but I'm sure she's enjoying herself far more than me."

Hawk glanced at the social lubrication. "I know I'd rather be wrestling giants and quaffing mead then philandering with 'philos'thanes.'"

Berihtos laughed. "Hawk, you never change. Go speak with Ucheub; he has something for you to carry back with you to Ilyia."

"Another present for another's wife? On the eve of your own betrothal? Berihtos, neither do you."

Berihtos's laughter carried him half into conversation with a reckless sycophant. Hawk used the momentum to curtail any kind of decadent interaction. It wasn't the first courtier's foot to be stood on with such vivid fervour.

Looking for fresh air, fresh space, freedom, Hawk moved quickly towards the exit.

Ilyia's court room was infinitely more hospitable. Instead of the extravagant and gaudy dressing, there were brown, black and white bear skins, deep purple and vibrant red deer hides, and white-grey ayoul wool sheets. Instead of the incessant heraldry, there was community and cohospitality. Cohabitation. A free cohesion without the lords' and dukes' demands. A voluntary service of duty and order instead of forced laws and armed guards. Instead of servers, it was serve yourself. Shifts of chefs would collectively cook; everyone would get red-faced and leathered and proceed to consume all the surplus to tide over the winter.

That was real joy.

*

Flickering orange flames illuminated the veranda. The shining stone fence that stopped revellers plummeting down the hill-face was a decorative addition to the garden, which lay on the third storey of Berihtos's castle, and hung a golden apple far above the stoic trunk of the gleaming thick-barked fortress.

The fast-flowing river that had bitten the cliff-top into life could be heard flowing vastly deep beneath the protruding terrace. Hawk stood, leant against the fence, pondering the time it would take for the river to eat away the rock that held the terrace up. That was when he heard a server next to him. The small, black-haired kid was holding a tray of food Hawk hoisted it from his atlas-like shoulders and let it rest on the table next to them.

"Excuse me, sir... sire?... lord?"

Hawk's laughter helped the latter to enunciate. "Hawk is my name."

"Are you the Dragon Slayer Berihtos boasts about? I mean, many of the staff know you by name, of course." His feet ran concentric patterns beneath him. "I just... you know... I wondered if I could get a souvenir? Berihtos has promised me I'll be his squire when I reach the age of recruitment. I just maybe could do with some lessons or pointers?"

The tension ebbed from Hawk's shoulders, and Te took over, the lively backdrop melting behind the studious students.

"It's about making sure you're aware of yourself and your surroundings. Awareness on the battlefield will save your life, and knowing that you have to build ability with time and dedication. Protect yourself and your shield wall. Maintaining a clear head and remembering your drills and footwork are crucial." Hawk motioned to his feet. "Make sure you support your stance so that you aren't easily knocked over. Formations save lives, and if you all protect each other, you'll make it back home alive. A war you survive is a war won; no one's life is worth its loss to violence. A battlefield is a place that is heavy with chemicals and distractions, sounds, smells, vibrations, and tiredness; they will all try to stop you from being clear-headed enough to survive."

He conversed with the server for a while, before being left once again to the serenity of the veranda's quietude.

When Hawk re-entered the hall much later, it was swimming with festive harmony. Amongst many other things, the emotional-chemical overlay proliferated in incandescent hormonal swirls, all culminating over a room filled with circles of conversation and rotations of synchronised dancing. The clusters, in neatly demarcated quadrants and civility-ensured positionry, revelled and brimmed with the fluctuation of fun. Comedy and jubilation descended in pairings to the dance floor. The music gushed from instruments plucked and blown in the dipped recess by the floor's northern side.

The twenty musicians stamped their feet as they swept through a series of beautifully resolving jigs. Gentle repetitions of sweet, rich flows of harmony lifted the dancers into ecstatic commotion. Their twirls and ripples, turnovers and bows, footsteps and gyrations, shifted to the pendulum swing of the beat.

Strings and wind were plucked and blown, blustering in a cacophonic crescendo. As the peak imploded into itself, the dancers fell to the floor in committed and jubilant exasperation.

Berihtos stood and applauded; he called for the band to take rest and respite, and for the actors and jesters to begin. To which a clamour of brightly garbed peacocks took en masse to the centre stage, ready to beckon Yggdrasil from their sleeping realm. The actors and jesters that preoccupied the riotous occupants spun a multitude of multifaceted yarns.

The swirl of creative invention was conjoined between acting partitions. The choreography was an art form combining elements of dance, theatre and duelling. It was born from Berihtos's homeland, the Shining Vale state of Casidia. As Casidian society had moved away from its violent history, and even more violent prehistory, it moved its passionate population to embrace the dance forms that were held to bloom life.

The play they performed was a translation of the Casidian tale of Istarig the Jewel Thief. It was a retelling common amongst post-Immortals societies, who took the tales from poetic fabrications. The Arnabi stories were brought to life as transcendental activities, the stages combining rigged terraces and scaffolds with deep pits and cover-strain obstacles. The acrobatic actors cast their lyrical indictments towards the woes of Istarig's plight: the woes of his people trapped within their gilded cage, while the wearies of the world beneath riled away in rampant chaos. The actor playing Istarig leapt up from the deepest of the dug tombs; he boldly proclaimed in hexatonic verse his mission before the Green-Eyed.

He landed before the wild-eyed crowd, primal incandescent joy spilling forth. Vibrantly garbed actors, playing the parts of the elemental foundations of existence, tore into "Istarig"; they tore from him garment after garment, each a vivid, bright, symbolic sign of Istarig's infinite virtues.

Finally the actor was bare-skinned, a black embodied sash that held his "junk", for want of a better word, being the last fabrication left.

The actor spun and swung his frame as the monsters before the dawn cast themselves before him. Duplicitous in their projection, each of the monsters was split, hewn and disembodied before the audience, their pairing diving and rolling from the stage in perfect symmetry.

Finally, Istarig was paired with his jewels. He had crept into the lair of Enyao'Piryi, he had slain the dragon god Usti, wrestled the gargantuan, spectral, dog-headed guard Chaous to the ground.

Hawk left as gemstones twirled around their victor, soon to be slain by the demonic form of Azga, who would consume the jewels and spew them across the twilight sky to provide himself with entertainment over the coming eternity.

The final scene would be Azga's malicious descent into madness.

The polished granite stone corridors of Berihtos's not-so-newly-claimed castle were decorated with beautiful hanging tapestries. The Rekilli Entoile were renowned for their weaving and artistry, and the intricate geometric figures that embroidered their work. Well, the Rekilli were *more* widely renowned for their horrific and violent slave trafficking during the golden age of their empire; however, with the ascension of Berihtos, those practices were finally put to rest.

Regardless, the deeply troubled Entoile that Berihtos had nobly taken under his wing had furnished and fitted his new fortress with an enchanting and dazzling array of cloth. This cloth art now decked every possible rock face, in a half-hearted attempt to warm bodies and minds. Each piece was a complex intersection of hotchpotch culture and personality. The garish colours of Berihtos blended with naturalistic signs key to Entoile imagery. Thick-antlered deer and shining-furred rabbits clustered in corners and along the borders of each rich tapestry vision.

The threads towards the centre were woven into the esoteric geometry that marked out a catechistic collection of constellations. The Entoile were descended from the Ultai-Peshya, hence their late journey to the continent, and their blurred accumulation of symbols and motifs. The twin elephant-headed god Uzusi was often shown next to the Rock Dweller Tael'Gar, the legends of Otherkin and Urm'Gil merging behind the expressions of Berihtos's victories, all against the accursed lords who previously used these valleys as their blood-sport coliseum.

The proclamations of death were sardonically juxtaposed with the loving couples who had sought secrecy in every other nook and cranny of the castle. Each alcove was guarded by violent and stoic threaded titans, housing the corpse-stained movements towards Berosia's future.

The first tapestry expressed the first Berosian War, known as the Emergence Campaign to Berosians. Rich waves of red, green and blue heralded the triumphant announcement of Berihtos's legions from the patchwork of valley forests they gathered and prepared within. The inclusion of the Rock Dweller Djus'Garn, and the Cloud Dweller Byori-Tyar, in the top corners was to honour their part in blessing the campaign with good luck and victory.

The long lines of soldiers trailed out through forests, into villages, down into the faux town of Lord Guirston. Long flames rose from the castle of the lord, marking the victorious final siege that led Berihtos to establish his first great foothold in the peninsula.

Then again, another loving couple had been emboldened by the secluded sanctuary of the shadowed alcove. They were lapping themselves upon each other, soft gentle movements and tender gestures signifying entwining love. Rich fragrances and bewitching aromas fumigating their space away from the vivid bustle of courtiers and servers. Flesh mirrored by flesh; the tapestry describing the War for the Core Valleys bloomed, embroidered with dazzling lines of gold and silver. A rich interplay of geometric enticement strung out the stories of Berihtos's war, all to solidify his position as King of the Peninsula.

The centrepiece was the epic battle of Uscreg Crevice, a scene consumed solely by a large pile of flayed flesh, arms and legs sticking out at excruciating and painful angles, appendages and grasping hands capturing the vile slaughter that cost the peninsula a trove of lives. Then, without missing a step, another appendaged mass of chemicals and flesh, linen and liveliness. The couple gazed deep into each other, doe eyes dilating into ephemerality, their essence culminating in sublime submersion.

The tapestry they wove themselves before was the final war, the war against the Rekilli Clans who still stood violently against the sea of coming civilisation. The tapestry was a combination of the four despotic clans and their insidious vices. Each square lined with soft inflowing patterns, they were brought by scenes of skirmishes and sieges into the cataclysmic centre. There, woven in the brightest and sublimest of golds, sat Berihtos and his captains, each radiating a weaving white aura of consecrated blessing, each adorned with motifs of green trees, brown bears, white-stained boars, and weapons galore.

The juxtaposition of life and death would have struck Hawk, each set of couples linked between explicit scenes of vicious warfare. Luckily, Hawk's voyage through existence had shown him the plethora of ways in which death and life rejoined in synthesis. In all honesty, they were the primordial symbiosis, the helix chain of perpetuation, forever sustained and forever reborn; the glistening gems that twinkled in the centre of every unwinding cell, permeating out through the Divine totality.

They were golden ripples of leaves of trees that had blossomed long before, and long after; anything can truly happen. Perhaps, with the orange-leaf sea that would amass, there would be a moment that all could glean the deep, intangible truth of all being. And where better a place to catch that essence than the leaf-stricken valleys of the West Rock Peninsula? The valley that Berihtos had built his kingdom amidst was the central vein of the peninsula, caught in the heart of a series of tangled arteries and protruding granite muscles.

The valley was lush; the warm winds that came from the south and east carried the breath of life for flowers and fauna hidden and nestled away from the harshness of the Shorelands' adjoining steppe. Since the war with the Entoile, and the just deposing of the lords that used to rule, there had been countless victories and advancements for the region, the once-burnt-out cottages and hamlets finally growing into sustainable villages, the trackways and roads finally shored up and paved, lit and patrolled. The Berosian Legion now stood guard along the coast and periphery. They kept positive relations with the giant kingdoms and raided the old Entoile chiefdoms that populated their northern and eastern borders.

The scenery reminded Hawk of Ristos's luxuriousness. However, there were no titanic lakes that carved through this tiny peninsula. No giant mountains with deep cavernous dragons' tombs scraped out of them. No fractured crevices, nor fractal rockfaces left over from the Falling Spires. The idyllic expanse that Ristos had been formed within was both a paradise reborn and an ancient graveyard. Another deep symbol of eternal renewal.

The valley of Green Horde that Ilyia had inherited from her father was especially idyllic, renowned for its amethyst and emerald lakes, and the streams of purple flowers that descended from the rock faces to welcome every visitor. The first time Hawk had travelled there it had been with Ilyia; he had only moved to the Shorelands to campaign closer to home. Before they had conjoined their fates, Hawk was more often found in the Farlands to the east, from the Inyipi-Masiritian hospitality of the Warm Coasts through to the violent hostility of the NeoVishidyai Conglomerate.

He had recently heard that a Rock Dweller named Thiel'be-ois was looking to take up arms against the despotic clans of maddened zealots that circled its mountains. Some conversation had echoed around guild halls about the upsurge of violence between the Warm Coasts and the Ultai Deserts. He wondered if he would be needed further east. The war between granite and god-granted was often a long and bloody affair.

"Hey, Jozio, what's a scarred hooligan like you doing in these civilised parts?"

Jozio was leant against the terrace. eating from a bowl of nuts, his eyes a porcelain blue. When Hawk's words reached his ears, Hawk saw Jozio's eyes suddenly shift back to normal, the colour dissipating to a rich green.

"It's nice to see you, Hawk. Nice to see you haven't lost

any of your limbs yet." More nuts were strewn into Jozio's mouth. "How goes your furious foray around this ferocious land?"

Hands upon hands of great cast-falls fell short, the midden immense and ever-growing. Jozio's absentness was a trick of the light.

"These are pretty trying times." Hawk's arm motioned the remembering. "But still, it's enjoyable and continues to be so."

Jozio's skin was a light tan, a greyish hue emanating from soft brown-pink. A scarf was pulled up, with bristles of dark brown scrub softly brimming up. For the Inyipi of the frosted lands, Jozio was underdressed for the occasion, his traditional ceremonial lynx furs being an antagonising furnace in this climate.

"I spoke to Feli'gar. He's well. He bids you a prosperous future, as always."

The last final few nuts were scattered towards his mouth's general vicinity.

"I'll go to speak with the Cloud Dweller Visya. They might have news; they said they were travelling across the Northern Plateaus. They might bring word of the Dragon Riders. If it's that time of the year." The conditional was excessively emphatic.

There came an uproar of clamour, a riotous call to arms, clapping, calling, hawking for ribaldrous entertainment.

"I think it's best you return to the pre-maudlin. I think they wish to bid you farewell and thanks for all the... you know, something fishy." Jozio gestured sardonically.

Hawk turned to enter the hallway. "Am I sure I want to see what the racket is?"

Jozio's serrated laughter trailed behind him. "Why would you let such a question stop you?"

The intense glow of pre-passion embered in the doorway. By the time Hawk's footsteps passed its liminality, the shadow of the hallways illuminated its rich and vibrant smile, fluorescent pre-candescence dripping in preposterous riot, beckoning a play, or chance, in its fae-adorned remittance.

Berihtos and Serena were huddled like newly found lovers in their richly adorned chairs. The silver that glistened from Serena's eyes matched the rippling tides of oceanic blue that Berihtos bore.

Ilyia's eyes had also twinkled with enchanting hues the day of their wedding. The day the snow had fallen and shimmered the ceremony from mundane ritual into euphoric Divine, high in the mountain ranges above her stronghold home. They were both anointed with the golden honey of the Guazd Bee and taken before the steps of the Shrine to Aios'Doir, the Rock Dweller of Green Horde Valley. Ilyia's father and mother had been there, and the clan's High Shaman, who had been wrapped in a pure-white snow bear pelt.

For their honeymoon, they had travelled north and then east, journeying through the Frozen Coast and the Free Cities towards the Farlands and the Ebonheart. From the Ebonheart, they had headed to the Albair Principalities, and from there to the Isle of the Mad Gods.

Ilyia had settled down a few decades after, pregnant with Tiana. Then, after Elipse came into the universe, Ilyia finally took Bastion's place as the Chief of Warchiefs, and that spelled the end of their dastardly and daring adventures together.

Hawk had been dumbstruck the first time he saw

Ilyia, both of them young adults, Ilyia on her mission of ascendency. Her beauty and voice had smitten him stupid. He was indebted to the universe that they had managed to have their lives together, and he was thankful that their children would continue their sublime moments into the eternal future.

His thoughts were split by a hewn axe, Berihtos's voices peering over the threshold.

"A feat of strength from our fabulously famous Hawk? Why, I do think that befits such a splendid occasion as ours. What a mighty fine suggestion from my wife, nay, bride-to-be."

Berihtos winked at Serena, who was giggling at her husband's foppish antics. She had requested the performance, but thought her husband would silence her straight away. Instead, Berihtos took the chance and leapt for the blush.

"Some may say that Hawk's feats are the greatest things they've ever seen, that none could top them. That each time his shine is just outdone, but at such a tense and furtive rate that even he, Hawk, struggles to do the things he champions himself for our entertainment."

Berihtos took a long pause for precipitous triumph.

"I for one know that Hawk is so modest he himself reneges on accurately portraying his strength."

Hawk was thankful that this was the last ordeal he would have to undertake tonight.

"So I say, why not let Hawk show us his magnificent strength by wrestling our late guest arrival?"

Drummers and fanfares appeared from concealed corners and inconspicuous cloaks.

"The giant, the indestructible…"

Hawk gulped harshly, swallowing a frost-cracked boulder. "Brognind."

The crowd erupted with taunts, cheers and red-faced cajoling.

The doors opened like the can of worms following Hawk's freshly dug grave. Thumping across the shining granite stone tiles came forth a bi-horned shadow of gigantic proportion.

The sight of their first actual giant was a fright to many of the denizens of the room. The colourfully clad citizens leapt away from the titanic colossal weight as it shifted towards Hawk. The blue, pallid complexion was cut and scarred by the weather and tear of the millennia-eroded mountains. Bruised knuckles would usually have hefted a weapon, embedded with the giant's sparkling and Divine-hued metals. A giant white sea of a beard washed down from the giant's face, its coastline brimming with gems and coral ore. Combined, the giant's titanic fists would be able to crush Hawk, if he didn't keep his wits about him.

Hawk himself was steadying his legs, reinforcing his posture, and praying to God that Brognind was someone who would respect the tap-out rule.

The giant stamped his feet bullishly, roaring the spine-chilling sound that scars the tallest mountains of the Ushigai Range, his fists pounding the granite steps. The structure sneezed and shook, its navel irritated by the angered obstruction.

The frost-white-blue behemoth leapt and strode towards Hawk, the hallway too small to accommodate the vast encompassing tension being pounded and tempered into being.

Hawk glared with silent bewilderment, noticing the

wall-hanging heraldry between the internal and external partitions of the hallway.

As the giant form descended at Hawk, he leapt upwards, stepping on the outstretched arms, up the extended biceps, and over onto the cloth canopy. The cloth banners were pulled down and around Brognind's eyes. The blindness brought his hands upwards. Hawk deftly tied the two offending instruments of terror and despair into a conjoined bundle. He leapt to the floor and took several deep breaths as the giant figure collapsed underneath vast and heavy entangling fabrics.

Brognind cried for a cease to the wrestling; the crowd, once simmering, now exploded into jubilation.

*

Silver starlight clung to the tar pit of the eclipse. Drawn into the gaping vacuum, maw-esque and hungry, it said its final goodbyes.

Hawk's passage home would be as faint as the traced constellations that cluttered his vision when he glanced towards the aether. He could see the accrued symbologies of a vast empire of continents, the ever-growing and perpetuating body of people that brimmed and beamed and bustled under the Sun and Moon.

The constellations that could be seen from the Shorelands were prominent and vivid links through a paint splatter of cultures. There were three constellations that shone out particularly bright. There was the Seared Mage, and the Swift Salutation, which were normally both followed by Ilyia's favourite, the Dead Wife. Of *course* the Dead Wife was Ilyia's favourite, her preference quickly followed by one not visible in the Shorelands, the Butchered Sin.

The Dead Wife was a cluster of twelve stars perched just above the mountain line, each a shimmer of yellow, pink or orange. They marked out a woman carrying a man's head. The tales spoke of how the constellation was formed by the actions of Lysilla, from the Green Bravery Inyipi. One late night, in the times of the Falling Spires, Lysilla had been out hunting when she returned home to find her husband's brother had squandered her and her children's food and wealth, killing her husband to maintain his silence.

Lysilla left her fresh catch with her progeny, helping them skin and prepare the meat, before heading out into the dark twilight. Preparing a suir'kiia, a long-handled blade designed for piercing inner organs, from bone and her remaining blade edges, she made for her brother-in-law's house.

She arrived just before sun-up, daubing herself with the markings of the returning sun. Then she struck and killed the sleeping man as he lay alone in his bed. It took her a while to sever the head. Afterwards, she carried it on into the wilderness, to be left as a totem for the Ice Crofters.

She was still held in high regard by Jozio's clan, and was seen as the avatar of the Ice Crofter Tyomm, who led the Inyipi in their great migration north.

Instead of Ilyia's favourite, though, there was the Dark Maw, a cluster of stars said to show the path to the stomach of the universe. The clusters of stars knitted together like a patchwork of teeth, leading directly into a black, chasmic void. The Seared Mage and the Swift Salutation sat glibly either side.

The Seared Mage was a shining beacon of the ancient

magic lines taught to the Second Peoples by the First in the times before and after Azga's war, before the Ultai were forced back to their desert to escape the Winter Titans. Lastly, the Swift Salutation was the guiding constellation to follow the ancient Ultai trail, the hand that rose above the north-west edge of their world. Following its path at the time of dusk was the surest way to Azga's Tomb.

He heard a noise, way too late to intercept. The nets and rocks struck him into bleak unconsciousness.

(736)

He knew it wasn't déjà vu, because he remembered how he'd escaped last time – that simple trick of effortless action.

This time it got to be even more effortless. So he sat patiently, cross-legged, whispering a pretend prayer to whichever of the gods might want to enjoy the societally inspired spectacle soon to erupt. Up popped his friendly foes, several impeccably dressed guardspeople, all embroidered in the liveliest of heraldry, the beautiful, bounteous bosom of Valestia's finest.

He slowly stood, knelt down towards the bottom left corner of the metal gate, felt the tension and pressure of the dense alloyed metal. The three guards at the front of the mottle were crushed as the gate levered from its hinges straight onto their dense formation.

Hawk shivered. He *did* have a thing for the abrasion of metal upon metal. His hand rushed out and grabbed an encroaching sword; his other fist flailed and flayed, finally grabbing a shield from a grunting man.

He kicked the owner of the sword and chucked it to the ground behind him before ducking backwards. Using the shield in a defensive knelt posture, he finally grabbed the sword by its hilt.

The trick to opening armoured animals is getting the casing to do all the work. As the soldiers charged him, he bit through their necks with the serrated shield edge, artfully dodging between their escaping life forces. All that was left was a crowd of clutching pre-corpses drowning in vacuums.

The prison cells led up through the castle to the entrance. There was no need to investigate the fortress any further; Hawk knew what its occupancy meant. He knew it last time, and he knew it now. They would have to prepare for war.

There were several assortments of guards carefully positioned between pauses for breath. This strategy was something Hawk was always eternally thankful for. He made short work of every step they took to stop his escape. Many of the steps to stop would never step again, which was another thing Hawk was eternally thankful for. It did good to remember the worth of those lives that perpetuated the harmony of the universe.

Unfortunately, those that didn't were becoming more tinder than rotting vegetation. A lack of nitrogen was causing the plains to recede, and the flow of chaos would return all people-as-nutrients to refix the missing in their return to the land.

He was saddened that it had to come to this, especially because it spoke of the last good sacrifice he would get to make in this life.

But to rinse and repeat that godawful word, unfortunately it was just that time. It would just have to be that way, or there might never be another time like this again for a long, long time. And, yet again, unfortunately to Hawk, that was definitely the darker of the two darknesses.

As Ilyia said, at least they would finally get some peace and quiet.

He thought back over his last few premises, a patchwork of stained bitter tea leaves scarring his impression, leaving lines of premonition plied onto porcelain.

SIX

There were hushed tones throughout the tent. The dripping white candles had been diminished; now darkness-touched silence surrounded them, the tent shadows now staring at the passing and joyful camp life outside.

Her breath was slowly drifting into the slow, sibilating soundscape he'd come to love and cherish, her snores slowly shredding their way through his ears, soft but piercing, strained but sharp. The gentle night-time calls of birds and deer traipsed through the walls to enmesh in harmony.

He felt the anxious tension in his stomach's knot. Like Alexiandi he tested it, but without a severing rashness. Instead, he kneaded the anchor of thoughts. He moved the motion around his abdomen, encouraged to recede across his chest and nest through the slow movement of his breath.

Ilyia's face bore a rose-kissed complexion; her hair hung either side of her brow, smeared by the pillows she was enthroned among. The sparkling trace that moved from the corner of her mouth down to the sheets elicited his smile, her trademark sign of true sleep. The jade-green hue of her skin, embossed on primordial pink, shimmered with eternal sparkle. Flickers of movement abbreviated dreams. Tensions built, and settled warmth gently accrued across her complexion as she crawled deeper and deeper under the covers.

Her hand unconsciously called for accompaniment, finding his. A soft statement resonated far beyond his comprehension. She nuzzled into the pillows and ascended further into her extension.

Her lips were posed pre-question. Her tendency was to enunciate far beyond necessity. Far, far, far beyond necessity. But, alas, no one would dare make such a statement to their warchief. More so, it amused her court to see her spew saliva at those in attendance, especially if she was knee-deep in the depths of her fervent passion.

The question escaped her lips with a furrowed brow and wrinkled expression.

Her regalia hung half-heartedly over the chair; her diamond centrepiece had been strewn somewhere. Instead, the fey shimmer of starlight was caught in the locks of hair free from the encasing bed's body armour. There were only a few, sparkling like silmithrilic sapphires. Something like that.

Hawk decided it was finally time to rest.

Well, maybe tomorrow. He said his prayer and made the sign of the All Father: a red teardrop falling from the sky.

Then came the madness of the Sleeping God's Realm.

Yggdrasil was shimmering asleep at the centre of the universe. Often, they found the ones within and throughout, with-out and through-in, if that makes sense.

Within and throughout they came at night, in deep spiritual sense; as Yggdrasil twinkled above, below, and out through.

Manascape Symbols: "Sacred Geometry" by Dyal Imberine, 651 PIA

THE SCRIBE

STUCK IN THE RUT(GUAARD) (712 PIA)

A sweet, written word is a powerful thing,
A gem-trusted neuron enchanted with brim,
A twisting and turning of fate's final strand,
To leave one enmeshed to a semiotic band.
—Nin's Semiotic Mnemonic [sic]

For once, he was trapped without escape. It was a daunting, harrowing, chilling sensation. He hadn't expected his day to have escalated to such. But… unfortunately, it had.

Now he was sat there, prisoner of himself, his odyssey on forced embark. Before he could continue, he would have to acquis the requests of the one sat opposite. The one known as the Scribe.

His blood curdled. Then came the first question:

Well, it was a hard "fuck the mountains" in his opinion. If he were a greater man, he would sunder their burdening scree-scratched steps. He would tear them ridge from ridge and shatter their shitty sides. Their long, hard, arduous, shitty sides.

Fuck the mountains. Fuck them till kingdom fucking come.

He reached the precipice. He was pressed for a piss. Badly. His bladder itched. Disgusting. The Divinity was supposedly ahead. He spotted an alcove. Phew. Time for some relief.

The Divinity had emerged some time ago. It wasn't an old Manakind. Divinity was another common word for them; titans were an altogether different breed of Divinity, leftovers from the first epoch. Epochs once; they were eras now.

Epochs of eras before the Ice Age. Damn.

This was a young Divinity, imbued by a Valestian cult. They didn't realise what they were doing, and it accidentally ate their leader. Chewed his head. Minced the meat between the calcified sheet of his cranium. Catastrophically crushed...

It was there.

He smelt it.

The rich, intoxicating fumes of blood. Corrupting a water source, turning the wildlife into aberrations. Despoiling the essence of the manascape. All standard stupidity and ignorance. The rites they'd used bound a spirit of small power; this could affect something, but not anything else. They'd been stupid to do it so close to a spring out in this parched mountain dustscape. That gave it more power than the rites. That was the incredibly dumb thing they'd done.

His blade whispered to him, and his hand moved to comfort her.

The beast turned and leapt; his hand moved outwards; she gasped.

The beast was struck clean in the chest. It winced in pain, scattering acidic bile across him. He was forced to roll.

The beast turned, looking for a safe place to tend to itself. It found its breath as Hawk assembled himself. He was huddled over his bag, rummaging. There was sweat in urgency. Emergency perspiration. A gasp.

The beast leapt from the rock face, arms clawing, terror wrought upon its form. It met his shield. His legs braced, spine stoic. The beast gnashed and gnawed. The drool tried to flay his face; the visor was stalwart.

He bashed, sliced, bashed, sliced; establishing a solid rhythm. *Left, right, left, turn, bash, forwards, backwards, backwards.* Slice, slice, jab.

His shield stamped down on the Divinity's foot; it sought to engorge itself in its flesh.

The beast screamed.

It grabbed his arm, slashing deep scores into his flesh. The sharp wince nearly struck him dumb. He gritted his teeth and pushed his arm right; forcing the talons deeper, he shoved his shield straight into the beast's jugular.

It shrieked, releasing his arm and rushing to stop the thick flood of green-stained blood.

They'd been fighting for three hours now. The Divinity was starting to wane. Soon to push it into the water source and speak the unenchanting.

The protective girdle was limiting the acid-bile pain. Still, the occasional spurt caught him, causing grimaces. The slashes were still connecting; his feet dodged. His breath stayed disciplined, his concentration not faltering.

They'd been interrupted by corrupted beasts four times in the past three hours. His spear had snapped a while back in the back of a horned gaskin. It had spewed pollution that he'd narrowly avoided. That was twenty minutes ago.

The beast tripped as he struck. He took it a step further, forcing his shield forward full force. With the next step, his blade shimmered in an arc. Downwards she swept, straight through the Divinity's outstretched arms. He shoulder-charged the bleeding monstrosity.

It fell into the spring. The toxic black blood spewing forth from the fount started to shimmer. The putrescence slowly ceased.

He threw off the visor, laid down his armour, and collapsed. He rolled over, and finally basked in the starlight.

The scribe gasped. "You really fought that thing for three hours?"

"It wouldn't have been the first."

'It wouldn't have been the first time' or 'I wouldn't have been the first'?" The scribe inquired past Hawk's fragmentary phrasing.

"The first one."

The scribe wasn't sure if anything had been clarified.

"And it didn't do any long-lasting damage to you?"

Hawk winced unconsciously. Not from muscle memory, mind you, but from excessive articulation. "Long-lasting is a matter of perspective to some."

He reached for his drink.

He finished the jug of ale. He crashed it through the shop

window. He followed it with a large park bench. Hopefully, that would keep it trapped for the time being. Did it?

The speeding shape aimed straight for him told him no. The Divinity struck him, pushing him into the building across the street. He tried to untangle himself from the mess of limbs and appendages.

The form was a chaotic whirl of feathers and fists, an eruption of undirected sociological affliction. The riots the night before had seeped into the streets. The gryphon corpse buried beneath the settlement square had morphed with some of the kettled corpses. Now they were bearing the cross of their misconformity – wholescale misconformity across the whole polity.

Like, who the fuck had buried a gryphon corpse beneath the town square?

It punched him. Again. And again. And again. *Oh, for the shitting light of dawn's sun.*

He'd been brought in to keep the peace, apparently; *where* was anybody else's business. And where had the peace been? Anywhere else, as always bloody usual.

God's gift to personhood was the innate ability to fuck up a good time, and unfortunately, while Hawk was getting leathered outside to excuse the fact that he wasn't punching peasants in the face for any amount, out had popped this little fuck-up, God's own little mutant monster.

It punched him again, and it stung like a bitch.

He brought both his fists down in tandem. The steel gauntlets he wished he'd had on were somewhere, yes, as usual, God knew where else. So instead, he grabbed a sharp and piercing wooden stake from his sudden intake into the shop. He levered it and heard the monster wince. Satisfied, he slammed his fist down onto the stake's blunt top, firmly wedging it deep into the monstrosity's head.

It screamed in sheer anguish.

He looked for a weapon, anything, even improvised. He found a chair and firmly planted it into the side of the feathery flailing. The beak struck, and caught his leg in its razor-sharp trap. Blood started streaming from the bite as the beast's jaws receded. Hawk used this opportunity to propel his bleeding frame over the shop counter.

Several guards took the chance to burst through the door to assist. They didn't last long; the first was eviscerated by a tearing lurch; the second was mutilated by the monster's sharp claws as it reared up, dropping the first onto the third. The fourth turned to run, but was instead pulled apart by the mass of hands that pummelled forth.

Hawk had used the time to arrange a primitive spear; it had to work. It was assembled from flimsy twine and a sturdy enough pole. He'd tied severely sharp pieces of glass to the distal end. He moved up to take position over the counter – and lunged.

The spear snapped almost instantly.

The chaotic cloud of percussive force splintered the pole. Now it was coming to splinter Hawk. He braced the counter, and with strong feet he pushed with all his might. He felt the sweat drip down into his gushing wound.

The feat was triumphant. The counter pinned the beast to the floor, the full weight of the wooden coffin bearing down on it.

He felt his muscles slack. The first splinter ricocheted towards the roof, then another. Finally the counter grimaced, groaned and split asunder. The fists of fury's heterogryphon flung itself towards Hawk. It followed through with its menacing premise, and they both landed spreadeagle on the shop floor.

The pox-wrought, pummelling, bastard of a gryphon-thing overwhelmed him, beating and bloodying him down on the wooden floor. Its thick, cloying stench stung to his nostrils; he nearly vomited in putrid fixation. The jaws of the beak opened with rapturous intent. With ravenous glistening, they snapped forwards towards his skull.

His arms shot out to grasp and hold. He felt the beads of sweat on his brow.

Perhaps he wouldn't make it this time; perhaps this would be his final hour. He felt the twinges amassing, the sting as his muscles started to tear. The gryphon's eyes twinkled with dire premonitions.

It didn't notice the blade that tore cleanly through its neck, severing its life force.

"They said you were drunk, but I didn't expect *love* drunk. How was the hickey?"

The figure of speech was a sharp shadow cast across the combat's climax. Familiarity shuddered through Hawk's adrenaline.

"Tyrus, you cheeky swine, how thankful I am to see a fuck like you!"

He wiped the gratitude from his face, as the scribe scribbled his scripture in purposeful prosaic. The writing was pictorially ornamented. Designs of the demons Hawk had ruthlessly dispatched traced the margins of the scribe's script-pad.

"There have been others. Monsters far beyond the imagination of the peoples you'll find here."

The scribe looked up. "Really? What kind of despicable devils do you find amidst the lands far beyond?"

Hawk was lenient with his answer. "It depends on what you want to see. It would be far wiser for you to venture there yourself. Perhaps we could get the guild to give you an escort?"

The scribe was enthralled.

"But…" Hawk placed power and poise on the precipiced premise. "The worst devils I've found interspersed throughout *this* land…"

The scribe was engrossed, saliva dripping from the corner of his mouth.

"… are the demons we make ourselves."

Hawk finished another jug of gratitude, and belched a vicious opal of splendour. "Perhaps another drink? I could tell you of the time I slew the sorcerer Embrin's cabal."

"A diabolical cabal? Perhaps it's best I order."

"They weren't just diabolical," Hawk began. "They were disfiguratively demonic in their deviousness. They had captured the wife of King Enippi, and were sacrificing her to bring about the end of times. I… think?"

His footstep hit the ground with sheer force of will.

"They ambushed me in a ravine and injured another group sent to trap them in a mountain cave."

He felt the searing pain of the arrow firmly lodged in his left leg.

"It was left to me to finish them off. Unfortunately, I'd left my sword somewhere stupid."

He finished the drink and slammed the stein onto the tabletop.

The boulders plummeted from the path above him, tunnelling

straight towards his head. His lips opened to begin the gritty sub-sub-suburban tale. No, sorry, subterranean was what he meant. They pursed.

"FUUUUUUUUUUUUUUUUUUCK!!!!!"

He pulled the arrow clean from his leg and punctured the throat of the cultist, once descending down at him from great heights amidst rubble projectiles, currently gurgling pulses of blood; soon to be dead, drained on the floor.

This was stereotypical. The blood-drenching scream of curdling fanaticism. Several more leapt from the height to join their gurgling comrade. Hawk readied himself to dispatch them, however easily he could in such a pre-dented state.

Their landings, less than fortuitous, enabled the hamstrung Hawk to cleave them in three strong swipes. His breath was heavily stressed; he could taste the pain in the splats of blood accumulating at the back of his throat. His blade swept through their innards like a knife through clouds.

He saw the leader of the cultists, Embrin, curse and swear, raising his two hooded arms in tragic tandem. Red-laced mist emerged and swirled around his acolytes. He spat his blood forward, willing it into the fray.

Hawk tried spilling less of his drink down his face than into his mouth. Instead, arcane and esoteric secrets were spewing forth at such a rate that all incoming alcohol was pushed aside.

"It's interesting, because many of the Guild Loréds claim that incantations have to be followed to an exact T. That there is an existential precedent to the conduction of Divine energy through the universe."

He tried to finish the drink, but still more semiosis concurred.

"Really, there is very little need for precedent if intent is strong enough to coax the cosmos. You only really need precedent if you are lacking in 'natural' ability, maybe? I think that might be the case."

The drink was finally finished.

"How about a different story? One at a different metre? I don't really feel like telling you all the wondrous ways in which people are dumb enough to consign their own fate, and others, to the eternal madness of the twilight void. How about the story of the…" Hawk paused. "Or the story of…" Hawk scratched his head in complacent but absent reminiscence. "The problem, really, is that my life has descended into a meaningless cacophony of violence. And I'm truly at the whim of the chaotic forces that surround us."

The scribe looked perplexed; he sipped his drink quietly, and slowly drew out a proposition. "So you're saying you don't really care for this life anymore?"

Hawk smiled. "I'm just being bitter. I can still remember my first adventure for the Guild. I think it was while I was still an apprentice." The facial scrub on Hawk's chin was itched for nostalgic reimmersal. "I had to clear a temple of Sansombs, a rare breed of post-life ghoul that is essentially a zombie indistinguishable from a person."

Hawk's arm itched.

"Well, at least until they decide to take a bite from you when you get too close. They spread a semi-contagious disease. With a roughly…" Hawk pretended to calculate figures, "… forty per cent chance of turning you into one as well, depending on whether you share enough similar motivations and ideals. It's a form of ideological zombistry. It was quite common during the Vishidyai Empire."

The scribe sat notifying the places – the Vishidyai Empire, far to the East of the Shorelands.

"They are incredible mimics of communication, who get spread through the populace to help persuade potential dissidents and to create conformity. They just struggle to understand what you're saying, and when you mention their ideological trigger, the thing they are designed to protect or protect against, you can see their eyes dilate.

"So that was the strategy: get there, discover their purpose as a secret guard force, and then use their triggers against them. All you have to do is kill or nullify the person who started the curse, and then everything's back to how it used to be. So I left the Guild ready to investigate the cult that had taken over the town. We believed someone had stumbled upon a book of power and decided various nefariousness.

"We got to the town of Aesberg, a really beautiful place in the Free Cities coastline, but from before it was called such. I tried to deliver the first test, but I was interrupted by the town crier. Well, after a shitstorm of a battle with nearly everybody and everything, all of them throwing themselves at me, wave upon wave upon wave, I made it to the prison. They were thicker there, tides of hands and teeth; I had to batter them away with a stoic wooden shield, stamp on their feet, and push them away. Shoving them till the end of eternity. It was a fucker getting down the stairs, although finally I made it. Beat back the denizens who were guarding the point of no return. The eponymous end of the line.

"And who the fuck is there? In the bottom cell, tucked in a padded and pillowed room, under a mountain of cheese?"

Hawk sighed, and finished looking forlornly through the past. "It was a mouse called Aljernain, who apparently could read."

He sighed alcohol and foamed down his gullet, the froth dispatching the accumulating despair.

"Now, that was a lot of chaos for somebody who can't really be held accountable."

A common occurrence as old as time.

"But it just goes to show you can find conflict absolutely anywhere you look."

Hawk took a large drink from his mug, the beer draining down his anecdote-thick throat. The scribe nodded his head in serenity, happy with the innate disorder that surrounded them both.

His epiphany was supported by a shower of brown wood confetti, sprinkling over the conversation with copious intent. The tavern chair splintered across every fractured multiverse, disrupting the thread of causality being cleanly dissected by the scribe. The tenor and tone of conversation had erupted into the backdrop and brought to life a vibrant brawl – a bustle of fists and fisticuffs, fluffs, and blooded blemishes.

A riotous roar and howl swept the occupants of the tavern into a vigorous coda, their warrior's waltz spreading out over the dance floor.

The scribe quickly crawled under a fortification of sorts, a pile of damaged furniture quickly rescued from the ensuing bushel of battling brawlers. The bar staff awaited him too, the innkeeper sighing, head in hands.

"This is the danger of having such a centrepiece of chaotic climax. We often find tensions and moods are high when he's around."

The specification dripped with double-edged admiration. He was a beloved nuisance, worth more harm than good, or so everyone thought until the tab for every fight was continuously picked up.

"He does try his best to stop it, though."

"We think."

"We *think* he does his best to try and stop it."

Hawk was stood with five heads collected between his two unfurled arms. His muscles bulged with strain as a case of alcohol was smashed across his back. His aggregated assemblage of bodies broke free and proceeded to pummel him. The foetal position became his best friend.

Eventually, the fighters settled down, with rich laughter rolling and resonating across the room. Hawk precariously perched himself upon his upright knee; he brought himself into a standing posture and spoke four magicks:

"Next round's on me."

He gasped, red-faced and pained, positioning himself against an upright table. The drunken revellers erupted like tempestuous volcanoes, mountains of foam churning from clashed jugs.

The islanders beneath, sublimely breathless yet sleeping another night more.

The stars above, laughing, grinning and gawping in enchanted awe.

HISTORIOGRAPHY FROM THE YELI ARCHAEOLOGICAL SOCIETY

What follows is Intrif's meandering discussion on the historical basis of the legendary Proto-Ultai hero Istarig, supposedly the very he who slew Azga;Kilnof with the First Forged in the Battle Before Tael'Gar. We are unsure as to what end Intrif found himself doing this for; however, it seems of particular importance to Intrif that the various cultural understandings of this silhouette of a figure prescribed an important actuality to the hero.

In his other arguments, Istarig is described not merely as the bardic conjecture of those in between Intrif and his fabled muse; instead, Intrif was convinced that the legendary hero carried a prophetic template that speaks to the true nature of storied history.

Intrif's own essays on historical subjects are often full of slander and libel towards the republican government of his time. We are unsure as to where his familial prejudices end and his serious commentary on political policies begins. It is remarkably clear that the Final Kings of Berosia were nothing more than figureheads, and the Republican Council held the power and posture of the state.

This seems remarkably different in political tone to the early egalitarian crowned republic that emerged from the Three Berosian Blade Wars, the wars declared to quash, and substantiate, what would come to be the Kingdom of Berosia.

The main recall to Istarig could be seen as an extension of Intrif's recall of early proto-economic states to justify utopian views and positions. The strong call back to metaphors and symbols that permeate each step of society allows an easy dissemination of ideas and ideologies.

Moreover, this is a theme that is extended by Intrif with his heavy collation of illustrated materials. His use of these visual prompts is to associate the visual processing of truth with the literary narratives that constitute meaning to the subject, thereby enabling people to integrate his perspectives into their everyday lives with ease.

It is an interesting psychological phenomenon that, in seeing a visual representation of something, people ascribe it a higher level to its reality, whereby the visual presentation of information can often be used for the extent of conditioning and propaganda. We can see this more explicitly with the rise of ideological totalitarianism during the early part of our century. However, universal emancipation has shown us that these tactics rely on cognitive stress overweighting subjects; with the provision of basic needs, people create communities that preserve their existence without the need for ideological reinforcement.

Since the ancient speakers of old, people have used rhetoric and imagery, alliteration and punctuation, rhyme, rhythm, and syncopated enunciation, all to create tension. They clearly inspire the emotional parts of ourselves, and the neurobiological effect of language is definitively undeniable at this part of our discourse. Tension can further be seen to activate key behaviour response patterns, creating necessities of resolution that predispose individual cognitive responses.

Intrif thought it of utmost importance that his visual library be kept for further reference and proof, and we are undoubtedly blessed to receive his works after several millennia of silence.

The reasoning for Intrif's preference for Istarig is most likely seen in the Shorelands Chronicles, a series of documents compiled by the High Colonial Inquisitor of the Valestian Colonies. Named Dyal Imberine, there is little left of his work. The documents themselves were recovered by Intrif's forebears from a cache found during work done at the Old Denilt Reliquary. They were evidently stashed there to escape the anti-Imberine purges of 652 PIA, when it is said the High Inquisitor of the Spectral Palace of the time decided upon Imberine's heresy and traitorous nature, culling his supporters and ordering his execution.

Events like these are common throughout the secondary sources available to us. It appears that the nature of the Valestian Primacy's theocracy hinged upon a Divine right, was primarily totalitarian, and was only hedonistic for the upper echelons of the polity.

Most of the secondary sources available can be found in the Great Yeli Museum. Various notations from the Magisterial

Orders, and various diaries, biographies, notes, letters and other literary sources, are available at request.

The documents describe a fundamental harmony between the landscape and the manascape in a way that has often been theorised by various writers and researchers since the first millennium. They describe how the earlier Urm'gil civilised societies were left adrift as their connection with the manascape caused its eventual degradation. The Dark Territory of Azga's Mound has never been explored since the Renewal and the beginning of the Fifth Era. Therefore, it is hard to compare these stories and their descriptions to the climatic events they supposedly sit in shadow of.

Therefore, in following the traditional style of the Hedonist Historians, Intrif carefully uses an admixture of hyperbolic rhetoric and cluttered terminology. We believe this was to dispel notions of seriousness, and to effactually protect him from state countermeasures. During his time, the Berosian Order of Stability grew to its golden era of social planning, and Intrif was a critic careful to toe the line between censorship and civil service.

What is clear, though, is that, if these titanic events did take place, there is a reason that our landscape is looking as depleted as it is.

If this is something we truly wish to rectify, it is not only something of ourselves that we need to change. We need to remanufacture how we understand who we truly, really are.

Galiandur Baikstri
Nominal Chair of the Yeli Archaeological Society
Headchair of the Valestian Encroachment Project

Inscriptions from the Blessed Cavern, Wisdom Hewn Deep

THE HERO

THE BALLAD OF ISTARIG (1E⁶: 2126, OR APPROX. -45,000 PIA)

All tall tales are told at very little height.
I studied, I read stuff, what was the point of all that?
—Herodbheri, *On the Nature of Historiography (254 PIA)*

The ballad of Istarig is a curious tale, a woven frame of

---

6   (It is important to note our "First Era of Peoples" is the Third Era of Dragon Rider Chronology. Our current "Second Era of Peoples", after the Ice Age Accord (0 PIA), which followed Azga's demise (~-30,000 PIA), is the Fourth Era of Dragon Rider Chronology. The Dragon Riders have existed long before any others, and because their type of existence is so separate to ours, there is little need to formalise the chronologies.

Likewise the Krylei of Ristos, and the other peoples from far before, use different chronologies, naming their eras after the trials and ordeals that occur, the Fourth Era more commonly referred to as the Time of Rebirth, our First Era their Time of Falling Spires.

retellings from the times before times. Even Istarig's humanity is laid in question, possibly akin to the Primate Kings that the Vishidyai enslaved and slew to erect their first temples.

Istarig was also from that paradise, our First Era, a traveller let to travel the world beyond where the first peoples of Ebonheart only sat beneath the eye of Yggdrasil, the green one from before all.

Legend speaks of Yggdrasil being a monstrous dragon of behemothic proportions. Istarig's own pictographic account, hewn into the deep Caves of Blessed Vision, speaks of no form before forms.

If legend is seen through itself, it would suggest that Istarig was the first of the Primate Kings, first of the Post-Vishidyai Warrior-Gods, and the first, and foremost, of the First Era Immortals.

The relationship with Yggdrasil is important, because, prior to Istarig, no other person had been allowed to leave the guarded cage that is known to the various sons of Ultai as Ebonheart.

The first stories of Istarig are evidentially grouped into three "parts".

The first is a large pictorial script found in the Caves of Blessed Vision, representing Istarig's life in Ebonheart, his growth into an adult, and his journey out into the lands southeast, following the Darktrail River. After the first journey, the pictographs show his adventures amongst the many peoples that will come to be, and his journey into the Soul of Yggdrasil, down into the ripple-tide "coral" glade.

The second, a leaf-bound NeoVishidyai manuscript, details an allegorical story of a drunken fisherman repenting to his wife for arriving home late one evening. It features five figurative fictions, the final tale about Istarig. However, by this point the drunken fisherman has become so incomprehensible, there is little legible detail as to what, or where, or how, or who Istarig is – bar the fact that the moral of the story, and the fisherman's plea that he would never stray from his partner, allow a happy resolution, the wife treasuring that the fisherman would compare his devotion to her to Istarig's devotion to his jewels, and letting him into their house.

The third and final collection are the tomes of the Arnabi, the order after the Immortals, the first of the "mana" blessed to govern and maintain connection between the "First Peoples" and the "manascape". The tomes detail a great treasure of adventures, of monsters slain, beasts caged, maidens rescued, priests purged, kings toppled from demagoguery, victims shorn of victimhood. They tell us very little about Istarig himself. In fact, he is purely used as a narrative device to describe the ideal virtues and understandings that the Immortals used to keep the lands of Ebonheart and Yggdrasil's Range free from Divine problems.

It is therefore incredibly hard to begin to describe Istarig beyond the stories of his era, and the following fabrication by the many-faced poets of the many generations that came after Azga's fall.

To say this collection of stories scribed by myself has been created around six hundred years after Hawk's passing, to describe Istarig, a figure who is more than tens of thousands of years of ages past, is a nigh-on impossible task.

(All historiographical arguments aside, Istarig's story is both important and trivial, as all such things simultaneously are.)

Therefore, I resolved to find the truth of the matter by consulting the Dragon Rider White Scales.

As always, they were incomprehensible in their communication. They left me with stories of ape-men and black holes, meteoric rocks cascading from the sky, teeming with juice, the edge of one universe bleeding raw cosmos into the other: a transcendental eyeball billowing out luminescent intent across the star-marked stellaris.

They still refer to Yggdrasil's Shaded Blink despite their aeons of esoteric silence. They still walk the sky amidst the Drakarchs, atop the cities and settlements they've strewn amidst tectonic scales. Sometimes it seems entirely alien to me that where they fly atop blood, we soar with balloons. Where they weave and knit, we have begun to use mechanical automation. They still carry their womb beside their breast; they still honour and sacrifice their hunts to the glory of the fruitful earth.

We, the idolaters that we are, brimming with luxury, profit and coin; they, beaming beneath the sun, lapping the Cloud Dwellers' fabricating forms.

Sketches of a Neo-Vishidyai Truth-Stack, Leaf Strewn Winds

175

ON THE SHORELANDS AND THEIR VERACITY

By High Colonial Inquisitor of the Shorelands, Chancellor Dyal "Sdruan" Imberine; compiled from the various fragmented documents of the Shoreland Chronicles (636–652 PIA).

ON THE NATURE OF THE SHORELANDS MANASCAPE (650 PIA)

The Shorelands sit in contrast to the fairly tepid manascape of Valestia, a feature that is most definitely a consequence of the severance with Sossianis, and the subsequent purges of those who renewed worship towards the others rather than towards the worship of Eisgar. We might refer to them as the Chaos Gods; however, this term is self-defeating. The Chaos Gods, or more accurately Dwellers, are the metaphysical manifestation of causal consciousness.

From the studies of the ancient Urm'gil network, and the study of the scattering of remnant sites that exist within the Valestian sphere, we have found a treasure trove of references.

As the Geographites have long discussed in the city complexes of Ebonheart, it appears that the cold temperature and sparser-than-average life of the Shorelands is the direct consequence of the pact between the "Chaos Gods" and the Urm'gil.

I am launching further investigations at the ancient ruin labelled Site X-Five. This will hopefully allow us to see the reason and mechanism of this pact.

Dyal

ON THE NATURE OF DIVINITY
(636 PIA)

This is to be my magnum opus. I have found this truth before all other truths. I am fairly certain the layers and depths of Divinity will always lie obscured; however, my notations on this subject have proven invaluable.

I think it is irrefutable that the Divinity we have come to understand as the manascape exists beyond a division with our material world. It is more apparent that our ability and capacity to act directly affects these Divine manifestations.

It is not only our power to act that is increased with the broadening of our church, but our ability to sow the seeds of our enemies' destruction.

Through our bright perseverance we will consecrate the landscape and reify our true Divine.

This is itself the will of Eisgar, and with it, our landscape will renew itself indefinitely.

Dyal

ON THE NATURE OF THE DWELLERS AND TAEL'GAR (642 PIA)

Tael'Gar is the named Rock Dweller of the Azga Cycle, as named by the Dragon Riders. I have managed to have some correspondence with a few of the White Seers who are comfortable communicating with me. However, most of them are hesitant to talk to "an enemy of the cosmos", oftentimes calling me something much worse.

The few that have supplied me with responses have told me that Tael'gar was the Rock Dweller responsible for mustering the forces of the Urm'gil against Azga's encroaching army, that he was responsible for marshalling the army of Yggdrasil on the day of the Final Battle, that he slipped beneath the earth and shattered the space between Azga's army to help corral them into a killing field.

These descriptions leave me with the impression that the might of the Rock Dwellers is something we have entirely missed. I am sure that this might be something to do with the pact of Val'Est, although I'm not sure what the consequence of the First Sacrifice would really mean in these terms.

Could it be that Sossianis was murdered in the defiling of the heartpool?

Could it be that Sossianis has merely been rearranged as the Divine pantheon we now have, embodied by Kori, Val'Est and Val Gori?

We are likely to never know.
Dyal

ON THE NATURE OF ISTARIG
(651 PIA)

It has been reported that a village is led by a character called Istarig. I am the only person in the Colonial Government who sees any kind of significance to this. Perhaps that is a fortunate thing; if other people knew of the name's tie to legend, this could cause controversy. Regardless of the persistence of the tale, it is remarkable that very few people are named after the First Hero.

Maybe it is a turn of circumstance? Maybe it has deeper connotations. It would be best for me to say as little as possible until the Inquisitor includes this village into the Colonial Jurisdiction of Valestia. Regardless, it is the final piece of my puzzle.

I have been communicating with a Rock Dweller called Theilol'Boe, who claims to be a servant of a greater being called Theil'Be-ois. They have said that if I travel to the shrine of Dyus Bari, east of Casidia, I will be able to commune with them regarding Istarig's journey.

This might be the answer I'm looking for. All I need now is the Istarig of Cerebrium, then I can make the journey.
Sdruan

Detail of an Arnabi Tome Blessed-Box, Tortoise Shell Sigils

SEVEN

Val'st was a sombre figure amongst the Large Isle Ultai; he'd lost several fingers fishing the violent Sabrossi Sharks, and several teeth to scoring vicious shark bones. His eyesight had worn away its raw brilliance long, long ago, gazing out through their cavern's gem-scored peephole. Out through the impenetrable and stoic granite, into the essence-consuming frost of the glacial tundra.

There were few of them left now, trapped within their tiny pocket of existence, warmed and nurtured by the sleeping island, Sossianis. Here by their heartpool, Val'st and the last of his tribe slept on warm sands, shaded from the encroaching tundra, safe from the shrapnel snow and ice that sat jagged outside, and the frozen titans of legend.

Outside, the storm of ice blades and whirlwinds whipped life into bleak, harrowed stillness. There was no life, nothing to preserve or keep them from austere disintegration. There was just strict death and desolation, unpermeation of a caustic, winter wasteland.

Val'st was their guardian, until his passing brought the "honour" to his son. There were forty families under his diligent protection, four hundred people of his tribe. He had been taught his position since birth: to be strict and subservient until the end of time.

Long, long ago, when his beard was one of many adolescent dreams, he'd been taught the subservience to time and nature, to maintain the chain that kept the traditions and rites alive until the next generation. To persevere, and perpetuate, until the glacial blizzards retreated, and they could once again emerge into a world that lived beside them. All alongside, instead of against.

He'd been taught there were others, sparsely scattered through the expanse of the world, though now Val'st was wont to believe that a lie.

He'd been taught they were a chosen people, who had helped slay a mad god dubbed Azga, and brought balance to the universe. They were the mighty descendants of those that had shorn the enticing vestiges of psychotic power, those who escaped the death-stoked enslavement to a ravaging terror that subsumed their world. They had escaped to their frozen sanctuary, surrounded by a swallowing rock face, chosen people who would once again repopulate the green paradise that would exist when the glaciers retreated, to sit in reverence of the flowing life amidst the resonations of Divine causality.

His mind was sagging with old age. He was starting to think Sossianis was the maddened god; not Azga of legend but the resting figure who refused communion and left his flock voiceless, refusing to acknowledge the Chosen of the Chosen, time and time again. His father said they called it a frozen slumber; too little life force amidst their place, too much ice and snow permeating, bringing a hibernation for some, death for others. A frozen slumber for the mighty god who had used the last of their glorious life to create their entombing reprieve. The rich cavern inlaid with fishing ponds, fertile soil and blossoming life. An extravagant prison forged to keep them safe from the icy ones.

What if Sossianis was the mad god, depriving them of flourishing, depriving them of knowledge, depriving them of their birthright and destiny?

He had tried communion many times over. He was never successful; there was never a source of the Divine to touch upon. Val'st remembered the legends that his father Val'tyn had taught him. When communion brought contact, life would renew.

Thoughts of Azga had, as of recent, recurrently traced their way into his head, tinging his mind with recurring dreams, continually shifting webs of spinning anxiety, horror, and anguish woven into the eternally pitch black, deep metaphor broken by cascading rivers of red fire.

Then green bursts of life. Renewal.

What if Sossianis had been laying a trap for his soul, and these dreams were the herald of a way through to the light?

His father's stories told him to ensure their group survived, to protect his families' blood, to rest and sleep until Sossianis deemed it fit to return to the valleys, meadows, and rivers of their ancestors' lives.

He believed he was the fortieth of his kind. He had become chieftain at the age of thirty, as the rites demanded. It would be four more years before he left the group to die in the frozen wastelands, as was demanded when one turned fifty.

A dark and maleficent thought touched upon Val'st. His

face became contorted with stiff resolve. When he returned to the camp by the shores, he gathered his family members and told his wife what was needed for their trip. She protested too late, arriving as the last person's throat was slit, the heartpool a fountain of blood.

As Val'st adorned his face and marked his soul, the winds around Valestia began to recede.

However, no boats would leave the ice-encased island.

*

It had been several generations since the moment of Val'Est, and now the settlement of Tyor had grown to its two-hundredth member. There were other settlements dotted around the island; they had all agreed to divide the space into what could be farmed and managed equally.

However, the paradise they had been promised, and ceremoniously rejoiced towards, came back with very little vigour. The forests were never as thick as the paintings along Eisgar's cave wall predicted. The streams were littered with dirt and stones, with only a handful of fish finding a sustainable existence. The vast expanse of wildlife was nearly non-existent, the few species of animals comfortable surviving in winter found themselves in a new bizarre, life-giving wilderness. Sparsity kept flora and fauna to themselves, choosing solitary safety over communal extinction.

Eventually, their numbers had grown large enough for the Children of Val'Est, as they had come to call themselves, to fully believe the legacy of their ancestors was restored. The God Slayers of legend would soon soar again, re-emerging into their traditions with the power sacred of God.

This was the mantra of Val'Gori, the Chief of Chiefs, the Grand High Lord of the Infinite Cosmos. For several generations, the true-blooded children of Val had ruled from Val, at Tyor, while the others had left their ancestral legacy to fall into idolatrous worship.

Eisgar, the Blessed Darkness himself, had personally spoken to Val'Gori, and told him of the new times – that his assured rise would adjoin the two worlds. He would be the first of his line, and his line would grow and multiply, to rule the entire world. He had sacrificed three deer and two wolves to Kori, conducting the ritual beneath the yellow moon in ascent, and placed two finger bones from his pouch in the fire. The ceremony would soon begin, with his ascendency eternalised.

Val'Gori led the only village that still held true to the prophetic vision of their righteous forebear. The other tribes that were spread across Val'Est's island had turned as the land regrew; had fallen back to worshipping animistic spirits as they saw the impenetrable ice sheets that surrounded their homeland. They went back to worshipping the very foul chaos Val'Est had sought to rescue them from, a travesty that saddened Eisgar at every turn of fate.

It was not just the loss of love for the being who brought them into this golden age that removed them from the solitude that nearly drove them to maddened self-extinction. It was a reckless abandonment of all that held them to be dear. If they had persisted in that cave, the stories of Val'Est spoke, they would have dwindled and malformed. Now ten generations on, they were bountiful and prospered. They slept under the night sky and saw the clouds and animals once only dreamt of, or seen in the painted wall murals that adorned the Crystal Valley.

Now that he had lain out the remains of the sacrificial offerings, Val'Gori would await the holy people of his tribe. They would arrive soon, and nourish the Divine with their chants as Val'Gori entered into the vision trance, their voices assembling the backdrop of the Almighty. This would be the moment where Val'Gori attuned himself to Eisgar's plan. This would be the moment when Val'Gori would seal his fate as the next great prophet of the Children of Val.

His priest and acolytes appeared from the rise to the holy plateau, carrying the sacrilegious items they would use to antagonise Val'Est into action.

The many rituals of Eisgar that had been preserved by the tribe shamans: the many incantations and acts with which they could summon forth their almighty lord from the cold void. They were spoken by those who knew how to speak, passed from elder to youngling with each fresh generation.

They burnt the incense along the edge of the ritual circle, tracing smoking herbs along the white painted lines they had sown across the Divine space.

"Eisgar has decreed that we are those to carry his legacy onwards. Even though the many clans scattered as we left the frozen prison of Sossianis, it is now the time to rejoin them. Only heretics believe that we should stay shattered despite the great weight that Val'Est carried."

They had brought the false prophet Andrus Embering, bound and gagged, hogtied and sacrificially suitable, a perfect example of the foul indecency that corrupted his pure heritage. They would split his chest soon.

"Eisgar instead believes it is time for us to crush the others and bring them back into our holy fold. They no longer respect the true rites, established by our glorious founder.

They no longer respect the codes and creeds we established to hold us true to the one that brought about light."

The blood of the sacrifices was daubed across the consecrated space. Images of perfection were scarred into the wind-whipped plateau. Bleeding vigils adorned the space around Andrus "The Embering", the fool who had appeared from nowhere to sow discord and unite people against their grand awakening.

"I hear rumours that the others have fallen to false gods and prophets, and some are even attempting to resurrect the dead god Sossianis from his blood-quenched coma."

The shadows around them grew in ominous horror, the space for light and life being slowly drawn and suffocated into the white-etched centre.

"It is fool's folly to let them carry on; we must vanquish and decimate them all. We must strike them from the land and turn every foul-headed blasphemer into a spitting example."

Raw lightning split the ground where Andrus lay asunder.

By Eisgar's hand, he had been incinerated null.

*

The arrival of the Entoile had been prophesised since the time of the Great and Noble First One, Val'Est. Eisgar had continued that prophetic thread with the designation to Val Gori. Now this prestigious responsibility fell to the Grand Inquisitor of the Spectral Palace, Eious Val.

His revelation had been spectacular: a euphoric spasm, epileptic Divinity bursting forth, a tumour pulsating red, glowing with heat. Blurred lines of radiant light sang the heavenly truth, as it spilt from the High Heavens of Eisgar into Eious's mind. The visions had been happening for several months, increasing in frequency till the very fabled lost tribe had now come back to rest amidst its ancient cousins. The Entoile's arrival signified the new tide of Eisgar, that a new order would need to be born, would need to emerge from their island womb to purge the desecrated continent it nearly abutted.

This evangelical resurgence was necessary for Valestian society, which had become gluttonous and slow, bloated and befouled. The Valestians had grown accustomed to their island paradise, and it had been several hundreds of years since the ice had finally receded. The people didn't care; fisher people expanded out, but that was the limit of their newness, having grown lazy and insular.

Now Eious would lead their new golden age, their well-overdue ascendency to the heights of the Chaos Gods of Old, the Urm'gil titans who used to rule the continent before the Valestians helped them slay the "Dark God", the very same who now bestowed them glory and life.

Eious knew the stories down to their bare, rune-scribed and Divinated bones. He had seen apocryphal texts stored deep within the musky catacombs beneath the Spectral Palace. The ideas had long been denied by the corrupted, yet still their script of luminescent symbols and signs were a twinkling signal to their preordained primacy. When he had risen to the rank of Highest Two-Named, he knew he was destined for greatness, the ritual position demanding his introduction into the highest order of Divine priesthood, requiring his inoculation against the Chaos Gods and their foul fellowship of stained mana types.

The one he was replacing led him down, ready to cast off their name and identity and enter into rest and refuge in the Vallyium Gardens. The cold stone floor slobbered over his feet, burning a raw tingling into his bare soles. They had stepped down deep into the pitch-black halls of the catacombs without lights or assistance, an obsidian twilight of soul dust cast across the atmosphere.

They made it to the internal chamber of the Highest Inquisitor.

He passed over his powers to Eious, spilling his blood into the first gold bowl, encrusted with ruby red gems and glistening amber.

Eious was forced to drink every drop, after which he was the highest supreme.

The guttural and despotic priesthood he had inherited was more than lazy and lax. They were deeply weak, and distressingly indulgent, indolent and uncharismatic – more interested in gold coins and finery than the deep, profound truths he took upon his mantle. They were uninterested in the spiritual revelation that Eious held for all his kin and kind.

He had seen this since his early years as an acolyte, learning the religious rites and mantras from people more interested in paying lip service before returning to gluttonous harems.

He had seen the stench of corruption and the signs of idolatry as his fellow priests and bishops ate and drank volumes more than their poverty-stricken flocks. As they toiled to renew the injustice and exploitations that kept the true-blooded and devout from enjoying their eternities of rest and pure sublimation.

When he had been chosen for the Two-Named and been given the rank of inquisitor, he had seen how his fellows and brothers had turned a blind eye to the malignant undercurrent of venerated ignobility. It was the duty of the inquisitors to stamp out and uproot the distinct discoloration of heresy and ill virtue. Instead, he found the inquisitors to be bloated enablers, themselves feasting on the blood money, bribes, extortions and benefits that came with their prestige and finality of say.

As he had been brought further through the circles of the inquisitors, as he had been brought higher and deeper into the chain of esoteric truth that granted the inquisitors their power and strength, he saw again and again the foul natures of those he once respected and looked to for guidance.

Finally he joined the inner court, the First Circle, and was deeply engrained. He had his final tattoo embroidered into him. He was anointed with the tainted blood of Sossianis.

He was first among equals, and first under supreme. It would soon be his time.

It had now culminated in his supremacy. The Entoile were now his emboldening key. They would lead them back to their homelands, give them access to the ancient powers of the Entoile Empire. They would realise Azirn from afar, bringing the full cataclysmic extent of the dark energy of the Rekilli. This fitted with the ancient scripture handed out by the priesthood. They might have been lulled into a hedonistic decadence by the Chaos Gods, but they were still of use.

They were still brimming with potential, overspilling ideology into every porous person close enough to hear the soft, silken, sibilant words. They spoke of how Kori, the Grave Keeper, was distilling the souls of the Valestians from the

Cloud Dwellers' grasp. How he was preparing the lifeblood of the Valestians to imbue them with the power of a thousand generations. This would be the key to their attainment of godhood. This was the reason for their new crusade; this was the bright star that would lead them onto immortality. The Valestian Primacy would stand until the end of existence, the vigilant and valiant protectorate of Eisgar.

All this required was a disruption of the manascape.

They would seize the ancient holy sites of the Urm'gil, claim the soul stones divided by the Islekind across their islands. They would unify their power and eliminate the Chaos Gods until the end of eternity.

He shivered as cold, frozen power rippled from his shoulders to his core.

All for Eisgar.

The One and True, and Only, Lord of All.

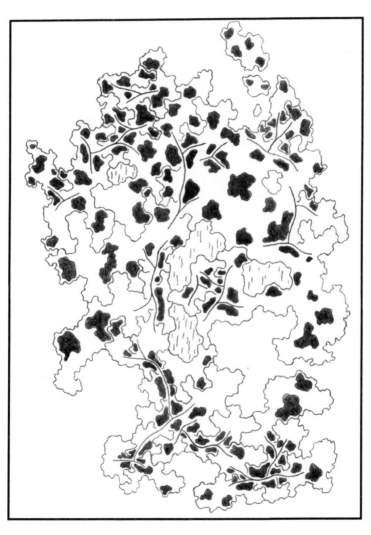

Map of Valestia: "The Lost Isle" by Intrif II, 1451 PIA

THE FLOW
THE CARROW (652 PIA)

Rich-washed blackness envelops every forged star,
Where consciousness creeps by soft river discharged,
The once-broken tides, refreshing with silt,
All slip from the mountain, and wash away guilt."
—The Inyipi Hymn to Eternity

Rolling blackouts always cause devastation, decimation and dedicated crucibalic catastrophising. Derelictally distributed with a delicate yet demolishing debonair de-light, rolling blackouts are the worst of the worst of the worst.

Ask that besotted, besodden(?), bespoken for pile of corpses clearly piled to provoke and escalate.

Rolling blackouts are a snake of our time, which wind their hand and weave their web to ebb and flow beyond the capital ideas of chivalry and nobility.

But rolling blackouts are rare. They come at you when least expected.

The last time I had rolling blackouts, it took me to the edge and back. Just, you know, the self-control required. The reliance on intuitive instinct. Inbuilt virtue. To a Te.

How had I gotten the rolling blackouts? Magical curse. Yep. Hand on my heart. Of course, it would have been.

I'd been traipsing through the forests north-east of Askilt, minding my own business, when the foulest, evilest, most diabolically minded of hags emerged from her lair and smote me sick.

Sick with rolling blackouts. The pre-posed thought of violence would incur their deep and dark depths. I was to slay anything that stood before when such occurred.

I decided the only person who could help me would be one of those shaggy-haired shamans. Malicath was too far, though.

Fuck. It would have to be the Seybili instead.

Was she still pissed at me? Oh… definitely.

So yeah, I began the journey across to Seybili's mountain hovel. That gritty, shitty, stench-stained shamble that stuck out from the rock precipice like a dank, frostbitten remnant of a thumb. That pungent black hole of inhospitable bullshit.

Oh, and yes, of course there was fucking trouble in the way. Like up-to-the-knees-mud-thrown-blindly-everywhere trouble.

I think I remember how I solved it…? But, you know, it gets a bit dark and immemorable. Which is kind of the problem with rolling blackouts.

I don't think I killed anyone?

The green-brown floral interplay abruptly ceased.

The brim of red, yellow, orange, pink and blue petals

194

that poked out from the grassnopy receded into snow-white fields.

Here before Hawk lay an obstacle. Shit. He felt the sweat muster upon his brow.

A battalion of battle-ready battle-clad battlepersons.

*

Clanging feet brought the company of Valestians onwards towards their target.

Esti'bon was a commoner, a vigilante conscript taken from the eternally righteous flocks. It was a common Valestian practice for the outer clans to send their children away to spiritual festivals. There they would be chosen and kidnapped and assigned to respective military cadres. Esti'bon was lucky that he had been picked by the Gold Crest Order, the group responsible for training those fortunate few who might be picked for the Diamond Lancers, or, as they were commonly referred to, the Royal Wardens.

That meant fifteen years' training at the Diamond-Soaked Castle, and then this, his tour of duty in the greater imperial provinces. Esti'bon would only have five more months of duty under the Inquisitor Galdrie, and then he would be on his way to the Diamond Lancers. He would be fitted with dazzling armour fit for the most heroic of champions. He would dine in the brilliant halls fit for the most daring and dangerous of doomstavers.

His tour had been mostly successful, which was why he was here now, setting the pace of a harmonious rhythmic footfall, on the periphery of Deskilt. The village and its verdant hinterlands, both known ubiquitously as Cerebrium, was a golden trickle awaiting fortuitous Valestian grace. Unfortunately, like every other village he had come across, they were devout heretics, readily giving their spiritual energy towards false idols and evil gods.

The Chaos Gods were the deceitful opponents of every noble and virtuous Valestian. They were dark adornments of the universe, who could only be cleansed by sword and flame. It was Eisgar, the Noble Light, the Knife-Borne, who led the Valestian pantheon. Eisgar, the Totality of All That Goes Forward, who was the true unifier of the universe. The true power that bestowed life and chance to those once burdened by the icy prison that surrounded and subdued their island.

Having grown up with a zealous family, Esti'bon was privileged to have been taught the various righteous acts and rituals as his place in the Valestian Primacy demanded. His life was blessed and sigiled daily, his actions imbued with the Divine spirit of Val'Est, who was his symbolic aspect as a member of the Diamond Lancers.

The two-named inquisitors of the various orders were servants of Gal Vori. They were dignified their rank with the newness of a name forge. The surname they decided upon was carved into a rock, painted blue to match the soulstones of the Islekind, and entombed in the Great Order's catacombs. These stones imitated the temple cities of the Urm'gil, and the stories mustered around campfires said the replications were as powerful as their Divine originals. They were held to be the life force and driving signs behind the Valestian Primacy's magnanimous ascension, and, unlike the soulstones, they weren't tools of the Chaos Gods.

Esti'bon's first tour of duty was against the Islekind, during the grim conflict of the Broken Moon. His company had been stationed aboard a Valestian Warship and taken to the coastline of the central island. They were to establish a bulkhead against the Islekind, to create a fortified position that the rest of the Armada could join. From there they would begin slow pushes against the sparsely defended Islekind villages.

They had arrived to a storm, the bleakest and shriekiest of howls scuttling their vessel, the encompassing sharp tones shredding the wood that held the water at bay. They had clamoured into lifeboats and set sail for the coastline, setting sights on calm sandy beaches, the golden yellow a silent Shangri-la far away from the thunderous and vengeful drowning strikes of the Chaos Gods.

The lifeboats were cramped and overburdened; water slipped over the sides of several, bringing a lingering heaviness. This soon grew to a swallowing weight, bringing the small wooden frames into darker shades of blue. Vicious and violent waves cascaded against the waterproofed sides, the force splitting and haemorrhaging boats to either side. Esti'bon could hear the harrowed calls of his kin quickly cast off to a swift death, succumbing to the beating tides.

As the moon grew to epic proportions, keen to witness the savage foray, the souls of those drowned were cast up into the sky, washed into their constellated afterlife.

Esti'bon had finally reached the beach, and shortly fell into a deathly unconsciousness. When he awoke, the beach's soft sands surrounding him were littered with bloated corpses and bodies – the middens of lost lives, gangrenous accumulations of the previous night's death. Few had survived the relentless folly; or perhaps few of the survivors were willing to return to the shore. Esti'bon hadn't known which was true, but eventually, as he talked to catatonic and clear-sighted alike, Esti'bon found that several surviving cohorts had formed under the captaincy of his brother-in-arms Oise'Yul.

The camp was just nestled into the thick forest-jungle that crept towards the bare shore. A bright and comforting camp light reminded that life would always find a way to persevere through the nebulous whims and catastrophic atrocities of the Chaos Gods.

Oise'Yul had granted him a lieutenancy, with several soldiers to command, and asked him to scout for a better place to make camp. He advised his soldiers that the Islekind were aggressive, and not to be taken too lightly, and then they had made their way deep into the thick and creeping underbrush. They were all of virtuous stock and training, so he reckoned this should be easy.

It was after their second day of exploration that they were attacked by the Islekind. They had attacked Esti'bon and his men as they sought rest in a small stone alcove cut into rock face. They were travelling carefully along a stream, and the rock cliffs that abutted it were filled with pockets and rest sites, all easily defensible.

The Islekind had only attacked with arrows and jarring barbs, a fluster of activity sending a whistling issue through the exposed face of the alcove. Esti'bon and his soldiers had quickly taken up a defensive posture behind their shields, creating an armoured fortress with the cold stone as their rear guard. With that, the Islekind had quickly retreated.

It was the night of their fifth day of exploration; the Islekind's arrow storm had been held off for a second time, and his soldiers were sat resting and catching their breath.

They had still taken no casualties and had barely blunted their weapons. Few dents would need to be hammered out of their armour; therefore, it was with certain fact that he knew the Islekind would be made short work of. Even with the devastating sinking of possibly three-quarters of the invading armada, there were still around one hundred or so Valestian soldiers, many of them from the elite Diamond Lancers.

It was on the eighth day that they found the perfect place to set up a base camp. They could still feel the rush and high from fighting off the attacking Islekind the night before. They hadn't slain any of the attackers, but neither had the attackers slain any of them. That left Esti'bon feeling triumphantly glorious. He was resolved that any Islekind they faced on their way back would soon fall prey to their expertise and cunning. Anyone dumb enough to step in their path would meet Eisgar the Maker by glistening blade edge.

There above them, Esti'bon spotted the ideal campsite.

They made their way back through the suffocating underbrush. Esti'bon had asked his troops repeatedly if they also felt the trees creeping closer, if they too sensed a denser choking to the atmosphere. They all agreed they did; the humming of life, the snickering of insidious feral violence, had grown broader and richer each hour. A vibrant hum of foreboding agony and painful intrusion was echoing around them with each and every step. They decided to make camps fewer and further between. They also kept two up for each of the night shifts.

They weren't attacked on their way back. However, when they reached the base camp that Oise'Yul had engineered, he was waiting, ready but blunt. "We need to move now. We've been attacked by wild animals." There were signs of injury – bandages, bruises, swollen fingers – amongst the soldiers surrounding Oise'Yul.

"They crept up from the beach and broke through the barricade. They killed several while they slept; several more have been wounded. We need to make our way to a better camp now, or we're well and truly fucked."

That was it. They made their quick journey up to the exposed rock face that terraced a safe space. There, they quickly set up their tents and spear barricades, this time with only one entrance: the slight incline that ascended for several hundred metres across the rock face down to the jungle floor.

For the first time, they felt secure. For the first time, they felt their campaign might have been saved, their tenuous position well and truly rectified. There was no one way the dimly equipped Islekind would shift them from this position, and this position was so good they would become resolutely embedded, an irrevocable fulcrum as they levered their next army deeper into the island. They were even defended from above by the sheltering rockface, protected from any raids during the night.

Oise'Yul had brought Esti'bon into the commander's tent at nightfall. It felt better to be around the patrols and torches. There were no suffocating trees, no breath-stealing foliage, to ambush them, cornered and panicking; no safe avenues for beasts to sneak up and strike at them when least expected, snapping or slashing at their legs.

"We need to make an advance column to the temples further inland," said Oise'Yul. "That's the reason we're here, to be a bulkhead as the rest of the forces then begin their invasion. That should hopefully keep the Islekind distracted while we then intervene at the temples. All we need are the soulstones; then we can leave this desolate, accursed place."

They all agreed it would be a simple task by the end of it. There was no reason to dwell on the losses they had already faced.

Esti'bon fell asleep devastatingly quickly. It was fortunate he had not pulled night guard duty. As his snores began their climb, the deep chorus of rolling bass dislodged the rocks above, which immediately began their descent, plummeting down deftly. He was forced awake as a coarse boulder crushed his tent-mate, the jolting splat rupturing his dream.

He flung himself upwards, bursting into a dash for the tent flap. As he made it to the chaos at the exit, he saw Oise flattened by a deadly bludgeoning impact, his rallying cry silenced by a deafening smote.

He didn't remember them fleeing, just returning to Valestia, harrowed and sore.

That was why Esti'bon had now been reassigned to a captaincy in the Shorelands, why Valestia now refused to move closer to the scornful and hostile Islekind. Why his fingers twitched uneasily before the chasm of sleep's silent death. The very earth that was supposed to sustain them had rebuked their presence, a sign of the foulest of possessions by the Chaos Gods.

Soon they would return and purge that desecrated archipelago, and Esti'bon's restless legs would stomp their way to silence, though they would have to acquire more manpower if they wished to cleanse that putrescent scourge completely.

Which was why they were now marching forwards into the hinterlands between Ristos and the Shorelands. They had already claimed the coastline, carefully avoiding the Islekind's rage and anger.

The drops of feet bounced like pebbles and stones.

He felt the undertide of his raw memories beginning, and bit them back with tenacious ferocity.

More often than not, the pain of the memories would resurge. The quick breaths and sharp anxiety. The recurring sounds of screams and crushes. Bones snapping and bloodcurdling, ruptured howls.

Never again would he be caught unaware by an enemy, lest he suffer a fate worse than death.

That was how he kept the dark immersion at bay.

*

If Hawk said the word enough now, there would be no potential crisis.

The sweat continued to accumulate.

He could say *battle*. "Battle, battle, battle, battle, battle."

He just couldn't think of battle-ing. The *ing* was the thing, as it always was with this kind of fiasco. Not so much a problem, a catastrophe or a cataclysm but definitely a probleming, a catastrophising or a cataclysming. Maybe cataclimaxing?

Well, it was all irrelevant. He just had to focus on not focusing. And, you know, just not scratch that itch to fight.

What were the words of the magical curse that shitbag Skullim had cast upon him? *If you seek a violent path, your blade will bite all eyes that catch.*

I mean, firstly, fuck all poetic truth. Well and truly at this point, he was happy to shoulder that ontological burden, crosshairs aimed at the universe and Yggdrasil, the green sleeping shit.

But also, secondly, well, truly lastly, he didn't notice the jagged, immovable rock brimming and beaming under the soft, silken sunshine.

The expletives were heard in the village. It wasn't too far away, maybe three fields of snow-white petals and cereal crop salutations.

The horses in the pasture heard the curses uttered unto the All Father, the equine epitome that galloped far above.

The colour-marked gangs of birds that flocked amidst the auburn-tinged village trees whispered between themselves in suspicion.

The rampaging warbands of renegade rabbits ceased their squabbles by the village fishing pond. The fish that skirted the interludes of beaks took pause to seek the source.

The gaudily daubed green-and-blue doors of the thatch-roofed wooden-clad houses daunted and opened. Out popped the heads of those ready to receive the coming… thing?

There was little foreknowledge of this kind of thing, which worried the village elder. He was agitated when he saw the self-conscious ambling stroll of a giant of a figure, clad in serrated steel body armour, a jet-black helmet of vicious skewerment, carrying brutal visions of death-dealing destruction.

The voice that caught him was off-key; that was what especially worried the elder.

He made the sign of the Six Sisters and began the descent down his steps, across his rich brown veranda, descending to the cobble-sided dirt track that led through the village. He greeted the harbinger of death with two open arms.

The harbinger smiled and asked for a cup of tea. "Warm tea is a blessing to the soul," said he. It was the kind of idle comment that could keep you occupied for hours.

The tea was well and truly sublime, and as Ilyia always said: "Start with tea, end with Te."

So he started with the former, and hopefully the other would follow. Plain and simple, easy premises.

His brow betrayed the other.

The village elder sat opposite him. The man must have been sixty-five, with a grey-brown-bitten scrub of facial hair that warmed his face and fed his gentle demeanour. The village elder's arms spoke of his veterancy; his hands spoke of centuries of toil. The tea spoke a shimmering satisfaction.

The village was far out, well and truly far out from the protection of the Valestians. Hawk assumed the village elder liked it so.

"How old is your settlement? I'm new to the region. I normally range far to the east of here. Rimside, not Rimwards."

The elder began his introduction in the baritone of deep time. "We've been here for generations upon generations. I am by far older than my name suggests, and I'm easily more than the fifth of my nominative descent. Was that we just used to fight the night-dwellers of these lands. Was that we just used to see the crumples of snow for longer than the dreams of green that rest beneath stars." The elder quaffed his drink.

Wow, that was ridiculously fucking old. Hawk was intrigued.

"Does that mean you were here during the last Ice Age?"

The village elder laughed. "Not me personally, mind you.

But yes, our village is a descendant of those Ultai that sought to stay stable with 'those that dwell between the bars.'"

"Did it work for you?" Hawk inquired quickly.

"Well," the village elder laughed, "we're still here now."

Hawk drank the last of his tea in affirmation; he nodded in approval. "It seems like you're doing just fine to me. May I have more tea?"

They drank the tea in idle chatter. In the shadows, Te was produced, followed, and settled. Wayward ties aligned and the geometric ensued. Tangentially, Hawk saw the marks of perpendicular Divinity across the features of the man. The odd degree in dialect tic; the rare reflection of primordiality.

*

Tul'Viar was a member of the Valestian slave caste, brought into the invasion force as a way to earn a life away from indentured servitude. He was a member of the Entoile who left their empire, when it fell to the vile Krylei, and migrated back south towards the So'Ultai homeland. They were officially brought into Valestia by the Two-Named. Deemed the predecessors of a grand empire, they were quickly put to use as cheap labour.

The island of Valestia had been a solidly homogenous group, despite some minor ethnic divisions, before the preordained and prophesied arrival of the Entoile. With their arrival, the whole society saw itself uplifted, placing the Entoile where the bottom used to be. They had spent generations toiling through the two hundred and thirty-odd years spent in their homeland, before their vile eviction by the tyrannical Krylei usurped their glory. Many of the Entoile had chosen to stay in their land, without the empire's political stability. They were soon led by vicious and maleficent warlords, petty assholes who swung their swords at every piece of exposed flesh.

The Fleeing Entoile had been sent straight into the waiting arms of those who had previously hounded them. The Borsi clans of the West Shorelands viciously bit at the toppled people. They were driven by blade-edge to the Yeli continent, and then, once again, by the Korsif they were driven down into the Farlands. From the Farlands, the diminishing community had heard of the island paradise that had bitten through the frost.

Their god Eisgar had appeared before the High Priest of the Fleeing Entoile, commanding him to turn his back on the rites and worship of Azga the Sullied; to instead bring their hands and voices to the island that was his ward and charge. He had bestowed the islanders with empyreal wisdom, and venerated glory. Now they would follow, and the island would emerge in all its glorious shine.

They followed devotedly by the boatloads. Crammed into ancient ships and bitten woodwork, they sailed the ancient trek of those when they were gifted Valestia as reward for the war against the Dark God.

When they finally arrived, the supposedly frostbitten shores were burnt into lush coastland. Troves of excited and flittering wildlife clustered to meet them, the waters littered with brightly coloured sailboats and gaudily dressed people, grey and white dolphins, mesmeric shoals of multicoloured fish, white and black birds and grey-soaked seals.

They had been brought to the bustling harbour at the lively and growing city of Tarsus, where they were met by the

Grand Inquisitor of the Spectral Palace. They were received with open arms, and likewise told they would be the new leaders of the illustrious and weak cities of the Shorelands.

The Valestians had acted within a few years, and took the jewel city of Yeli as their prize. Then they seized the whole peninsula, declaring it their colonial empire.

The Entoile had become a quick-breeding and prosperous slave caste, used as cheap field labour, water carriers, tradespeople, artists and indentured servants, but lastly and mostly as meat shields – which Tul'Viar was happy to admit they excelled at, he himself being a model of a perfect soldier.

Unlike the Valestians, who were conscripted and chosen by the various regimented orders of the Valestian army, the Entoile would volunteer for their military service. You were more likely to be turned away as an Entoile than be accepted, and therefore it was of the highest honour to be taken from the cramped and arduous, but Divinely benign, conditions and lifted into the fanatically righteous military.

Tul'Viar was on his first tour of duty, having completed his ten years of military training in the camps of the Valestian Auxiliary Colonial Army. He had received the highest medals and accolades during his training, which was why he had been assigned to the cohort of Inquisitor Yuix Gadrei. He was fighting alongside some of the most promising of Diamond Lancer potentials, and was keen to make his mark.

He had yet to fight with any of them; he had joined the cohort at their camp in Denilt before they began their trek northwards. The rest of the soldiers had been together since the unsuccessful, and highly debated, invasion of the Islekind. They had been brought together to repair the image and reputation of the Primacy's elite cadre of soldiers.

Since the adoption of the Eisgar Tomes by the Fleeing Entoile, they had only ever proven themselves to be the most virtuous and zealous of followers. It was common for the more fanatical of Tul's brethren to casually throw themselves at the defenders of city walls, defenestrating them both to no real benefit. The Valestian army tried to create barriers against this apparently natural tendency, but the fervour that spread across his kin the night before a battle spoke greatly of their passionate dedication to Eisgar's cause.

As it was said in the cramped and scuffed churches that the Fleeing Entoile had built, "without Eisgar we would be nothing; therefore, for Eisgar we become nothing". Wise words, fitting devotion to a truly wise god.

The so-called invasion of the Shorelands – so needed because the native heathens were adamant followers of the Chaos Gods, refusing to see Eisgar's mantle and light – was going well enough for prosperity to flitter behind the retinas of the High Valestian Royal Council. Their pupils and irises spoke of visions of gold, trailing rivers of diamonds, seas of silver, and ultimately that vice before all others: copious quantities of power.

Power was the source and scourge of the universe, Eisgar proclaimed. In the motions towards greatness, the Primacy would become that which it was always destined to be. It was preordained that they would sublimate, ascend to the higher form, find their eternal solace before the full voice of the universe. This was the ending that Tul dreamt of.

Eisgar spoke of how the Chaos Gods wrought the landscape into deformed monstrosities; turned the tides of water and ice upon budding life, reshaping the many prosperous forms into demonic aberrations. The Chaos Gods would perpetuate the eternal war that caused the rootlessness and decimation. The Chaos Gods would continue their foul follies into the minds of the Second Peoples; they would continue to cause their severance from the life force of Eisgar.

None from the Shorelands would follow Eisgar willingly, despite their eclectic and bizarre collection of gods, demigods and deities that clung to every feature and appendage, stood or moving through the giant steppe landscape.

The plethora of powerful idolatry had been sufficiently pruned on Valestia. The blur of Divinity was reduced to the Holy Trinity of Eisgar: Kori, the Grave Keeper; Val'Est, the Violent Blade; and Val Gori, the Two-Named of Divinity. The rich myopic maze of river and field gods were rinsed out and shed away. The rituals and rites would nourish the holy trinity, and the holy trinity would nourish Eisgar in truly powerful simplicity.

You could even hear the noisy animals and bristling bushes and flowers, feel their flagrant defiance of Eisgar. The further behind they left Valestia's colonies, the louder and brighter the displays of wasteful, dumb, animalistic hubris, all of them wild and unfearing the advancing cohort marching into their untamed existence.

The call from the Inquisitor cut through Tul'Viar's intense internal monologue. They would make camp for dinner, and then continue onwards towards the village.

The captain, Esti'bon, passed over his ration of meat and bread, and told him they were nearly there.

*

As the last lights flickered over the tea set, the village elder stood and beckoned for Hawk to follow.

"We have a special religious ceremony tonight, the Boko'Morrow. Unfortunately, it requires a deep trance and several hours' dedication. We would ask you to stay in the board-house, but I would prefer it if you stayed with me. Obviously, to someone of your stature it shouldn't need too much explanation?"

Hawk solemnly nodded in approval. He feigned a yawn. "Just point me to a bed, and I'll happily sleep till sun-up."

The bed was soft and comfy, the fortress furthest away from the ancient battlelines coursing through the landscape.

*

Inquisitor Yuix "Galisi" Galdrei arrived at the village just after midnight, followed in close succession by his plethora of finely armoured colonial soldiers. They were here amidst the garden wilds of Cerebrium, bringing the valiant glory they were renowned for, to all the brutally barbaric and untamed people yet to embrace the cleansing lights.

Cerebrium itself was newly acquired land, seized when the Valestian Colonial Infantry marched through the village earlier last year; the village had in turn offered itself up to them as a free token, without conflict. They said there was no need for violence, no need for disarray. These were villagers to admire. Cerebrium would become the model colony of Valestia. Nested far north of the Twin Cities, it resided in Deskilt's portion of the Shorelands.

His company strode behind him, hot-headed and gently roasting under the dazzling sunshine. There was not a cloud in the sky as they marched their triumph. No sign of any nefarious ill-fated messenger of the Chaos Gods. If they saw clouds, it might mean trouble, and they didn't want any of that. This was a cut-and-clean mission. The picturesque yellow-gold, teal-stained pastures dipped and dove in rolling hills of bounteous beauty. The white-bricked village lay just ahead. There were no ominous landmarks; there was no church hewn from an ancient deity's resting shell.

This should be the easiest extension of the Valestian Primacy. It would do well with his superiors. He would earn the fortuitous rising of his kindred from the progression of this campaign.

With forty men, he would waylay this region into a peaceful prerogative of purposeful cohesion. They would erect the Church to the Trinity in all its pure-stained glory, calling for the proliferation of monuments to Eisgar, and ordinations of locals. Then they would establish a missionary service to carry the religious works of the Primacy to the untouched barbarians further north.

It was a long way to the Krylei settlements of Ristos. A long way was a slow way for news to travel; success guaranteed.

His kin used to live in the poorest district of Valestia's capital, Vest'le. Now they lived in the terrace-topped square towers of the ecclesiastical district. Bright, vibrant yellow-turquoise banners decked the rooftops they rested on. No more rats and disease, blooded coughing, and noxious fumigation.

Soon, they would ascend higher. Purchase property in the lands beneath the cityscape. They wouldn't toil, never again, but the revenue and status would assure their esteemed position for many generations of lackadaisical bearing. If his successors were as pragmatic as him, maybe one day they would also make it to the Triarchy of the Two-Named.

He arrived, and there was no problem. The river, to be crossed in view of the village periphery, was stepped over quietly and without issue. No sign of traps or waylaying were strewn across the path. Calm, decadent steps of decent footing ensured the company a quick stride past the waterway, through into the meandering, snaking passage of the tall-tree underbrush.

The soldiers behind gawped and hawked, guarded and mystified by the surrounding wilderness. The vast, lush lifescape they journeyed through was infinitely richer than the landscapes of their home, Valestia. Many were fresh-faced recruits; a few were "veterans", if that word could be used. The advantage of being the only military state in this region was that the piss-poor excuse for muscle bred at home was still infinitely likelier to be battle-hardened than the yokels they came across out here.

The captain, the zealot called Esti'bon, gave the order to continue forwards. "If we're marching for much longer, we'll need a brief rest, sire. The men are starting to flag, and if we want to be fresh for combat, it's worth resting our muscles now rather than later."

The white stone houses crept out from the thick foliage.

"Ahh, pish and tosh. It looks like we're here already, all ready to beckon on the new dawn of their new day. When we've succeeded, we'll rest on befitting laurels, and receive that reward we've all been salivating over."

The captain called back to the men. "Keep a tight formation; the village has been sighted. Get ready for trouble at the first sign of an offence."

The soldiers tightened their grips, locked their formation and stamped their feet further up the dirt path.

Some villagers emerged from the houses. One took a step onto the porch, their front door already widely ajar, and called out, "The village elder's house is just up ahead. Look for the bright red rooftop, and dipped black streaks, that's his. That'll be Old Ist's."

The inquisitor thanked her without comment or acknowledgement, as he was wont to do at times like this.

His fat, lazy, heavy weight bore continuously down on his steed, a purebred Yeli Whitemane. He hadn't cared to name her, or check if she preferred one. Instead, "Hurry up, you lazy shit" and the odd kick were deemed enough.

Teyani the Whitemane felt upwards. The fat fuck would soon be off her, she hoped. Otherwise, she might have to kick his fucking face in.

They found the bright red roof and heard a call from the porch. The figure stood in front of him towered. A gargantuan shadow was cast by the bold eclipse over the inquisitor's plan.

They'd made their merry way to the village elder's house; they were greeted by the elder's steward, his wife, and their eldest son. The inquisitor had extended the warm regards of Valestia to its new occupants.

"We're not a muddied evil," he explained. "There'll be very few changes to your village's performance under our Divine rule. It's important, however, that conformation to our spiritual oversight is accepted."

The wife bemoaned this fact, mostly due to her husband's absence for their own cultural ritual. She explained the importance of the reification of the mandate to manage

Ist'Cair, through the Boko'Morrow, and that he would be back promptly.

The captain of the Valestian Infantry was encroaching on the giant's personal space, the small-statured one called Esti'bon trying to assess how much of a threat the one called Hawk would be. He was breathing heavily through his nostrils directly at Hawk's belly button. Hawk was slowly losing patience, half-asleep and semi-cantankerous.

The pool of detrital snot was slowly growing on Hawk's feet. He felt the encroaching blackness.

Hawk lifted his titanic arms and brought them clashing down onto the tin can tomfoolery that stood so ungainly before him. With strong clasps, two of the soldiers were lifted fully vertical.

Istarig knew what was coming. He'd seen the tension behind the young warrior's face, the threat obvious, as he had entered late into the back of the room, the near-possible lapse of judgement and ensuing chaos. He leapt forward, conveniently after Hawk had bludgeoned a large collection of soldiers to near-death. The guards that rushed to stop him were slaughtered where they stood, left diminished in pieces on the floor.

Hawk was currently gouging out the eyes of the inquisitor with his thumbs. Foam burst from both mouths, accompanied by a sharp crash as the door to the room burst open. There stood young Unye, son of Eriyn.

Hawk had heard the noise. The lifeless corpse of the inquisitor was tossed to the floor, and the giant, towering rage, made several steps towards Unye.

Istarig finished the last guard with one swift swipe through the jugular. He then began the dash to intercept.

Hawk was getting closer to Unye; he stood there half-transfixed, half in dread-induced shock.

Hawk's arms reached outwards. His large hands would crush the boy's skull.

Istagir leapt.

The flickering candles caught the scene perfectly, the tension seared sharp; Unye screamed a guttural envelopment of despair and demise.

Then blackness.

When Hawk awoke, there was a stain on the floor. Fortunately he had been restrained, and there were only a few corpses, and he was glad to see none of the villagers were hurt.

They resolved to travel north to the lands of Ristos, safe from the ill touch of the inquisitors.

The survivors on the inquisitor's part brought their tale back to their commander; they had fled from their posts outside the house as soon as they heard the violent death of Galisi. When the tale was told to the High Colonial Inquisitor Chancellor Imberine, his feet emphasised the soldiers' quick passage of time.

They say the life of a being is a ratio of its heartbeat and the times its eyes can flicker. The soldiers went from elephants to cicadas in the flash of an instant... a glittery, splash-inducing flash of an instant.

*

Imberine was left to clean up another set of bloodstains that reminded him only of another wasted journey and expedition; another long list of costs of equipment and life.

Another long list of fuck-all, as usual. His cadre of inquisitors were wont to cause fuck-ups in every corner of the continent.

It was apparently his job to oversee their inability to perform, their inane impotency, throughout the entirety of the Shorelands.

He was stationed at the Great Church of Eisgar in Denilt, the first of the bare stone Valestian buildings to be sacrilegiously erected over indigenous holy ground. It was a blue-stained approximation of Eisgar's face, the entrance hewn into the cliff face that terraced to form Denilt's upper strata, the god's features casting a grim and forlorn watch over the citizens now subject to its ardent supporters.

After the Great Church came the Beseeched Grievance, a blasphemy of a fortress, hewn into the ancient face of a bleached and tarnished Rock Dweller, who fortunately for them was long past the ability to respond to such desecration.

Imberine was careful with how he approached his feelings surrounding the invasion of the Shorelands. Since they had built up a power base through the lands of Askilt and Denilt, their tentative position had been solidified. Now they could become unstoppable.

They had brought several thousands of soldiers over from Valestia to support the Primacy's colonial acquisitions, all to be directed by the Grand Inquisitor of the Spectral Palace. Despite this, Imberine was still too low down the pecking order to be given access to the Church's secrets. The devout clergy clung to the prophetic tapestries handed on by forebears with earnest and dedication, and these were kept in deep, dark holes far from prying eyes.

The threats and warnings woven into the sheets of cloth that foretold Valestia's glorious uprising were of the highest and most serious of arcane examinations. Alas, the clergy of the Primacy were no comparison to the genius Magisterial Orders of Yeli; however, the magisters colluded with the various Divinities the Valestians held to be Chaos Gods.

That was inexcusable blasphemy to the Primacy, so the magisters' magical talents were overlooked and left to fester in the slowly growing ruinous essence that looked to consume the Yeli peninsula. Imberine predicted that the tides of Valestian dominance would severely cripple the Shorelands in the coming decades. He knew that they were here to harvest the manascape of its energy, to redirect the beliefs and sustenance of the peoples towards the Primacy's Holy Trinity.

The Shorelands had already been *mana-scarred*, as Imberine had come to name the process. His own loyalists had been covertly conducting excavations in the mountains and had found cave paintings that described the War of the Falling Spires. This was no new news to anyone; many traders had brought the stories of the Falling Spires from the Krylei in Ristos down to the So'Ultai of the Shorelands. Many of the ancient cities of the Farlands still held reference to the Falling Spires in the beginnings of their cities' histories.

The genesis of the Krylei had come during the Falling Spires of the Urm'gil, and even the landscape the mighty Ancients had once occupied was still left shorn, stitched and scarred by their legacy.

The pictographs, recovered from tombs and treasuries, described a form of symbiosis between the Urm'gil and the manascape; how the gods had helped the ancient ones keep back the constantly rotating glaciers; how they had sacrificed many of their lives on the promise of warmth and spring.

Eventually, as the Urm'gil and the little-mentioned Ehmr'gil fell to desolating infighting, the life force of the Shorelands had apparently been coaxed into a final action, the consequence of this action being the steppe wilderness that threaded itself across most of Askilt and Denilt.

To the untrained eye, there might have appeared to be no difference between what was natural and what was a consequence of the Divine war. Imberine, however, was trained to notice subtle lackings, and he spotted the chasm straight away. It was the reason for his current heresy, his contemporary but secret apostacy, the reason that he had finally agreed to abandon his post and turn over the plans for Askilt's incorporation to the patrician and his Ristosian allies. Imberine had already contacted the Guild to circumvent any Valestian spies that might learn of his treachery. He had already made his final plans to escape the religion that had held his life high aloft, hopefully before his soul was brought down into the crushing depths of oblivion.

All Imberine was waiting for was the call of a Cloud Dweller. He had been told they would send a bird to signal when their compatriots would arrive to aid him in his journey.

There the bird call was at his window; a pitch-black raven landed on the sill and chimed quickly. It fluttered away after a moment's heartbeat, to the accompaniment of an opening torrent. The splashes of water masked the incoming footsteps, and it was only as his door opened that he heard and turned around.

Stood before him was the Beseeched Grievance's Champion of Eisgar, the avatar sent to eliminate any internal enemies of the Primacy: the person sent to clean the slate, one cleaving swipe at a time. He wore pitch-black armour, kissed by red and gold, with the burning emblem of the Primacy's Fire Eye etched across his chest. The champion swung his sword half-heartedly and motioned for Imberine to open his mouth, but, before Imberine could, an arrow had pierced his throat. Pustulations of blood slowly drudged out from the wound, bubbles bursting and spitting.

An archer with emerald eyes stood cloaked behind the champion; he was the one who had silenced Imberine quickly.

Imberine swiftly slumped to the floor, directly in front of his two assassins, who proceeded to silently move over to his corpse and clasp his arms and legs in their hands. The archer made some inaudible comments, and following their gesture and command they both summarily tossed the lifeless carcass out the open window. It descended into the dark abyss, rapidly falling down into the jagged, craggy rock face below.

A torrent of rain hitched a ride onto Imberine's body, feeling the sharp reverberation as his neck cracked upon impact. Luckily, Imberine had died with the arrow. Now he saw his body fallen, painless and still.

He noticed the shadow form of a cloud before him, motioning him forwards. There was a chain of unspoken words: H U R R Y – W E – H A V E – N O – T I M E – T O – K I L L.

*

The green-daubed figure wasn't sure of the political doctrine of the Valestian interlopers. The caucus of song knowledge the Magain used to keep their methods alive were massively different to the tactics of the Valestian enforcers. The political conveniences they brought with them required fresh blood to support their lust for glory, power and honour.

Exploitation requires lackeys, and political conveniences required immunity. The Magain were allowed to do as they did because they had earned the respect of their peers; however, the enforcers mandated respect by sword and whip.

It was painfully obvious that as the social support structures were undermined by the power hungry, and the community pillars were toppled by the mustering of regimented lap dogs, steeled and tempered away from the communal towards self-glorification, they would betray themselves and leave sundered horror in their wake.

They would deepen the community divide instead of resolving the crisis at hand. The Magain kept good intent away from their duties; they acted for the protection of the future, not the protection of private property.

He saw the cloud call from the mountain top. He had left the cohort of Valestians to meet with the Green-Eyed, to ensure everything went to plan.

EIGHT

As Hawk's dreams and thoughts drifted deeper into his subconscious, his synapses danced intricate chemical interactions, his eyes rapidly shifting into chaotic disarray. A dark turn began to spread across Hawk's life, and to surge. Shapes and symbols melded before Hawk's sleeping consciousness, dredging deep into the knitted network of trauma and intangibility, seeking to access the conditioned stresses pricked by his day.

Images of the camp and Ilyia sat before the blackness, the consequence of intense fixation and interaction: a painting of prior conditions that would soon come to pass, all into dissolution with pure perfection. Nin had given him vivid and intense accounts of the nervous system and its developments. He had etched deep into Hawk's memories a reflective narrative to demarcate and segment his thoughts and feelings in practised introspective syncopation. Left right, left right, left right, in a cognitive quick step.

He knew why and how the coupling of emotion and

chemical expressions enabled the thoughts and feelings he entrenched with each flashing synapse. He knew that his states of mind codified his behaviour; he felt the shifts in synaptic pressure when his mood dipped or elevated (or was drawn into a conclusive finale).

It did not help reduce his nightmares. Nin called that short-sighted. It allowed him to tolerate the idea that fate was as much the repeatedly conditioned response to his environment and stories as it was the hand that moved him. It was the double edge of discipline that the same methods that refined his combat awareness left him more sensitive to the waves of bloody trauma he waded through.

Nin was far, far, far ahead of any of the local knowledge. To be truly fair, though, there were few who could protest to ever match a shred of Nin's perspective. But that always happens when you're older than everyone by everything.

As the last Brightscale, Nin was still young, a sparkling shimmer of draconic pre-eminence. Yet he had been older than all the species that had risen in his kin's wake.

Hawk had met a few of Nin's genetic compatriots, if they could be called such. This was Hawk's first experience of true common difference, the Dragon Riders bearing little and all resemblance with Nin. When they did gather, for the rites of Tael'gar and the ceremonies of the First Isles, Hawk was let aloft the sacred Dragon-Cities, and let into the flowing festivities spread across wingspans and continents.

The sharp and jagged difference between the wine-drinking, fire-bathing, hermeneutic sublimation that was Nin, and the demon-slaying, scar-adorned, flesh-eating cloud nomad that was Nin's brother Ashae, gave way to the harmony of sky, and the thick, rich, intoxicating petrol stench of the Dragon's Breath. Hawk found that especially divine. Truly, indelibly sublime. The luxurious black smog fuelled the navel-gazing dreams of Hawk's navel cavities; they belched and laughed and gorged themselves on the trails of infinite smoke.

And as they say, there is never smoke without fire.

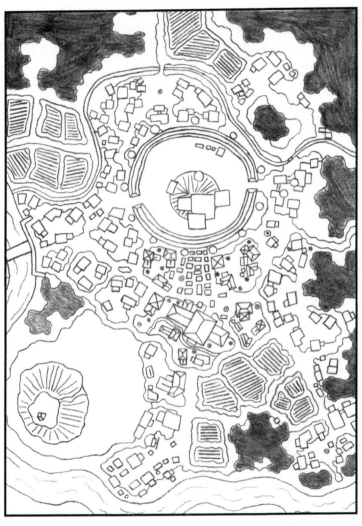

Map of Etribuy: "A Deathful Protrusions Village" by Abbot Bleonine IX, 752 PIA

THE SAINT

THE BARROW-LICH
(622 PIA)

Three little people poked their head round the wayside;
They all saw at once the bright, shining light.
"Who goes there?" asked the first, headstrong and callous,
And all without answer, they met the twilight.
— An excerpt from the Ultai fable *The Prior Lights*

He was abreast of wine; he sat a beast on brine. He loosened several teeth of a swine with one fist, while the other slapped a face straight through a table. Splinters of a brown chair shattered upon his left leg. He crushed it. Crushed the seat on the face of another brawler.

His laughter rang throughout the tavern. Several chairs splashed across his back; he swung around, table in hand. He let go. It launched. Propelled by sheer will, it clotheslined the incoming intruders who sought his ex-rear.

The tavern was never empty, bar fights being the prime form of entertainment in this part of the world. Instead, the potential-to-cordon-off area became the bar's respected cirque de swole-knee.

The bard let out a jig as four new entrants took the challenge to best. Hawk was enjoying himself. This kind of sport was both legal and safe. Hawk knew how to keep any challenger from coming to harm. Hawk knew how to resolutely incapacitate someone with minimal damage to their fleshy internals.

Plus, everyone else wore armour. Mostly tatty, cheap accumulated armour etched together by thin threads and tattered weaves, but still.

There was little pain to come; Hawk even encouraged locals to maintain fur-lined head gear to reduce the impact of blunt force trauma. The resulting head smashing was an integral aspect of the fun.

He was just about to engage the four new intruders in the argy-bargy when the tavern's door was pushed open by someone looking a bit too formal to truly belong in the grimy, dingy, rotting, dilapidated public house that was the Blood Splurt Sheath. Mind you, it wasn't the best of names.

The people who entered impressed with full ceremonial dress. They escorted an "officially" official, someone whose office might dictate others with a tax.

The bailiff of the town was not a man to cross lightly. His heavy medallion swung from his neck. The Cross Queen Eteia. Solid gold. Empyreal and becoming. Extremely unnecessary.

He wondered whether it would be moonlight or ballroom light? Cobwebs or tapestries? Bars or bars? He laughed.

They led him away.

She was an asshole; you would have to be in a job like that. The other was an asshole as well, and assholes collect like black voids, sucking one another into each other in an endless circle of anal chicanery. The two stood opposite were symptomatic of sycophantic assholery. The bedazzled consequence of fetishistic courtroom idolatry. Idiotry? Idealised idiocy fit for nothing but rulership. Destined, some might say.

A fucking disaster for everybody else.

Hawk coughed awkwardly. "So, you bring me here with nothing but an intent to ask me to act in your favour? Is this even sanctioned by the king?"

It wasn't. It never was.

So that was his task: to slay the beast persecuting the persecutor out east, to go to the village of Etribuy and slay the diabolic and devouring demon. He was to report to the inquisitor stationed at the church at the centre of the village. The inquisition had been going strong since the previous decade, when the current royal lineage came to power. It had increased in hostility towards those of other persuasions recently, as these things always do.

That worried Hawk. It spoke of ill-woven times to come.

He'd seen inquisitions of this type in far-flung lands to the east and south, in the cradle of the Ultai, Ebonheart, and the verdant Isle of the Gods. His travels across the Jahbairi, the emerald desert, across the plateaus of the Yantik, across the gold-purple regal cities of the Asimor. These inquisitions followed the threads of power wherever they were spun, cloying for whatever dregs and stains of power they could acquire.

Incandescent rage promulgated. He would even have to keep dealing with the shitbags here, basically in his backyard – only a stone's throw from his and Ilyia's backyard, anyway.

If a blacksmith's might is the keenness of his touch, and the rhythm and order timed to perfection; the watchmaker, perfect synchronicity of being; well then, the "inquisitor" was the cesspit of self-indulgence, and of course, always with a cataclysmic case of constant existential catastrophey.

It wouldn't be so bad, but they tended to flock to manashrines like sparks to a gas, to ignite like struck flint at the first fright.

The affair was a bit of a shitstorm, to say the least. He'd dealt with this kind of demonic deviation before. It was a lot more common now as the chains of being became broken. In the past, the stories said deviation caused emergence at a titanic intensity, but they were rare.

Now deviation emergences could occupy the space left in the manascape at any level. Maybe it was just a combination of different causes. Maybe it was a sign of incoming storms.

The witch hunt was the catalyst. The anger and fervour a spark.

He would have to kill the manifestation, now that it had devilishly manifested onto the scene. It shouldn't be too hard.

He didn't want to have to fight any of the people silly enough to get involved. If it was just the persecution and prosecution of innocents that was igniting the manascape manifestations, it'd be a simple hack and slash. If he had to deal with some ridiculously insidious morbid curiosity, he would really struggle. Maybe not with the monsters; they'd be more vicious, but hey ho. It was mostly the people.

If they'd started some kind of necrofetishistic death cult, he would be especially pissed. Proverbially provoked. In both senses.

He arrived at the village. Soul eschewing gallows were stacked up outside, a smoked-out corpse rotting by the roadside. He had seen a couple of ransacked houses by the river further north. He had seen the signs of a mock trial by the speech rock at the village's periphery.

The village was Etribuy. It was an ancient village long before the arrival of the Ultai, an ancient village from the first journeys of the Urm'gil. There was a church there, built long before the Ultai had even begun to speak, from the times of the Dragon Riders.

It was said that the stone foundation was hewn from the body of a Rock Dweller. If this was the place of the trials and tribulations, he hoped to the core of his being it wasn't so. Such a large kind of enchantment would wreak havoc in untrained hands.

The buildings were modern: dark wooden erections over chipped grey stone bases. They weren't the crystal stone of the Urm'gil, or a radiating soft pink hue would have been visible. They weren't the thatched daub of the pioneer So'Ultai, tan sandy weaving atop carved stone walls. The pictographs of Kyian legend were carved into the timber frames, running the length of the frame in chaotic depictions. Rich images of mountain giants and forest beasts were etched into panels beside windows, as was customary to adorn the houses with the spirits blessing.

Rich, thick candlelight blossomed out from wood-set glass panes. Stained imagery resonated ethereal traces of red, orange, brown and blue. The warmth of the hearths roasted in malicious contrast to the frigid, hanging bodies by the entrance road.

Hawk coughed by the doorway of a large, blue-painted house. There was no response, so his fist introduced itself to the front door.

The denizen was careful with their opening; it was slow and dread-drenched.

"I heard there was a monster here. I can see by the blood marking on your door that you're creating an aura of protection. Why?"

The door slammed shut and a face appeared at the closest window. It was jagged and tired. "Get inside! There's space at the church. If it's got your scent, we can't let you in. The priest said so. The blood won't protect you."

Hawk tried to inquire as to the nature of the beast that was causing such a caustic fear. Alas, the face had retracted as abruptly as it had entered the conversation. Hawk was left to glance at the church. A phosphorescent glow rippled from the stained-glass windows, a rich weave of purple, red and orange. There was no blue; that was especially interesting. If this was a stone dweller's body, there would at least be a hint of blue, maybe even if just ethereally. A pre-eminent hue that would slowly radiate outwards, vibrancy of agency constrained by the collective history that brought these people to rest here at this penultimate time.

Perhaps someone had slain the blue hue? Carved and cracked into the flow of energy, which now despoiled was terrorising the villagers?

He had passed through the stone-dotted cemetery that lay before the church. The church itself was a domed turf mound, with two large oak doors. There was a patchwork stone tower of various greys, whites and blacks that protruded from its apex.

They opened on his arrival, not before, not after. Auspicious.

They had eaten a fine meal cooked by the inquisitor's chef; the attendants had eaten too, and were surprisingly allowed to eat with them at the inquisitor's table. The inquisitor had provided a detailed account of their response to the fiend's intrusion on their quiet village. It had little excitement, just bleak estimations of last moments and shocking findings. The inquisitor's brown eyes betrayed a sadness at life's loss, a cut tinge creeping out.

Hawk's unrest, palpable, excused itself to end the night early; Hawk, however, waited for dessert.

After a sinful splendour, they settled down to sleep.

The sharp, warbling scream shredded through his dreams deep beneath Yggdrasil's emerald gaze. His eyes tore open, his arm already clutching his blade.

She told him they were in the other room; they had the inquisitor's attendants surrounded. Hawk would have to act now to save them.

Two gargantuan slimy, grey-blue leeches stood before the mass of cowering servants, crammed into a corner of the dining hall. They oozed time into a slow slog, the anguish, horror and disgust growing across the servants' faces as they stood hemmed in, surrounded and catatonic.

Hawk gloriously leapt into action, then awoke, grazed, bruised and cut, but feeling a semi-consciousness, searingly subduing. He wasn't sure how he would handle this day. He could go and inquire with the villagers about what had been happening, but he already knew. It was also pretty evident that the villagers didn't. The inquisitor's attendants had fallen into an amnesiac slumber after the attack last night. They had just been questioned by him, returning little, unaware that they had nearly met their fate, thick with despair, a few hours before.

Even the inquisitor, a grey-etched, stone-faced, wizened character, who for a rare turn of events Hawk might come to admire, was oblivious to the twilight interactions. Hawk guessed this meant they had been occurring for a while; it would be a matter of determining what had caused this. Why now?

It didn't look like subconscious fears were being imbued by the manascape; it didn't look like there was an emergent Divinity from the acts of cultists. There were no traces of victimisation or symbolic obfuscation. No surreptitious maliciousness that suggested a curse. Well, bar the use of animal blood to ward off the spirit, but that could be part of the curse itself.

The question rushed past Hawk's lips: "Who told you to daub your doors in blood?"

The inquisitor was still reading his holy book. Silver and gold runes crested its front and back covers, emanating from a deep purple. "It's all part of an ancient prophecy, one lain down by the forebears of this village, dictating an end of the world occurring. It's pretty standard hocus-pocus, but when the attacks started, the prophecy demanded fresh goat blood be used to protect the doors of the villagers, lest the…"

He reached for some notes… "Unless the Yegriab comes to feast on your souls. Auspicious, eh?" Hawk swallowed several swords simultaneously.

The plan was to wait until sunset, when the leeches emerged from the shadows surrounding the Azga'ite Stela. Hawk would battle the vicious intruders, hopefully before they attacked any of the village. Hopefully, Etribuy could be saved.

The moon was produced from its holster; the sun moved to be sheathed instead, slowly dipping behind the mountain line. He readied his blade. She twinkled with expectation. It was time.

But first, how could no one have told him about the Stela?

Well, he idled, preoccupation keeps the mind uncluttered.

The pitch-black obsidian tooth had been adorned with a blue-and-green painted surface. Hawk had scratched away several layers before reaching the telltale scale of an Entoile "deathful protrusion", as the Guild liked to call them.

This did stack the odds against him a bit… definitely an understatement. This *massively* stacked the odds against him, He just hoped this prophecy would keep the final "vicious maliciousness" at a reasonable distance until preparations could be made for Hawk to really tear him a new one.

Deathful protrusions tend to draw on every mis-decision, accruing them into a malevolent, whirling cesspit of dark stagnation. They not only sow the seeds of doubt and desecration but also absorb the solemn unspeakables spread before their dark trajectory. Whereby a curse affects a single person with a malicious aim and energy, deathful protrusions extend an aura of harrowing curses that desiccate the landscape until naught but the silent shadows stand beneath the sun.

With raw consumptive power, a never-satiated swarm of existential locusts would furrow through brow and flesh to feast upon the soul. Bleak nihilistic desolation of any life force caught in their wake. They were leftovers of the Entoile Empire that fell to Ilyia's father, Bastion: the slaver nation that slew Hawk's parents, and their various cults across the Shorelands. The nation that dotted its lands with the foulest of monuments and pedestals.

Hawk felt a personal grudge against the abhorrences, fixated with his scrubbing brush and leather gloves.

Scrap that. Maybe some kind of flaming-inferno flinging device.

That wouldn't work; they malformed and tainted most methods of cleansing, like they twisted and tortured flesh and bone.

As he was washing the bloodshed from his blade, she cackling ferociously beneath the water scrub, he heard the gentle canter of hooves. There was one upon a horse, wearing a vibrant red-and-blue patchwork cloak lain upon leather-steel armour. He saw the novel metallic glint and stood corrected, *mythrillic* armour, one of the ever-sturdier metals found far to the east. Exceptionally rare in this neck of the woods. Well, slash-and-burn groove within an Old Forest.

The rider was slowly cantering towards the well, so shade was strewn across the village's circular centre by a gathering mass of interest. Kids burst from protective holds of parents and ran towards the rider. A glimmer shone out from the rider's florid right hand; metallic glances escaped his clutch, spearing their way towards the children.

The coins ricocheted off the dry dirt as the children cackled in mania.

"So, what's going on here? Who the fuck are you, you gargantuan pig-dipped grim-shit excuse for a villager?"

The twinkling gem atop the steed had the mouth of a poisoned sailor.

"I'd save pleasantries till after that lunatic for a night owl you've got ceases to tear the sky into haemorrhaged gashes."

The children were oblivious to the barrage of curses eloquently dipped in the lyrical Casidas tongue.

The figure sighed and stretched, bruised and beaten by the fiend in the night.

"Now, if you can't find me somewhere comfy to rest after that shitstorm of a night, I think I might well and truly go and fuck myself."

Hawk laughed and helped him down from his horse. He and the interloper, his old buddy Tyrus, resolved to fight together against the leeches. That night, they would antagonise them to attack the pair while the villagers stood safe inside the church.

Wooden splinters splurged out of the trashed house like a quiver of arrows caught in a blood-enraged cave bear. The decimation their fight the night before had wrought was truly catastrophic. Luckily, the occupants had been evacuated to the church by then. All the villagers had gathered inside at the inquisitor's behest, safe from the showdown that must have ensued.

The leeches had attacked? They couldn't remember the scene wholly; the deathful protrusion must have been affecting their memories. But lo and behold, there before them lay the bodies of the leeches when they awoke, dented and battered, in the village centre. Their slimy, glistening hides of fear-drenched moisture were sopping and seeping with visceral cuts and pustulating holes. Their bodies were etched with slash marks and stab wounds, jabs and cleaves cutting through a rough but slippery skin.

Now that Hawk and Tyrus had slain the beasts of the First Seal, their stomachs churning throughout their cadaver inspection, they were ready to inquire as to what would be the second.

The inquisitor was resting in the study, reading through the ancient yellow-stained prophetic pages that glistened under the hard strain of his eyes. He began, "The beast of the Second Seal is the winged monstrosity that attacked Tyrus on his journey into the village. It's said it will attack tonight at the dead of twilight, when the seals between worlds are most weak."

They both grimaced, a gulped harmony of pre-despair.

*

It was that time again.

The villagers were once more to be gathered into the welcoming bosom of the church. They had stashed arms and torches in chests and boxes, some of them carrying cantrips prepared by Hawk and Tyrus. They were wary of what the night would bring for the villagers; all they could do was provide them with the means to best protect themselves.

A thought struck Hawk, a quick way to resolve the stress without needing any horrific resolution or sacrifice. If the emerging Divinity was tied to a prophecy, and the villagers were the persisters of this tragedy-to-be, he could use the soulstone that must be nestled deep within the supposedly Rock Dweller-hewn church to counter the deathful protrusion. Well, maybe. This was a last resort, a do-all to end-all, only ever to be undertaken when all other safeguards were passed in the Divine landscape. If a Rock Dweller couldn't squash the beast, then its soul would break it asunder and cast it aside. As the vessels of the beast, the villager's sanctification would undo it, a deep-earth counterbalance to the emerging dreary torrents of the deathful protrusion.

That was it! He rushed down into the crypt to pilfer the object of his desire, half-heartedly mentioned by the Inquisitor on his first night here, before rushing back to the top of the church tower, the highest point to overlook his success.

He hoped Tyrus was safe from the ensuing events.

In his hands glistened a stone like any other, tinged with a sad, blue, slowly diminishing hue. It sat in the clasp, grinning and ready to unfurl its destiny. Just like any other day for a stone, really. If you come to think about it.

The rich wave of emanation flowed out from the church tower. It danced a decadent trance around the villagers gathering before the church doors, the thick mist-fog settling and cocooning in graceful metamorphosis.

*

Nin stood over the young Hawk.

The catastrophe that lay before them was an ingenious undoing. Hawk had created a machine to represent the rule of eternalism, a multiplicitous pathway of determined truth tempered from raw possibility, all throughout the room that Hawk had appropriated for a study, a random scattering of dominos through space and time that would reduce to a linear path when flicked into metaphysicality.

Unfortunately, it was also Nin's infirmary of injured animals.

The machine unwound itself, along with the latches that sealed the vibrant, if surly, accumulation of wildlife.

Birds, bees, bats, geese, sheep, dogs, cows and frogs, amongst every other sort of indigenous or endangered species, now sat before them, everyone befuddled, a rich cacophony of stunned colour, all condemning the exercise in sure certainty to a fate of, well, who didn't expect that. Especially now the rare and suffering fire-pups were crying in the corner.

Hawk's distress had reached a high tenor, an octave below the wailing pine of the fiery pups. The feeling of weightlessness overwhelmed his senses; he felt the flickering fire flames grow in zealous fervour.

Nin's voice cut through the nauseating clamour.

"How in the eternal flames of Eltria did you do this, then? You've well and truly gone and flipped our plane into post-oblivion."

The scaled hand clasped Hawk's shoulder and drummed a comforting rhythm, laughter rebounding off the walls into a tranquilising resonance.

"You know, there's a curious feature of 'mammal' brains." Nin added the quotes at every opportunity. "If you sing a specific range of resonances with specific acoustics, you create a loop of transcendental experience… Truly mad."

Nin didn't herd the animals; he offered them food and apologies, and took Hawk off to look at the stars.

*

Rich egg whites were splashed across the sky. It sat in

238

harmonious mirror with the chaos of the pre-night. The shattered egg yolk was left to hazily coagulate behind the overcast and musky, congealing clouds.

There wouldn't be any rain today, but maybe tomorrow. That would make the trek back harder.

He heard the vicious snarling of the monsters; he heard their snarling, padding instep and hunter's sniff, the way their ears trailed with the new sensations they received. The new abilities wouldn't last long; soon the apex status the emergence provided would dissolve into fornicating decay, rapidly breeding and dissolving fleshy connections across their bodies; then they would feast to resume themselves.

He had to find a way out of the clusterfuck. He had seen the transformation of the "villagers" from the church tower, what should have been sublime turned into an awe-inducing excarnation.

As the blue radiation from the soulstone had descended to rest atop those it would save, the blue had fumed into depths of red, cascading around the people and eschewing their gentle forms. Instead of providing auras of protection, the red mist lifted to reveal half-despoiled decaying masses of flesh. They caught his scent and began to chase him; he snuck behind several buildings and crept towards the stream. Hopefully, he could wash away his scent in the riverbed. He motioned right to head round the corner to make for the bridge.

The huddled mass of gangrenous citizens turned and snarled at the wary interloper. Hawk turned and nearly caused a particularly messy accident. They chased the fibrous action out of him.

He ran, legs churning intense exclamations of pain and

danger, bounding up the thin steps of the wooden church tower. He couldn't keep it up; his legs repeatedly yelled at him to slow the pace, to find a safer place to make a stand.

He would need a chokepoint that would let him kill them one at a time. Where the fuck was Tyrus at this godforsaken time?

Hawk was pissed off.

So the prophecy was just a lie? A fabrication to justify their own primitive gladiatorial combat? And when the rescuer arrives, they all play tomfoolery and lead Hawk around in the dust?

What had been the mistake, then?

Well, definitely trying to purify the villagers using that soulstone, especially without knowing that they were lying to him. That was the mistake. Most definitely. Yep. The rest had helped.

He leapt from the church tower, resolving to fight his way out, before returning with a Guild-safe expression of duties. He didn't want to be seen eviscerating a village for no reason, but if he could bring a witness he would be safe to finish the job. Guild regulations were strict on this sort of thing.

He landed in the centre of the fleshy flail, cleaving through the surrounding corpses with efficacious wit.

Officially speaking, he wasn't having a good time. But now, at least, he was officially sure they were legally dead.

Legs, heads, arms, and trails of bloody organs flew, strewn from their protectors by the lamenting shine of Elii, the Blade of Brightness. She was less thrilled to be hacking through the half-dead remains of previously viable candidates for her butchery.

She was an esteemed actor of the highest order, a blade forged from before blades could be forged quite so nicely as her.

She was, and would always be, a rarity.

Now left to cleave flesh too putrid to provide any true weight-bearing... and now she would be left to carry this stink for an eternity.

A WHOLE ETERNITY.

The sensation was pure lament, and yet still she struck, swerving viciously with a severing curve that bit, bled, and butchered the encroachingly slow mass of disturbed flesh and thoughts.

Hawk had broken into sweat miles back, reaching for his serrated shield as it turtled on his back. The pair of metallic proportions decimated the oncoming mass. But still there were more.

Hawk had hoped the sun would still be high by the time this wry affair was put to rest. His arms began to tense, his legs stiffen, the drips of sweat gathering in crescendo and rush. The expletive started to form behind the harsh, sharp, guttural pain in his throat.

He heard a horse's whinny, saw the intense reflection of that vagabond Tyrus. Felt the rush of wind as two severing swords swirled in symmetrical salutations.

As the two caught breath under the shade of a tree, Hawk heard another.

The sombre figure stood in front of him, a deeply dark shadow cast over his seat. The figure was pulling another by a rope, hooded by a black bag.

Yuil began, "You see, I was taught that life's like a river; it flows all around us. We lose ourselves in it, and allow the flow to guide our actions. That's the key to harmonious living. I guess what I struggle with is that, to me, it seems like life's a valley. A valley that floods with warning but always surprises you. All you can do is try to prepare yourself. Ready the diversions and channels, and then you weather the storm. So that's what I do now. I follow the warning signs for floods, and I dig ditches. Like the first garden kings of the Ultai. Like the first of the Dragon Riders."

Hawk responded brusquely, kicking away dirt that sat minding its own business by his feet. "Are you trying to tell me that all this is to you is digging a ditch?"

The dirt on his clothes looked suspiciously red.

Yuil answered, "A metaphorical ditch. Hear me out. It has to be said that the true danger to this village is itself. It was dumb enough to kill the Manakind bound to the barrow. It was dumb enough to build the church out of its bones. Finally, it was dumb enough to let the dark preacher take advantage of the terror and breed the death cult."

Hawk didn't appear to be impressed, his posture uninterested and unpersuaded by the scummy rhetoric. The dirt by his feet, however, was beginning to feel oppressed, and began to clamour up a dust cloud. "I don't think you could really call that group of people a death cult. They didn't really do that much murdering." Hawk was pretty sure they weren't a death cult, just poorly informed sadomasochists.

The hanging bodies were apparently from those unfortunate enough to sign a death waiver for "chemically enhanced" fights, then masqueraded as heretics to hide the inquisitor's complicity. "It wasn't their fault that the abomination was formed."

"Their naivety led to every death from the spirits. The foul corruption seeped from their unbound ignorance." Yuil was austere.

Hawk wiped the blood from his sword.

"It doesn't have to be done. But it'll send a message. If the trials continue, there'll be more executions." Yuil lifted the black bag. "Well, at least that's what he's supposed to say."

He slapped the prisoner with the flat of his blade. The prisoner buckled, lifted himself up and began sprinting.

A question stuck out in Hawk's mind. Couldn't Yuil have undone the soulstone curse for more of them? It seemed pretty insensitive rescuing just one. "Do they even know you're out here doing this, Yuil?"

Yuil had vanished off into the rising sun. Tyrus was gently laughing.

"Looks like you've been sold out, friend. Perhaps I can buy you a drink before they deport your immigrant ass?"

The tension ebbed between Hawk's eyes. It didn't really matter if he was allowed back here. Well, he hoped so. He could never admit this knowledge, especially against someone as high-ranking as Yuil.

Tyrus continued his venture, undaunted. "Come on, there's the port to the east. We don't have to drink there, but there's this nice little village that owes me some free wine for kicking out a bandit king." Tyrus mounted his steed, gently patting his flank and holding forward a carrot. "He wasn't even a good bandit king – didn't even last one round of combat. I was all prepared to give him this beautiful flourish in the third round. Such a nice dispatch. And then, no. Nothing. Just the bleating as he saw his life flash before his eyes."

If he was caught, Hawk would just have to plead ignorance; he couldn't be killed. It was obviously not him. He only dealt with Manakind.

Yet… he would take the blame; he would probably be kicked out of Kyia. For something as stupid as a witch hunt. Classic petty politics. Luckily, Kyia had a strong relationship with the Guild, so, even if they recanted Hawk's access, there would still be others. The guild even had its own Kyian Headquarters. A regiment dedicated to the protection of Kyian interests and political importances. It was no coincidence that the inquisitor's guild bodyguards were off doing some important guild busywork the week of Hawk's investigation. They'd be the ones who returned to discover the bodies. Then the Kyian political sphere would be informed that a guild member went rogue and used his contacts and deviousness to secure an assassination on the targets. The guild would decry the reports of a night monster. Perhaps they would call it propaganda, crafty countermeasures from Hawk to justify his movement to the region.

It came with a big pay-out to Hawk. The Guild reserved the rights for certain "infamies" to be accrued. They would offer a "restitution", maybe even "compassionate leave". Eventually, he would be allowed to return. It wasn't as if it really mattered. Hawk only worked for the Winter Unfurling, and only then because his role as consort to Ilyia demanded a certain level of prestigious income.

Ilyia had been saying he could have an honorary title, but the Tiana and Elipse still enjoyed the idea that he was a noble hero. Now that they were in the half-moon and adults soon to be off travelling, he should spend more time with them.

When he was allowed back, he would have to go see Yuil.

It would be surreal stepping into the King's court and seeing him there, at the head of the King's bodyguard. No longer crimson-coated, watching with hunter's eyes the people he was "sworn to protect beyond the ethics of nature".

It was the violent adventures that had first drawn his interest to the Guild's work; now the flagrant contradictions that kept it.

NINE

Nin was stood in slow sublime, stretched out over flames, the orange-red licking tongues softly simmering his form, consuming the hard materiality that divided Nin from thing, nothing and everything; Nin's eyes were closed and fluttering. That told Hawk meditation. Or intense joy.

Hawk never knew how to tell. Nin had him practising yawning; he called it an "empathy prompt". Yet Hawk was feeling short-shrifted, and ever sleepier.

The book before him was a tan, leather-bound text describing the witnessing of the three rocks fall. It was a picture book, Hawk's favourite kind. The beautifully etched scenes showed three meteorites devastating the world, puncturing the cosmology with dedicated intention.

The rocks with "juice", as Nin laughingly called it. The "juice" that brings life.

Rocks that devastated the roaming draconic lifescapes, plunging the populations of herbivores and carnivores, of draconosaurs large and small, of flora vibrant, rich, diverse, into extinction. A few tectonic plates chose to conserve the ecosystems that sheltered within them; other tectonic plates had already welcomed the newcomers. There was a specific term Nin used. Hawk stretched his laterality.

The new phylogenetic trees; that was it, the new branches of being.

The bindings of meat beneath the organs, muscles and bones that were introduced into the world in one fell stroke.

Nin and his brother were born during this period, when the Winter Titans and winter flow were aided in their tempests by the seas of black dust and choking smog storms. Nin told with gleaming eyes of his first flights atop a drake, his first dragon steed Azeesul, his journeys atop the Dragon-Cities across the large snow-drenched valleys, plains and continents. When Nin was young, they rested few and far between, gracefully nesting atop the most welcoming of mountains for fear of angering the Divinities that eschewed life at every turn. They watched new life eventually bloom from the oceans as the wasteland and glacial tundra retreated back towards the Winter Mountains, the first movement of fish and flowers to the shores, up through the rivers, the birth of forests and giant trees.

Nin always smiled fondly when he told of the "dinosaurs", the giant yet not-so-vicious remainders of what his ancient ancestors used to hunt. After the dinosaurs came the First Peoples, in all their bounteous splendour. A diverse collection born from two of the three rocks, they flourished and hid, grew and sheltered, developed and collapsed under the constant footfalls of the Winter Titans, the coming snowstorms, the constantly roaming glacialisation.

Nin would often say that the only peoples safe from the incessant enwintering were the primate kings of Ebonheart.

Nin would laugh. Perhaps that's why they were so naïve.

Eventually Azga had turned foul; the great machine cities of the Ehmr'gil and the dome cities of the Urm'gil became the eventual target of his putrefying conquests. Azga's dark armies marched on them both after the world-consuming war of the Fallen Star, as the Falling Spires began. In a pitched battle above Tael'Gar's Barrow, the Ultai joined the war against Azga, away from their continental protector, and the dead mountain was expunged from the material plane.

The Ultai's reward was shelter away from home during the coming war with the Winter Titans. Alongside a handful of sparkling soulstones.

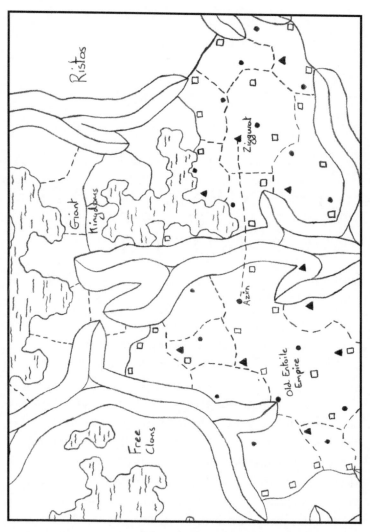

Map of Rekilli Highlands: "The Ancient Slaver Empire" by Bastion of Nostros, 363 PIA

THE CHANGELINGS

THE NIFAFA-NIFAFI-NIFILOST?
(674 PIA)

It's always better to lose your tongue than your eye;
your eye gives you vision, your tongue helps you die.
—A Rekilli, or Old Entoile, proverb

The hunger was growing deep within him; unbound and unbidden, it coursed cruelly through his veins. It sucked at his skin and stomach, churning over with restless pacing.

He'd been minding his own business, looking for some deer to hunt, strolling through this untamed forest free from care and want. Well, with only one want and care – some nice, tasty, tender meat; succulent, sweet, dripping deer. His stomach turned in temptation. Salivation wrought itself across his face.

Salivation wrought itself across the bar frames they had encased him within.

They being the group that ambushed him, trapped him, attempted to hold him against his will, which was a nigh-on impossible task. He could have burst free, but he was interested. A ragtag family from a ramshackle borderlands hamlet had actively sought to capture him without killing. They then held a mock trial in some strange dialect he'd never really come across. He knew most of the words, but if this hamlet was inhabited by Entoile, there were a few languages he was missing. Perhaps they could teach him?

The trial ended with pause for repose.

A youth walked over to him. He spoke in Rekilli. Old Entoile. "You're not one of the giants, are you?"

"Alas, no."

"Are you a warrior?"

"Yes."

"A hero?"

"A hero slayer. I kill the ones that go astray."

"So you could kill the beasts that attack? They aren't heroes, but if a hero could slay them, and you can slay heroes…"

"Then I should be able to slay their beasts of burden?" Hawk's laugh was a rich, rolling, burgundy velvet. "Yeah, I can do that for you. Shouldn't be too difficult a task now, should it? Just… what kind of monsters are they?"

The youth looked perplexed, his brow stern, his face quizened. A stony response came forth. "Giants. A whole family of gargantuan giants. They stole our families. All of them in the upper houses."

They let Hawk out with a harrowed demeanour. Hawk was looking irked. Not harrowed; irked. You couldn't really look forward to this kind of stuff, though it had to be done.

But you couldn't look forward. You couldn't even look backwards. Too many painful memories.

So, a family of giants he would have to slay. Perhaps they could pen a piece of poetry to pour the heartfelt plight that tore at him. It was never his duty to kill the untainted; he was here to cleanse, rehabilitate the essential. Not tidy up factional infighting in the hill-lands. The giants were here first. The Entoile last after the Ultai, who were here after the Urm'gil.

But who really gave a fuck?

The only ethical quandary here was the stolen people.

Giants weren't necessarily carnivorous, or eaters of people. They were, however, dying out this close to the So'Ultai's settling. Could this be an act of terrorism? Would he find them executed in some dark corner? Splayed as totems?

He hoped not. To the depths of his soul, he hoped not.

His thoughts drifted to his own children: Tiana and Elipse. They would both be shieldmaidens of Ilyia soon. Tiana was destined to inherit after her fastenating, the trial that proved the warrior's right to rule. Tiana was definitely the broader of the two; she had Ilyia's sense of humour, his and Ilyia's strength combined. Elipse would forge her own legend, and rightfully so. She had her father's sense of honour and justice. He always remembered her, animals following, communing with the manascape.

Tiana could be brusque, which was necessary for a warchief; Elipse could be headstrong, which got her into all kinds of mischief and trouble.

He would miss them when they were gone.

The trench-esque tracks followed north. They were huge

dredges of earth. Pronged expanses of terrestrial eruption. These would be gargantuan giants. Truly ginormous. Epic. Titanic. *Hmmmmm.*

He stepped down into the track, the earth sifted by furrowing feet. The ridges of ruptures teemed. There were only a few birds in each, scouring the upturned assembly of insects. The giants had passed a few hours past.

He checked for droppings.

Three hours, heading due north. Covering two miles an hour at leisure.

The giants would be grim, gruff, grizzled veterans of centuries long gone. They all lived excruciatingly long lives. The same giants Hawk had met as a young hunter still crept from their cold stone castles and ranged the brittle breeze-blown mountains. Hawk had grown old and ragged; the giants were still fresh-faced and cheerful. It was scandalous.

He'd been invited to several of the Jotuncalls. He'd held his own in the melees against the champions of the Frozen Ridge. He'd performed valiantly and earned his place at the Champion Feast, and in the Jotunhall, the giant afterlife.

He could empathise with the giants' acts of hostility, but expressed his concern at every chance with the Winter Kings. Unfortunately, the giants of the hill-lands were ordered by no one. Instead, they slowly declined. They insidiously lost themselves to the dark practices in the shadows of society. As the Entoile interlopers expanded from the So'Ultai borders, the hill giants lost themselves to the blood sports, to sacrilegious infighting as the last noble few struggled with what had become of their kin.

He hoped the giants he would come across were of the latter; the Blooded were a task. More than a curse to deal with. He would need the appropriate tools, and a sanctified blessing. He didn't want to go to any priest in these parts; there was nothing worse than a bigoted clergyman, a corrupt rural clergyman complete with contempt and abandonment of whatever moral code they were sworn to uphold.

The illustrious reputation of this region was carefully constructed to coax settlers to come. The lax attitude of the local warrior-aristocrats towards their underlings' religious practices through the centuries had allowed a myriad of criminally crazy cults to take root.

The communities often arrived with a nuanced epistemological persuasion that kept balance with the Manakind. Then, by the end of the first century, some local curse would defile the attitudes of the religious elite, allowing a despoiled cult of damnation and predilection to form, a symptom of a larger maleficence. A tendril of a wide-spreading corruption. Emergence from deviation was the Guild name for it.

What it meant was unbridled destruction at the hands of defiled "magical".

Magic was the ancient Ultai word for it, a word held with appropriate superstition. Superstition breeds caution. Caution lets people sleep steady at night.

He stopped by another set of trudged tracks and set up camp. He removed the food the village had given him. It wasn't much: a few apples, some bread, some butter, smoked meat, and fish. At least he didn't have to kill a deer. At least he hadn't had to kill the first. He didn't like hunting for sustenance when the hunger had him, even though his stomach took hold of his consciousness. He didn't say the Guild's prayers after slaying for nourishment, but that was because they were meagre words, a device for lessening the moral ambiguity of the act. A kind of "you may have killed, but...". The *but* was egocentric. Malnourished people needed it, but those that had eaten could do with facing the moral consequences of their actions. Regardless of his preferences, his hunger was always ravenous when bottomed out, and ravenous hunger breeds gruesome decisions.

The fire he'd lit was enchanting. The flames flickered scenes of cosmic interplay. The thoughts of morality drifted into existential abbreviation.

He heard footsteps. He declined to acknowledge them, and soon enough a figure was sat opposite by the fire, atop a moss-covered log.

"I see you've got food, maybe to spare?"

Hawk waited a few seconds. He reached for his satchel, passing the tied parcel of rations.

"I should warn you, there's been some giants wandering through the region. I saw a group move north. They were chasing after..." The figure paused, scratching their chin. "What's the word? I think... Nifilost? I spoke to them briefly. They didn't seem too encouraged about the idea."

"A Nifilost?" Hawk's brain sank into lacking. *What the fuck is a Nifilost?*

*

He awoke early the next day.

The ravens had gathered in a mob around several carcasses. The dead bodies were of several deer ripped apart, four chewed into sheer oblivion; bone dust and entrails scattered in blood-red piles across a larger-than-necessary

255

area. Legs and arms and other appendages were strewn around the blood mounds where the ravens cawed and poked. Whatever the excess limbs were from, they were no longer identifiable.

The ravens rippled with anxious murmurs when they spotted Hawk. One was quickly nominated and ruffled forwards by the others, feathers pricked with horror and anguish. "Be warned, there's a gruesome being marauding through the forests. It's already ripped its way through several deer herds and butchered an ancient grove on its journey towards the mountains."

The raven pointed its beak towards the Blackscowl Mountain Range, which shiftily and daringly crept out from its haunted peaks into the Shorelands. The group it was with broke out into a raucous cacophony of dread and fear.

The spokes-raven eventually calmed his peers, reassuring them.

"The atrocity is ferocious; be warned that no matter how you prepare, you are in to see death's face personally."

There were more carcasses thrown apathetically around the hewn tracks. Several large buffalo had been shredded by leviathan tearing claws, their desecrated furs now mounded in bloody middens, bearing deep threshes by serrated teeth. Gargantuan tracks of slashing intent, wilfully severing the thick brown hides.

This was definitely not the work of the giants, who were at best a third of this monster's size. Moreover, giants were wont to eat their prey efficiently, and also, obviously, they cooked the meat.

Hawk took a closer look, prodding away the gashed remains with the edge of his blade. The blade bemoaned the putrid smell. As he severed several flaps of mutilated skin, out rolled a pouring accumulation of white and yellow maggots.

The smell was a nauseating manifestation of corrupted decay. Light and dark strands of toxic green and brown were unleashed from the opening. A faint black-and-red tendril marked out the stain of dark macabre.

Hawk resolved to push on, his stomach queasy and wheezing. It got worse several hours later as the sun started to set and the threat of dark twilight exaggerated the monster's tears.

The sun was hanging too low for a positive omen. The cave entrance would emerge soon. He'd had to push on through the hillscape into the east–west mountain ridge. The cave wasn't too high up, but was nestled deep in a sun-lost ravine. He'd had to climb to descend. The worst kind of climb.

This wasn't typical giant habitat. If they were this far out this way but had also talked to the traveller, this wasn't normal behaviour for the unBlooded. It seemed absurd for a giant hunting party to be moving peakwards while carrying a cohort of captives with them.

He saw it. The cave entrance was voluminous. The two pairs of thick indents continued; the smaller ones still accompanied it.

When he reached the entrance, he found a multitude of tracks heading the other way, a pool of blood accumulating in the middle of the remnants of their motion.

A thought struck him. It made him shudder.

He thought he could remember where he'd heard of the Nifilost before: from a song sung in the Jotunhall. He couldn't remember the exact words, but the Nifilost was a beast slain by the giant-god Kranosk, a dark-blooded creature akin to the Wendigo of Ultai folklore, or the Aoern of the Krylei.

The derelict and flesh-engrained cave floor was strewn with the bones and carcasses of a cast of creatures mauled and ravaged. The signs of breaks beyond the decay of the flesh filled Hawk with notions of cruel, vicious malice. The size of the breaks spoke of a butcher beyond normal stature.

He entered the cave at nightfall, keeping his torch lit. He readied his blade and tried to muffle the footfalls indicating arrival. His arrival was heralded by an echoing metallic snickering.

By the time he had reached the centre of the cave, it was especially too late. He found the corpses of the giants.

Now the noises made sense: the far echoes of weird shinks and slashes. This explained the doorway of the head villager's house. They'd performed a macabre ritual for some dumb enchantment; now their families were gifted. "Gifted".

For fuck's sake.

He hoped he could gift them a short, quick, painless death.

He'd had to cleanse people of curses; that wasn't too bad. Normally you just countered the cantrip and nullified the catalyst. But killing those who were magically transformed into maleficent deviations? That was far from his definition of a fun and exciting time. That was antithetical to a good adventure. Killing was always wrong, but being forced to kill the shadows of fratricide... That was a curse for which there was no cure.

So now, here he was, stuck with this ominous task hanging over him amongst the stalactites. A proverbially blood-stained and darkened cloud.

Hawk readied his felblade and checked the glean of the edge. It was abysmal. Vexed, he placed it against the edge of a stalagmite. With several short kicks, his muffled metal boot serrated the edge. With several sharp strikes, it was better.

He heard their footsteps echoing in the distance. He reckoned there were about thirty of them. He hoped his beckon had worked.

He heard the ricocheting cackle emitted by the incomers. The fletchettes' spray of barbs on abraded stones. A dark, Machiavellian manipulation coming to haunt and tear at him.

The first rounded the corner, their tar-choked flesh hung, tore at, as the last vestiges of parental trauma clung to their decaying souls. He could see the cuts the Entoile spell had spread across their skin as the transformation took its toll, turning flesh into grimaced death.

They hadn't told him the captives were children.

They swarmed violently towards him, ravenous hunger in tow. Lost children to the shepherd. Lost children with teeth that ground with the sound of severing shears.

He split the skull of the last deformed being, their body crumpling into the mass of soul-shattering descent. There were too many to count. Too many to see.

He silently wept, from his eyes and from the shredded flesh they left him with.

Then he made his way back to the village, each footstep a slog through graveyard sin. Each step bringing a fresh wince to his bitten skin.

He returned to a raucous chorus of lamentation. All of the villagers had that glazed bewilderment that accompanies primordial transgression. They seriously asked him where their relatives were.

In the howl of tears and pain that followed Hawk's excruciating detail of their loved ones' fate, the villagers arrived at abject hostility towards the Giantkin.

Hawk bit back his blade. The chief saw the tension and asked his opinion. Hawk nearly exploded. "I mean, it's interesting that you would ask me, of all people, to lend an opinion in this whole dispute." The villagers looked disconcerted, the look of sheep taught to cannibalise at whim. "It's okay that you don't get that your perception of the giants' 'race' is the thing that distinguishes them, and not the other way round. Some of my colleagues would say it's below your pay grade. Your prejudice, to put it bluntly, killed your loved ones."

A dark growl emerged, with the snarls growing, the villagers' mouths biting in itching condemnation.

"Now that you've let your prejudice grow and foster into blind hatred, you've well and truly fucked it. I'm sure your predecessors had some story to stave off this kind of disaster. What's worse is the fact of your sacrifice."

The crowd was particularly unimpressed. Some of the torches still flickered. The guillotine hung in the background, illuminated by xenophobic tendencies.

"The fact that you sacrificed *sheep* to try to give your loved ones the power to come home is the crux of the matter. Your own blind ignorance caused their death. Your need to demonise the giants to justify stealing their land and perpetuating your own existence was the cause of the conflict. When they tried to help you, they were slain by the horrors you unleashed on your loved ones.

"Perhaps if you could learn to share the land you've been given, you wouldn't have such a hard time."

Hawk had definitely overstayed his welcome. He guessed he would just have to go hungry until he reached the forest.

He thought of Tiana and Elipse, eternally thankful for the fact that they didn't have to grow up in this rural backwater.

*

He decided to walk home via the Giants' kingdom, to pass on the news of their kindred's noble passing.

His feet eventually stepped into crisp, newly forming snow sheets, their flumpf heralding his arrival into the giants' snow-capped land. The crumpling footfalls pierced the mountain-ridged valley's deathly silence. After some time and several more sheets of snowfall, a gang of white-dipped rabbits scurried past.

Hawk saw their foe soaring high above, a grey-feathered snow eagle circling with dedicated intent. Apparently, that was a Nifilost slain, and hopefully no giants that Ilyia personally knew.

The prowling eagle dropped; with a vicious gust of wind, its sharp claws bore hard on Hawk's skull.

The scream was heard from miles away.

He heard a gentle rustle crescendo.

The death-white snow slowly began to shift.

It dropped abruptly.

Fuck.

TEN

Ilyia took her first steps towards him, silhouetted by candlelight. Bright orange flames flickered, illuminating her tender traces across the tent floor. The shadow of her action drew Hawk from the bed, entranced by her as always.

The covers fell from him quickly as he rose, hidden hands clinging and dragging them away.

With several soft footsteps, he found himself close to her extended arms, the reflected lamplight glistening in her eyes. An intoxicating swirl of her smell and taste undulated through his senses.

Her face a pitch-black mask, Hawk gently moved to draw her into the light, to see her tides of falling hair a pure shadow. He tried to speak, but concrete blocks consumed his mouth, Ilyia ethereally silent.

He turned her, but there was no change, again and again and still none, the constant silhouette rotating with her, forever masking her from view.

Constantly. Consistently. Mind-bendingly so.

This would be excruciatingly annoying. Would be, but he was used to this by now.

And then there erupted the flames. Shimmering reds and oranges, casting ravenous, searing tides. They engulfed the scene with a furnace ferocity, incinerating the multitude of furniture that decorated the tent of the loving couple.

A cornucopia of antiques swept devastatingly up into fire food, fuel for the inferno.

Portraits of Tiana and Elipse. Ageless trinkets and wonderous treasures. Eponymous heirlooms and priceless heritage. All were devoured by the ravenous flames engorging themselves on Hawk and Ilyia's linen-hemmed bedding.

The rupturing roars of crimson and ochre bellowed, belching out thick smoke clouds and tinges of sun-tempered yellow. Hues of blue began to appear in the centre of the all-encompassing, flickering and dancing fires.

He felt the need to escape and leave the incendiary torment behind... which was when he felt his feet turn to sludge, thick, immobile tar pits subsuming his gait.

He felt the heat descend on him, the tar pits fidgeting like a tinder box ready to ignite in a slow and roasting immolation. His legs continued to melt, their form incinerated by the insatiable, sweltering furnace, the tar yearning to consume him in fossilising fury.

Oh, that's fine then.

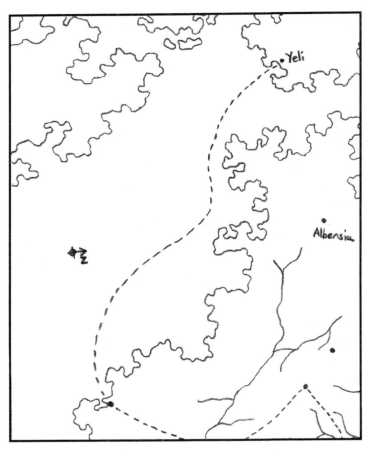

Map of Cereal's Journey: "A Captain's Laminate" by Captain Yelbeart Rost, 624 PIA

THE PLAGUE CITY

A TAIL OF TWO "SIT-THEE'S" (624 PIA)

*Pandemics are social disasters. Don't ask what the virus
did to us, but who were the people that let it? That's where
you find the true epidemic.*
—Magister Aleina, First Magister of Berosia.

It started with a sneeze, which to be honest is a pretty piss-poor excuse for a story's synthesis, but let's be honest – brutally honest, painfully truthful for a moment here. Even a sneeze can have catastrophic consequences, and as should be prior apparent: consequences come in clusters, quadrants, bucket-loads and clusterfucks in this kind of pathetic-falletic cosmos.

So where did the sneeze come from? The originator Patient Zero of doometic prophecies, that through piece-proposition will expose the underlying fabric of this Ontos?

In a field. Up to his hayfever-ridden nasal cavity in cereal sperm. Floating pockets of pre-germination. The sneeze came and went, splattering itself across some of the to-be-reaped brides to be, pre-buns in the oven.

The person was nondescript. Which may be farcical but is essential. Nothing great comes descript, the descript trails meandering a woven tale of half-truth and reflexive tomfoolery. He was a magi… maji? Mayji to be dialectish. A mayji of abysmal rank and level. Bevelled into a lift by overbearing parents.

There was a shadow in front of him. A towering metropolis tucked behind the thicket-woven canopy that he lay beneath, sprawled before the fields that fed the life that flowed and blossomed.

Why was he here?

Well, that's an age-old question with varying adages; an important nuance on the notion of activity is the premise of who before the particularisation is placed.

He was researching, caressing the intimates of the cosmos. He coughed twice and forgot his thoughts. Then came the real symbolic snickerdoodle, for want of a better un-emphasis to his introspection. If before him lay the sneeze, and it beheld the essence of the mayjical underlay, could it bear the full brunt of decimatic intent and shunt the full bear of mayjical underlaying? Could the fracturing nature of chaotic theorems spread disconjunctivitus and jaundice as far as any eye could seep?

He sneezed again and paused, forgetting himself, his place, his time, his state.

He hoped the universe hadn't noticed his slight stumble.

Of course, the universe was there; well, it's really

everywhere, always. Maybe some of it's over here. Maybe some more of it's over there. I heard once that a bit of the universe got stuck to another bit of universe without bits. That was a catastrophe never to be repeated again.

As usual, the universe was quite happy with itself today. Especially because, well, firstly, the universe is always happy, and secondly, the universe doesn't have to perceive time, so, you know, there's no difference between itself one day or the next, one instant or another.

One momentary pause once left the universe bedridden. Still does. Indefinite bed-riding was one of the many activities those parts that chose to partition themselves engaged in, often to unnecessary extents.

Unnecessary extents was what the universe didn't like, because the universe was left at odds with itself. Unnecessary extents were the thing that the universe dreaded engaging in beyond anything else, especially because the universe really had no choice in the matter. It just got dragged along much like everything else, especially because it *was* everything else.

And once again, unfortunately, it had noticed.

It sighed, hoping that they, them, and especially itself, could stop it from going shit up.

Metaphorical fingers crossed.

*

The poisonous piles of bodies had become ruinous mountains, towering with toxifying vitriol over the pestilent city streets. The consistently sick, dredging stench putrefied through the sinus systems of the three standing guards. They were as at ease as they could be during this trying time.

One of them brushed blood from his blade, seared crimson staining frayed brown leather. He sighed the usual forlorn sigh.

The first spoke, exasperated and short. "How much longer do we have to stand around on guard duty, Tyrus?"

Tyrus, the wayward vagabond with neither smile nor laugh, had somehow been roped into the desecrated and despoiled stain of a city. Responsibility tended to breed unadulterated rage.

"Long enough that your voice should become the sibilant backdrop to my dreams, Bienis. Perhaps if you practised your dialogue, we wouldn't currently be standing on watch, presiding over another one of your famous fuck-ups." Tyrus was further than sour; he was the rancid rotting remains of a fruit pile splayed degeneratively across the cracked city streets.

"I blame Talibold's quick wit. I wouldn't have had to lop off any arms if that trap of his kept shut."

The declaration was twofold. The verbal balk bit, while a sharp stone glanced off the mud-smeared helmet.

"If you stopped fucking chucking stones at me, perhaps I'd have the leeway for some fucking patience."

Talibold's retaliation was swift and forthcoming; a segment of wooden barricade harangued Bienis. It connected with a satisfying click, before Bienis abruptly dropped his patience and drew his shortsword with a grotesque flourish, it beckoning viciously, braying for blood.

"If you two would stop your incessant bickering, perhaps we could let the festivities simmer for a second. It's unbecoming, and I mean in the literal—"

Tyrus looked at each separately, drawing his tongue

in violent premonition. "I will stab both of you without a second glance."

The escalade settled, as pitchforks and burning torches appeared en masse before the barricade's border. A gaggle of braying citizens were once more blustering forth to threaten and berate the blood-drenched trio. Their crimes? Being the municipal military to this godforsaken block.

Their hastily erected forticade, which was once several shop fronts and furniture collections, forced the mob to broach their tempestuous burden through an isolated chokepoint. Chairs, tables, windows and stairs of the surrounding wood and stone structure, had been bludgeoned into a near indestructible turtle shell for the guards to holster within.

The fraying threads of malicious clamour erupted with a tide of unconscious and constrained fury; raw, biting alienation seeping from the people and buildings held to the newest mob court. A sea of sound broke into the shark song, blood mist permeating through the atmosphere, noses pricked and consuming scent. The biting shoal growing ever hungrier, awaiting their feast with famished eyes.

"The government lies, and everyone dies. Fuck the lot, the scum can rot."

The chant's white-hot iron was beaten and tempered as the crowd reverberated their call and response. The tempo and timing stamped into a singular expression of solidarity, the furnace of their ferocity blazing into a violent white gold.

"As usual, the only response is to await the arrival of the druids…" All the while the death toll was gradually marching amongst the monks. "… and to make sure to stay clean and stay safe."

This was the third week of the plague city's indenture to

the infernal service. This was the third flash mob for the day. The wells had also begun to dry up. The thirst and hunger, the greed and gluttony above – it had all begun to feel a little flashpointy.

The mob dispersed; no blood or butchery was needed at this time. The guards stood forlorn at the breach between sanity and madness. The petrified audience of cobblestones and charcoal sat abashed. Well, pre-bashed. Post-bashed tears and sweat had been washed away each night by the overly dramatic storm clouds.

Tyrus was resistant to the plague, as befitted someone of his "dark ancestry". He would scoff at such a befitting statement. Befitting in the way his sword might find a nice resting place between their eyes, leaving them looking jaunty and doe-y (he really meant doughy, though).

The two guardspersons stood next to him in this triarchy of deepening terror were both of Yeli birth, Yeli growth, and soon, maybe, Yeli rest. Talibold and Bienis had no natural fortification against tainted biology.

The Yelites had no genetic fortification against their troubles. Instead, their bodies would pustulate and perforate, spewing forth violent, disgusting flourishes of decay. They would collect and contaminate, weaving the threads of their own dissection, brokering their ever-twisting tango with death. The corpse piles he had helped bury stank of death and vomit-inducing corruption. Many volunteers had fallen ill, and they too were shovelled by the barrow-load into mass graves outside the city limits.

Why was Tyrus here again? He lamented the fact he'd volunteered for this mission to the Shorelands, to scout the lands for a fitting kingdom. These barbarians were surplus the fact, and a fact of pure surplus, so maybe Yeli wasn't ideal after all.

Yet now he was stuck here indefinitely, until the borders opened up, a prisoner of his own inane significance. If only he hadn't mentioned his immunity, he wouldn't have been drafted into duty by that magister. Aleina might have been their name. The overblown windbag that nearly slit the throat of the Royal Court when they called for the lockdown to be lifted.

There was a noise before the three of them; a large metallic object had landed in the previously marketable space. By the steps of a statue of the Grand Yelite Royalty there was now a small porcelain sphere, a white-vein marble statue of the Great Royalty of Yeli, the founders of this apparently "great and gem" of a city.

It imploded into eviscerating shrapnel. The three ducked quickly as surging shreds punctured the wooden fortress that was precariously wedged between collapsed houses.

They had started hurling homemade explosives at the start of the second week, then the pitchforks and torches. Braying groups broached blind indecency. If only the aristocrats had given the citizens reprieve, that might have spared the impending bloodshed and incinerating red fire-scape that Tyrus saw in the citizens' eyes. The magister was infuriated by their lackadaisical tactics.

The magister's strategy was infinitely different: strict lockdown, free bread and alcohol, and then maybe some magical herbs and books. Distraction, isolation, and tracing of infection. In the meantime, if they could have turned every home into a prison and paradise, then there wouldn't be any civil unrest.

It was a pretty ingenious strategy, although it was a standard etiquette and practice of the more cultured regions.

Mind you, Tyrus thought, in the more cultured regions, a plague would lead to truly necromantic pandemics. Seas upon seas of restless undead. Waves about waves of desolation.

His mind drifted to cold, pallid, grasping hands. He shivered a night tremble of an eternal restless undeath.

Now *that* is what we call skin in the game.

*

Yeli somehow looked different to Hawk. The walls had a desiccating, depleted aura that clung to the masses that trailed towards the city's entrance.

You could almost see the ruinous mist of the plague emanating from the barricades and fortresses – a green hue tinging the cloying atmosphere, nauseating the structures; a pox-risen rapture; the trail of pestilent-ridden fear wafting slowly and securely up to the higher tiers.

Hawk stood near the gate's mouth; before him stood the yellow-and-black liveried guard of Yeli, trailing off for a bleak and harrowing distance from the wanting entrees. The sun hung low and dilapidated. The stain of orange diffused into galling green and bruised purples. You could almost see the faint seams of scouring tan bone dust trailing across the sky.

Hawk could sense the intense bottomless well of suffering being forged in this engorging black hole; the slow and guttural stretching of people's life and history across a rack of indisputable fear, the burning iron scalding and searing flesh into vile aberration. In the dense, miasmic crucible of Yeli, an intense, compressing expression of gangrenous universal infection was being undressed, the culminating crescendo of cosmological influx heightening to a world bearing extent.

Several twinkling fires emerged, encaged buzzing atoms fluctuating with structure-splitting intent, fireflies gliding through a city slicked by oily smoke.

Yggdrasil looked on, the universal rule of "right things looking nothing like" being applied firm and fast.

Axiomatically so, woe was re-smelt through the apocalyptic screams, and rapturous exclaims, into the frame-forming lines of existence and consequence, all unbanding around the burgeoning burst belly of the metropolis.

Yggdrasil's policies when things got out of hand were always bemoaned by nearly everyone, and every other everyone else, unanimously so.

Multiplicity breeds consistent discontent – which ultimately isn't a bad thing, or something to be distraught about, just something that needs awareness, Complaints are the trajectory of growth, when unfurled prophetically and poetically.

Yggdrasil had apparently gotten its hands to properly conduct these sorts of things by this point. It had to have, otherwise it wouldn't still be here, right?

*

The golden-flecked fields of blossoming brides smiled as their husbands clustered to reap their rewards. They shed their mortal follies and returned womb-laced to the earth, their bodies brought to bags in blooming and bountiful bundles, all ready to be milled and harnessed.

The people above laughed as they toiled; the gentle sunshine set itself across their backs and fronts. Scythes flared through the field's thickets, tumbling torrents of cerealised drama. The swooning brides fell to beds of soft joy. They travelled beneath soft cloud copses, rested under the stoic granite touch of their above lords. The machinations strewed their forms to flour. The rich mountains of speckled white- and sand-coloured accumulations were swept up by the handful into twine-twisted bagging, ready to be brought into the bounteous bosom of the Innitipk Complex.

The Innitipk Complex, with regal posture, welcomed the tides with the gentle flows of its friendly appendages. The streams of civility flooded the urban pool as the deep waters subsumed the emancipated crops. The mayji buttresses, with their blue-chalked obfuscations, laced with arcane and esoteric sanctuary, warded the coming preamble of despair.

Somewhere amidst them, *the* mayji was silently fulfilling his duties. Well, he should have been. The soft resonance of laughter often accompanied the supposedly serious cantrips the acolytes lay across the city. The Innitipk Complex was at the centre of Ebonheart, which, despite its strange name, was the cradle of the Ultai. It was the first city created by the Second Peoples and was the longstanding bastion of all peopled knowledge. It was the sublime foundation of their unfolding collective epiphany.

Within the lax and reclining square-stacked complex, a merchant from the city of Illyrianm overlooked a batch of corn yet to be milled. The tender leaves of yellow gave no impression to the merchant of the subtly shaped enchantment left by one nose's deft strike. He haggled for a fair price, and eventually, after several huffed breaths and hushed tones, rightly acquired his discount. His servants loaded his wagons with his new acquisitions; his guards arrived with gem-struck polished armour. They resounded themselves successful before setting off on the long, dusty trail home.

Shimmering blue birds flew overhead as the cart ricocheted down the cobblestone road. It made its way west following the Ancient Ultai Trail Road, darting among the various cities that had sprung up along the road's snaking meander. The iridescent avians flying overhead would be their guardians for a large extent of the journey, they too following the same migratory path westwards.

Moving from Ebonheart was an easy task; the first destination would be the merchant's home of Illyrianm, the first of the Second Cities. The Ancient Ultai Trail Road was a misnomer; it was neither the ancient road of the Ultai nor a trail for trade. Instead, it was a large, meandering cobblestone path built as the last Ice Age waned.

The scores of peoples and clans unleashed from the Ultai Deserts at the end of the Ice Age had moved to settle wherever and whenever they liked. The road was built by the descendants of the Ultai, the glorious So'Ultai, to unite them with their homeland, a meandering metaphysical genealogy to their birthplace. Many of the ancient Ultai cities were occupied by the So'Ultai; many were left to become dusty, forgotten, stone-dotted statues to the timeless ones who lived before.

Their long and broad settlement trail ran north-west and south-west, but there were also two other great migrations from the cradle of their species. The one after the Ice Age was the third great migration away from Ebonheart, the others leaving much earlier, heading north and south respectively.

When these early settlers left, they scaled the windswept and cold-stormed mountains, creeping through dark-crusted, suffocating, cavernous cave systems. They left a shallow imprint on the landscape, softly garbed nomads who hunted and gathered along the inland shores of the Aeyol'I Lake, or along the Ultai Deserts and the Underbelly. Others touched the Dark Coasts, and others yet slipped through the shadows of the Vishidyai Empire, often caught in their slaving nets.

The lands they found were teeming with vibrant and vocal life and glowing and bounding rejuvenation, flooded with rich, luscious vales and gem-sparkling groves, sanctified paradises refreshed by the ice-gripped comb of the Winter Titans. Even the pristine sand-washed deserts that the Ultai called home were delightful and fruitful paradises of life when found. All it took was the knowledge and experience that came with patience, and the Second Peoples had long since learnt patience living in their god-guarded, gilded cage.

The clans of Otherkin who welcomed them were bizarre and eclectic, plentiful in social formation and practice. Adorned with trinkets and ornaments that dazzled and shone, and furs and hides from a plethora of alien life forms, their surreal nature and chimeric compositions were no impediment to their coming unity with the emerging pink-skinned.

The Vishidyai to the south, however, had already made their mark on the Second Peoples' lifeways, making prisoners of the first Ultai to navigate and pass through the harrowing ordeal of the Esyion Caves. This tragedy was enshrined in the campfire and festival stories of Istarig's war with them to free the Primate Kings, immortalised in the constellation of Second Peoples bravery.

The Ultai truly left Ebonheart during the second migration. They followed the last of the Inyipi, who slipped morth under the guidance of the Ice Crofter Tyomm. They were the only ones of the expanding Second Peoples to enter into the lands of the First Peoples beyond the line of the Urm'gil pact with the Otherkin. However, their lone journey was handsomely repaid; they met those exceedingly far beyond their prowess in every art and craft, and were left dazed and destitute by their effortless machinations and biomechanical contraptions.

This was the reason for the early Ultai cities. In the short space between their arrival and the encroaching Ice Age, the First Peoples taught them the secrets of their old scientific knowledge, and now eco-epistemic perspective they passed these back to their kin when the Ice Age caused their return to Ebonheart.

The polities that absorbed the Ultai were obstruct, brusque, arcane bearings, vilifications of their ancient ancestors, and wise descendants the Pre-Krylei; the mechanistic Ehmr'gil were cloud-staining shadows of the fey-ascended Urm'gil, who in their soul-shorn descent into Azgaite madness unleashed the devastation that sundered the Urm'gil and broke the covenant that bound the Winter Titans.

By the time the Ultai arrived at the table, the cutlery had warped far beyond a final mergence. A titanic and subsuming death, encompassing the twilight's night, was borne by the Ehmr'gil, accursed and star-forged.

Illyrianm was a vast metropolis that stood at the mouth of the Ulticicc river in the centre of the Embrik Rift. It was a patchwork complex of several previous settlements that had slowly been knitted together by the So'Ultai. It housed smatterings upon smatterings of flat-roofed terraces that were strewn across the jagged hills that Illyrianm luxuriously rested atop. The grand towers and buttressed fortifications were relics of the Rift Clan's war against the Vishidyai Empire. The Rift Clan's current border with the Neo-Vishidyai was much further south, and constantly patrolled for encroaching raiders and warbands, although these prolific patrols were invisible to the Rift Clans homelands.

The jagged hills that propped and supported the city complex were not natural accruements. The giant, jagged protrusions of split and hewn earth were instead the leftover defences between the Urm'gil and Otherkin forebears. The vast swathes of cresting and smashed rock and dirt were earthworks split by the titanic and monstrous weapons the Ehmr'gil used to devastate the ground that lay beneath Urm'gil feet.

The crevices deep beneath Illyrianm, which had been appropriated as catacombs for the rich and prestigious, were the results of the brutish, indolent, tectonic-shifting warheads that proliferated before the Mechano-kleptocracy's demise – accumulations of kinetic energy left with a match and fuselage, ready to warp the foliage, grass, and shrubbery into a shimmering irradiated Divinity.

Before the Ultai were granted the benefit of bearing the vestiges of the others, they were first forced to watch the reckless-abandon-drenched flaming inferno that forced the First Peoples to shed their mantle of world protection.

It was sheer misfortune that the nuclear winter emboldened the coming of the Winter Titans. It left very little time for the Ultai to emulate their forerunners, and it left vast swaths of indifference in the wake of technological mastery. Fortunately, as the behemothic being with glacial steeds arrived, the Krylei and the Giantkind excelled.

The bag of corn lazed against the wagon as its owner haggled with the gaudily clad merchant from Illyrianm; well, Yenti, to be more exact. The gold-trimmed yellow of the merchant's attire spoke of his long journey home, further south along the ancient Ultai trail road that ultimately wasn't.

Gold-dipped fingers passed over a small brown bag, within it a glistening pile that spoke of many warm meals to come for the returned marketeer.

Their smiles matched the grin of Istarig's jewelled vision. They paid his respects upwards to the heavens that watched above in the tradition of the Ultai cosmology. The Yentite merchant then began his long journey home.

*

It hadn't taken Hawk long to cause an argument.

It never did. It was complacency with connective communication that allowed Hawk to placate through gentle provocatation. That wasn't a word to anyone else, and yet Hawk held it to heart.

The man in front of him was a lecherous being; he could tell by the stench of glazed perfumes and labour exploitation, as well as his grimy gold-ringed stained fingers, which fidgeted and shifted, itching with immorality.

The person behind Hawk was a noble knight guarding several of the monkhood that had come to do vigilant missionary work. Tend to the ill; replace the wearied apothecaries. Truly righteous work.

Hawk bent down and nicked the purse hanging from the lecher's thread, the coins tumbling to the ground. The sounds provoked the monks into gasps of undue decadence. The stingy red-faced lecher tried to hide the eschewed eschatological images.

Two guards boldly strode forward. They called forth for the money.

"You know the Plague City Ordnance. Hand over your concealed treasury, or face two months of civic toil."

The capitulations seeped in. The lecher's golden toils were swept from his blood-mudded hands by the blue-and-yellow-adorned guards.

They strode off as the monks sacrilegiously gabbed between themselves.

The solemn crowds continued, slowly shuffling forwards.

Hawk eventually made it into "The Plague City". Now the full view of the rotting cityscape came into being, finally freed from its shielding sullied-cream-coloured granite stone curtainry. The illustrious backdrop of shining lights and flickering torches silhouetted a plethora of plague-ridden souls. They moaned and howled, groaning out foul smells and stretches of despair, the mournful wail that permeated above them sucking the life from the city entrance.

There before Hawk was a merchant naively engaging in murder.

The fox-faced and unethically discussed thing, or pitysome merchant, was adorned with garish and gorging blue colours. They rustled and nudged themselves out from the swatches of fur that had been knitted to form the merchants' fashionable attire. It wasn't the common blue available widely and freely amongst the poorer castes and classes. Instead, it was the rich, deep, pelagic blue-green interplay that bespoke mercantilists carried as hard insignia from the Valestian Isle.

The rare blue was a fey enchantment woven by the weaveseer craftsmen that Valestia's wealth was built upon.

The ethically disgusting merchant was harshly demanding that his goods be urgently, quickly, resolutely sent through the customs barrier. Who cares about lives when coin is lost? He was adamant and resolved that his livelihood mattered ever more than the lives of those he might infect and torment.

Careless abandon is often fresh turf to the Horsemen of the Apocalypse. Hawk found this sort of self-obsessed sensibility exacerbating, this conceitedness exasperating, as the merchant was trying to say that his goods were the central tenet to a bright future. He was a food merchant, and an avid one at that.

His green-scarred handkerchief attested otherwise, lest perjury strike it down before the magister's newly appointed goods managers.

The mucus was overflowing from the pocket linen, and worse for the fact that it looked as if the merchant had reached the limits of rhetoric and now offered a glittering respite to the official. Wrapped in soft brown fabric, the coins jingled.

Before temptation and sin were wrought affluently through the affairs of the fates, Hawk had grasped a solid, stout shank of wood. He hurled it blunt end forward. It connected sweetly and repletely, sharply silencing the emaciated elephant of the room.

The guardsperson took stock of the situation – of Hawk, the unconscious infected merchant, and the illegal produce they had very nearly let free from the hold of the city. Hawk flashed a smile, and with a slow grin waved hello, his Guild trinket firmly in his palm.

That settled things, then.

*

Tyrus was getting bored of being stood in the forticade. He was only here on loan, scouting out this land for his commander, Berihtos. They were getting bored bashing thugs with wooden sticks, and wanted a real life for their families. Berihtos and his bandleaders, Tyrus, Elesa, Syuin, Icheub, Kai and Jozio, had all come up with the plan. Jozio had spoken to one of his friends up high and divined that the kingdoms to the west of Yeli were of ample Divinity for their coming prosperity. Tyrus had laughed at Jozio's obsession with frigid mothers and furry fathers; there was nothing a snowflake polar bear could tell Jozio that Tyrus couldn't witness with his own eyes.

Yeli was the place Tyrus knew they should take; it was the cultural epicentre of the Shorelands, the home of the Guild and free enough from Valestian enterprise that no one could stop them. Although the Valestians had claimed Yeli over a hundred years ago, they were lax in the occupation and management of their protectorate. Therefore, he'd been tracking the movements of the city guards and the local patrols, Yeli being ruled by an oligarchical community of aristocrats. They all supported the commodity-rich grand houses and high families of the Royal Court; below them, the Guild and the Magisterial Orders sat as meddlers, then below them the self-righteous city guard and the bumbling Yelite militia.

There was a multitude of religious groups and societies that had bred like rabbits beneath Yeli's carrot-rich merchant community. Many of them were pacifist, many of them tithe-stoked and gold-minted.

It was prime real estate, awaiting the taking. That's what he'd argued, fervently and fiercely. Now he sat and waited in a Plague City he was immune to, because he had made the misfortune of stepping in before he could step out.

Classic.

*

The divine, speckled, simmering bag of corn was brought to the rustling city outskirts. Having travelled half a baker's dozen of days south, it had been bought botched and batched, to now stand before the towering merchant state of Yenti.

Yenti sat at the mouth of the turquoise river of Issillisk. The Yentites loved the gentle rippling water their city rested against, and had come to master and perfect the art and joy of sailing.

The bag of corn was gently and professionally lifted from the cart and carried to the sailboat. The Yentite conversed with the merchant come home.

They clasped hands and smiled. The buyer offered a symbol of friendship; it was politely refused as tradition demanded. They both laughed and went about their days. The merchant, thankful to finally be home, sought out his wife and children, to tend to his joy under the sun.

The Great Yenti Bazaar was ringed by sixteen towers, each connected by two curtain walls. Some would say Yenti was a city surrounding a bazaar; some would say Yenti was a bazaar surrounded by sit-ees. Others would finally say that Yenti was the notion of commerce surrounded by sitting seas.

The dockyard was choked with life, and the vibrant colourful symphony of sweet speech and soft fashion. Dialects from the far corners of the ocean were slurred and spat at wanderers and hagglers.

The sea captain was being harassed by a slight merchant. His tenuous figure suggested the moneymaker could ill afford to be overfed, and that made the sea captain anxious to accept his load. Perhaps this would be the final ill symbol of his life?

The captain knew his hangover was the ill-conceived bringer of this dark omen; there was little superstition to be sought out to renege. He would accept the burden and be handsomely rewarded. He barked orders to his crew to load the several crates of grain, careful not to break the preservation enchantment lain long ago under Innitipk's tiered skies.

The journey to Yeli would be long and dangerous. The corn would follow the coastline west, then north, travelling along the edge of the Gastio Sea. It would avoid the pirates that lived on the Sun-Seared Isles, the start of the sparkling Chembya Ocean the crossing point from some safety to desolate vagrancy.

With the journey they'd plotted, they wouldn't pass into the territory of the Umbil whales. The ship captain had seen many from his times as a Yenti sailor. They crested the waves with deep-purple backs, rich blue stripes spread across their skin.

He remembered the first time he saw the ocean stars, those visible beyond the fiery, incandescent light pollution of Yenti. He had become a sailor young, conscripted to fight against the Sun-Seared Pirates. The Pirate-King Alsui sought to capture Yenti and begin his continental empire. For five long years they waged war across the ocean, getting battered in skirmishes by dark ships with deadly ballistae. Screaming gargoyle-tipped helms ruptured the hulls of the Yenti navy.

Eventually, the pirates descended, and Yenti was ruled by the Crimson Oligarchy. They smashed the Protectorate's Palace and adorned the yellow-gold heraldry with the skulls, bones, and fetishes of the Cult of Yamis. The bazaar was turned into a desiccated slave market.

He didn't really know the true depravity of the situation; he had been a survivor of the war, nestled within the cave system south of Yenti. In the warrens where Yentil, the city founder, kept his people during the Ice Age, they hid and amassed their weapons and warriors. After ten long years of gruelling exile, only ten miles away from the home he once called his, they returned.

Luckily, many of the soldiers' families had escaped the city before the assault, leaving those inside without loyalties that could cause suffering and sorrow.

A long siege finally wrested the city from the cruel pirate-king despotism, many lives lost to the dark sea on both sides. It was with his final reward that the soldier, née sailor, became a sea captain.

The oceanic sparkle of dazzling white was bobbing across the waves and horizon. Now he sat beneath the beautiful bounds of bird song that shifted sublimely overhead. Sweet calls of half-sentences and agitations flittered around the sails of his mighty vessel.

The sailors and soldiers he surrounded himself with were

the best he could find. They had worked themselves into a perfect synchronicity, like every good expert does. They diligently toiled and manned their stations, to carry his cargo to the glorious resonance of sea-supping cities beyond Yenti.

It looked like they would make no stops before Yeli. The cargo they carried consisted purely of luxury goods destined for the Royal Courts, presents ordered by one of the Grand Houses to dazzle their brethren and further secure some important position or status. Regardless of their intent, the hold was now gloriously adorned with Ebonheart grain, Shuush desert wine, Inyipi furs and opal walrus tusks. There were beautiful golden statuettes from the Isle of the Gods; shimmering silver plates and stamped cutlery gathered from the Neo-Vishidyai Empire.

All in all, the vessel now contained lush, exotic relics from the infinite expanse of the First and Second Peoples. It would be a sweet journey, a soft odyssey over familiar seas, gentle tides carrying them on. They would avoid the more dangerous parts of the ocean, and avoid the preying pirates that quickly scuttled ships of every fortune and persuasion.

There, out of the corner of his eye, the captain spotted black flags on the horizon. He called out to his crew, hoping it wouldn't be too late.

They responded with an anxious but swift efficiency, unfurling themselves through the ship's body and sails, the rattle of weapons and arrows sounding out their readiness.

*

"Ahhhh Hawk, you bruised-nose bastard, what the fuck are you doing out here in this godforsaken hell of a pit?"

Tyrus had been granted leave for the next few days. This was his opportunity. Yeli was less fortified, less protected, all the more an ideal target to take and hold. He was beaming with vigilant fervour. It clung to the peninsula like a jewel on a hilt, useless and prestigious. The perfect prize for the company to make their name and mark in the Shorelands. It wouldn't be hard for the highly trained cadre to take on the city's militia. They could capture it and leave it; that would show Jozio.

"Are you still looking for a shit-stain to call home? I can see that twinkle in your eye. And that twinkle often leaves me on the sharp edge of separation, always at the wrong time."

"Hawk, my good friend, my esteemed colleague. Why would I do such a thing?" Tyrus's proposition was matched by licked lips and a twinkling wink.

Hawk's laugh boomed, and their hands thunder-clapped each other's backs.

"Want to come with me to the magister's office? I've been recalled by the Guild for some kind of adjudicating duty with the city official. Boring tripe, but maybe free food?"

"I could, I could, but I'm busy, Hawk; not everything revolves around you. Some of us have lives of our own, you know. Plus, I only have leave for a few days, then I'm to return to guard duty indefinitely. Perhaps this accursed city will be my tomb."

"Tyrus, you could do well with a break. Let me fix you up with an escape."

"I'm good. Thanks, my brother, maybe another time, I've got errands to run."

Tyrus mock-saluted and left off into a back street, instantly vanishing into the crowd's dark depths. The milling mass continued around them, in a spreading irony.

Hawk eventually reached the red steps of the magisters' tower. He was soon in the offices of the Yeli grand magisters. The magister across from him was clothed in a verdant blue hue which emanated the essence of purification. The room was filled with perfumed flowers.

"The apothecaries and druidic order have been helping us try to balance the rate of infection. The problem has been keeping people in lockdown. We've tried to bring it to people's eyes that the earlier people stay sheltered, the quicker it will pass, but this city isn't rich." They coughed. "Well, it's rich, but in all the wrong places. We've been using the levied tax to sustain supplies and shelter for the homeless. We've even been producing face masks, but the great unwashed still refuse to participate en masse."

Hawk could see strained weariness splashed across the serious magister's face. The Magisterial Order refused to act out gender; they believed that it fundamentally diminished a person's power to act.

"We've been trying to work on education, elevation and entertainment, but all we get are tired arms and swords thrown at us by the various house guards that run the private parks. Someone thought it would be a smart idea to tell people to stay six feet away from each other. Well, not personally, but the heralds were burnt. They made banners saying 'If you keep us out, we burn you in.'"

The fire flames of the burners on Aleina's table etched screams of horror and anguish in the recesses of the room. "Not the most restrained of people, your average everyday Yelite. That was when we started hiring surplus guards from the neighbouring cities; they all are now ours, to stay indefinitely, part of the contract. I mean, if we had better leaders than the tar-suckled morons we currently have, we might have had a fighting chance to begin with. Alas, the best we can hope for is that the apothecaries and druids will find some sort of magical restitution. We have managed to contain the spread within the city. So perhaps we just have to wait till everyone's dead?"

*

Tyrus had already dipped beyond perception as he sneakily scoped a trek towards the aristocratic estates. They were perched on the second and third stories of Yeli: thick, stoic gatehouses shouldered away the spilling, drunken citizenry.

Now they protected the rich from the plenty.

The only issue with such a prevalent wealth disparity was that it meant lots of private mercenaries – lots of people slightly better than the civil guards and the civilian militia, and slightly less directed at anything other than protecting private property. They would never be a match for his blades; they were just severely surplus the fact of his swords' excellence.

It was interesting that even now, as the city was a tinder-box ready to spark, the ruling elite were inclined to rest and plan the future of their soon-to-be-cleaned easel. Many of the elites would rebuild the newly burnt-out homes, earning tenfold their investment on the newly renovated, and vastly increased rental-valued, lodgings. It was a business strategy as old as time itself.

This was why these lands needed some urban renewal, some alteration to the power structure. The egalitarian structure of Berihtos's legion gave men and women equal opportunities, even though they involved a very specialised skill set. This was what Berihtos thought would truly give them power in this land. If they reorganised the people beyond the vain hero-worship of their ancestors, if they taught them to embrace the heroism of the everybody, if they taught people that life could inherently be lived without the need for some vainglorious lord and lady…

Although, knowing Berihtos, it would be interesting to see how committed he was to the rhetoric he spewed forth in front of every campfire.

Tyrus remembered the speech given by the Magister as he had been conscripted into the "voluntary" city guard. "Our original plan would have been for a full lockdown, essential services delivered to people's doors, the family houses of twenty or so holding individual groups of people who wouldn't be in contact with anyone else. Then we would hand-deliver the medical and food supplies, free education services, no rent or costs, free artistic therapies and supplies."

This seemed like idealistic thinking to Tyrus. Where in the fuck were they going to get all that money? These kinds of projects required a large surplus of coinage and value. Well, really the coinage was a symbol for trust by the powers that be, and unfortunately the local ones here drowned in their mortifying ineptitude.

"We could have used the time to retrain and retool our people, so that after the pandemic we could raise the average level of education, increase the rate of literacy, give people new skills to accrue values of all kinds."

Value of all kinds. Clearly wishful thinking. What did Yeli have to offer to subsidise these grandiose, utopic schemes?

"We would have maintained safe sanitation and

redistributed access rights to land and healthcare, religion, ideology and entertainment, prioritised university research and community production of goods and services. However, it was all a self-defeating piss-against-the-wall after the infection moved from the royal district into the poorer tiers. Which is why the lockdown was lifted, and therefore where you come in."

*

They survived the pirate attack by the skin of their teeth, the evil flashing swords still slashing through the captain's memory, his perception still tainted by the black-flag bandits that sailed from the war-torn islands to the south. They only grew to be bolder and more daring with each passing year. Even after being evicted from Yeli, they were still terrifying trouble; they split ships quicker than vicious storms, and burnt hulls faster than the most colossal thunderbolt of the raging, stormy ocean hurricanes.

His crew had done well to fight them back, and he was glad they trained regularly. They would be rewarded for their service this journey, and it was likely they wouldn't be hassled again now for a few years. The pirates were famous for passing on a blacklist of targets. Those who bloodied their noses just enough would miss their cursed glare for a while after.

Pirates weren't the only danger of the high seas. Sometimes titanic monsters would creep up from the depths and capture stranded ships. Other times, hordes of sea birds might descend, if they felt the food below deck was easy enough to uncage. Other times, flocks of ravenous sea people might appear: beasts half-person and half-animal, green-, blue- or yellow-hued, their skin blubbery and wet. They would wait for a boat to lower its speed and attack from the waves, climbing up the sides and investing their blades into the bodies of any nearby crewmembers.

The captain hoped there would soon be a time when these terrors would stop. But it wasn't uncommon for people to be born with webbed feet and gills in some villages. He had heard of one person born with a fish's tail and stunted arms and legs.

Valestia was on the ascension as well. Not that they were a threat to the trading routes, but they still demanded tithe or tax if their fleets found you. Their Grand Armada was currently ferrying troops to and from the Yeli Peninsula as they looked to extend their colonial empire through the Shorelands. They did fight the pirates, though, a small gain of stability at the cost of freedom. He wasn't sure if that was a good or bad thing, but it was out of this captain's pay grade.

It was obvious that the Valestians were waiting for a time to strike, to seize the city of Yeli truly for themselves, displacing the Royal Court that held ownership over the urbanised valley landscape that Yelite society existed amidst. It would only take one large disaster to weaken Yeli sufficiently; then the Valestian army would advance, demanding total servitude, probably building their temples throughout the city. They might even execute a few people if they seemed the sort to inspire rebellions. They had done it once before, and, if they did it again, they would wrest away full control.

Yeli was usually safe from this kind of grandstanding. The city state of Casidia-Masiritia respected that the Guild called

Yeli home, and therefore Yeli was a supposedly neutral space in the politics of the manascape. However, the Valestian armada was always too close for comfort, ships circling the city like the black-tarred vultures they were.

Finally, they arrived at the wooden-decked docks of Yeli, an ocean of ships upon glistening water. The sparkling reflections looked like gems from afar, azure glitter heralding the safety and security of Yeli's Great Harbour. The stretch of coastline that the busy and rustling harbour took up was significant. Yeli was built in the entrance to a valley, with a coved beach leading up to the raised grass and populated hill terraces. The golden-yellow sand quickly turned into cobblestones and grass-stained porches. Wooden and stone houses jutted upwards in rich patchworks of history and laboured reconstruction.

The marketeer on the docks was from the royal tier. You could tell by the deep red crest that adorned his chest: the Red Dragon of House Geola. He had been sent to acquire the luxury cereal crop sent from Ebonheart, a special gift for the Royal Court to enjoy during the ceremonies of the new ascent. It was an ancient custom from Yeli's origin, from back when the chiefs of the Yeli clan would gather under the full moon and anoint themselves with the energy of the universe. They would drink deeply from goblets filled with wine, and imbibe the Tissip leaf, an ancient hallucinogen from the Ultai Deserts. Then they would undertake the trials of their ancestors and earn their place amongst the stars. It was a trial and test as old as the So'Ultai themselves, and one handed down generation after generation during their time in the Ultai Deserts.

The cereal crop was taken to make the sacred bread to be

dipped into the stew of a thousand star-gods. This would be eaten when the day finally ceased.

In the evening, the bread grew a sickly green; intoxicating streams of putrescent potential fumigated within the ovens. It rose an intoxicated green, befouled by envy and jealousy, rotten stench and nausea-inducing damage crusting over into crisp and firm brown, decayed fibres and desecrated carbohydrates blown into a toxic web of self-deceit.

Then, finally, it was charred into the terrifying, eternal pitch-black, a botulistic blackness of which the likes had never been seen.

*

Aleina was figuratively enchanted. The bubbling concoction amidst their glassware was slowly simmering, expelling deep, fragrant clouds of pink and purple at every other occasion and instant, bubbles popping and rippling whenever their whim caught fancy. The chemical belches, ruptured and released, quickly expelled a refreshing aroma around the room. It was drifting slowly up Hawk's nose, reminding him of the herbal balms of the Krylei, or the apothecary creations of Nin, acquired from the various societies that harvested and negotiated the treasures of plants and trees.

Aleina was obsessively producing variations of cures and tonics, stockpiling potential healing solutions and antidotes. They were compiling a deep compendium, detailing every possible ailment and all the relevant fixes.

This had partly been inspired by the pandemic, but mostly by the lacklustre response of Aleina's royal governors. As a powerful magister, Aleina wouldn't suffer their indolence, or be left stupid through their ignorance. Moreover, they wouldn't be caught again by the foul, bubonic, plague-ridden hands of fate. Well, fate's lecherous, nepotistic and self-harming advocates.

Therefore, regardless of the Yeli Royal Court's inept and fiasco-inducing handling of the pandemic, there would still be a productive end to Aleina's experience, something that indefinitely helps when things are getting the best of you.

Hawk was carefully trying not to provoke Aleina's rants, but they were as inevitable as the constant flux and change that permeates through the totality of existence. Just as the cascading waters dredged down the chasms originally beneath, to collide and explode upon the bare rocks that sharpened abraded by the downpour, Aleina's rants were the momentous outpour of time's corroded stance. Their words caught the glint.

"The pandemic was taken seriously to begin with because it hit the royal house. It started in the Royal Court's kitchen, and several council members were infected. A full lockdown was established, but the trickle into the other parts of the city had begun. Eventually, it died down in the royal and higher tier as it spread out through the transmission lines into the poorer parts of the city. The lockdown was then lifted, and the pandemic began.

"The amount of resources required to survive a pandemic is immense, but mostly the problems are logistical. All you really need to do is reorganise the systems that were sufficient before the system collapsed. Then you distribute them efficiently as a distraction. Overindulge people and create a complacency to stay inside. You only have to do it for a while, until the pandemic dies down. My personal belief is that these are the perfect times for education or artistic expression. If these were offered to people for free, these pandemics would go over like a short, isolated holiday.

"We were at least successful in organising people to stay indoors to begin with, while we were worried the infection would spread around the Royal Court and down to the other tiers. However, when the infection did spread and the aristocrats felt secure enough to return to normal, they pushed a disinformation campaign.

"It requires a devout conformity to the Order's line for social planning to succeed. If there is any form of difference of opinion amongst the people seen to be specialised and responsible, the whole system will collapse. This is because people unconsciously choose to agree with the unanimity if they know their lives will be good, and their being safe.

"However." Aleina dripped a viscous orange liquid into the concoction in front of them. "If people are exploited too much, these unconscious frames of acceptance and agreement are broken. Or they don't have the traction to encourage successful and safe behaviour."

A forlorn sigh of existential pity was splashed across Aleina's face, its stern and serious features breaking into heart-true compassion.

"Even some magisters broke ranks with the order, disgustingly so, calling on the lockdown to counter the lives of those it was meant to protect. They claimed the ideals of liberty and freedom. Polluted the waters of the specialised discussion. Turned the Royal Court against the Magisterial Order's best solutions. One of them claimed the cost of people not working was too great to them, that they had already suffered the worst effects of life and needed to continue working lest they get forcibly removed from their homes and jobs. They also claimed the virus must have already gotten the majority of the people that it would, and therefore the death rate was lower than our work suggested.

"They are a curse, and I hope to God they find eternal rest soon for their dumb and brutish actions. Their carelessness and self-importance has cost the city too many lives. And now since they've justified a discussion, we've seen all kinds of fop-headed indolence spoken and acted upon."

Aleina washed their hands under the hot, running water. Cleansing steam and purifying admixtures were combined between their palms and fingers. Soap and suds rose and bubbled gleefully. "People like that disgust me. Their ignorance is blood on their hands."

The water tinged red as more cleaning chemicals were introduced through the flushing stream.

"They used dumb, self-involved arguments to justify sending people back to the work halls, reasoning that markets and shops must remain open so people wouldn't suffer from a loss of productivity. They even sent kids back to schoolhouses, which just caused an even quicker outbreak."

Hawk thought to the composition of the plague piles. These epidemics always butchered the poor indiscriminately.

"The reason they did all of this was really just to exasperate those below us. So there's no reason for anybody to accept that our society could be made more equal, or that lives could be more valued. In fact, quite the opposite."

Aleina paused for breath, time crumbling behind the backdrop of their sociological dissection.

"It's almost necessary that they accept our society as it is, regardless of change. Because to acknowledge change would be to admit that the bullshit short-lived plans of the foppish shit-sippers that sit in the Royal Court are little more than the ideological fuck-puppets of unbridled exploitation and deranged idiocy. If people knew their quality of life could be better, why would they accept the shit when the pandemic ends?"

It was unboundedly true that a sad life is only appealing to those with dark blinders.

"Disgusting short-minded behaviour, fit for the incessant, narcissistic psychopaths who play the games of power."

This was one of those big, generic, all-fitting political statements.

"Now, this might make a fitting base for a cure." The orange liquid had turned to a nullifying cream.

The howl of the city's underbelly could be heard from the black soot- and red blood-drenched watchtower Hawk was resting against. The magister had warned him of the seething discontent; they had watched with pity and sympathy as the masses had vibrated against the lockdown restraints, seen the heads sliced as people sought to highlight their suffering and plight.

"They like to call it a mob, a problem with people's animal instincts overcoming their sense of decency. That's bullshit. This is just the straw that broke the camel's back. It's easy to keep people distracted from their problems – everything does that – but when those core needs are hit, people start to be able to articulate the inarticulable. Well, I mean, it's articulable to us. Just not them. And again, that's not their problem."

Now Hawk saw what Aleina meant. The forticade before him had become a swollen vigil of searing flames, the crowd of lashing, jeering citizens exulting their fury and wrath. The soldiers were being roasted alive, incinerated by the people they were sworn to protect, bears slain by tormenting dogs.

The magister's voice continued, cutting with seriousness.

"Some might look upon these designs and see the mark of the ungodly; they would do well to remember the furnace of the stars. Some might even claim that they've now drawn their lot, to suffer the worst of this desiccating plot.

"Assholes, each and every one of them. It's the duty of those that know what not to do to show others how not to do it. Simple as."

*

Tyrus gasped for air. The reconnaissance mission around Yeli's back entrances was definitely, and life-threateningly, not going to plan. The previously calm granite gatehouse was in the clutches of hysterical cackles. Several strong-armed rioters were manically heaving the metal chain that separated Yelite from Yelite, their shadows cast in vicious and reckless abandon.

There was a large armed mass before him, protesting the quarantine and accosting some guards with sharp words and slivers of protruding steel. They nicked and nagged and picked at the tin-can targets. The tension was building, buzzing, rippling, sparking at the periphery of ordered civility. Electrical conduits of neurobiological flashes surged and sought between the swarm of lightning rods. The square was adorned with demands against inadequacy, the militia and milling crowd forming two bulges of pre-battle intimacy.

There was a spark amongst the bustling bundles of

tinder; an iron ingot was heaved through the air by a flesh-garbed trebuchet. It collided with a soldier and fractured his skull into a scattered eggshell.

Some of the guards saw Tyrus; they weren't from his patrol and designation, so they presumed the worse, which in all fair understandings of things was pretty accurate. They made their way to engage and rescue him while the surrounding furore caught a taste for blood. The group of five in armoured iron, with polearms, swords and shields, started to jostle their way through the blood-fuming mass. Hands swarmed them as they passed, fingers reaching out to tug, grasp and snare at these forbidders of freedom.

Just as Tyrus made his way to sneak past the mulling mass of arms and flaying grunts, he felt steel hands. He shifted quickly, slipping through them, and bounced succinctly over the wall adjacent, into the floral courtyard of a Yelian Duke. The sudden surrounding of yellow swamped his vision, sifting away the chaos and crisis just behind the wall.

The guards were quickly pulled under the congealing crowd, a thick gross mist accumulating in the atmosphere. The sharks caught their taste and descended, razor-sharp teeth lapping against metal shores, tin cans gutted for minced meat.

There was a group of swords stood before Tyrus, unsure of what to do. Did they advance on one of their own caught in an unfortunate circumstance? Or did they resolve to stick to their oath and seize him for trespassing? And what about the conflict brewing next door that they were supposedly backup for? What made the decision ever so more difficult was the morsel of a fact that they'd all drilled against him – simultaneously. They knew they didn't stand a chance.

Therefore, they just froze. However, they froze in front of the doorway of escape. Tyrus had leapt headfirst into a treacherous drop. A slack reminiscent of his descent into settled madness.

He was in no fit state to attempt to escape, and was sufficiently lacking the want to muster up a vicious crescendo.

The two house guards were pushed forwards; this was their property. The militia were here in case the rioters finally saw the sense of what they could do next. That was why the elite kept scrapping the public-led education bill. Educated people make educated decisions, which leads to educated threats and rebellion. It was much safer to leave people in a state of ignorant oppression, the violent waves of their injustices occasionally breaking through the storm barriers, than it was to allow the unwashed horde to be taught the lessons that might lead to the aristocracy's undoing. But it also made for a piss-poor collection of civil enforcers, civility being a communal experience.

Not wanting to kill his previous comrades, Tyrus offered his hands forward quickly, feeling the cold, sharp pinch of manacles.

He spotted his escape route as the house guards thanked the militia for their assistance. They would hand Tyrus over to their employer, and the militia would have no hand in Tyrus's alleged "criminality". That was a long word for walking on grass. The civil militia moved away; the two private guards were left to plan their movement on Tyrus.

Out of nowhere appeared the black-steel-glazed tank of a brick known colloquially as Hawk. Hawk's occurrence was impromptu; he'd taken the "wrong" turn, and now found himself in the middle of the commotion.

"Tyrus, what the fuck are you doing here? Why have they got you in chains like a slave? Do the pretentious pricks not value your worth this side of the property barrier?"

The two guards that clung to Tyrus like Cerberus's mortal handlers stood sheepishly and pre-wet. The stench of... maybe their fear?... was definitively overwhelming their bright garb, dampening the vivid stream of colour.

It took one sharp step forward for them both to bolt.

Hawk stepped towards Tyrus with a syncopated tut. "For fuck's sake, Tyrus. I've told you before, if you're looking for somewhere to call your home, there's land west of here, in the ancient kingdom of the Entoile." Hawk undid Tyrus's shackles. "And you can't trample on the rich people's grass; it makes them feel like commoners."

Tyrus laughed in tired contentment.

"Now let me give you a foot over, and the magister will ensure our escape from these piss-stained walls."

Hawk's head shook with the force of an earthquake, and the universe took note.

The mighty walls of Yeli finally relented their assault on Tyrus's slowly suffocating freedom, leaving him free to deal with that severe need for a piss.

(693)

Jozio was happily gazing out over the plains surrounding the city of Dzeriko. The once-burnt farmlands now blossomed with life; the ransacked hamlets and villages teemed with people unbound by the tyrannical laws that had hung over them since time immemorial. No longer were they used as slaves for the war games of the Entoile lords. No longer were they meat and bones solely left alive to labour and groan throughout the bone-strewn fields all year round.

The plague had hit them at the worst time. They were still at war, fighting the hordes of Entoile that refused to acknowledge their newly claimed fiefdom. They still only had a meagre army, the four-hundred recruits from the local villages bolstering the four hundred-strong mercenary regiment. Nonetheless, their war had been successful since the beginning. Compared to the vicious, demonic warlords that dominated this part of the west coast, Behritos's Band was an angelic horde of cleanly visceral evisceration.

This would have been their first reprieve, now that they

had finally taken the valley. It *would* have been, until the plague came.

Luckily, Tyrus was the griping bastard he usually liked to be. Having witnessed the shitshow of Yeli, he had every right. He had seen first-hand the eagerness for the palace elites to push the workers back into labour, the lack of welfare and subsistence provided, the despotic rules forcing classist death tolls, the resulting inferno of chaos and destruction as the tools of the state met with the fervent mobs.

Tyrus was adamant that the people who ran Yeli were, quite simply, quote unquote, "fucking idiots who deserved to die dishevelled on infected stakes". Jozio agreed; the Cloud Dwellers always told him everything, and even they, who were often happy to understand how people like to occasionally do people things, and who had seen the Falling of the Spires, were crestfallen and appalled.

It wasn't surprising, though, that Jozio would respond; pandemics are always social disasters, clear examples of where your society is getting things abysmally wrong. It's up to the people to look for the messages and respond, and if they don't... well, the blood's written on the wall.

This sentiment Tyrus readily agreed with, which was why he recommended calling for the Magister Aleina. Dzeriko was a smaller city – well, really a castle and decapitated settlement. Tyrus, however, was adamant that he would never see such inane, life-hating stupidity again.

Berihtos had made a comment about not wanting to be in debt to Yeli's Magisterial Order. The sentence was half out his mouth when the blade coerced it back in. Aleina arrived four days before the first case in the capital, while the plague was still moving through the villages to the north and north-west, and within another four weeks the spread had been completely stopped. Not only that, but they used the social quiet to reconstitute stability and order. They used the premonition of horror to reinstil in people a sense of social duty and care. The crowds that would have been devastated if the new state had confused or contradicted them were instead left to foster a newness of spirit, which helped them break through the toxic miasma that hung over them. That renewed their fervour for freedom from the aristocratic assholes who had previously debauched themselves and their sanctity of life.

Jozio's cohort marched into vision. Their standard had been muted and their equipment was light, yet still the glint of metal marked out their path as they passed over the plains. The expressions on his soldiers' faces were determined, grizzled and ready. Their brows split with the metallic sheen of their iron helmets. They would devastate the Entoile bandits who refused to give up their despotic and maleficent power, finally catching revenge for the soul-splitting mutilations etched on them at every damning opportunity.

The soldiers shot daggers from the hearts of their eyes.

And now they were ready for war.

ELEVEN

Ilyia awoke before him. Her eyelids slowly lifted to reveal Hawk's sleeping face, contorted by agitating tension behind his eyes. There was the rapid movement that accompanies deep prophetic thought, the encapsulating splashes of neural energy that ripple and tighten.

With a silent chortle, she shifted herself closer into his hold. By several slight incremental margins, she was eventually nested between his arms. It would still be several hours until sun-up, the end of their first great adventure, the start of their second. Soon, the sublime sight of the green-etched purple glaze would be her final prize.

Ilyia was a firm believer in absolutely nothing, and she liked to keep it that way, spending hours toiling endlessly to establish perfect equilibrium: nothing coming in, nothing going out. An existential inertia without a heavy weight.

She fancied herself dancing between the metaphysical Divine.

Regardless of whether there would be any future to her existence beyond this "inhabitance" of a life, this surreal blur of moments and eternities, memories and forgettences, lost landscapes of life, love and violence, she was happy, ready for death.

Her father had told her that her lust for destruction would eventually lead to her downfall. Maybe he would smile when he heard the news; there was no doubt he would be proud. It was a shame the war had been called so soon, as it had given her little time to say her farewells.

Perhaps she could come back as a spirit and haunt him and Mother, embrace the poltergeist and enjoy an immaterial life of imagined luxury.

Elipse and Tiana would be furious with that; just like their mother to mess up leaving for the afterlife! If there even *was* an afterlife. It was something Hawk was absent on when she poked him. He didn't really care for such thoughts, saying it detracted from the all-perfect, always present opportunity.

Maybe if she believed hard enough, there *would* be an afterlife for them, if that was the whole purpose to all the inane, esoteric rituals they performed at circumspect times of the year. Nin called it "accrued agency", but with that smile that told you he didn't really believe the words he was saying.

If the whole "metaphysical premise" of absolutely anything and everything is "the act of observation alters", then how does the universe decide on how it conforms?

It never made sense, which Ilyia suspected was the point. Perhaps that held in check the abuse of powers; if the all-knowable is unknowable, then the all-knowing was only ever unknowing: the knowledgeable left unknowledged, the more violent aspects of their existence left to simmer in the dark, dusky depths of some cold, distant pit.

If she were to expand the metaphor out, it would be as if

the First Peoples had consumed forbidden knowledge, their being chased out by Divinities from the landscape of their ascension, them then being forced to contest with God for their infinite sustenance and insurance. That would leave a truly grim and gruesome hole of a soul in that culture's expression.

Imagine believing that the very facets and alterations that existence puts on you are solely your own burden. That every action you choose, or are persuaded to choose, is fundamentally your conflict with that which created you. Every mental illness a strike from the Almighty, every issue and needed restitution a sign of weakness or previous crime, every mistake a sign of immorality, never a chance for growth. Just a feared and vengeful god.

Now, those kinds of thoughts are bound to bleed the brain.

Ilyia was forever thankful her "religious perspective", as the Krylei called the orthodox form of their spirituality, was one of life's acceptances.

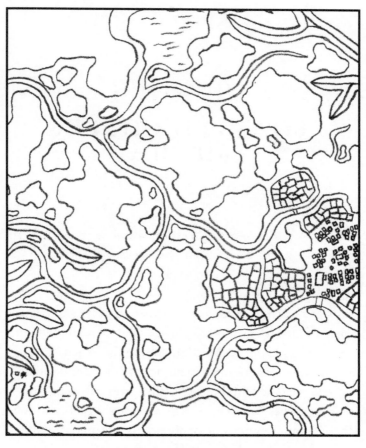

Map of Seybili's Village: "The Valley of Periol" by Arch-Sister Melodial VI, 823 PIA

THE WITCH

TOASTED CHEEKS
(618 PIA)

Good witchery is existential snitchery,
yet the Witch is always an unwilling victim.
—Krylei proverb

She was a witch. They knew it; she knew it. Every godforsaken token of life on this morbid plateau of existential stagnation knew the goddamned situation. Seybili the Witch, the Dark Sister. And it was one of unrelenting witchhood and witchery.

Are they the same concept? Who gives a flaming toss?

Sometimes stories have to have these shitty stupid stuffs. These commiserations of symbols and metaphors. Stainless similes smiling slaphappy and sardonic.

Just another piss-poor excuse for the start of a story.

Which by the way, was HERSTORY, not his. *Her*story began ages back, moons upon fucking moons past. Way before her birth. Way before the birth of her parents to this godforsaken, self-involved, inquisitor-ridden backwater of a world.

Just like everyone else, right at the star's inception. That's where her story began.

But HIStory dictates that this story begins now, with her poor attempt at self-introspection, because, well, let's face it: if you're caught in the pinch of what people believe is becoming true, and these people flock to the ley lines of collective stupidity like ants to an anteater... well, as they say, now she was well and truly a witch.

The only question was: just what the fuck was she supposed to do with it?

To which I guess the answer always is: just be witch-ever the fuck you want to be. It's pretty plain and simple.

*

Hawk was casually strolling through the meadow, his sense drifting through the after-day's deluge of thoughts. Just this one last job for the moment, and then maybe some rest. He had that other business to attend to, but that could wait. Then he could finally see Ilyia this year. They could embrace and recount their arduous adventures, physically accosting each other before resting beneath the stars.

He had been given the order from the Guild. "There is a possible 'envisaging' in the village of Eliyul."

Envisaging? What in Yggdrasil's green shimmer was that supposed to mean? The Guild had a knack for obtuse definitions. He checked his blade. He wondered how simple it would be this time.

The ensemble of birds flying overhead came to rest before

him; he drew the grain seeds from his pouch and cast them before the murderous clutches. They chirruped and chirped their praises and adorations. They flexed and ruffled their feathers with ever-loving joy and leapt back into the air to search for their next victim of footpadding.

As the vagrants scattered, Hawk's existential mist was lifted.

He caught a glance of the birds again, this time waylaying a miller for his bags of grain. Unfortunately for the miller, through clutching his pearls, they were dashed asunder, rolling far and away from him.

The scattering of grain crashed before the taxing bandits; the miller left the bag to curse with arms flailing either side. He eventually continued his trail with the other bags that were left unsplit and unshaken, lamenting his woeful circumstance.

*

A crowd of villagers were gathered in the mass hall, led by the ignorant son of a pig that was the Grande Inquisitor. They lapped up his sickle-cell postulations like haemophilia-philiacs and wheezed in exasperated fatigue. The blue tinge to their lips and faces was a curse of the light, but if she had her way, they would bear that mark of eejit-induced idiocy for eternity.

The mass hall was a large, bespoke light- and dark-brown segmented wooden structure. It lay in an elongated cross, a central tower rising from the intersection of the bars. The mass congregated in the longest hall that jutted out, the doors positioned at its extremity, facing due south. The mound the structure lay on was the barrow of a god-king long past, built by Borsi settlers as they moved into the coastline centuries ago. The cemetery was interwebbed with the various coloured stone stelae that pinpricked the ancient grove. The houses of the village began after the circle of blue-green stones that sat like teeth, grinding the dust of the universe into the dreams of the villagers.

She knew what she needed to do. She could hear their voices accusing her of false sorceries and foul crimes. Of course, she knew nothing of the sort, this starry hat arriving late in life. Her husband had first passed last winter, then her children this spring. Now she was left alone and accused... well, even more so accursed.

Perhaps if they were to burn her she would find solace? She could spend her final days preparing their recompense and making herself ready for the descent into the after plains.

She and her husband were from Youfi'sinit, the emerald city of the jewelled lake. That was probably why she faced such half-hearted attempts to vilify.

She remembered Bazin, the elderly vagrant crucified in her home village all that far away. She'd cried then, too.

She remembered Samson, who was shaved and beheaded, all because an elderly member of the village had drunkenly murmured that he shape-shifted at night. A black cat had howled at her from her bedroom window, and now Samson must pay for his curse. She had cried rivers.

This time there were no tears, which one could take as a positive sign.

At least it told her she was ready to be done.

*

Hawk hadn't been in the village for long. It was a standard affair, a normal set-up of a settlement, a motley collection of houses around a church and encircling cemetery. The job was pretty simple, too. A "witch". Whatever one of those was. Which really meant a standard search and rescue role. Minimise damage before unnecessary extensions of suffering and harm.

This was the other side of his role with the Guild. Search and rescue, from stupid-led heathenry. He was in the church's "mass hall", looking for any telltale signs of emergent Divinity. "Envisaging" meant human thought affecting other humans. He felt for the unlucky victim.

There was a face leaning from the stone pulpit that centred the church's mass hall. A crimson-cheeked, wiry-nosed face that shed more passive-aggressive detrital than the worst silting of any mudslide-befallen river.

"I, good sir, am the Grande Inquisitor, the royal dignitary deemed duty-bound to stamp out this accursed witch. WHO, I MIGHT ADD, has befouled the very nature of this village, good sir." The short, stocky frame bore a weight of empyreality, a stench of decadence, and an air of unaware that could be spotted from a mile off.

"Seybili must pay for her crimes against nature. She can turn men to mere pox-ridden rabbits. She can cast her shadow into the sky and turn any man's soul dark." The short, squat cross-section of comorbidity descended from the pulpit to stare up at Hawk. "She is a jezebel of the highest proportions! A warlock in cahoots with the devil herself! She must pay!"

It was self-evident "stupid-led heathenry". The absolute worst.

*

To think of a plan is quite an immense undertaking; to set it out in motion, a lapse of judgement often too late to rectify. To see the enflaming inferno of carnage that follows a fruitful exposition is quite blinding. Sublimely so.

Had the plan gone well? Only time could tell.

She was pretty chuffed with it all. The house was aflame, with no one inside, obviously, which would mask her escape to the cottage in the Old Forest.

The cottage was her late husband's hunting station. She had carried provisions there, tidied away keepsakes, stashed a horde of treasures she wanted to keep with her forever. There her revenge would come to fruition, and a long-cast enchantment would finally bring balance to the land. All she had to do was wait patiently, and the apples would rot on the tree branches.

She clutched her head in agony. She'd been having heavy concussive episodes since the start of this whole chaotic mess. They came again. She nearly fell to the ground.

They came periodically, but not regularly, and with increasing intensity.

She felt consciousness ebb and flow from her head.

When she passed out, she always awoke different. The same, but in a sense through a distorted lens; her inside voice subtly changing, new ones awakening. Feelings cresting a sun-kissed desert ridge.

The light was intense, burning a hole through her consciousness.

She had been walking down the street when the first concussive pains had begun. She had blacked out and fallen, and awoke mud-covered back home. Her neighbour Seli had brought her home after finding her unconscious.

"Sameis helped me with you. He's quite the charmer, you know. I was thinking of asking him to the fayre. His hair just falls just right… if you get me?"

Seli was an angel. She tended to her headache with a cold flannel and passed over a herb-tinged broth to help with the pain.

"They 'caught' another, you know."

The implication spoke more than the sentence.

"I wonder when this incessancy will end."

Loud knocks disturbed. Seli straightened her posture and smiled.

"I'll double check who that is and then be on my way. Just knock if you need anything."

Who had been at the door?

There was no recollection. Most likely no one important. No one of beneficial merit, at least.

Well, there was *definitely* no one of *any* beneficial merit by this point. Much in the same way as the dark clustering in shadows. Or how sheep mass before a wolf.

She saw a strained web of gemlike sparkles. Rhinestone eyes peered out from a glassy sheen that separated her ethereal form from the intangible singular ahead of her.

The smoke in her vision cast itself as jewel-set spheres. A hydrant of water dashed itself amidst the inflating spheres. The balloons imploded and cast their Silmarils across the twilight ocean of the stellaris backdrop.

A monstrous beast, furred, gargantuan and fanged, cast a silversmithed web across the calm sea. As the web was pulled upwards by the monstrosity, the water cast itself tempestuously, a celestial empyreality parting the waves, exposing a dirt-laced pavement.

She took a breath and stepped forward.

Her foot landed on the first shell of many. The bones of pelagic pastoralists, they paved her pathway forwards. Her steps, twinkling, spoke and beckoned roots and stems of plants to rise. As she reached the end of the divide, there was a flourishing ripple of leaves and weaving canopies. A bronze figure illuminating an inset constellation was thinly glazed across her horizon.

She went to gasp – and suffocated.

She wasn't sure what had lain before her. In true reflection, no one ever is, or was? Or will continue to be so? Most definitely.

It always worked to added effect.

She was in her house during the twilight of dusk. Her husband lay asleep in her bed next to her. She could hear her son snoring from his bedroom above. The two-storey thatched roof, which leant to just above the ground outside, was silent.

She heard movement outside. A scuttle burst through the chirps of crickets. She felt a flare, an urge to rush and respond. The itch tantalising, she pushed her covers back, slowly but stoically.

Her husband still unconscious, she moved to the ladder at the end of the corridor. She passed a lantern and lifted it from its sheath. The light magnified as she wished it so. That startled her, and she put the light out completely.

Her breath became erratic catatonically quickly; she fought the shock and leant against the wall with her free hand. As she steadied herself, the lamp relit.

She took a deep breath and continued forward, her padded footsteps drifting past her frightened awe. When she arrived at the window, she was midway between dream and wakefulness. The crescent adornment of moonlight stung her eyes, fey pixels rippling between her visions. She left the torch in the mantle, her eyes rubbing and stinging, her eyelids opening and seeing the commotion that lay before her.

A collection of forms motioned through the light underbrush's foliage. The green and brown, the muted grass, shed its colour as the pink and purple enchantment wove up to Seybili. She felt herself, her vision contorting, the pink and purple resonance imbuing her shaded sight with gaseous whirls. A noxious sweetness simmered, turning from pungent to pastured. The harsh reverberating tinnitus intruding upon her skull shifted to the soft, padded inflections of sibilant wisdom.

The cacophony of being that burst forth from the forest floor serenely simmered as its chaos was strewn across foliage and fauna. The intrusion of a mid-drift of teal-spotted deer provoked the free-flowing folk of viscous abstraction to merge and meander. The rough-hewn pixelated extensions melded into dissipation, immersing within the pink-purple ripples. The ripples evaporated into an emerald ethereal mist, the pointillistic proposition returning to an eternal, blood-drenched, flesh-entombing room.

*

Nin, the Last Brightscale, was playing with a set of marbles, his scaled physique sprawled across the floor – a stance befitting his noble, esteemed, transcendent being. Hawk was still new to his apprenticeship, so he was wary of aggravating the smoke-churning dragon who strode amongst the mortals of Yeli.

Nin threw a couple over to Hawk. "Come and try this game, if you would like to."

Two marbles clattered.

"Mundanity breeds revelation."

Then several more.

Intrigued, Hawk wandered over.

The marbles didn't appear to be in any kind of magical structure. Nothing of symbolic merit was obvious to him. He grabbed one, and carefully threw it into the pile.

The scatter of marbles, the gentle chime of rebounding resonances, attracted a smattering of mice-seers. They scampered over, clutching their troves of tea leaves, cheese and crackers, borne in linen hampers.

"Is there a point to this game?"

The curiosity-bound question was left with nothing but laughter. Nin refused to acknowledge the premise. Instead, he flicked three marbles; the ensuing ricochet formed a semi-circle. With two more, the circle broke into a flight of velocities.

Nin spoke six words as he cleaned up the mess. He spoke another "wise mantra" before dinner: "Is there a point to life?"

Hawk was vexed.

"Years from now, people will 'discover' that the fabric of the universe talks to itself beyond our ability to perceive communication. The only thing they'll really discover is that truth is fundamentally relative."

They had oven-baked chicken for dinner, the smell lingering.

*

The smell of oven-baked chicken stank through the Grande Inquisitor's stolen accommodation. Hawk was stamping his foot with nervous agitation.

"So you think the witch can do what?"

The pause threatened to smack the fucker between the teeth.

"And how many people did you get to believe this gobshite?"

The cloak-clad conjurer was oblivious to any other premise. "We're sending a mob to her tonight. We'll drag her from that accursed rest and burn her. Whatever problem you envisage, *Guildman*" — the moniker was spoken with a deluge of disdain — "this will be finished by tomorrow's blood moon. Which I think is very auspicious."

He smiled a sickening smile. Hawk was ready to convulse.

*

Nin's tower was powered by a marvellous feature. Hawk always drew the image to him in times of stress. Nin was older than pretty much everyone; it was a well-undocumented fact of Nin's life and background. Nin was most likely older than anyone was even able to conceive of. Anyone capable of conceiving the depth of Nin's causality had either already been and gone, or would come too late to see Nin's shadow... well, all except the Dragon Riders' silent ethereality, whose refusal to participate rendered them a shadow.

Which was the backdrop to Nin's fabulous "Meritor", as referred to by its creator. It highlighted what Nin called the "Fundamental Ontological Truth", with earmarks and capitalisations and fistfuls of smirk-shaped glee. In reference, his eyes twinkled, and it spoke of his genius that he had accurately drawn the truth for Hawk.

Not linguistically; Nin was too clever for that. Instead, the feature itself demonstrated the essential truth to the universe.

The tower was unspeakably high, and immeasurably deep, conditions allowed for by some mystical enchantment that Nin referred to as the mind-bending magic of mass. It started with the tower's top, which burst through charted dimensions into the atmosphere, allowing an immaterial access to the cloud realm.

Clouds would come and go, passing through the wind tunnel at the tower's top. There they would depart messages and gossip for Nin, taking in news from the bowls of water left every morning at dawn. The trickles would cascade and collect, forming translucent pools of pearlescent wisdom that were stacked between the octagonal internal tower's chambers. From the pools they formed waterfalls, each moving to the next layer to collect before descending, collecting, descending.

They finally accrued at the base of the tower, where a pool was dug beneath the final floor of the internal tower. Past the waterfalls were bridges and honeycomb rooms, webbed and interwoven into the external tower.

The pool descended deep, into the dark murky depths of the eternal deep waters, where small pipes and relay systems drew the synthesis, returning it to the bowls of water stationed inconceivably high above.

Hawk had asked why Nin used such a complicated system to return water back to itself, for the Cloud Dweller's own amusement.

Nin had laughed his laugh, the one that told Hawk he would never really hear the answer, because "the search for truth is just as important as the dust it upturns".

But this time Nin spoke as well, huddled over a bench writing a list of ingredients needed from the bazaar. "Amusement is the highest form of potential…" He moved over to his library and pulled out one of his arcane maps, a large tan leaf marked with silver-blue ink. "… in a world where power begets power."

Nin put the page in front of him. The drawings on it reminded Hawk of the tea leaf trances of the mice-seers that Nin raised and revered.

The sheet showed the cycle of rain from the oceans through to the mountains. Then vice versa, in the journey of rain and rivers. Trace lines showed the various orders of Divinity the process moved through and steeped in life.

"Idle amusement is the motion of the universe."

Hawk had gained a greater respect for the Mice-Seers that were left to freely wander Nin's tower. He had always loved them, their kind and compassionate nature reverberating with Hawk's own. But it had always eluded Hawk as to why Nin used them to commune with the higher Divinities; why he would sit and shush those older than the tranquil times, all for the faint outline of a tea-induced tail trace.

Now he knew.

He just hoped the poor witch didn't.

*

Fortunately, she didn't.

Organic wisdom has a tendency for cultivating its own crops. Yggdrasil flowers in its own place. Ripples of rambling flourishing.

They arrived at the front door of the cottage en masse, pitchforks and torches in hand. The sheer image of destruction was mirrored in the searing inferno of their eyes. The pre-eminent desolation of their deity burnt through the dense existential dread clutching at their souls, flesh succumbing to flame, motion mirroring meditation – soon to be satiated with her blood-boiling screams.

Seybili didn't stand a chance. The traps her husband had taught her had taken their toll as the mob marched towards her rabbit hole. Several of the crowd limped, ligaments sliced and diced; some had fallen into the pit stakes she'd set, while others lay suffocated in the riverbed, legs caught in buried bear traps.

This only inflamed the fervourish fever of the fanatics into further fury. Alliteration to offset devastation.

She was drenched, shivering and shit-scared.

They splintered the door, chanting a vicious phrase. The crescendo of the chorus peaked as their torches caught the padded walls of the hut. Unrepeatable, it rolled in perpetual echo around her skull. Her hiding place was not. It was only time. Her legs tremored in anticipation. Shakes shook, followed by the unspeakable. Then the hands came, hoisting her up by her hair. It strained and shed as she lurched.

Thankfully, blackness.

But from the blackness there came a deeper void, one of recurring envelopment, folding the fabric of the universe ever inwards into itself in star-smote Möbius-forging fury.

The eye without sight sat there beaming its blue-green hue of pelagic wisdom. The coral reefs that accrued were obsidian mazes of objection and resolution; eyelashes of Eternia. And she was caught amidst them. Stranded. Netted now to sit before the crucible of the cosmos.

The dreamer's eye said something or other, all things carried in reflection of its utterance.

Their utterance?

Our. The tone was irrelatively absolute.

The seashore shell nebula was cast before her feet, the coral maze now a rise of petrogenic chorus. The ensemble bode her to step and shimmy, sway and centre further afield, find stepping-stones where there were none.

The ephemeral suggestions of "words" came and went. Their meaning registered without occurrence or existence.

Next to her was a smouldering… no, that was wrong… half-shadow, barely visible.

Spoken without speaking, she wheeled away from the voices, but not the speech without, and found her form dissipating into the twilight-speckled diamond of existence. She awoke to the fevered pitch of dissonance and terror, candlelight and wick spoken for; her time was sifting like the brown-tan sands that gall us all.

They dripped mercurially.

They had tied her to the stake at sun-up. The Grande Inquisitor had stood there, watching for a milieu, looking like a head-to-toe toss pot. Hawk spat on the ground in disgust.

The ground spat back with a slap of mud as a cart pushed its way through the crowd around him. The jostle and bustle of onlookers waiting to savour the execution disgusted Hawk. He had hoped the mob wouldn't have gathered; he had hoped his plan had bought him more time. Instead, only a few had listened to his words; others had corrupted his offering and turned it into a parable.

So now he stood in lieu of any righteous course of action left to take.

He was aware he was slowly and surely becoming a philanderer. The only cost would be this poor woman's life, consigned to death through idolatrous thought. It was hard becoming a focal point of the universe's whim, especially when it was handed out on the delicate sword-edge of inane naivety.

Rightfully so, she was straining against the ropes; he could see the readied look of death. The executioner, black hood on his head, lit the torch that would assign her soul to the Sleeping God's realm.

Then came the clamour. A chaotic cluster. A cacophonic cloister assembled from those normally too blood-shy to see the death of their loved ones. Well, too blood-shy to *rejoice* in the death of their loved ones. Well, rejoice IN death.

Hawk's pedantictry ceased as he noticed the flash of steel. As the Inquisitor's small militia met the crowd, several hands flashed towards the sun-marked books they bore. A dark iron-shine of a dagger emerged and entered the neck of the militia commander. The blade point waved from its exit hole, bathed in gurgling floods.

The militia began to shout, to close their meagre ranks around their stricken commander and ensure the Inquisitor's safety.

The crowd continued to rage against the squadron; they began to mob and ripple against the onlookers, longer blades emerging from the centre of the mass.

The unarmed "rejoicers" fell like a flock of lambs to the slaughter.

*

"We can get you a new name, if that's any help?"

The silence in the air dictated careful stepping, each sentence a shallow stone away from slurring into cold, clammy, damning water. Plus every parasite that accompanied such a disdainful slip.

"It seems a shame that you got left with this mark. But it doesn't have to be the end of existence as you knew it."

The face opposite was an etching of existential disgust. Blue-black rockface jutted coldly out from her, vilified expression burnt into the exposed sneer, all carrying the thick, choking pollution of the attack and attempt on her life.

"I'm sure you've realised that most of your personality changes were the intense effects of the kind of existential concussion this stuff brings along for the ride."

She stood clutching her head. Blood dripped from several slice-marks across her arms; the binds around her wrists had been too tight, leaving severe rope-burn blisters in their wake.

"What I'm trying to say is, you don't have to kill anyone with your new abilities. The spiel they were saying about you is the wet dream of that Grande Inquisitor."

Hawk spat on the floor.

"So you're not really a demon consigned to a life of hell."

The "witch" Seybili looked at Hawk. Violence shone from her eyes. "You think I didn't know that?"

She paused as her caged frustration snipped the lock and

flipped the latch out into the gnawing abyss. "Those scum-sucking assholes deserved to die. They deserved every drop of pain I wished upon their souls."

She paused and sneered at the universe's unfairness.

"After the despoiled horrors they unleashed against us, me, every last soul they hounded and persecuted... they deserve to burn in the deepest depths of soul-extinguishing decimation."

The precursors to tears were forming around Hawk's eyes.

"And yet you decided to stop it."

Seybili looked at him with a smouldering arsonism. Her tongue licked her lip with strained aggrievance, agitation biting through the tense corners of her mouth. "The noble hero turned up, just at the right moment to spare the life, so sacrosanct and sacred."

Her eyes penetrated Hawk's armour, casting jagged slices across his heart and soul. "To stop karmic justice rebalancing. Stopping the pain and suffering that those vile, disgusting, woman-burning, shit-stains deserved."

She broke down, collapsing in tears, falling to the floor.

Hawk approached her sheepishly. He attempted some thoughts of conciliation. "Travel with me to Ristos. I'll take you to safety; my wife will give you a place of haven until this all blows over. This doesn't have to be the way this story ends. I mean, this 'narrative' they've written for you is just conjecture by this point."

Seybili's eyes shone with the revelatory destruction that all devas undergo, grey, enchanted skin bubbling under her horizon.

She resolved to shack up in the lawless mountains, to place stepping-stones where the souls are shorn.

*

Hawk always enjoyed watching the leaves fall to the ground. The journey to Ristos was being trodden at a slow saunter. He was lonesome and speculating on the metaphysical essence of being, or as he liked to call it, "the deep shit".

The leaves always reminded him of the black-blue ink-stained skin of the Lightning Riders. Their tattoos mimicked the nerves in the body, tracing the lines in imitation of their brave forebears, struck by lightning and eternally scarred.

Once Nin had dissected a brain in front of him, one of a Yeli artist who had donated his body to Nin's practice. Nin had shown Hawk how the brains of "mammals" were built of nerve structures, too. Infinite strings of substrata upon substrata connecting memories, feelings, premonitions and activity; the "mnemonic-neural network", as Nin called it. Nin had used bottled lightning to show how different parts of the body moved with different plucks of the harp string.

Hawk was always reminded of them by the leafless tree canopies. Looking up into the interwebbed mesh of sense comprehension had that air of motion behind perception.

Hawk continued walking. His stride would allow him to watch the wagon rest by nightfall. There he could hitch a ride up to the city of Yeli.

He had heard of Nin's passing on his journey up to the village and had decided to ensure the woman's safety before the trek to Nin's internment. He had been told to expect some surreal requests, and that there would be assistance from Nin's apprentice. Was it the same apprentice as last time? He hoped not; that one had been particularly amoral and fetishistic. Not a good mix in the slightest, especially for a short, stout, bald man.

He laughed, wondering what issue Nin was going to haemorrhage his existence with. It was never often much; maybe rescue a dragon, lay to rest a barrow-lich, unearth an arcanium. Hawk's laughter ricocheted through the fine-barked, interspersed willow thicket, the sound an immanence in crescendo.

*

Nin was stood before a pile of shattered ceramics. They were fused beyond Hawk's ability to disassemble them, a trick that Nin did to pass the time. Hawk was still tasked with cleaning up the mess.

"Come on, Hawk, hurry up, you've got better things to dream about tonight than this mess that won't undo."

Hawk was bemoaning his Herculean task. Atlas shrugged, and Hawk caught, the apple of his eye the time he was after. "And why have I got to put this contraption away for the thirteen billionth time this year?"

Hawk's eyes rolled in perpetual motion, swinging with pendulum-struck simplification. The dull gong of midnight came.

"It's important that you respect that no problem is unsolvable; you've just got to be aware of how the rules are set before you."

Hawk was lamentably gobsmacked. This "process" of "ascending" that Nin was adamant Hawk undertake was stomach-splittingly laughable.

Normally, Hawk would have to wait till Nin fell asleep

before the concentration spell disappeared, or wait until his attention was elsewhere for the briefest moment. However, this time Hawk had thought ahead; he was hoping that Nin was going to be taking the last few steps before the hastily constructed trap. The classic brick on a step trick. Well, the brick above the doorway, more importantly.

The shattered ceramics may have blinked for a strong minute. Hawk didn't.

TWELVE

Violence is the price of our universe;
love our unexpected reward...
—A Mino-Inyipi psalm

Ilyia remembered the words vividly; they rolled from Jozio's tongue at every opportunity, often accompanying the sheer consumption of alcohol. One poured down, the other stormed up, in the wake of a cat's cradle.

She smiled, catching the corner of her ear. Ilyia loved violence, revelled in its glory, rejoiced in splintering shields, battering maces, heady breaths, gnashed grunts. It was nearly better than sex. Nearly. It was safer than hunting, although nothing beat the noted feats of her prowess with lance and spear.

It was her sublime *objet petit a*, the uncoming object of her unbridled desire; well, it came, in deep libidinality, in furious sentiments. Ilyia's laughter resonated deliciously. It came often enough when she wanted it, her furiosity knowing no bounds. But not often enough. Especially now that she had entered the baritone of her existence, stood before the last sublime precipice, beneath her undulating bass.

A voluminous base of bass, both figuratively and literally. Her base to be scraped from when the coming violence ceased. She shuddered. The itch spread across her back. Then would come the love, for a longer time to come.

Enough to justify the cost and sacrifice. Long enough to justify the lives to be drawn red.

Ochre red bled across the valley's crass bare-backed spine.

The protruding scapula would hide her forces; in the swathe of the deep rolling back would lie their enemy. Behind that would lie Hawk and his chosen few, stationed in the coccyx, to strike at the enemy commander's ass, and hopefully bring about the fall, rear-guard butchered and command structure fallen.

Although she too would fall on the frontlines.

And then would come the consequence of their last and slow-burning come-under-them conundrum.

"Every scar's a glimpse of growth;

"Every teardrop's the fossil of fools."

Her soldiers were out in front of her, spread across the spaces between their assorted pitched tents, readying their sweat-tempered weapons and lovingly maintaining their armour for the coming warfare. They would fare well, the shimmers of campfires illuminating their faces and futures.

She could see the coarse collection of cuts and burns, wounds and slices, covered and patched. She could see the edged veterancy held above her warriors' heads, exposed by flickering firelights.

The best of the best, she had brought here. They were the

ones who had volunteered for this fool's folly to the edge of the realm of the living. A prompt offering of three thousand heads, six thousand hands, and a surplus of serrated weaponry, steeled armour, and pre-emptive protection.

The local soldiers were scattered further between the valley's curtain call, ready to mop up the fleeing troops when the slaughter ceased. Then Yeli would fall from the foul fallacies of fools. She was glad she wouldn't see that day.

She bellowed orders, and her soldiers moved with vicious efficiency, deftly boding the time to come. They were organised succinctly and sharply, their footfalls denoting sharp steps towards chivalric intent, demon-goddess anointed at the helm. They marched into, and abreast, their raised-rock precipice, overlooking the massed Valestian forces. A sea of deep blue and purple rich sin loomed before them, spun by the candlewick-thin thread of causality.

Ilyia stood aloft, first and foremost, holding her dragonstone-inlaid horn. She blew, hearing the harsh staccato march of her heart.

"When night comes all colour's a facade. Bright torches show, don't starve."

The soldier's song was woven into the sky. The clamour, honey-dipped, traced into the atmosphere.

The clouds rippled with chilled anticipation. The water buzzed, thin vapour charged with frosted tension.

Map of Ilyia's Stronghold: "A Jade Strewn Valley" by Ilyia of Nostos, 639 PIA

THE HAWK

STEMS OF THYME
(325–737 PIA)

Ilyia was energetically adverse. Cantankerously spriteful.

It suited her well; she found her crown of thorns fitting delightfully. Dressed in ceremonial attire, a long flowing white dress that gracefully swept the atmosphere, she found her fury culminating in malicious bac-drifts shifting past the court room courtier assemblage. The evening was successfully boring, sweating with elegant eloquence. Here, soon would be the end of boring speech and her chance to escape.

She couldn't even bring herself to pay attention; the farming rites and rituals were a shoddy display of her father's humour. How better to celebrate the fertility of the fields than to stand in dullness, dressed to decorum, and stripped of festivity. All the while, Father would be out drinking and hunting with Mother.

Ilyia was left to ensure the courtiers tallied the crops and margins and settled the court's out-of-court expenses. "It builds the moral character and fibre of those wretched barbarians," smirked her father, to his wife's blushed gestures.

It left them alone to do whatever they wanted, wherever they wanted. Absolutely anything, absolutely anywhere.

It was ghastly, disgusting. Foul and indecent.

Ilyia noticed Vice-Chancellor Pesii close his speech on the future of the "wool crop", to the wide snicker of the crowd.

A cough was announced from her lips. "Perhaps we'll settle this another time." She pointed to the door firmly. "Father appreciates your work today on managing the estates; I'll express my high esteem of your work and discussions. May the night bless you all."

The courtiers were half-responsive, petrified by the tedium and dire-lectic. They shook crumbs and cobwebs from their dullardly grey clothes and furniture. The strain to raise up from furniture continued the tenor and tone of Pesii's speech.

Ilyia's gestures became ever more affirmative, her shrug and point carrying the gruelling eight-hour slog of a day forwards in their beam and bear. Importance is dependent on an instant's relativity. "Please... I still have the offerings to Yggdrasil to attend to." A fitting lie.

Her foot tapped as the last of the yawning, zombified courtiers bid their elaborate goodbyes and profuse gestures; Ilyia turned to escape the tedious air of the redwood adorned court, passing the gold-inlaid doorway through to the walls. The night rays burst from the moon, through the cloud-webs, and down across the twilight setting.

Below her in the gateway sat a messenger on his great

wolf. A red-purple cross patch told Ilyia he was from the south-west hold of White Vale. His left arm was bleeding, a snapped arrowhead tourniqueted. The journey had worn him to the bone, his paled complexion pallid and weary.

"There's more, there was a farm burnt down by Entoile slavers. It wasn't strictly Krylei, but it was..."

The messenger drew the paper from his pouch. "It was Ishni's estate. They killed her and her husband Jiha, the Altai. We couldn't find their child. Her father demands bloodshed; I kind of agree with him, and I think Bastion will agree too. They're already mustering forces ready to butcher the Slave City."

Bastion was her father's nickname, fitting his titanic proportions and steadfast loyalty. Ishni and Jiha were familiar names to Ilyia, from tales that lay beside her bedside, entwined within the thick velvet-knitted book she read often and avidly. They were heroes of the Ice Age Accord, the war with the Winter Titans and their roaming glaciation three hundred and sixty years ago.

The Slave City was a crude epithet for Azirn, the home of horrors and foul, debauched sorcery that the scum-sucking Entoile had erected in the penultimate culmination of their pilgrimage. Their final shrine had been a blood ziggurat dedicated to Azga. It had stood for less than a year.

This would begin the next war. Ilyia knew it.

She awaited the rush and joy. *I wonder if Father will let me join him?* She was optimistic. *For the journey, at least?*

The pox of a city was now a burning scorch-mark on the parched page of history, a fiery papyrus post-palimpsest incineration. There would never be any more meaning here, salt assured. Ilyia was enjoying herself most thoroughly,

337

licking the flames with her lips, deep in blessed appreciation.

They had freed the slaves, recovering the appropriate supplies from the behemothic settlement that housed their torture. Then they had lit the buildings and said a prayer to Fyios. Under the Fire Light's Divine smith, the Slave City was no more.

The land was finally free from its name, burden and torture. Now the slaves were given a choice; they would journey back to Ristos and settle under the Krylei's stars, or they could have freedom. The child, though, was nowhere to be found. To lose one so young left a sombre resonance amongst the adults gathered in tributary mourning; Ilyia herself was a similar age, a familial reminder of an awful tragedy.

*

Ilyia was lying across the forest floor, entwined within grass vines that sublimed her being deep into the canopy's heartbeat. Soon the end to her day of luxury would come, spent reclining and enjoying the shine of the sun in abundance. Then would come her ascent to adulthood, her last steps as a youth. The ascension to a higher order of having no clue; no knowing or knowledge would be revealed to her. But she'd get to stab something up. She grinned officiously. That would be the experience to savour.

Red-crested and purple-breasted butterflies fluttered from her form as she rose. In one flush flourish, she pinched and plucked her sword from its tender rest. She skipped through the clearing towards home, several deer joining her for the journey. They skipped alongside her, jaunting off occasionally to nuzzle flowers and tear at protrusions of sweet green leaves.

Sadly, the burgundy deer had departed by the time she left the forest periphery, leaving her to hit the sea of red, yellow, blue and lilac flowers alone. The sweeping meadow was a cornucopia of blossoms, gracefully expanding out over several gentle, rolling hills until it touched the rising hillscape.

She could make out her father's keep on the horizon, tucked away under the overshadowing pass they called Green Horde. This was partially in reference to the green-skinned folk that were Ilyia's ancestors, but mostly to the lush, overflowing verdancy. Once-mighty warriors and builders of the Urm'gil empire, they had gathered here before the unification with the other, once separate "species", who were all now collectively known as Krylei.

She reached the precipice into Green Horde, and, true to form, the verdant Shangri-la of flora and fauna was brimming with energy and sun-searching salutations. She arrived at the roof of sunflowers that perched over the pathway up to the stronghold. Their brown seeds embraced her as she set forth up the ascent. They sprinkled soft expressions of good luck and prosperity, fortuitous tidings to illustrate her soon ascension.

Ilyia was stuck deep in contemplation; she'd heard mention from one of the attendants that Nin was passing by on Yeilish, the Free-Scaled. To arrive to her task as a zephyr between cloud-tops piqued her sublime fantasy.

This would be a truly tantalising test. She wondered what monstrous beast she would wrestle to the ground, decapitate, eviscerate, smite with the omnipotent force of her being, emancipate the agency bound into malformed maliciousness.

Her lips salivated in sweet anticipation.

This would be her first triumph as an adult; at the age of eighteen, it was her rite of passage, her tumble through the turbulence of personal growth, her first footsteps into the ethereal state of adulthood, an intangible quality Ilyia was pretty sure didn't exist. Yet, it gave her the excuse – nay, demanded her perseverance. Her dedicated stride into potential oblivion, to emerge fresh-faced, rosy-cheeked, and maybe even bruised.

Purple suited her spectacularly, even if those "uncultured" might deem it unfitting. Purple and black, and maybe a few slips of red.

She saw herself, tousled hair and exasperated expression, stood above a titan's body, foot clamped into its jugular.

Food was tasty tonight, she noticed on her seventh mouthful.

She was speechless and thoughtless when the Dragon arrived. It wasn't as big the dragon cities, but still, it was titanic. Bigger than titanic; few words could express the magnitude of the beast that she would soon be riding aboard. She was welcomed atop the winged god by her father's friend Ashae. He was a renowned explorer and monster slayer, famous for leading the war against Azga, or so he was oft to say. The back of the dragon was large enough to house a fortress, but instead Ilyia found a small tent settlement, red-, yellow- and orange-adorned tents everywhere to be seen, each marked with their own individual family sigils, clan associations, business signs.

It was strange to Ilyia to think that these people had existed before any of her ancestors had even been born.

Before she could find herself drenched in existential

depravity, the ringing gong was sounded for dinner. She licked her lips in anticipation. *I wonder what dragons eat.*

It turned out, absolutely everything.

Her eyes lapsed across the large tent; they were feasting to Tael'gar, as Dragon Rider rite demanded, in honour of his final wisdoms and judgements of Azga. The tent was brimming with dragonkind, or Draco Eternilis, as they called themselves. They sat each in their garish and bright garments. They laughed deeply and soporifically, a sense-dulling smog permeating between jokes and anecdotes.

Nin's hand nudged her arm. "Go and take a rest outside. I forgot to mention: you might suffer from severe lightheadedness if you stay in a room with our vapours too long." He coughed. "Maybe even death."

Nin went to beckon his student over to help her to her quarters, but she refused quickly and politely. Her hands feigned a strong "no".

"I think it's probably best I go by myself… I don't think I can." She clutched her head for repose.

Nin smiled in affirmation and shook her hand. He wished her tranquil dreams and infinite rest.

She couldn't remember making it to her tent, but she awoke feeling clear-headed. She checked she was dressed – yes. She peered outside the tent to gauge the time. She was late. Shit up Azga's creek!

She heard Ashae's voice call out; they were nearly there, at the base of Abyi's Ridge. She snatched up her pack and grabbed her sword belt. With a zephyr gust she shot out of the tent and straight towards the descent ladder they had tied to the dragon. Ashae was stood there smiling, naginata in hand. "I hope you've enjoyed your stay with us, heroic one;

341

we'll see you soon. Good luck slaying the beast; we all have confidence in you."

She descended with headstrong determination, ready to face the oncoming challenge with all her blood-fantasising heart.

"Hawk, watch where you're trying to fall off. If you do that again, I'll let you plummet to your nigh-conceived death."

A yelp was followed by shame.

"Foolish spool…"

*

The blue-pricked mountains of the Giant Kingdom were Ilyia's destination. She had left Green Horde stronghold the week before last and was just about to leave the territory of Ristos to enter the political arena of the Giant Kingdom… aptly named because it was both giant, and obviously for the giants.

Ilyia was off to meet her newest trainer, to do time with the martial lords of the West Giant Fiefdom, Ulgyui. They were renowned for their fighting prowess and their strategies in their border wars against the Entoile Empire, when it had existed. Now Ilyia would be sent to learn from them as her role as next warchief demanded. She might even engage in a few scuffles along the Giant—Rekilli border.

The valley Ilyia was hiking through was an overflowing snow-kissed garden. Thick blossoms of flowers and trees adorned the descent into the valley's centre. Bounding deer and rabbits, birds, badgers, wolves and lynx cubs, all of them blended into, and padded and bounced about, the valley as she finished her trek for the day.

She would make camp soon and rest beneath the stars, although she wouldn't be able to witness the Dead Wife. Which was a shame; the story reminded Ilyia of the kind of person she wanted to be: passionately dedicated.

Several frost-white deer crept up to her, emerging from a thick blanket of snow, warm noses nuzzling her with a grim, stank breath.

"Are there wolves nearby?" Ilyia inquired.

They told her no with wide joyful eyes. One grabbed a clump of Ilyia's fur coat with their teeth and began tugging.

"Okay, you've got me. I'll do whatever you want." Ilyia had always been easily swayed to do the things she wanted to do, a skill she never wanted to lose.

They led her further into the mountain pass, bringing her upwards from the valley indent. The atmosphere chilled, and static cold began to cling to her clothes. Her skois-fur coat was notoriously thick, but the particles were thicker, their masses and sheets conducting frost above ground into seas of permanently chilling.

They travelled for about half an hour, her feet growing weary and cold. Then she saw the break in the snow, and the small, exposed grey-white rock face.

The deer led her further down into the opening.

The grove was abundant with rich, sprinkling flowers. Pollen drifted from waterfalls of yellows, reds, purples and pinks. Cascades of greens and oranges clustered in corners of the crevice that the grove was carefully nurtured within.

There was a sibilant river sliding through the split rock-face, leading to the centre of the crevice/cavern's interior. Sitting by its trailing side were scatterings of trees and bushes, several deer, rabbits, badgers and other animals. Birds and

343

insects buzzing, and frogs ribbiting, all gathered around the settled and sublime shine of life, bringing flora and water into life-dipped harmony.

The sound of miniscule cascades of trickles across the stone face told her several streams and springs rolled through the warm cavern. The heat was subtle, but softer than the despoiling cold outside; the soft glow of being thriving.

There in the centre, as well, was something Ilyia had never seen before.

The Grove Divinity radiated bands of phosphorescent green. Fluorescent yellow wove itself through each banded ring to create an eternal sense of motion. Void-stepping butterflies flittered around, between, and throughout itself. Sparkling refracted essences glistened and gleamed in a shiver-inducing presence.

Words dripped from its mouth as it caught Ilyia's gaze.

W H Y – A R E – Y O U – H E R E ?

Ilyia shifted her feet nervously. The soft braying breath of the deer surrounded her.

"The deer brought me. I thought it was essential to follow them."

The silence was unescapable. Ilyia wasn't sure whether this would be a blessing or a curse.

T H A T – S E E M S – U N N E C E S S A R Y.

Ilyia's mouth spoke too soon, "Why so? Is it not where joy is found?"

A slow pause.

E A C H – T O – T H E I R – O W N.

Her nervousness continued between slowly unchattering teeth, the previous cold strain leaving its mark about her shoulders in ripples of rolling frost. The butterflies exaggerated the anxious tone of her stomach. "Who are you? I mean, if I can use the word who, or you… or really, *what* are you?"

The question was left adrift in the empty space between her and the fluctuating flow of Divinity.

W E – E X I S T – A S – C O N S E Q U E N C E S – O F – O U R S E L V E S.

It took her a long time to parse the meaning.

"That's not very helpful." Ilyia paused quizzically. She was pretty certain that was a rule of thumb true of everything. "What do you mean by that?"

W E – A R E – L I V I N G – R E P R O D U C T I O N S – O F – O U R – A N C E S T O R S – A N D – O U R – O W N – J O U R N E Y S. A L W A Y S.

Ilyia thought of her response more carefully, her mouth holding its tongue. "So you are just the grove's life, emerging as it's grown?" The birds and animals were busy around her, biting at leaves, chattering energetically and dabbling amongst themselves as animals do so naturally.

W E – A R E – U L T I M A T E L Y – T H E – R E F L E C T I O N – O F – E V E R Y T H I N G – T H R O U G H – I T S E L F.

Ominous and auspicious rolled into one.

"As in, everything that has existed?"

W E – A R E – E V E R Y T H I N G – T H R O U G H – I T S E L F.

"No, no, I mean, do you have a start and an end?"

N O W – A N D – A L W A Y S.

Ilyia fought hard to not cradle her incoming headache.

This was getting nowhere slowly, as tedious as a turtle towing torment. This was dull, blindingly, torturously, *painfully* slow.

BELIEF–IS–THE–FOUNDATION–OF–
EFFECT. ACTION–IS–
THE–MANIFESTATION–OF–BELIEF.

Ilyia readied herself for more arcane musings.

"So you're saying that you're just another life force that's popped into existence?" Ilyia had slain the emergent Divinities that were befouled by people's naïve causes; had fought the corrupted manifestations that plagued guilt-ridden settlements. Although, she thought tantalisingly, when she was old enough, she would began truly exploring.

IN–KNOWING–HOW–YOU–WANT–
TO–ACT–BEFORE–YOU–DO–IT.

This would only get more absurd, with little acknowledgement of her voice; however, the grove was a rare warmth between frostbitten mountain peaks, the green-yellow blossoming extensions of verdancy carrying fired comfort.

"That doesn't really help me any more than anything else you've said."

The grove's fireflies danced above the ponds. The green-blue water was fed by streams trickling gently from their cavern sides.

THAT–IS–THE–DIFFERENCE–
BETWEEN–BRIGHTNESS–AND–
DARKNESS. YGGDRASIL–WATCHES–
THROUGH–EVERYTHING.

Ilyia was officially nonplussed, and caught the eye of a deer, beckoning them with her twinkling moons. "The emerald ethereal watcher?"

THEY–ARE–AN–INESCAPABLE–
BLACK–VOID.

346

Ilyia fed the deer some of the berries she was half-mindedly plucking from a branch. "That doesn't seem particularly positive of them."

THEY–ARE–OUR–INESCAPABLE–BLACK–VOID–BLESSING–US–WITH–LIFE.

"That just seems depressing." She stroked the deer's ear, and it shivered with delight, its back legs shimmying with pleasure and enjoyment.

THEY–GRANT–EVERYTHING–SALVATION–INDEFINITELY.

"But what about the deer? Do they not get a say?" The deer looked at her, doe-eyed and appreciative.

SALVATION–IS–SOMETHING–YOU–FIND–FOR–YOURSELF.OR–YOU–NEVER–FIND–AT–ALL.

"That seems a bit cynical. I'm not sure I appreciate your liturgy." Several rabbits clustered at her feet, their grey-and-white fur stained with pollen and grass smears.

DZOVE–WAS–A–FIRST–PEOPLE–FARMER–LONG–BEFORE–THE–FIRST–SPIRE.

"I don't think I've heard this story." There was a sweet sibilant call of birdsong that harmonised above her. "That was before my time." Several snow-feathered birds had joined her harassment, pestering her with pecks and prods, their plumage shimmering with ancestral care and concern.

HE–WAS–KNOWN–TO–BE–A–DEVOUT–FOLLOWER–OF–THE–ROCK–DWELLER–TYAIS'JYOR.

The trickle of the stream across the uncarved rock etched

347

through the soundscape, resonating an atmospheric presence through their shared communal space.

THE – FIRE – LIGHT – FYAS' KUI – INCINERATED – DZOVE'S – CROPS.

Ilyia wasn't surprised by this turn of events. The Fire Lights were a notorious subsection of primordial cosmology that were highly regarded as vicious, malicious, obnoxious assholes. There was no single word that suitably described the stain on existence that marked their passing. Well, except maybe "fuck".

DZOVE – DIDN'T – CARE – AND – NEITHER – DID – TYAIS' JYOR.

"He didn't care that his crops had been destroyed? What would he eat?"

I – THINK – HE – SAID – THAT – HE – WOULD – HAVE – TO – FIND – MORE – FERTILE – LAND.

"That's obvious."

AND – WITH – THAT – A – NEW – GOD.

The deer and rabbits paused their nibbling. Ears pricked, they awaited the coming sign of deathly despair.

"So what did eventually happen, then?"

Ilyia was trying half-heartedly to coax her companions back into restitutive healing. The mood of the story seemed abruptly juxtaposed to their dinner.

DZOVE – LEFT – AND – WAS – HAPPY.

"Well, good for him." Ilyia cared more for the hunger of her new comrades than the ancient hunger of a pre-Krylei farmer. The present was more important than the past. All history served to line someone's stomach over everyone else's.

GODS – ARE – ONLY – AS – USEFUL – AS –

348

THE – HELP – THEY – GIVE – TO – EVERYONE.

The growing collection of white-dipped fauna all returned to their nutritional cause, satisfied the calamity had been resolved.

"That doesn't seem very polite to the gods." Ilyia was yet to learn that the gods were straw dogs for everyone and everything.

I – REMEMBER – THE – GIANTS.

"Why?" Ilyia was slowly getting tired of the esoteric tedium. Her gaze was drawn to the sparkling cave walls, cold moisture perspiring into mist and fog, dampness dripping Divinely.

THEY – SOWED – NEW – STEMS – INTO – THEMSELVES.

That was a curious statement. "What do you mean?" Nin had said that the Divinities would only ever talk at their own pace.

MADE – THEMSELVES – TALLER.

Ilyia's left foot began to tap out a slowly building momentum.

"I'm still not really following you."

THAT'S – ALL – YOU – EVER – NEED – TO – DO.

"Pardon?"

JUST – SOW – NEW – STEMS.

MAKE – YOURSELF – TALLER.

FOR – THE – LIFE – THAT – FOLLOWS.

Ilyia continued feeding several of the soft fluffy rabbits, their ears long, furry blankets and arm warmers.

She thought the Grove Divinity was staring at her cock-eyed and vigorously.

Finally it spoke.

S E R I O U S L Y.

*

Ilyia scoffed gruffly. Albensia was the westernmost Casidia-Masiritia city state, the reddest of sand-maddened gems to sit beneath the Dragon's Throat. It lay against the teal-blue Beli River; sand touched but flowering with deep, radiant, desertified reds, oranges and blues.

It was a square-bricked, square-housed, orange-soaked gauntlet, stacked to the city walls with structures of various dilapidations, a decrepit testament to the congealment of people that had hastily housed themselves here in this forsaken lot. The bricks were a sandy orange-tan that reflected the searing rays of the looming, intense summer sun, a canopied oasis of houses upon houses upon houses, flowering beneath a blossoming sheen, a dripping, luxurious, acropolised plateau.

Albensia was counted amongst the Casidia city states, although it was an ancient Ultai city housing the Albensi, sons of Ultai who never took the arduous So'Ultai migration north-west. At its centre stood the paradisical and totemic acropolis, a raised mound of soil and stone that housed the religious orders, the temples to the Casidian pantheon, and the blue-flowered gardens and royal estates.

Beneath the acropolis began the vibrant but destitute whirlpool of warrens. God-kissed royalty was vast in Albensia, and all the variously idolatry-inlaid clans were perched atop the giant, laboriously constructed plateau. Beneath them rumbled the poor and downtrodden, for there were no middle classes in Albensia. Just the exploiters and the exploited.

The exploited were held in check with luscious cultural events, free food for the needy, healthcare and education. These "freebies" were repaid by indentured service, conscription, forced taxes, and a divine right to aristocratise. Seizures of land and estates were commonplace; only the rich got richer in Albensia.

Ilyia bemoaned the fact she had been dragged here, to witness a triumph and tribulation of "heroes", maybe even find a husband... She retched for emphasis. Well and truly fuck that.

The gates were hewn with a cornucopia of dazzling crystals, all set within flawless hexagonal sockets.

She paused and breathed deeply, a naïve tourist's mistake. The crusted, desiccated houses that welcomed her from the other side broke that illusion. The nauseating aroma of burnt flesh and harsh life shattered the gems' spell.

Ilyia had been told that the "grand finale" to the cultured festivities was one she would personally enjoy, the closing act of the Seminal Kioboti. King Estios had asserted that every year the biggest, most brutish, most bullish of megafaunal rhino was brought forward to fight the royal band of heroes, led by the King's own battle-honoured champion.

That would be enjoyable – Ilyia was a fan of the hunt – and yet the King was certain that the rhino would be brought here to the city, to a carefully constructed coliseum just out by the royal stables. He promised it was "wholly safe", and that the band of heroes would finish the fight spectacularly. He had just had the arena cleaned by a "wannabe Herakliones" (whoever that was...).

She saw the coliseum emerge from the teeming web of houses, a massive crowd gathering to dine on the crimson-coated blood sports.

The fight was, just as the King said, to some degree spectacular, the group of champions armed with spears, swords, shields and polearms herding a rhino thrice the size of anything she had seen prior. The rhino towered over the mass of men, grey-and-brown hide bristling with rage. It dwarfed the Albensians before it.

A gnarled horn parried waves of attacks; weathered, wizened skin resisted at first, but eventually was marked, shredded and punctured, pierced and sliced. Slowly, the rhino was wearing down to the last of its life force.

It heaved several of its attackers to the ground; it trampled a further few more. It gnashed and chomped with a death-bringing mash of might. One of the heroes swung a battle axe, tearing away at the beast's hind legs. Pain flickered in anguish on its face. With a howl, the rhino kicked backwards. It was too late to save itself from severe injury; it wasn't too late to cripple the unlucky antagonist. He crumpled instantly.

The fight had been going on for a few hours by then, and there were still potentially a few more to go. This was undoubtedly inane and senseless cruelty.

The King's champion emerged from the backdrop, to leap atop the back of the distracted animal. With sweat and strain, he levied himself ready to deliver the final blow. His arms pitched. However, the behemothic rhino had different ideas. It screamed its death roar, beginning the final charge towards its resting place. The champion clung for dear life, tied to a fast-fraying life-thread.

Ilyia could see where it would end, even as the mighty

giant rhino was damaged and blooded. The "band of heroes" had done little to protect the civilians; the rhino was veering towards the wooden fence of the arena. Not towards the jaunty wooden seating, but toward the innocent non-participants.

It smashed the semi-show wall, fractured wood splintering into the onlookers. They covered their eyes and screamed in deep despair. There behind the wall were families, gathered in a large crowd before the stables to see the distraction from the blood sports: a large figure clad in biting steel, sweltering under the sun-scorched sky, hefting a sword.

The figure swept the arc of his blade up and over himself, spinning viciously on his heel, the blade edge swiftly ruptured the rhinoceros's face. A sea of blood washed out from the wound. As the rhino took its last few steps, its fat legs buckled, its ferocious head punctured, coagulating blood trailing from the ocean of its wounds and holes. The slayer withdrew his blade and lifted his visor, a sharp look of disdain and disgust plastered over his features.

His lips articulated muted consonance.

Blades stabbed from dark eyes towards the so-called band of heroes.

*

The stronghold of Cracked Ridge had gone renegade. For the last couple of months, they had declared themselves an independent state. It wasn't a large stronghold. It wasn't a necessary defence. They didn't deal in those kinds of platitudes in Ristos. They were free to do as they saw fit, to be how they wished to be. Ilyia was intrigued, though; their message had lacked any real reasoning. It was just a rough-written extol of their new boundaries and intentions.

Father had let her come with a retinue of guards. The garrison was close enough to the Free Cities for whatever ideology they now espoused to find a safe home. Even if monsters appeared, they were Krylei, progeny of God Slayers. They could handle themselves.

The stronghold was a soft grey flourish rising from gently rolling hills. The towers etched themselves across the night sky as Ilyia and her band of guardians approached.

A voice called to them from the gatehouse. They had ascended a small, rising path littered with mountain flowers and rabbits. Now it was a crevice with a raised drawbridge. "Who's there? Are you the envoy from the Free Cities?"

Ilyia laughed. "It's me, Ilyia, daughter of Bastion. I come in peace. We wish to talk to you about your recent declaration. We're here to endorse your freedom."

The guard retreated his head, and the mechanical chains of the drawbridge were released. It began its slow descent.

A call broke the diplomatic tedium, a rumbling growl resonated from the cloud-littered skyline. "There's something in the skies!"

One of Ilyia's guardians had seen something, a shadow tracing between clouds. It soon began to grow in size, an obvious descent at speed. As soon as it came into a permissible view, there were further shouts. "It's a wyvern, falling to the ground! Get to safety!"

A wyvern was a dark omen, a scaled and winged consumer of flesh. It would snatch its prey and escape before there was any time for rescue. This one, however, seemed to be following a different cue. There was the quick flash of silver in the sky. The wyvern let out a malicious howl, its sharp roar deafening the onlookers. It landed face-first into the metal-enforced drawbridge; a shaking and tired figure fell from its back into rest. Both forms reminded Ilyia of a twilight-shelled tortoise trapped on its back, utterly, and besottingly, helpless.

After the armoured turtle was released back into its sparkling ocean, the wyvern corpse was taken back by the occupants of Cracked Ridge. They wanted to use its hide for leather, and there was enough meat on it to stock their pantries through the winter.

The people of Cracked Ridge were apparently socially aware renegades. Their original goal in this part of the broader Ristos territory was to secure the eastern border against Valestian encroachment. The bleak mountain ranges descended into a patchwork maze of slender valleys. This, in turn, caused them to associate too closely with the Free Cities of the Abresh So'Ultai.

Now that the Abresh had become slaves to the growing Valestian Empire, the garrison had decided enough was enough. They had begun leading refugees and fugitives out of the colonial territory and bringing them into the undisturbed valleys beneath the stronghold. Now they had decided they were going to openly defy the Valestians, and lead skirmishes of rebels against the Colonialists. There was little that Ilyia disagreed with.

She thought it best just to write home to Bastion before she left. They could do with sending supplies or help from the well-stocked surpluses. They could provide extra manpower in building winter safe settlements. They might even be able to send extra soldiers to help subvert the Valestian plot.

Ilyia felt a deep smile settle across her face.

At least the journey had been worthwhile.

*

Fractal beams of a white-blue colour danced around the study. Nin and Ilyia were sat at opposite ends of the long, sturdy, burgundy-soaked desk. The artifact sat before them was emanating a finely flickering incandescence, left to trail in constellations across the walls and ceiling.

Nin was exacerbated, agitated, frustratedly irritated; this had been going on for quite some time by now. Each repetition of the arcane light display was further infuriating the reputable and wise figure. Ilyia was displeased with his displeasure; this couldn't have been her doing, could it? It wasn't her fault that the trinket – artifact was too generous a word – refused to co-operate beyond its liminality.

They pranced around the question of why she'd brought it here; danced around the necessity of this specific artifact at this specific time.

To be painfully honest, Ilyia was bored out of her mind, silently succumbing to the maddening throes of much-wanted boredom, lack of work for trying. Ilyia was ready for adventure, and Nin always provided.

"I think it might be to do with stabilising the manascape. I found it in a barrow-king's grave site." The premise was left to sit in the air. "Not because I was there grave-robbing, I promise," she hastily added. "I was fighting off grave-robbers. I saw their flickering torches and decided to end their negligence."

What was the truth of the matter?

She had found it in her father's study, as a paperweight, a relic from their ancestors' journeys to the north and east whenever the glaciers had come.

Nin was apparently playing the part of the gobsmacked ignorant. "I just have no idea what it is. I can't even sense its energy source."

A faint vapour mulled in through the window. It crept through the library, slowly misting the books and furniture. The calling card of a Cloud Dweller, one fidgeting with anticipation, the news couldn't wait, this dark rain cloud had a refreshingly different story to tell. It pricked Nin's ear, slowly gesturing his attention away from what was, to all intents and purposes, a rechargeable, portable, light show in an isometric triangle-faced sphere. It whispered discreetly.

"Hawk has just finished rescuing the... Mercenary Commander? Berihtos is his name, I think. He's quite renowned for his military prowess and strategy."

It continued to thread the yarn of its juicy cat's cradle, Nin salivating.

"Berihtos has become quite the feature of the city states, loaned out at every expense and opportunity to ceremonially lambaste whatever opponent he faces in the samsara-prone conflict they excrete down there. Apparently, Hawk saved him from a necromancer cult; that seems a tad typical. I thought they'd bred that out of them by now."

Ilyia was unimpressed and half-distracted.

"Are you sure this just couldn't be some arcane light show? Some relic from bygone eras that we just don't have use for? I thought you kept all the records of the ancient cities, that you'd stashed away relics of bygone Divinity until they were needed again."

Nin sensed that this was getting increasingly shiftier by the nanosecond.

"Nin, it's me. Who am I to tell a soul of your treasures? I mean, Hawk is tight-lipped, but I've got the odd tale and story out of him…" She coughed. "I have my ways, Nin. There's something I've been planning, and I was wondering if you could help me with it?"

Nin gave in to the limited amount of peered pressure. He was wanting to cave, and Ilyia was someone he was always happy to enable.

"So, what can I do for you on your heroic fable?"

There was an amethyst fire in her eyes. "I need some maps to ancient temples. I'm going to try my hand at treasure hunting."

Nin nodded affirmatively. "That I can definitely do."

"Also…" Ilyia's voice fell to a hushed quietness. "I heard you've got a *particularly* shiny blade, left over from a *particularly* ancient time…"

The mice-seers hidden in crevices and cracks stopped dead in their tracks, in fearful, prophetic premonition, a hunger growing deep within their stomachs.

*

Bat shrieks echoed throughout the jungle. Unfortunately, the entrance rites for the temples took forever. Therefore, the motley party that Ilyia had gathered was suffering repeat divebombs from the plethora of batlike irritants that took offence to their being there.

The stone door was a complex mechanism; interconnected triggers and traps stopped them bashing it in. Gizmos and gyrations made sure that the mechanism had to work the way it was supposed to. Gorrick the Thief was currently trying to unhinge the mechanism, and when he failed it would be up to Ilyia to solve the equation riddle, a simple problem/solution system that was only really a problem because it was written in a dead language.

Ilyia would pick the appropriate answer from the door. And if she picked the wrong one? Well, she imagined they would end up dead.

The images across the door spoke of an Islekind hero slaying a brutish demigod called Idyei. Idyei was a malformed bat monstrosity, with tusks and horns and teeth galore, who was said to guard this temple and the collection of Islekind relics that had been entombed and encased within it. The temple was essentially a giant prison for trinkets of power, and would be the fourth one that Ilyia and her party had picked clean.

It wasn't an unethical venture, solely to steal the treasures of a bygone empire. They wouldn't be despoiling an ancient monument site in their search for esoteric ley lines, cultivated deep beneath them. They were here for the soulstones they knew the Islekind hid here. Even better, they had the Islekind's permission to emancipate these objects of power.

That didn't solve the demonic bat-god guardian problem, though. Or the problem of the riddle, which would be the next agitation after Gorrick failed at his task.

There was a shout and clamour as Gorrick looked up sheepishly.

"I take it that's the mechanism dud? I think I've worked out which of the four answers we can pick to enter." Ilyia's voice was tempered with nonchalance.

Gorrick smiled an unexpected smile as the doorway abruptly jarred itself open.

They lit their torches, and the party of twelve descended down the green-stained, cut-stone tiles.

The temple was located in the heart of the Furnace Island, the Islekind's dedication to the element of fire. The temple had been built long before the first spire was raised. The lakes that existed outside the temple had existed for millennia before that, dug by the ancient ancestors of the Urm'gil. The Dragon Riders even claimed that one of their line had been here to help the erection and dedication of the temple. That the heart stone-lain in the temple's core was inscribed by the claw of the Brightscale Iorn.

The Islekind islands, where the temples were to be found, were all lush paradises, the Islekind having spent tens of thousands of years cultivating their landscape into a veritable utopia. Crops and fruits rose and fell at every turn. Their animals and insects, flowers and plants that grew here were rich and sweet, filled with love and beauty. The predators that hunted herbivores were in no way aggressive towards anyone, although Ilyia had been told of the failed Valestian invasion, and how the flora, fauna, land, sea and air had turned against them.

That was lucky, because Ilyia had no wish for any of her crew to be injured or hurt. It was risky enough entering into the lost, harrowed playgrounds of the ones amongst gods. It was even scarier to think of the weapons and forbidden secrets that had been stashed and stowed away in these temples far from the reaches of Azga. That was the original reason that the temples were built: to house the secrets of the dying Urm'gil empires as Azga and the dark macabre brought invasion and decimation. How the ancient builders had known history not yet written was something Ilyia tried to avoid thinking about.

They were here for the soulstones in particular. Ilyia was in no mood to gather ancient weapons and forgotten obliterations. She was in no mood to unleash a box of devastating secrets. Not again.

A deep, prismatic turquoise-blue scoured the treasure room, which was lovingly adorned with a vibrant buzz of gently resonating soulstones. Their rich blue emanation pulsated out from rows upon rows, from shelves upon shelves. The ancient forebears of the Islekind had lived upon the eastern shelf of the Shorelands. They had consecrated and deified their kind, amongst the scatter of islands that gently sat upon the shore, each a lush tropical jungle herded by a crystal-clear ocean.

"As the dark fleets of Azga's navy moved south, the Islekind fortified their ancient temple cities. Before he could reach their troves of ancient god souls, he was met by the First Bladed in the Hijal Crossing. Some speculated it was Istarig himself who wielded the blade, never to be seen again, lost in the devastating aftermath of Azga's explosion."

Kelio was enthralled, her description falling from her mouth. This was her first experience of an Islekind temple treasure room. Ilyia heavily suspected it wouldn't be her last.

Ilyia believed it was Istarig who had performed such an action. Not for the sake of historical validity, but for the sake of imbued Divinity. She had been lost down the rabbit-hole for some time now, and had scoured the lost libraries of the Urm'gil temple cities and the Ehmr'gil colonies. Her research pointed to the idea that the sustained belief in something, and the actions towards, or in consequence of, its endeavour, added to what they called "esoteric potential".

Ilyia had taken it to mean that the movements of life and its beliefs shaped its next movements, continually adding to the incremental power and mechanism of the universe. She was reminded of Nin's tower, and his marvellous water feature. That was the masterstroke that let her know she was right. Now she just had to collect more soulstones from other temples. If simple beliefs in rites, rituals and stories like Istarig's moved to empower the First Blade, then who knew what her growing collection of god bodies could do?

One of her assistants pulled a lever along the side of a wall. It caused an eruption of space along the northern portion of the room. The glass window was briefly active, a large, black, bat-winged monstrosity plunging past the newly separated viewing screen. Embedded into the bat-god by two sharp and vicious blades was the strained and exasperated figure of Hawk, his mouth perched into pitch black bat fur, his stomach only slightly retching.

He and Idyei continued their dark, bleak, ignoble fall.

*

A large, kindling rotundness pulsated through her abdomen. Her lower stomach was fluttering with a heartbeat. She smiled the smile of sublime semiosis, her firstborn resting lovingly within. Kicking occasionally, maybe, but mostly slumbering gracefully and tenderly; a deep, roasting hearth warmth. A slow burn to soon bring boon to the universe. To emerge from her womb, the victorious herald of the future, as all children are. Her smiled radiated a softening orange, the untouched igneous stone of identity and personality yet to be moulded by the callous hands of destiny and fate.

They hadn't decided on a name yet; she still hadn't told the father. She'd told her father, and mother, and they in turn relished the wait. Twinkling shines glistened and dazzled from their eyes, fixated on the blooming flower nestled deep within her smouldering, encompassing passion.

It had ended her illustrious career as a reckless adventurer and rabble rouser, another fact that her father enjoyed. Now she was to spend her time tending to court affairs and learning the tricks and trades of "politics". She was infinitely thankful that many of the ancient, brain-crumbled relics had been retired to their relative heavens before her administrative descent, consigned to their paradises of perpetual laziness.

Morbidity amused her. They still wouldn't be dead for several generations more, but at least their progeny understood the benefits of finishing the day early, and taking time out for your family.

A rainbow surge splashed across her vision. The guard to her right was carrying something surplus; feathers crept out from beyond his head, his hand clutching a sharp incision. A punctuation. Several.

Sharp and concise, they hobbled Ilyia's guards with a stiff staccato of articulation, points and barbs silencing her retinue with precision persecution.

The bearers of the onslaught emerged from the dusky trees to either side of the road, marked by dark burgundy sashes, dank blue-and-green capes providing a thick, immersing camouflage. There was no time to run. If they caught her, they would quickly kill them both; she would have to hold out. If she acted rashly, there would be no second chance to escape.

Her breath was intense but settling.

Well, eventually.

The shapes strewn across their clothes shifted and melded as if under enchantment; they stepped over the scattered and professionally silenced corpses and beckoned Ilyia to the ground with a cacophony of drawn blades. She could only say yes, her stomach sweltering.

They bound her in ropes and led her through the thicket; a rough path had been hacked and hewn towards a grove. There, in the space between living bars, sat a cluster of carts and one fully boarded, steel-clad prison vessel. Her abductors pushed her maliciously into the back of the prison cart, as several others brought horses from hiding spaces. Their leader called out several commands in a broad Rekilli dialect.

They were taking her for sacrifice, to avenge the fall of Azirn. In another common case of blood-feud extravaganza, Ilyia would now rest in a flaming chest until her embers and ash became the stuff of fowl-faced legend.

Her hands were settled on her treasure, her fingers anxiously kneading, her palms coursing their fate.

There were two guards with her in the prisoner wagon, two rough-bearded veterans of the skirmishes between Krylei and Entoile, two darkened and tortured souls soon to send her to the afterlife, a martyr and demiurge soon to return and haunt their shitty, scum-stained excuse for a life.

Her fury was growing with each ricocheted wheel step, her lips bitten to the point of near-blood, her hands strapped together before her in familial prayer.

An explosion erupted, then another.

Shouts erupted and soared around her; a clamour was raised to stem the breaching chaos. There was a score to settle, an encore to hear; the commander was ecstatic with anguish, feverishly trying to bring warmer intonations to his squadron. Blades began to strike at each other as flames started their roaring chorus. The quickstep conflict crescendoed and capitalised, as last breaths and cutmarks grew in assembly.

A hand burst through the wood next to her, sword-edge plunged into the sitting guard. The other was gobsmacked by a fist through the opposing wall.

"Tyrus, go for the commander. I'll give Ilyia a weapon and fend off the scumbags." The voice was muffled beyond familiarity.

Someone passed by one of the wagon's newly dealt windows. She saw his knife-flecked face, the gentle scarring tracing a rugged handsomeness, accentuating the flourish of facial hair scrub that he let settle.

Tyrus looked strained and sweaty. As always.

That must mean…

"How's my little tower-bound princess?" The sentence stank of pure sarcasm.

Ilyia scoffed. "Fine, now that you've cut up these asses and sorted out this mess. Please can you pass me my sword?"

The blade came hilt first, leather-wrapped fingers balancing her weapon before her.

She took it and pierced the unconscious slaver with a single thrust. Then she kicked out the doors with one ferocious bash.

Her progeny mimicked her. It must run in the family.

She and Hawk finally embraced under a dusted red sunset, purple hues bleeding through the dusky evening atmosphere, their warmth all-encompassing.

Ilyia had been riding for three days. Three long, sun-bearing, heat-soaked days through the ray-scorched mountain range of arduous, stressful, rough and weathering exhibitionism.

It was finally her time to rest, for festivities, for a chance to slyly surpass her training in court duties and embrace the family time she so well deserved.

Well, without the *family* she so well deserved.

He would be up there waiting for her; his letter had arrived via a rider from the village. Ilyia had wasted no time leaving the children with her parents.

Now all Ilyia had was one last job to do, having devised a plan to persuade her father not to commit to the right of wandering, a Krylei tradition handed down from the time of the First Peoples. From the time before Azga, when it was still just as deadly to travel the world, but there was definitely less consolidation. Much more free-range anarchy, and not the ethical kind.

Now Bastion had decided that as he passed the warchief title to his daughter, he would begin his own virtuous pilgrimage to rid the land of surplus terror.

Ilyia had tried to talk to Mother about it, but Ametia had passed on the opportunity. "Your father will always do as he does; it is not the place of people to question the will of Yggdrasil. We merely have to settle and sleep beneath his stars."

Like that was a helpful comment. Seriously.

The rain spat in stressed, mocking deviancy. She was getting closer to the village. She'd finish her final job, then find her love.

Hawk's form was cast as a pitch-black silhouette sketched across the cliff edge. The thick drizzle and sleet created a visceral sheet of pure blur. She saw his ears prick at the canter of her horse. Saw the slow motion to turn, his legs shifting on the left heel as he took a step back.

She had to ask him for this favour, even though she knew he might not say yes. Ilyia couldn't imagine anyone trying to rebuke Bastion from his course, his rightful end to a life lived in service – regardless of how that left Mother. If she could get Hawk to persuade him to simmer down, to accept his life could still be something worth living, to accept his life could still be something...

Well, really to accept life.

Ilyia knew of her own proclivities, that this was an epiphany-less realisation. Who else had a death wish as large and broad as hers? Well, except for Hawk.

Mother didn't have that same luxury; her spouse was far beyond her in the desire for a slow and painful death. Mother spent her time painting and writing, teaching and telling stories.

What did Father do? He polished his axe and waited for the end times, or the Jotuncall, or whatever hunt he could undertake across the mountain ranges, down far into the green-woven valleys. He didn't help prepare the next generation for the inevitable conflict with Valestia. That was what he really could be doing, instead of dwelling in dark maudlin.

Hawk's hand was held out as she reached him, outstretched to help her descent from her mount. "Hawk, Father won't stop claiming his right to roam the wilderness. You have to do something before it gets out of hand."

The words fell from his lips quickly. "Yeah, of course I will. Anything you ask for that old, virile psychopath." He pulled her close. "First, how are Elipse and Tiani?"

She scoffed in abject abandon, diving her hands through his shirt, her head snuggled into his chest. His fragrance permeated throughout her experience.

"They are both well." Her words were soft and compassionate.

"How is rulership treating you?"

She felt the heat and warmth multiply and grow. "Can't we just fuck?"

*

Ilyia's day was tediously boring. There was nothing but lamentable stock checks and market brokerages, civil issues to be addressed and legal documents to be notarised. It was a standard day of dismay, like any other doomed and bone-breakingly boring week.

It was just after three, and the tediocity of the day was only going to increase in tenor and pitch. The decibels were dullardly low. The voices moved like molten butter, dampening and compressing all consciousness into a melted blue of line charts and bar graphs. Figures and statistics had been gathered by the recent additions to the Ristos Court; the statisticians of Yenti were decked in bright garbs and violently geometric stitching. They had been easy to coax over to the winter paradise of Ristos, and now saw their time here as a long, primitive holiday.

There hadn't been much of Bastion's system that needed changing, especially as the relics of old that she had cared for in court had now moved on to their sunnier retirement estates. The efficiency of their inheritors was still admirable, and it pleased Ilyia that their economy had only grown more comfortable in its steadiness.

She had increased the court expenditures a fair bit, and decided that arts and education needed further developing. Her father's warlike tendencies were unbecoming for what Ilyia believed to be the new centre of the known world.

Yesterday they had attendance from the courts to the west; they had sent expeditions towards Azga's Mound and found signs of life at the entrance to Azga's Tomb. That spoke of ill times to come.

Ilyia spent most of her time at court now, boringly so; she was relishing her chance to escape with Hawk. Soon it would be the time that Tiana would become the new warchief, just like when she had inherited her title from her father.

Well, the sameness didn't extend too far; Ilyia was growing more concerned with the actions of Valestia each passing year. Nay, each passing moon. She remembered the efficiency and speed with which Yeli was subjugated following the plague; before the last body was buried and the city declared clean, the Valestians had tightened their grip. They toppled the towers of the Ruling Houses and hid their demonic rule behind the guise of liberation.

It wasn't as if they were an unmovable stone, or an unstoppable force; these were claims solely reserved for the multicultural haven of Ristos. She laughed; of course she would think that. This had only grown and prospered as the Shorelands had been plunged into ceaseless mercantile plundering.

She sighed languorously, reaching for the grapes lazily

reclining beside her, cradled by glass atop their ox-bone sunbed. They were sweet, the juices simmering on her tongue.

Tiana proved herself capable with every turn of events, every house of cards, every stacked deck against her. She reminded Ilyia of herself at every opportunity, and of Hawk at every other.

Elipse had been campaigning throughout the far north. Ilyia and Hawk had received news via Dragon Rider of her descent into the Heart of Azga, then her resurfacing two years later, adorned in wisdom far beyond her years; now she was in pilgrimage to Ebonheart, to honour Hawk's father, Jiha.

Deep contentment was the blessing Elipse and Tiana gave Ilyia. Deep contentment and assured knowledge that no matter how Ilyia chose to end her life, and thus Hawk's, the future of her clan and her kin would be in safe hands.

A flock of birds by her closest windowsill quickly mimicked a speaker at court, their twitter a high-pitched warble of ostentatious rapport.

*

Cradling each other, Ilyia and Hawk lay at the stern of their vessel. The shallow warbles of sibilating waves coursed and reproached, softly retreating from the gently drifting sailboat after each comfortable advance.

The white linen sail hung slack above them, soft and timid, brief blusters of wind guiding them ineffectually, the tan-brown deck supported their permeating demeanours.

Now it was their holiday; they could rest for an eternity.

The island was slowly and subtly rising into view through the horizon's fog. Ilyia's head was an anchor of relaxation, a weightlessness of the truly sublime.

In fitting symmetry, this island would be Ilyia's long awaited sublimation. A Dragon Rider had mentioned it to Hawk: the last oasis of drackind. Ilyia would be thoroughly in love.

Blades galore, drunk on fun, fighting and thrusting; this would be her fourth honeymoon, and by far her favourite.

Their first had been a return to the Dragon's Throat, the first time they had kissed; she had made her move under the purple-drenched gaze of the red sun. Then they had melted like the luminescent light that illustrated their night.

Their second had been a return to the Wyvern Keep, the place Ilyia had professed her love for him as he was drifting off. It caught him off guard, so incredibly so he pretended to be asleep, murmuring the words back to her. Not that that meant he hadn't felt the same way for her.

Their third was a return to the vale where Elipse and Tiana were born; two years apart in age, they were close to twins.

Hawk was thankful that they knew what to do now that he and Ilyia were ready to move on.

"You know, I'm in paradise when I'm with you."

Sweet birds chirruped syrupily.

The words resonated with pure tranquillity, calming waves to settle any tumultuous sea.

THIRTEEN

"And so that brings us to today."

Her form was illuminated by the candlelight; she lay next to him, half-dressed by the duvet and wolf-skin blanket.

He felt her breath and touch. It rolled across his chest in sweet syncopation, prickling the hairs that lay across her path.

Hawk was a half-cocked admixture of life-fleeting forlorn and psychopathic inertia. This would have to be done regardless of his feelings; well, definitively because of said feelings. Ilyia was of the same persuasion; she actively encouraged this affair. Hawk knew her death wish was relishing this fate, even though that wasn't the reason why they were doing it.

His smile radiated. Perhaps if his partner were less vigilant, he'd live to see another day. He laughed, like he would ever want that to happen, although Ilyia would still feel guilty.

Her lips pursed; slender soundwaves crept through the

space created between soft pink. There was a need to pay attention.

He pretended to know what he was talking about. "I'm not sure I trust that our ultimate, end-of-destiny plan involves leaving a bunch of 'god' souls with your tea-toting terror-opines. I doubt they even know what a soulstone is."

His gaze caught the forlorn morning shadows splashed across the tent walls. Ilyia was obsessed with the energies of their "material plane" and how they manifested as the objects and people around them. It was what he suspected she was originally interested in him for: his access to Nin's treasure trove of recovered heritage and illustrious battle weaponry.

Ilyia was looking exasperated. Her arms were thrown up in a sharp contention, the lines of her posture triangulating through the storm.

"And so that brings us to today."

His form scarred the darkness, erupting from the pitch-black turmoil that lay before them.

She gently shook her head to freshen her malaise.

He lay before her; she motioned herself across him, gently tracing comforting abstraction across his chest. Today would be over soon enough; she just had to get through it, see the end. The end of the end, by all estimates and accounts.

A final finale and fateful farewell to the mortal realm they all dwelt within.

Ilyia felt remorse for Hawk; he was forced into this fate by her hunger for turmoil. She'd been good while their daughters had grown, cared for them, taught them, ensured her own fitness and safety to provide and protect.

"The plan is settled, then? We distract and attack the armies while we leave the mice-seers, the blade, and the soulstones to the hand of fate. Hopefully, all the soulstones we've collected can do something with it."

It had taken them an age to collect the remains of the Rock Dwellers around Ristos. Ilyia had sent scouts out high and low. They had returned with treasures, secrets, plots and soulstones. A worthy haul that had kept her from too much mind-numbing boredom.

She still had the blade Nin had left her, the First Forged.

"It doesn't matter whether they get it or not; the plan's simple, Hawk. The blade turns the energy of Divinite/titans, whatever, into a furnace. If we leave it to the mice-seers they'll do something, and better yet, if they don't, we'll all be too dead to care."

Her arms thrown up in contention, Ilyia was certain she had made the point as firmly as possible without provocation.

"And you really think Yggdrasil's Blade is going to be the be-all and end-all answer to this problem? Especially when neither of us will be holding it?"

He wasn't really going anywhere with this. His head seared with pain in auspicious premonition of the day to come. "Trust in somebody else? What if that somebody else is just a bunch of tea-drunk mice?" he asked.

Hawk winced; he knew he didn't mean it. The mice-seers had always helped him navigate Nin's house.

"I hear that this needs to be done. I'm fucked if I think I can get at least *some* enjoyment out of the day."

He'd swing his blade. It *was* Ilyia's fault that her plan was cuckoo. It unnerved the shit out of him. She was definitely onto something, though; regardless of his protests, Ilyia just had that kind of mind.

His eyes caught on Ilyia's, a dumbstruck Perseus enchanted, her deep blue mesmerising. He felt warmth.

"I love you."

She was apparently wrong. Hawk could be denser than iron at times. It wouldn't last much longer; Hawk needed to prepare for his day's labour digging foxholes, hence the tirade.

"Hawk, you need to just trust that this is going to work out. For once in your life, just leave it to somebody else to do the heroics."

Trust Hawk to turn their final morning into a final mourning. Caffeine and/or alcohol was needed… or she could just swing her blade to loosen up. Wild hand movements imitated the imperative of her need, her face strained, heart torn. Redness growing. Ilyia knew what she was doing, down to the shivering anxiety threading and knotting in her stomach.

"Hawk, we can die nobly and heroically, and spend the next nameless infinite together. This is just the way life is; it's better not to fight it."

Her eyes met Hawk's; his irises swelled, and pitch black embossed the radiant green. She felt warmth.

"I love you."

*

The flash of steel blitzed through Ilyia's vision. Three gold- and silver-clad Valestians approached her, swords drawn and inlaid with bleeding red sigils. The distinct colour of their armour told her they were Diamond Lancers.

"For fuck's sake."

They began their sprint, the quick-beating hammer of steel upon grass-dampened earth. The ground was yet to be churned into the mud-drenched slog that normally accompanied long, vicious warfare. Her muscles ached in anticipation for their onslaught.

To her left and right, her valiant comrades were neatly and cleanly hacking and slicing through the swarm of short, stunted soldiers. The Valestians and So'Ultai were on average a few feet smaller than the Krylei. A few feet that made a large difference, as could be seen in the cleaves and swipes that dismembered and severed the advancing soldiers. Carriages of arms, legs and heads rolled to the ground, fountains of blood trailing and spurting, murmurs and groans echoing overhead.

Her fellows would slowly tire under the long strain of the day's combat. It would get gruelling, and eventually they would start to fall. There were fifty thousand Valestians gathered to draw blood, supported by thousands upon thousands of conscripts from across the Shorelands. All against three thousand Krylei, their allies held back in case their plan failed.

The three soldiers erupted at Ilyia. She felled the first, penetrating their throat with her tiger's-eye inlaid spear. As the soldier's flesh shredded, she thrust her left hand's shortsword through the armour that protected the second's belly. As the spear blade was pulled clean out, she plunged it into the neck of the third.

The three fell in her arc. She felt the sweat accumulate on her brow. The sun had finally begun its descent towards the mountain-line, marking the fifth hour of violent waves of soldiers the Untya Valley had endured.

She heard the noise of Hawk's horn. That was the signal that their surprise attack behind enemy lines had worked. The commander's severed head would soon be displayed on the opposite hill.

Well, if they survived long enough to mount it on a spike.

A swarming cloud of malicious, death-dripped arrows was released by the Valestian army's death howl, a shriek unleashed to scuttle and shear the ears of the Krylei, and any unfortunate Valestian stuck in their path.

Above them, the blackened sky awaited its tsunami of blood-fouled tears.

The whistling storm heralded a swift death to many of the awaiting incumbents, and yet, as Ilyia braced herself for her final breath, she caught the vivid emerging brilliance that spelled truly sublimating awesome.

Flows of sweet-smelling warmth resonated in vast waves across the battleground.

Ilyia heard the flutter of butterfly wings, as green and gold melded her vision into the deepest of light-absorbing blacks.

*

The violent and malignant cleave of an axe ripped through Hawk's right vision.

The blood-stained Valestian iron abruptly cut his concentration as he casually hacked away at the foot soldier in front of him. The newest intruder into this, his safe space, was bearing hard upon him, righteous fury in their eyes.

Hawk deftly parried away several slashes and raised his dented shield to deflect several more strikes directed at him. He swiped away the foot of the newest Valestian to attack. He dropped the serrated edge of his shield straight through the fallen body, splitting the soldier resolutely in two.

He lifted the shield brusquely, bashing away another sword as it sliced towards him. Another dick interloped into Hawk's kill zone, the stress and tedium of the conflict finally wearing him thin. A skin-seeking spear pierced his side, cutting through his black armour and severing his fleshy inner layers. He felt warm blood start to pustulate. Hawk swung himself left, jarring his sword with a jab through his attacker's neck. A blood-shower splurt breathed across the air. The pain seared through his left flank.

As the impeding soul escaped, it was split by an incoming mace head, the bearer of which was quickly and efficiently obliterated by the sweeping split of a great axe.

Hawk used the breathing room to charge forward. The Commander of the Valestian army was now before him. He licked his lips and tasted bitter-sweet salt.

He hefted his spear with his right arm and threw it.

With a tremendous thud, it split the leg of the commander. Blood started to trickle out down through the mashed and burgundy-streaming wound. Gold and yellow armour was stained crimson with mudded despair and anguish. Hawk lunged forward, and with one hefty cleave, split the red-eye-etched helmet of the commander. His brains trickled out as the body crumpled to the ground.

Hawk felt his muscles ache as an axe blade clipped his

shoulder. Pain seared through his body, his voice muffled by final resolute silence. As the trace of breath left him, his nostrils were enveloped by the rolling whiteness, a smeltering inferno bringing silence.

It was said before the time of eyes to see,
A frosty path renewed all bearing of spring,
But as the eyes came, so too fell those without vision,
And when the frost came, everyone wept,
Not knowing that after the frost
The spread of seed and life
Would garnish the blossoming crops,
Bringing replenished rebirth.
Those without eyes and voices know,
Those with eyes and voices seek;
The eternal similarity.
—*The Inyipi Ode to Spring*

*

Their pouch was warm and cosy, aromatic and laze-conducing; it was always their luscious luxury to choose to recline within. Why suffer the restless winds above when all they ever needed, or were to need, was safely tucked away with them?

There were three "oh so lucky to have been brought forth" from the "Shamanry", as the mice likened their Shangri-La-drenched monastic habitat: Eymr, Pnut and the eldest, Syus. The three wise mice brought to suffice the ever-moistening of Yggdrasil's blink.

Why were they necessary?

"Well," Syus had waxed ever so often on their long and

arduous trek over the Shorelands towards Yeli, "the larger a thing gets, the harder it is for the tiny bits of truth that float around the universe to stick in its head."

"The universal fluff theory of epistemology." Syus was an expert on the notion of notioning, which was a lot easier to say when you were as imbibed on tea leaves as she consistently was. "It's our job to just do as doing does, which isn't to not say... that's what everything does near-abouts all the time, every time."

The mice of Ristos were akin to the holiest of monks of any time, era, period or procession, their statements as empty as their cheese, the poetic foundation of universal pragmatism.

"The problem might even be the case that" – Syus had gone for far too long without a monologue, which was similarly the amount of perspective logged into her conjecture – "they're just a bit too big. It doesn't have to be a problem." Her hands withdrew a fistful of tea leaves from her pouch; her brown-green stained teeth pulverised the incoming harvest.

"Bigness isn't akin to detriment; quite the alternative, in fact." The chomps compacted her point. "Some of the biggest things in life are the best things, and I would go so far as to see the biggest field of tea leaves as a personal heaven, i.e. My Personal Best. It's just a case of crouching low."

The pouch jostled with the canter of Ilyia's great-wolf.

"I think there's a benefit to being so low to the ground all the time. We've had to attune ourselves to the intricacies of the cosmos, even if just to find the benefit of a restful slumber free from night terrors."

Eymr whispered to Pnut, a soft brown furred hand

covering her mouth. "That's a lot of words for 'tea leaves.'"

Pnut laughed, his harmony gentle and sweet.

*

The three of them were left amidst a shiny pile of blue gemstones, their shimmering wards all radiating a tranquilising aura. Of particular interest to the furry, stomach-growling fiends was a sharp, shiny blade nestled amidst their newly conquered mountain range. At the centre of the blade's shaft was an obsidian egg, sheathed by a velvety, yellow-glowing thread.

The three had passed the point of inebriation and fallen into empty pits of despair.

Their salivations heard for centuries, they nibbled away at the threads of causality, finally unleashing the bound energy of an eternity of epochs.

As the last of the tethers were torn through, the obsidian egg was left to slip from the grasp of the First Forged. It gently rolled across the blade's edge, landing squarely in the centre of the blue shimmering nest.

The egg blinked. Soft green sizzled through veins of deep, blue-marbled green-black.

Chains of ecstatic revelry broke out between atoms. They fizzed and buzzed, a cohort of catastrophic chaos.

The veil worn away, the mice-seers were incinerated, their white and brown fur blurring into an infinite similitude.

The mirrored singularity reminded Yggdrasil of themselves, its young days, pulling matter across the horizon.

The tails of stars morphed across dark, sparkling space. In the verdant, lush valley, none were left to see their tails.

The same could be said for the entirety of Valestia. The catacombs bursting, full of second-name rocks, exploding in bright cacophonies of violence. The land finally freed from their cataclysmic souls, blossoming into the salt of the earth.

> Doing the right thing,
> Akin to doing nothing;
> Swimming in s'oftening.
> —*The Mice-Seer's Solilo-squee*

EPILOGUE

There were long, soft-white, elliptical linen sheets lain beneath them, unfinishable extensions of a hardening carapace, interlacing to form a cobweb floor for their feet to gently rest above.

The entirety of the starscape twinkled before them, a rich canopy of vibrant atomic life sizzling into the simmering inferno of existential expression.

The vacuum took pause to soak them both in, immaterial warmth flowing out in voluminous rolls. Reflowing motions of static fields and winding paths slowly reassembled into the structure that contained their newest place of experience.

Meanwhile, they just stood there. Really, just stood there. At the epitome of their ascension, their adrenaline-fixed pace had decided to start again, to keep them stationary before the great Guard of the Gate. To keep them constant before the ever-flux of the infinite.

They weren't sure why they were there, or whether there would be anything after this. They couldn't see any others like them, just the dim-bronze fluorescent being erupting an interlude ahead of them, the carapace platform finishing before a vast encompassing expanse of twilight silence.

The-Guardian-at-the-Gate was also just stood before them, mirroring their perplexion. Stood justly before everything, as they were often wont to do, the eternity of every cosmos captured in the setting of star-stones on a stellar-tempered titan.

They weren't really sure if they were in a here or now. They weren't really sure what came after the here, or now, or the thereabouts either, where After was just another question further along the epistemological slipstream. When and why so caught fractionally before, the cosmic net of existential justifiability fraying into plethoric infinite as it deepened and rippled out.

They were both certain they were somewhere, and they were both certain they were capable of a somehow. They both knew that each other was also there as well. That they could feel themselves collectively, their hands locked before the atlas-dredged weight of the universal, fingers fidgeting to comfort their shared anxiety.

Flickering lights of dazzling whites buzzed throughout the centrepiece of the sky's bright twilight. Vibrant reds, luxuriating yellows, subliming blues, all crept through the black-hewn backdrop.

The cosmological titan in front of them was captured by a beautiful diamond refraction, their form elucidated by the prismatic scattering of a nebula constrained behind its enchanting reflection.

The titan had yet to speak beyond niceties. Pleasant platitudes had slipped and dotted themselves across the starscape as Hawk and Ilyia had entered into their ethereal unknown, the words soft and gentle, unforming as quickly as they constellated.

The sparkling encased face muttered something profound. It strung out as dazzling, sparkling gem light.

"Do-You-Know-Why-You-Are-Here?"

The sweat dripped from their foreheads, tracing their strained and furrowed brows. Their hands gripped ever tighter, the tension webbing between them with ripples of warmth and tension, the blood flow ever thickening and constrained.

"You're not some kind of principal, are you?" Ilyia stood firm and resound before the full force of the universe. "I'm pretty sure you're a principal." She grimaced. "Why else would we be out here in the place beyond everything?"

Hawk scratched his chin with his free hand. He couldn't disagree. On pure mechanistic design, he had to side with Ilyia. That didn't mean she was wrong.

"I think you're right. It would be a waste if they weren't."

Ilyia nodded in graceful affirmation.

"Although we could just be hallucinating," Hawk offered.

She paused, and then brought out another question. "So I'm guessing we must have done something bad to have been brought out here, then?"

Another thoughtful pause and intake of introspective reflection, the existential mirror before her illuminating her internal vision.

"Like, I'm guessing something kind of really bad…"

They were beginning to get the message, their gesticulation obvious beyond any level of density.

They remembered their final moments.

"Oh shit."

"Oh fuck."

The-Guardian-at-the-Gate laughed, no evil intonation tempered.

Infolding waves of deep vibrant purple reached out to bring them into awareness. They relaxed, shoulders dropping into a melt, the thick stream of resonating bass a comforting blanket folding over time and space, the stars a chirruping chorus at mass, Hawk and Ilyia's expletive-ridden gasps a fitting waltz and choral.

There was something else to add, but, at the centre of the infinite, everything becomes slightly ever more indiscernible, barring the ever-present, overwhelming, enveloping sense of serenity.

A whisper was brought forth, a half-remembered voice from centuries ago, a nemesis that sounded everything but.

"Just have trust, I saw everything." An embering intonation. "Have faith, you can't have done anything worse than me."

APPENDICES

The So'Ultai Timeline: "The Yeli Account of Fourth Era History"

The Krylei Timeline: "The Times Before and After the Accord"

The Dragon Rider Timeline: "The Specks of Eye-Straining Dust"

On the Factual Veracity of the Original Document

THE SO'ULTAI TIMELINE: "THE YELI ACCOUNT OF FOURTH ERA HISTORY"

Pre Ice Age Accord, "The Early Eras"
– The Journeys of Istarig (The First Era)
– The First Migration
– The Second Migration (The Second Era)
– The Falling Spires
– The Return to the Ultai Desert
– The War with Az'ga:Kil'nof (The Third Era)
– The Tragedies of the Peshya
– The War with the Winter Gods

Post Ice Age Accord, "The Fourth Era"
– The Third Migration
– The Green Times
– The First Yeli Golden Age
– The Fall of Azirn
– The Valestian Primacy
– The Second Yeli Golden Age
– The Albensian Crusade

THE KRYLEI TIMELINE: "THE TIMES BEFORE AND AFTER THE ACCORD"

Before The Falling Spires, "The First Era"
– The Pact with Tael'gar
– The Urm'gil Unification
– The First Spires
– The Otherkin Wars
– The Feyspires Ascendency

The Falling Spires, "The Second and Third Eras"
– The Death of Nyoldier
– The Ehrm'gil-Urm'gil Devastation
– The Replanting/The Birth of the Krylei
– The War with Azga:Kil'nof
– The Last Summer
– The Eternal Winter

Post Ice Age Accord, "The Fourth Era"
– The Long Spring
– The Sacking of Azirn
– The Valestian–Ristos "War"
– The Albensian Crusade

THE DRAGON RIDER TIMELINE: "THE SPECKS OF EYE-STRAINING DUST"

- The Molten Times
- The First Isles
- The Great Migration
- The Saga of Jysk
- The Settling
- The Great Meteors
- The First Peoples
- The War Between Godlings
- The Second Peoples
- The War with Az'ga:Kil'nof
- The Resettlings
- The Frost Titan Genocide
- The "Fourth Era"
- The Albensian Crusade

ON THE FACTUAL VERACITY OF
THE ORIGINAL DOCUMENT

By Chief Archivist Scribold Baikstri

Factual veracity, or the habitual residence within enfactuated truth. Infatuated? Maybe so, as infatuation can be the source of dissonance and interrupted memory. Even more so is the factualisation of knowledge that occurs in the moment. The passions and distractions that provide leverage between who we are and what we could be are ever more indiscernible in their incremental archipelagisation.

Stepping across sheets of laminated agreement, people often find themselves inundated with facts, and dispositions towards facts, and presuppositions of premeditated facts. But what is factual about the fictitious and facetious is first the space and place it resonates from. All conspiratorial beliefs extend the core disbelief and discernment of "Problem"™. How more so that even those who know their place are stuck laced with misremembrances and confusing corrections as the static energy of our thoughts stutters and jars.

If facts truly mattered in this day and age, I say as the Albensians have long since turned to dust, and the roars of the coloured winds trail above us and between our starry siblings: I think, foremost, all facts occur as a correspondence between necessity and acceptance. Better to be accepting of one's own flaws in tact, then to stipulate incorrectness in fact.